LONDON LABOUR AND THE LONDON POOR

broadview editions
series editor: Martin R. Boyne

HENRY MAYHEW.

[*From a Daguerreotype by* BEARD.]

Fig 1: "Henry Mayhew."

LONDON LABOUR AND THE LONDON POOR: SELECTIONS

Henry Mayhew

edited by Janice Schroeder and Barbara Leckie

broadview editions

BROADVIEW PRESS – www.broadviewpress.com
Peterborough, Ontario, Canada

Founded in 1985, Broadview Press remains a wholly independent publishing house. Broadview's focus is on academic publishing; our titles are accessible to university and college students as well as scholars and general readers. With over 600 titles in print, Broadview has become a leading international publisher in the humanities, with world-wide distribution. Broadview is committed to environmentally responsible publishing and fair business practices.

Library and Archives Canada Cataloguing in Publication

Title: London labour and the London poor : selections / Henry Mayhew ; edited by Janice Schroeder and Barbara Leckie.
Other titles: London labour and the London poor. Selections
Names: Mayhew, Henry, 1812–1887, author. | Schroeder, Janice, editor. | Leckie, Barbara, editor.
Series: Broadview editions.
Description: Series statement: Broadview editions | Includes bibliographical references.
Identifiers: Canadiana (print) 2019015702X | Canadiana (ebook) 20190157119 | ISBN 9781554813391 (softcover) | ISBN 9781770487215 (PDF) | ISBN 9781460406779 (HTML)
Subjects: LCSH: Working poor—England—London—History—19th century. | LCSH: London (England)—Social conditions—19th century.
Classification: LCC HV4086.L66 M38 2019 | DDC 305.5/690942109034—dc23

Broadview Editions
The Broadview Editions series is an effort to represent the ever-evolving canon of texts in the disciplines of literary studies, history, philosophy, and political theory. A distinguishing feature of the series is the inclusion of primary source documents contemporaneous with the work.

Advisory editor for this volume: Juliet Sutcliffe

Broadview Press handles its own distribution in North America:
PO Box 1243, Peterborough, Ontario K9J 7H5, Canada
555 Riverwalk Parkway, Tonawanda, NY 14150, USA
Tel: (705) 743-8990; Fax: (705) 743-8353
email: customerservice@broadviewpress.com

Distribution is handled by Eurospan Group in the UK, Europe, Central Asia, Middle East, Africa, India, Southeast Asia, Central America, South America, and the Caribbean. Distribution is handled by Footprint Books in Australia and New Zealand.

Broadview Press acknowledges the financial support of the Government of Canada for our publishing activities.

Canada

Typesetting and assembly: True to Type Inc., Claremont, Canada
Cover Design: Aldo Fierro

PRINTED IN CANADA

Contents

Volume 2

Volume 3

Acknowledgements

Henry Mayhew's project has been called "Sisyphean." Indeed. As we naively embarked on our research, we did not fully appreciate how much scholarly labour would be required to see this edition to its completion. Mayhew worked with a team of assistants to produce *London Labour*, and this project similarly would not have been possible without the generous assistance of numerous people. We were especially fortunate to conduct three graduate seminars in 2016 and 2017 on *London Labour*. Students were involved in researching and writing annotations for the volume, and much of their work is included or reflected here. Most importantly, our students helped us navigate the many twists and turns of Mayhew's labyrinthine surveys. We would like to acknowledge our students individually: Fatema Alhabib; Hamza Ali; Mariyam Alqahtani; Rachel Aquilina; Allysa Bolzon; Rebecca Boucher; Jessica Clark; Sarah Cole; Caroline Dodd; Laura Gaylard; Mary Giles; Michael Gregory; Kaitlin Griggs; Francine Harris; Melissa Hawco; Jenna Herdman; Emily Keays; Jessica Koswan; Elisa Lattanzio; Patrick Leech; Tristian Marsman; Sharon Newton; Jana Patterson; Neil Ripley; Chelsi Robichaud; Kristina Sundin; and Montana McLaughlin Tom. Their enthusiasm for the project, and their spirit of collaborative inquiry, spurred us on.

Many colleagues supported this project with their astute questions, suggestions, and advice. We would like to thank Christopher Anderson, Donald Beecher, Constance Crompton, Sierra Eckert, Sara Hackenberg, Anne Humpherys, Audrey Jaffe, Priti Joshi, Paul Keen, Julie Murray, Tom Prasch, Janice Scammell, Richard Stein, Emily Steinlight, Bertrand Taithe, Herbert Tucker, Andrew Wallace, and Daniel Williams.

We would also like to thank our team of excellent research assistants. Jenna Herdman has been with this project since its beginnings; her intellectual contributions and practical assistance have been integral to its development at every point along the way. Her work and dedication to the project are reflected on nearly every page of this volume. We have Henry Mayhew to thank for drawing Jenna into our scholarly community. Our deep gratitude also goes to Francine Harris for research assistance and to Karen Suurtamm for her critical acumen and manuscript preparation in the final stages of the project.

We are grateful to the Social Sciences and Humanities Research Council of Canada and the Carleton Office for Research Initiatives and Services for supporting our research for this edition. We also thank Marjorie Mather and the staff at Broadview Press for their enthusiasm for this project; we are indebted to the insightful suggestions provided by the anonymous reviewers of the book proposal. Our thanks go to the library staff at the MacOdrum Library at Carleton University, the British Library, and the Guildhall Library.

Last but not least, we owe a huge debt of thanks to our families for their patience and support. Jan thanks Chris Wiebe, Anna Wiebe, and Sylvia Wiebe. Barbara thanks Joel Westheimer, Michal Leckie, and Ben Westheimer. They have shown us why our labour matters.

Introduction

Every so often a work emerges that redefines how its readers see and experience their world. Henry Mayhew's *London Labour and the London Poor* was such a work. It had a profound impact on its early readers, from William Makepeace Thackeray (1811–63), who celebrated its "wonders and terrors" (93), to George Martin, secretary of the newly formed Street Traders' Protection Association,[1] who contested the images presented with a barely contained venom. It sparked discussions, debates, public meetings, theatrical productions, and public readings that extended its material into ever-wider circles. Its ability to draw readers as diverse as Thackeray and Martin and everyone in between was part of its accomplishment. *London Labour*, produced between 1850 and 1862, offered its readers an experience of an aspect of London they encountered every day and yet had never before considered closely: "the undiscovered country of the poor" (p. 47), as Mayhew put it in his Preface. But of course Mayhew's readers had seen the poor, and poverty was no discovery for the poor themselves. What Mayhew offered, rather, was a new and transfixing angle on poverty that variously captivated, antagonized, and enchanted his broad readership. And despite the temporal gap of over 150 years, *London Labour* continues to impress and dazzle readers today. It presents us with a remarkable compendium of the people, places, and things of London as it also captures the complexity of a world in a period of rapid transition.

Consider Mayhew's encounter with two street exhibitors, one of whom demonstrates telescopes (Fig. 13, p. 233) and the other microscopes (pp. 227–34). Both exhibitors evince a keen interest in the science underpinning new technologies, as well as an aptitude for colourful descriptions of what these technologies enable the human eye to see. Both are squarely situated in an emergent capitalist economy in which they calculate what they can make from street exhibits by contrast to their trades, a tailor and a shoemaker respectively, and determine which form of labour to privilege (they opt for a combination). The inventions of industrial modernity, indeed, made visible what had hitherto been invisible to the human eye: worlds in a drop of water, planets spinning in the solar system, and the whole of London laid out from above.[2] Mayhew reports on these aids to

1 Ole Münch notes that this society was "established for the sole purpose of defending traders against Mayhew" (63).

2 In *Mysteries of London* (1844–45), G.W.M. Reynolds famously brought together the city of London and the drop of water: "A drop of the purest water, magnified by that instrument some thousands of times, appears filled with horrible reptiles and monsters of revolting forms. Such is London. Fair and attractive as the mighty metropolis may appear to the superficial observer, it swarms with disgusting, loathsome, and venomous objects, wearing human shapes. Oh! London is a city of strange contrasts!" (58).

seeing with palpable wonder. In another very different context, however, just as he is beginning the project that will become *London Labour*, he reminds his reader that a theory too rigidly held causes the mind "to see only those natural phenomena that it wishes to see" (*Unknown* 10). He was attuned, in other words, to the ways in which frameworks for seeing—the mental parallels to the microscope or telescope—direct how and what is seen. For Mayhew, this point involves distortion—"warping" is the word he uses (*Unknown* 10). At the same time, however, in his efforts to present the experiences and voices of the people themselves, Mayhew sought to present their world unwarped.

Mayhew was drawn to the creative, lively, and punishing life of the urban streets as well as to the many new technological advances he everywhere encountered. But if the techno-industrial revolution brought water drops and night skies into view, if it macadamized the streets and produced the steam that drove engines, it was also the source of many people's impoverishment. Mayhew recorded the often brutal conditions of people's lives and the inadequacy of social and political redress in mid-nineteenth-century England, using new forms of investigation afforded by industrialization itself. His work, however, is not an unwarped, unbiased, or "authentic" picture of the poor. We always have a figurative microscope or telescope that brings our world into focus, and to communicate, to use language, to be part of a community, is to internalize what we often call biases but what are in fact simply the necessary conditions for communication. To communicate, in other words, is to draw not only on new technologies—from newspapers to microscopes—but also to use words that, as Mayhew makes abundantly clear, come with their own histories of struggle and contestation. To call someone a scavenger, for example, is not simply to offer a definition but also to invoke a richly layered history. And to *add* actors to established communities—as Mayhew's *London Labour* does—is also to recalibrate the ways in which language is used, the accents and inflections it carries, and the relations of power and authority it enables and contests. Mayhew's work is vital to our understanding of working-class culture for its record of the shifts that arise as new communities mix and interact and new understandings, new lenses on lived experience, become integrated into daily life. Mayhew gathered together material that others had not considered, and he presented it in new, immersive, and compelling ways. This presentation, which is bound up in the complex print-culture practices of his day, involved the invention of new forms for new life histories, new modes of data collection, and the juxtaposition of an array of diverse material drawn from a range of sources. Indeed, as we will see, Mayhew's approach to the world of London labour and the London poor combines at once the microscopically fine details of people's lives—as Mayhew walked the same streets that they did, entered their homes and workplaces, and listened to their stories—as well as efforts to offer the telescopically long view, the general theory that would enable the social reforms he sought.

Mayhew's desire to provide a "cyclopedia" of the life and labour of the London poor speaks to his desire to capture the whole of London life at mid-century. That his work remains unfinished therefore, is no surprise. It also bears remembering that both the encyclopedic range and the categories and classifications he developed to contain his material, as well as the overflow and incompletion, are inseparable dimensions of the story he tells. Previous government commissions and surveys had often reduced the lives of the poor to statistical tables, and there was not yet a non-fiction form established for conveying their voices, their stories, and their knowledge. Mayhew's descriptions brim with excitement about the prospect of such an account "from the lips of the people themselves" (p. 47). In this context, the poor came into view not as aggregated numbers, not as statistics, not as examples, but as people.

If Mayhew drew his own lines around this material in an (unsuccessful) effort to rein it in, so, too, did subsequent editions of his work. In this edition, we have tried to capture the texture and reach of *London Labour*, and this has meant also maintaining some of its repetitions, contradictions, and inconsistencies. Indeed, its kaleidoscopic array of material is inseparable from the form through which it is conveyed. We have sought to demonstrate that Mayhew included not only the street biographies for which he is perhaps best known but also a remarkable range of other material to capture what Raymond Williams, in his definition of culture, calls "a whole way of life" (*Culture* 18). Our selection also seeks to foreground two areas that other abridged editions have not: Mayhew's attention to the vital interconnections between humans and non-humans and his canny fascination with a green and sustainable London. While inscribed in the struggles of Victorian poverty, Mayhew's recognition of animate and inanimate ecologies anticipates today's environmental concerns about sustainable practices, landfill, resource extraction, overconsumption, and climate change. *London Labour* is also a fascinating case text in book history and print culture studies. Like that of many of its subjects, whose livelihoods were dependent on an economy of salvaging, recycling, and repurposing, the story of the production of the volume form of *London Labour* is a story of contingency and incompleteness, plenitude and precariousness, resourcefulness and improvisation that offers insight into the diverse and competing print platforms that defined the production, circulation, and reception of print at mid-century. Like the microscope and telescope, it changed how readers saw in ways that continue to inform us today and that remain to be fully appreciated.

"The Metropolitan Correspondent": Mayhew's Life and *London Labour*

Henry Mayhew's life and career is a study in contradiction. Although he was the son of a wealthy London barrister, Mayhew (1812–87) himself was frequently penniless. The originator of one of the most important

London periodicals of the nineteenth century, *Punch*, he lived in impoverished obscurity for the last two decades of his life, shifting from one rented room to another. Intellectually drawn to systems, taxonomies, and process, he was seemingly unable to complete almost any project he started, including his magnum opus, *London Labour*. He was a font of brilliant ideas and promising start-ups that often failed to launch, or, if they did, flopped miserably because of his own mismanagement and financial profligacy. Politically, he recognized and deplored the violence done to workers in the relentless pursuit of profit, building complex theories of wage labour from the data he collected. Yet he also blamed people who were impoverished by their work for their immoral habits, sometimes relying on hackneyed stereotypes circulating as truths. He was a prolific talker who suffered periodic bouts of depression in which he could neither write nor speak. He married his best friend's daughter, only to make a disaster of the marriage and his relationships with his in-laws. He served time in debtors' prisons yet was invited to give expert testimony before parliamentary committees. He hobnobbed with London's literary elite but seemed to prefer the company of weavers, ex-cons, and buskers, even inviting them into his home on occasion.[1]

Yet none of this is surprising when considering Mayhew's literary and social milieu. For all but the most famous and successful, the life of the working London journalist was chaotic and unpredictable, a guaranteed and stable income hard to come by. For Mayhew, sudden changes of fortune were the norm rather than the exception. In July 1845, for example, he launched a periodical called the *Iron Times*, one of over a dozen papers attempting to cash in on the railway-building boom. When the speculative bubble burst, Mayhew fell into serious debt. He filed for bankruptcy in 1846 and fled to Guernsey the following year with his family to avoid creditors. There he began the work of rebuilding with his wife Jane and brother Augustus, the three of them pumping out a series of comic novels over the next few years under the name "The Brothers Mayhew." If there was a pattern to Mayhew's life and career, it was a cycle of failure and renewal, great bursts of energy followed by seasons of avoidance, bankruptcy, and despair. Twice he was forced to appeal to the Royal Literary Fund for cash advances to keep himself and his family solvent, sending the very kinds of "begging letters" that he scorned as "literary forgeries" in his articles on screeving in *London Labour*.

Mayhew's curiosity was one of his greatest professional assets. He wrote successful stage farces, satirical poetry, an educational treatise, books of travel and popular science, comic serial novels, books for children, and, of course, the sweeping social surveys of London's marginalized poor that made his reputation. His versatility with comic commentary and serious social issues can be glimpsed in a snapshot of the years

1 See Humpherys, *Henry Mayhew* and *Travels*, and Anderson for further elaboration on Mayhew's biography.

between 1848 and 1850, when he published a satirical domestic novel, *Whom to Marry and How to Get Married!*, a stage farce called *The Image of His Father*, a fairy tale entitled *The Magic of Kindness*, an article on the cholera epidemic in the *Morning Chronicle* newspaper (see Appendix C1a), and the first number of *London Labour*. The latter of these titles signalled his career transition from mostly light treatments of topical and domestic issues to more serious examinations of social and political questions. The biggest break of his career came when he began reporting as the "Metropolitan Correspondent" for the *Morning Chronicle*'s "Labour and the Poor" series in the fall of 1849 (see Appendix C1b). Broadly liberal in its politics and supportive of public health and sanitation reform, the *Morning Chronicle* rivalled the *Times* in its importance and profile. As the series evolved, Mayhew became interested in skilled trades such as tailoring and silk weaving, and in the unskilled labour of dock workers hired by the day to perform some of the most difficult, dangerous work that could be found in London, literally hauling by hand the earth's resources—coal, wine, tobacco, sugar—off British steam ships and into massive dockside warehouses in London's East End (see p. 263).

It was in these same East End neighbourhoods that Mayhew encountered many of the people he would later interview for a new venture. Late in 1850, his stint as the Metropolitan Correspondent for the *Morning Chronicle* came to an end over political differences with the editors of the paper. In December of that year, Mayhew launched *London Labour and the London Poor*, a weekly, eighteen-page serial sold at railway book stalls on Saturdays for the relatively modest price of two pennies per number.[1] Weekly circulation was approximately 13,000 copies—a respectable number but far below other competing publications such as G.W.M. Reynolds's *Mysteries of London*, a serial "penny blood" that sold 40,000 copies per week (Humpherys, *Travels* 24). Shifting focus from the established trades, Mayhew trained his gaze on an even more precarious and "wandering" subgroup of London's poor: the "street folk," starting with the costermongers, who earned a meagre living by selling produce and other consumables in London's streets and markets. A nascent ethnographer, he was interested in the whole of their lives: the nature of their work, their earnings, their homes, family and kinship systems, political and religious beliefs, linguistic patterns, and entertainments. He further divided this "class" of street worker along ethnic lines, drawing sharp distinctions between Irish, Jewish, and English street sellers. The speakers of *London Labour*, often named for the labour they performed or the products they sold in the streets, were vividly drawn by Mayhew; readers responded to his "characters," such as the watercress girl, the nutmeg-grater seller, book sellers, mud larks, bug destroyers, crossing sweepers, and tom-tom players, as they would to characters in a novel. Judging by clues provided

1 John Seed notes that a periodical at this price would be worth 10 to 15 per cent of a costergirl's daily income and "perhaps something of a luxury" (544).

in some of Mayhew's interviews, his respondents seemed to answer his questions with a mix of willingness, suspicion, and bemusement.

The interviews were supplemented by two other forms of representation: photographic imagery and statistical tables, both of which were associated with progressive modernity and documentary objectivity. Each number of *London Labour* featured a wood engraving based on a daguerreotype by Richard Beard (since daguerreotypes could not yet be transferred to paper).[1] For Mayhew and his readers, the daguerreotype—a forerunner of the photograph—was still a new and rare form of image reproduction and signalled a greater sense of scientific accuracy and a more neutral gaze than a hand-drawn image. Accordingly, the visual subjects of *London Labour* are frequently positioned frontally, gazing directly at the viewer (for example "The Mud-Lark," p. 180), or, when in profile, engaging in their work (see "The Rat-Catchers of the Sewers," p. 209). The attribution that underlined each image—"From a daguerreotype by Beard"—advertised the text's savvy with new technologies of representation and assured readers that the images, and by extension the interviews they accompanied, were "accurate, neutral, and bona fide traces of 'life as actually spent'" (Clayton 28). As Owen Clayton points out, however, the images in *London Labour* are a hybrid of photography and hand engraving, incorporating both the incisiveness of the camera and the picturesque imagination of engraving.

Another key component of *London Labour* was the statistical tables that aggregated and abstracted Mayhew's data. His text was typical of the wave of interest in the quantification of information and the use of the numerically derived "social fact" as a basis for formulating public policy that had begun in the 1830s. Mayhew and his assistants collected data on everything from weekly to annual wages, to the number of people employed in particular trades, to the quantity and price of commodities sold per annum in street markets, to the amount of rubbish removed from London streets in the course of a year, to the profiles of applicants to homeless shelters. Like photography, the statistical table was an increasingly authoritative form of representation of the real conditions of daily life in which many placed their hopes for the tracking and amelioration of poverty, disease, and crime. Yet many, including Mayhew, remained wary of the claims of statistics to convey an exact or entire picture of the social body. He prefaced one of his tables with the proviso that "all the statistics in this work are ... an approximation to the truth rather than a definite and accurate result" (p. 154).

With the growing interest in statistical studies, Edwin Chadwick's massive *Sanitary Report* in 1842, and the many published Blue Books (parliamentary inquiries bound in blue covers) on the social, labour, and

1 Richard Beard (1801–85) opened England's first photography studio in London in 1841 after securing the patent rights to the daguerreotype process in England. Many of the illustrations in *London Labour* were engraved from his daguerreotypes.

economic conditions of the poor, there was a new appreciation of the hardships wrought by the industrial revolution. Mayhew called his survey "the first 'blue book' ever published in twopenny numbers" (p. 47), and it arrived at a time when readers were eager for more information about the changes they were witnessing. Mayhew proceeded on the assumption that the interviews, statistical tables, and images were mutually reinforcing—different but compatible ways of representing the same picture. Yet it was the testimony of the people that he emphasized in his 1851 Preface to Volume 1 of *London Labour*, calling his collection "the history of a people ... in their own 'unvarnished' language" (p. 47).

The heterogeneity of *London Labour*'s speakers is matched by the text's welter of genres, including travelogue, governmental report, popular fiction, scientific treatise, oral history, and documentary of the present, to name only a few of the most prominent. Mayhew's vast collection has always been difficult to categorize for contemporary readers accustomed to firmer generic and disciplinary boundaries. Yet we might read the generic instability of the text less as a sign of Mayhew's indiscipline than of his unbounded curiosity. Mayhew was not the only author to cross disciplinary boundaries; as Humpherys notes, "there was ... a literary and journalistic tradition behind a survey of street life that assured an interested audience" (*Henry Mayhew* 114). Fictional and semi-fictional accounts of "criminal" and "low life" characters found in popular street literature of the previous centuries had morphed into the Newgate novels of the 1820s and 1830s, Charles Dickens's descriptions of London life in his literary sketches, industrial or "Condition of England" novels of the 1840s by Dickens (1812–70), Elizabeth Gaskell (1810–65), Benjamin Disraeli (1804–81), and Charles Kingsley (1819–75), and a steady appearance of "slum journalism" by middle-class writers like Mayhew himself (see Appendix E). What united much of this writing was a concern on the part of writers with revealing the real conditions of life and labour among the urban poor in London and England's industrial towns and cities, often for the purpose of provoking improvement (as defined by middle-class norms). Mayhew shared this focus but, unlike most other writers of his time, credited the people themselves with information of value to the country as a whole; these people, as we will see, also returned Mayhew's gaze.

"An Epoch in Our Social History": Social and Political Developments

A tripartite conception of England at mid-century imagined London, smaller industrial cities, and rural and agricultural regions as separate but linked entities in the nation state.[1] Mayhew, the "Metropolitan Corre-

1 This three-part division is apparent in the *Morning Chronicle*'s "Labour and the Poor" series, for example.

spondent," anchored his interest in London and in the technological and industrial innovations that were helping to draw people from the countryside and into urban centres to seek employment. The centuries-long process of privatizing or enclosing common grazing lands led to economic migrancy and urbanization that increased in pace and scale between 1750 and 1850. The legacy of industrial displacement that followed can be felt in *London Labour*: one of the more remarkable features of the text is the continual sense of people's movement into and out of London as they outline for Mayhew the contours of their search for a livelihood. The rapid expansion of the rail system in the 1840s further facilitated an increase in population flows across the country (and served as a significant employer for a mobile male workforce). The rail system linked London to other urban centres across Britain, making possible a sense of London as a networked hub through which people and goods could circulate more easily than ever before. Accompanying this ease and speed of mobility, however, were social anxieties about the promiscuous and even threatening circulation of dangerous elements—criminals, vagrants, and other perceived sinister types—who could easily "infect" the social body in much the same way as noxious, free-floating, airborne agents were held responsible for some of the century's worst outbreaks of disease, especially cholera. Emigration to England's urban centres, a lack of adequate housing and sanitation infrastructure to accommodate the rapid population influx, and the increasing mechanization of industrial manufacture resulted in huge social shifts that were felt at every level of society. Homelessness, insecure employment, and periodic outbreaks of disease in crowded neighbourhoods were some of the most obvious signs of hardship among the working poor of London. While revolutions had been brewing in many parts of continental Europe and many feared similar uprisings in England, it was the industrial revolution to which many contemporaries attributed the spread of cholera and the rise of Chartism in the 1830s and 1840s.

Described as "*the* industrial epidemic" (O'Connor 32), cholera seized the popular imagination when its first outbreak in 1832 prompted detailed inquiries into the living conditions of the poor. Reports and studies by medical professionals and government officials such as James Phillips Kay (1804–77; later changed his surname to Kay-Shuttleworth), Thomas Southwood Smith (1788–1861), Edwin Chadwick (1800–90), and Hector Gavin (1815–55), albeit in different ways, explored the connections between poverty and disease by entering into the communities of the poor where cholera hit hardest.[1] Much of this work, which contributed to the passing of the Public Health Act in 1848, approached the problem of poverty systematically, implementing house-to-house surveys in an effort to capture regions as comprehensively as possible. But even

1 Christopher Hamlin illustrates how the focus on sanitary reform in these studies often shifted attention away from other forms of social distress—such as food, housing, labour, and wages—that demanded attention (16–51).

so, the reports often contained sensational elements, with intimations of incest and incipient revolution, and soon attracted the attention of journalists and novelists.[1] In the wake of the second cholera outbreak in 1848–49, baffling to scientists and sufferers alike with respect to its cause and its cure, Mayhew's revelatory article "A Visit to the Cholera Districts of Bermondsey" presented a graphic account of the devastating results of cholera on one poor neighbourhood of London (see Appendix C1a). With its grim details and passionate call for action, Mayhew's article bewildered and appalled readers and led to his commission with the *Morning Chronicle*, as noted above. At a moment when methods of inductive research and fact collecting were still in their infancy, Mayhew embarked on an ambitious analysis of poverty for which he had little training.

If the pages of *London Labour* are informed by the spectre of cholera, so too are they informed by the rise of Chartism in the 1840s. Chartism was a working-class political reform movement whose goal was to alleviate social and economic inequality. Having been excluded from the modest democratic gains of the 1832 Reform Act, which granted votes to certain property-owning adult males and relaxed other restrictions on voting rights, working-class organizers presented three appeals to Parliament between 1839 and 1848. Chartists demanded greater political representation in a six-point petition, or charter, calling for reforms such as universal male suffrage, equal electoral districts, and the abolition of property ownership as a condition for candidacy to the House of Commons. Although the petitions were accompanied by millions of signatures, Parliament rejected each charter. The wealthy and socially conservative elite who dominated Parliament continued to cling to the notion that poor and working people neither required nor deserved access to the franchise, and that their needs could be met by a paternalist class of lords and masters. Despite the failures of the Chartist movement, it was clear that democratic reform was on the horizon; many of the Chartists' demands passed into law within the next several decades.[2] The *Morning Chronicle* series and *London Labour* appeared in the wake of the defeat of the third Chartist petition in 1848. Like many in his social class, Mayhew's avowed attitude toward Chartism was one of "casual bias" (Humpherys, *Travels* 106) and suspicion of the Chartists' "revolutionary" motives. Yet his theories of poverty and its causes had much in common with Chartist thinking and rhetoric, and the Chartist press tagged Mayhew as a defender of the poor (Taithe 17–18; Anderson 114).

As Chartist organizing peaked in the 1840s, mass starvation brought on by the Irish Potato Famine and the systematic eviction of tenant farmers by landowners resulted in a huge increase in the number of Irish refugees to London, other parts of England, and indeed the world as a

1 See Leckie, *Open Houses*, for an extended discussion of print culture's role in social and political reform efforts.

2 Gradual extension of male voting rights, for example, occurred in 1867, 1884, and 1918.

whole. Mayhew records an ethnocentric bias on the part of the English street folk toward the Irish, regarding them as "intruders" (see "Of the Street-Irish," p. 76). Mayhew himself indulges in stereotypes of Irish people, referring to them as ignorant, unkempt, and idle. The perception that Irish immigrants were crowding an already unstable job market by "stealing" employment from English workers led to further unrest in an era already beset by industrial strikes, lockouts, and work stoppages related to global capital flows and laissez-faire trade policies. Mayhew's surveys—for both the *Morning Chronicle* and *London Labour*—are replete with accounts of men thrown out of work by obsolescence and redundancy as technological innovation and steam-powered factory production outpaced and replaced traditional home-based manufacture.

To cope with the changes resulting from a general population increase, rapid urbanization, and the social dislocations of industrialization, Parliament had already passed the New Poor Law of 1834. One of its provisions was to address chronic poverty by providing relief to the able-bodied poor only in workhouses rather than in their communities. One of the intentions of the new law was to make conditions of life in workhouses so unbearable that it would drive the poor to seek any kind of work rather than endure the privations of the workhouse—a hybrid homeless shelter and prison. Yet as previously noted, jobs were often hard to find; the Utilitarian philosophy propounded by Jeremy Bentham (1748–1832) and others who underwrote workhouse policy assumed a steady and stable supply of employment. Variously referred to as the "Union" and the "Great House" by some of Mayhew's speakers, the workhouse in practice housed mostly the elderly and the sick, yet the mythology and social stigma around it loomed large in the lives of the urban working poor, for whom it was a place of last resort. The idea that any kind of work, no matter how exploitative or ill-paying, was preferable to unemployment was the ideology on which the New Poor Law rested. To the "gospel of work" promoted by Thomas Carlyle (1795–1881), George Eliot (1819–80), and other prominent Victorian writers, Mayhew added his own formulation, a three-part classification system he defined as "those who will work, those who cannot work, and those who will not work" (see Appendix C2a). This formulation allowed Mayhew to impose a moral hierarchy on the people he surveyed and to provide an all-encompassing structure that could both explain his society and organize his findings.

Yet what counted as "work"? Mayhew did not, for example, view street prostitutes as workers, classifying them as "those who will not work." Mayhew did understand that work and poverty were related—that poverty was a structural problem rather than an indicator of moral character or individual failure. As Eileen Yeo observes, Mayhew "wished systemically to establish conditions of employment, especially wage levels, in the metropolitan trades, relate these to the life style of the poor and, at the same time, explore the industrial causes of low wages and poverty" (61). This goal is most apparent in Mayhew's *Morning Chronicle* letters, but it is also evident in *London Labour*. Mayhew was restive with existing proposals for solutions to the social problems he recorded and sought to compile new facts that would lead to more measured social and political responses. To convey his material in this way, Mayhew required a new approach.

Method and Theory: "My vocation is to collect facts, and to register opinions"

If the work that became *London Labour and the London Poor* has struck scholars as unwieldy, repetitive, and disorganized, abridged editions often suffer from the opposite problem: they iron out the oddness of the text to present a volume that is more contained and coherent than *London Labour* actually was. In the process, what is distinctive about Mayhew's methodology can get lost. Its sheer volume, for example, is necessarily downplayed in scholarly editions like this one and others. Mayhew's approach to his material may be summarized in a single word: more. He was constantly collecting more data, more examples, more testimonies, subdividing and extending categories, and expanding the purview of his project in seemingly unchecked and unlimited directions (see Appendix A). With each new fact he collected, he identified new areas that yet needed to be pursued, in a never-ending search for material. And it *was* never-ending. As noted above, *London Labour* was never completed, and the work projected to follow it, *The Great World of London*—tellingly, an expansion of his *London Labour* project to include the entire city and all its demographics—was also never finished.[1]

Indeed, part of *London Labour*'s accomplishment is its dizzying range of material in combination with its sheer quantity. For the *Morning Chronicle*, Mayhew wrote 82 letters of around 2,500–5,000 words each. Some of this material later entered *London Labour*, for which Mayhew and his assistants conducted over 400 interviews, some of them collective, including over 700 respondents.[2] In the original volumes, this material is organized under classificatory systems that do not always hold or are interrupted to introduce entirely new material. Tables, illustrations, summaries, etymologies, extended commentary, and excerpted material from other works are also introduced to support and extend the reach of his coverage, but here, too, the text often veers off in unexpected directions to follow lines of inquiry not immediately self-evident from the preceding material. In an abridged edition, some of this hodge-podge is nec-

1 Many of Mayhew's works were unfinished. The part of *Great World* that was completed was a survey of London's prison systems, later sold in a bound edition called *The Criminal Prisons of London* (K. Williams 238).

2 See O'Day for a breakdown of Mayhew's interviewees by gender, age, marital status, and occupational category (xix–xxiii). For good overviews of his methodology see O'Day and Englander; Humpherys, *Henry Mayhew* and *Travels*; K. Williams; and Taithe.

essarily reduced, as are the repetition, unevenness, and eccentricity of the material.

While his own working notes have not survived, Mayhew does frequently comment directly and indirectly on his approach to the material he collects and records. Inspired by Francis Bacon's empiricism,[1] Mayhew sought to apply "the laws of inductive philosophy for the first time ... to the abstract question of political economy" (*Labour and the Poor* 6). His goal, in other words, was to collect information to formulate theories rather than to begin with the theories themselves. This approach contributes to both the strength and weaknesses of his project.[2] On the one hand, he allowed himself to follow the facts where they led in order to produce a diverse, varied, and novel work; on the other hand, it became increasingly impossible to rein in his circles of inquiry as the project expanded exponentially. Humpherys, for example, notes that his plan to capture the costermongers through two interviews with a costergirl "inflates like a balloon" (*Travels* 68), with more and more interviews added to comprise 61 pages of the volume. This inflation offers a detailed picture of the costermongers but it also leaves much out with respect to other material related to the London poor; the costermongers, after all, comprised only about 30,000 people (*London Labour* vol. 2, p. 1) of the total population of London, which numbered over two million at mid-century. Further, as many critics observe, Mayhew does not address servants, the largest grouping of the London working classes, in his work at all. *London Labour*, then, features the voices of a mere sliver of London's poor and working class, and a fraction of the number Mayhew intended to interview when he began the project. Nevertheless, it gives the impression of encyclopedic totality.

This impression of totality stems, in part, from the most distinctive and oft-discussed aspect of Mayhew's work: his interviews with the poor. They were conducted on the streets, in the homes and workplaces of the poor, in the *London Labour* offices, and in Mayhew's home. In keeping with his inductive approach, and to bolster his claims to authenticity, he frequently flags his neutrality and the fact that he records interviews "on the spot" and uses direct transcriptions (*Unknown* 105). Mayhew's debt to inductive philosophy, then, drove both his commitment "to contemplate as large a number of facts as possible" (*London Labour* vol. 4, p. 3) and his desire to avoid bias.[3] He maintains that if the reader thinks his material

1 Empirical approaches to social science, based on Francis Bacon's (1561–1626) promotion of a scientific method underpinned by inductive reasoning, were on the rise in Victorian England. For Mayhew's most explicit reference to Bacon, see *London Labour* 4:1–3.

2 Several critics, for example, note that his methodology is inconsistent or unsuccessful (see Humpherys, *Henry Mayhew* and *Travels*; Taithe; and Prizel, among others).

3 Several critics have noted that Mayhew's methodology mirrors the more haphazard approach of the scavengers and street folk he documents: collecting material that has been discarded and reworking it into something of value (see especially Choi, Samalin, and Joshi).

seems fantastical, it is the reader's failure of imagination and not an error on the part of the author (*Unknown* 105). But the interviews are not exact transcriptions. Because Mayhew worked from shorthand notes, John Seed writes, he "transformed his raw materials into coherent prose, smoothing out repetitions and hesitations and *non sequiturs*" (538). With most of the questions edited from the text, moreover, Mayhew's interviewees seem to speak in an unprompted monologue that lends credibility to the details they related and allows for a vocal immediacy and often an intimacy that were unparalleled up to that point. Carolyn Steedman's research on the watercress girl also indicates that at least sometimes Mayhew merged two to three interviews together to create a single "composite" portrait of a character ("Mayhew" 550). In addition to the "individual" interviews, Mayhew interviewed large groups collectively on the docks, in the low lodging houses, and in workers' halls to produce a concise and united account of the views of marginalized groups. Mayhew's interview team was also composed of many collaborators. He typically worked with a team of researchers, and *London Labour* was itself very much a collective, composite project. While some sections of *London Labour* have been attributed to specific authors, others are likely the work of many writers working together, and at least one collaborator, Henry Wood, contributed so much that Mayhew felt he should also be considered an author of the work (see Preface, p. 48).

Just as Mayhew's interviews are not exact transcriptions, neither does he avoid the biases of his period. His prejudices emerge both in the Introduction to *London Labour* (in which he compares the poor to native tribes in other countries) and in many slighting comments throughout the work. Nevertheless, he is also alert to the brutal inequality of existing social relations and many times reminds his readers that they should not judge until they, too, have experienced what it is like to live weeks on only bread and water, to lose family to cholera, and to seek, but not find, viable employment. As Mayhew put it in one of his many public speeches, "[i]t is easy enough to be moral after a good dinner" (cited in Thompson, "Mayhew" 51). He seems to have had a rare capacity to enter into the lives of the poor, and his writing records many encounters of intimate confidence, surprising detail, and sympathetic regard. Further, the more he learned about the lives of the poor, the more he seems to have adjusted his own views and theories.

Untethered from governmental interests, Mayhew was able to obtain information in unconventional ways. What his data collection lost in its haphazardness, it gained in his willingness to venture into areas previously unexplored and to offer accounts less indebted to the restrictions imposed by already established forms. He believed that his inductive approach shielded him from the seductions of "cobweb philosophy" (Appendix D5), by which he meant political economy as practised and promoted in very different ways by Thomas Malthus (1766–1834), Adam Smith (1723–90), David Ricardo (1772–1823), John Stuart Mill (1806–73),

Charles Babbage (1791–1871), and Andrew Ure (1778–1857). Instead of a loose, abstract, and flimsy "cobweb" theory, he wanted to develop knowledge from the firmer ground of facts lodged in experience. This point of departure led him to the conviction that the growing disparity between wages and labour was not best addressed by the free market principles promoted by many political economists but rather by the introduction of regulations to protect workers.[1] Mayhew had seen too often the impact of unrestricted competition on the lives of the poor (Taithe 179); he recognized that the "market" would not stabilize this discrepancy on its own and that the poor suffered as a result. He makes several brief efforts to articulate this theory in *London Labour*, but its most extensive treatment is found in *Low Wages* (an off-shoot of *London Labour* and another work that he did not complete) and "Answers to Correspondents" (a paratext of *London Labour* discussed below). Mayhew's criticisms of free trade, his support for trade unions and protectionist legislation, and his consideration of labour and living conditions in any calculus of economic and political policy, have led many critics to identify him variously as a proto-socialist, a theorist of poverty, and a theorist of exploitation. Others feel that his critique was not radical enough. A gradualist who did not believe in revolution, Mayhew left a series of forays into the most volatile issues of his period as he sought to establish a new comprehensive theory that was never realized.

Priti Joshi has usefully organized twentieth-century scholarship on *London Labour* into "three chronological waves: the 1950s 'rediscovery' of Mayhew; the 1970s debates about the 'real' Mayhew; and the 1990s examination of his work as cultural 'thick descriptions'" (97). The first wave is represented by the reissuing of *London Labour* in a series of editions from the 1950s, through the Dover Press edition in 1968 (and Frank Cass in Britain); the second wave is represented by the very different, and often opposing, approaches of Gertrude Himmelfarb, Eileen Yeo, E.P. Thompson, Karel Williams, and Anne Humpherys; and the third wave is represented by Catherine Gallagher, Regenia Gagnier, Audrey Jaffe, and Christopher Herbert, among others. This edition offers much material to support scholars interested in pursuing any of these approaches. But it seeks also to broaden Mayhew's contribution by taking up one point, noted by Joshi, that has not received the same amount of critical attention—the ecological Mayhew—and by adding another—print culture. In almost all of the critical treatments of *London Labour*, the question of the form of *London Labour* is raised; for some its idiosyncrasies, inconsistencies, and incompleteness are cause for lament, detracting from both the theory Mayhew might have otherwise formulated and the force of his study as a whole; for others these same qualities are an integral part of what Mayhew accomplishes and speak to his work's greatest strengths.

1 For good overviews of Mayhew and political economy, see Gagnier 79–82 and Taithe 33–44.

What the critiques and applause alike demonstrate is the critical role of form—the work's organization, style, and tone as well as its means of dissemination (serial, book, letter, and so on). In this context, Mayhew's position in the mobile and dynamic field of print culture merits closer consideration.

Print Culture and *London Labour*

London Labour has long been familiar to readers for its vivid depiction of costermongers as well as its indelible characters. But its attention to working-class street economies and cultures of print has received relatively little attention in the scholarship to date.[1] Mayhew first began to treat literary culture as an ethnographic category of interest in his investigation of different social groups (see "The Literature of Costermongers," p. 60). He then attempted to tackle working-class print material in a series of commentaries, interviews, and statistical surveys under the heading "Of the Street-Sellers of Stationery, Literature, and the Fine Arts" (p. 87). The 64 articles in this group, comprising almost one-quarter of Volume 1, covered everything from vendors of used books to street poets to begging-letter writers, the latter of whom Mayhew viewed as little more than con artists who preyed upon the gullible. As relayed in *London Labour*, print culture informed every level and layer of life. But *London Labour* is also itself positioned within a complex and lively print field. Our second orientation to print culture, accordingly, emphasizes not print culture *in London Labour* but *London Labour as* print culture—that is, *London Labour* as a print culture case study. From its origins in the *Morning Chronicle* through its many print forms outlined below, it exemplifies not only the complex print circuits of mid-century London but also its print history from the Victorian period to its current forms. In short, *London Labour* enlarges our understanding of working-class print culture and readership in mid-century London as it also extends our understanding of the production, circulation, reception, and shaping power of print.

Although access to formal education was irregular until late in the century, England was becoming a nation of readers, as demonstrated by increasing print literacy rates and a growing availability of affordable books, newspapers, and magazines for the poor.[2] Broadsides and chapbooks with woodcut illustrations, popular song lyrics, true crime, melodrama, "last dying speeches" of the criminally condemned, and a Radical and Chartist political press organized by and for working-class people

1 Humpherys and Taithe both address these issues in their pioneering work on *London Labour*. See also recent discussions in Hack and Münch.

2 See Altick; Brantlinger, *Reading*; Rose; and Vincent for discussions of nineteenth-century mass literacy in its social, political, and literary dimensions.

attracted huge, overlapping audiences. Pirated versions of middle-class serial novels, sometimes abridged, such as Charles Dickens's *Pickwick Papers* (1837), were available in cheap editions and in unauthorized stage adaptations. Penny dreadfuls—long-running serials that sold for one penny per number—sometimes lasted for years at a time, attracting readers in much the same way we consume television series today. In the 1840s, weekly illustrated newspapers became the most popular news medium for the working classes, and it is no accident that Mayhew employed this publishing mode for *London Labour*. Two of his chief rivals were *Lloyd's Weekly Newspaper* and *Reynolds's Weekly Newspaper*, mass-circulation papers aimed at working-class audiences (for *Reynolds's*, see Appendices B3–5).[1] Just as important to this lively, expanding print culture was the continuing prevalence of oral forms that had long characterized urban street culture: reading aloud, ballad singing, theatrical performance, storytelling, and street calling (oral advertising, or what Mayhew called "pattering," see p. 88). Print did not replace oral culture and vocal forms of communication; rather, print and oral communication supplemented each other in a continuous feedback loop.

Though often addressed to a middle-class reading audience, *London Labour* was nevertheless deeply invested in working-class reading and listening cultures, both borrowing from and reporting on them. The pages of *London Labour* accordingly offer a critical window into working-class print culture—its production, content, marketing, circulation, and readership—in the first half of the nineteenth century that had not previously been available to middle-class readers.[2] Like many other middle-class novelists and journalists of the second half of the nineteenth century, moreover, Mayhew's work helped establish a distinction between "highbrow" and "lowbrow" reading, even as it blurred the line between them. As a working journalist himself, Mayhew readily recognized the sale of street literature as a form of income for London's poor, and the circulation of print texts, visual art, spectacle, and oral stories as a cultural practice that could illuminate the "hidden" world of London's street folk. Street sellers of literature—"the 'paper-workers,' of the 'pattering' class" (p. 88)—had not been discussed at any length in the *Morning Chronicle* series, thus introducing a new category of street folk for Mayhew. His articles on "Cocks," "Strawing," and fake pornography (see "Of the Sham Indecent Street-Trade," p. 106) betray his fascination with a "class" he defined as more intelligent yet also more deviant than the costermongers. Predictably, his reporting revealed his own moral attitudes and assumptions. Patterers were, in his view, an indicator of a broader social failure: they had been taught to read

1 Weekly circulation for *Lloyd's* between 1850 and 1855 climbed from 49,000 to 96,000; *Reynolds's* circulation was 49,000 by 1855 (Altick 394). By contrast, *London Labour* sold around 13,000 copies weekly (Humpherys, *Travels* 24).

2 See Levy and Mole's *Broadview Introduction to Book History* for an overview of key concepts in print culture and history, such as materiality, circulation, remediation, and readership.

and write, but their moral conscience was undeveloped. The moral shortcomings of the costermongers could be more easily excused by their lack of education, but the patterers, who should have known better by virtue of their superior intelligence, had chosen a "roving life," having slipped from "settled" to "wandering" forms of existence (see "Of Wandering Tribes in General," p. 50). Their supposed aversion to legitimate work and any kind of authority was evidence of their danger to the social order. In a culture of increasing print literacy, the distinction between writing and speech served as an important line of division separating workers from non-workers, entrepreneurs from beggars, documentary truth from false advertising, order from nuisance.[1]

Despite Mayhew's outward contempt for the pattering paper-workers, he was clearly fascinated by the literary culture of the streets and was not above recirculating material that might have been excluded by a more fastidious editor than himself. Crime, raunchy humour, natural and human-made disasters, dramatic military battles, jilted lovers and revenge plots, the lives of the rich and famous: these were the kinds of narratives that attracted broad audiences (as they still do now). Mayhew used *London Labour* not only to collect the dramatic, tragic, comical, and mundane life stories told to him by his informants but also to compile and reprint the stories they told to each other as news and entertainment in their homes and neighbourhoods, in turn allowing access to texts that Mayhew's middle-class readers might have otherwise eschewed. *London Labour* is thus a compendium of both print and oral street literature and other kinds of ephemera, some of it already passing into obsolescence by the time Mayhew arrived on the scene to document it. Many of the entries on street literature included in this edition are rich in cultural, historical, and literary reference, offering readers an immersive experience in Victorian London's print culture (see "Of the Death and Fire Hunters" and "Of Street 'Ballads on a Subject,'" for example).[2]

London Labour's publication history is as rife with drama, plot twists, and cliff-hangers as any of the stories told in the more popular print culture venues. For readers interested in Victorian publishing practices, Mayhew's text also serves as a condensed introduction to the key elements that defined the field at mid-century: celebrity, advertising, copyright, multi-format publications, plagiarism, paper economies, and new forms of speed associated with new technologies. When Mayhew's association with the *Morning Chronicle* ended late in 1850, he quickly set up

1 A letter to *Reynolds's Newspaper*, published on 7 September 1851, contested Mayhew's representation of the patterers, even calling into question the very term "patterer" as inauthentic. "Let it not be believed that we take to the streets because we love the life. Nothing but stern necessity forces us, in the absence of all other means, to adopt our present mode of living" (Martin 7).

2 Articles on Punch and Judy shows and annual Guy Fawkes spectacles in Volume 3 of *London Labour* reveal Mayhew's deep interest in the venerable traditions of folk entertainment (43–72).

shop in London's Fleet Street—later moving to 19 Wellington Street[1]—to start the weekly *London Labour and the London Poor*. The first weekly number of *London Labour* was published on 14 December 1850. By June 1851, Mayhew had amassed enough writing to be able to reissue the first 26 numbers of the series in a bound volume, complete with a preface and dedication. This is the only volume of *London Labour* over which Mayhew ever had complete editorial control. Weekly numbers continued until February 1852, with plans in place for the issue of Volume 2, when the project came to an abrupt halt over a legal dispute with the printer, George Woodfall. What followed from that point was a complex series of stops and starts that historians of the text have often struggled to piece together.[2] Mayhew returned to the project in 1856, with the intention of reviving it together with his publisher David Bogue, who had by that time bought the copyright. But plans were thwarted by an illness Mayhew suffered in October 1856, and by Bogue's sudden death in November of that year, and Mayhew never returned to the writing of *London Labour* in any significant way after that. The production of *London Labour* accordingly raises questions of authorship in relation both to the volumes on which Mayhew worked (usually with a team) and to the volumes on which he did not (to what degree were they based on Mayhew's interviews and research? who chose the selections and how? how was the ordering determined? and so on).

In 1861, copyright for the series was sold by Bogue's executors for one thousand pounds to the publisher Griffin and Bohn, who reissued the series in three volumes, adding a fourth one in 1862. This four-volume set is the form by which most readers encounter *London Labour* today, either in print, online, or in an abridged edition like this one. Volumes 1 and 2 were intact and complete, but Volume 3 was hastily padded out by an unknown editor at Griffin and Bohn with unfinished material from 1856 and recycled content from Mayhew's earlier investigations for the *Morning Chronicle*. The overall organization of Volume 3 is random and chaotic, containing none of Mayhew's characteristic introductory pieces or framing mechanisms, while Volume 4 contained only 37 pages contributed by Mayhew (an expanded version of his taxonomy of the "workers and non-workers of Great Britain" [see Appendix C2a]), even though he was credited as the author for all four volumes. Mayhew's name still carried "brand recognition" in the early 1860s, which the publishers capitalized on, although Mayhew himself never saw a penny from the sale of the copyright or from sales of the 1860s volumes. By the end of the century, *London Labour* had gone out of print and did not resurface in a

---

1 Wellington Street was the location of the offices of *London Labour* as well as many other influential newspapers and periodicals, including Charles Dickens's *Household Words*. It was also home to a number of booksellers and publishers, making it an important print cultural hub in mid-Victorian London. See Shannon.

2 See Humpherys, *Travels* and *Henry Mayhew*; Taithe; Schroeder.

significant way until the mid-twentieth century and the issue of the Dover Press reprints of the four volumes.

Mayhew's social investigations appeared in three separate but linked formats, each of them aimed at a different socio-economic audience: daily broadsheet for a middle-class readership, inexpensive weekly serial for working-class readers, and bound volume for a more upscale audience. This repackaging of material into different formats was a common practice in Victorian publishing, one that enabled writers and publishers to recycle the same material in different platforms aimed at different segments of the reading public.[1] Each weekly serial number of *London Labour* was sold in a cheap paper cover or "wrapper"—what Mayhew referred to as "the *waste* pages" to highlight their disposability (qtd. in Taithe 118, emphasis in original).[2] This supplement to the text featured printed advertisements (crucial to the financial viability of any periodical publication; see illustration, p. 344) and "Answers to Correspondents"—letters to Mayhew from readers, followed by his replies (see Appendix D). The wrappers, which were not included in most twentieth-century reprints of *London Labour*,[3] were an integral part of the series, containing sometimes lengthy debates on questions of political economy, Mayhew's theory of wages, etymology (a surprisingly robust line of debate between Mayhew and his readers), and other topics. Using the "Answers to Correspondents" as his main source of evidence, Taithe concludes that the readership of *London Labour* in its weekly serial format was diverse but "mainly comprised working-class and lower-middle-class men and women" (23). In addition to its various print platforms, *London Labour* also appeared in multiple oral editions. Mayhew later remediated the text himself by adapting and performing some of his more dramatic interviews for platform readings, ventriloquizing the voices of his interview subjects. One of these performances, *Curious Conversazione*, included printed scripts sold as souvenirs outside the venue.

The complex publishing history of *London Labour* encapsulates many critical issues in the sociology of print and literary culture. It demonstrates the extensive reach of print in the lives of the working classes (from letter writing, begging letters, billboards, and broadsides to the wrapping of foods, among others), as well as the reach of *London Labour* itself as it circulated through diverse print avenues in different forms to different audiences at different times. Despite the apparent textual coherence afforded by a bound, published volume like this one or those of the past, it is diffi-

1 Catherine Feely notes that a weekly paper Mayhew co-edited in 1832, *The Thief*, may have given him a model for both the "Answers to Correspondents" column in the later *London Labour* and the repurposing of previously published material.

2 See Leah Price's *How to Do Things with Books* for a discussion of printed "waste" in *London Labour*.

3 See the 2008 Wordsworth edition of *London Labour and the London Poor* (O'Day and Englander) for the only other abridged volume that includes selections from the "Answers to Correspondents."

cult to approach *London Labour* as an ordered, intact "whole," since it is often hard to say when something was written, why it was set alongside something else, who wrote it, and how it was received. That said, this edition, unlike previous editions, includes information on the provenance of selections, date of first publication, and authorship (other than Mayhew), when such information has been available. *London Labour* was, if nothing else, a text that constantly exceeded its own boundaries, both in its internal logics and its material appearances in multiple editions, bindings, platforms, and formats.

Ecocritical Mayhew: "The Same Wondrous Economy"

On 1 October 1849, Mayhew published a lyrical leading article on ecological patterns of decomposition and recomposition in the *Morning Chronicle*. Mundanely, the article is a paean to the recycling potential of excrement of all sorts. More profoundly, it expounds on Nature's astonishing economy: what is used in one place returns in another in what Mayhew calls a "doctrine" of "universal Compensation" defined by the "mutually dependent" relations between humans, animals, and plants ("Nature" 6). And indeed, what was used in one place—Mayhew's *Morning Chronicle* article—returns two years later in *London Labour*. In the *Morning Chronicle*, the article is the third of three leaders on diverse topics. In *London Labour*, Mayhew interleaves it, in its entirety, into a section that addresses London dustmen, nightmen, sweeps, and scavengers (p. 186). On the one hand, this reprinting is a nice example of the recycling, or "return," of print that is part of the print culture focus highlighted above. On the other hand, however, it can be read in relation to a new turn in Mayhew studies that takes up the topic of ecology.[1]

With his wonderfully vivid depictions of "characters," it is easy to forget that Mayhew always positions these characters in relation to the wider human and non-human worlds of which they are a part. The London of *London Labour* is dynamic, open, and unfinished, defined by multiple, mobile, and often overlapping relations that defy containment and classification. Nothing is definitively pinned down. Nothing is definitively resolved. The human and the non-human are equally agential in surprising and sometimes volatile juxtapositions. Mayhew's oft-referenced account of the watercress girl, for example, links the city to country and watercress markets to agriculture, as Daniel Williams has demonstrated. The long section on songbirds at once categorizes them, lingers over the large nets used to capture them in country fields, describes the fatalities arising from their transportation to the London markets, dwells on their possible extinction, and marvels over birds painted green to fetch higher prices. The many selections on rats present the rat as fearsome rodent, valued pet, skilled

1 See Choi; Leckie, "Henry"; Pemberton; Samalin; and D. Williams's recent work in this context.

scavenger, helpless pawn in rat-killing matches, and food for the hungry.[1] The relations between humans and non-human living beings are followed throughout these pages in which the rat's capacity to defy or unsettle all boundaries serves as an analogue for the descriptions as a whole.

Mayhew is also attuned to the country *in* the city and the threat that industrialization posed to long-relied-upon ways of life. Where were the parks? What was the impact of urban pollution on the growth of vegetation? When he turns to London chimney-sweepers, themselves a trade on the decline, Mayhew begins with a discussion of chimneys and coal followed by a discussion of air pollution (London's infamous fogs) and the problem it poses for the growth of flowers, fruit, and green goods. He charts a range of ingenious efforts to measure air pollution, from hanging a large veil between two buildings to capture "black portions of soot" to testing the "blackness" clinging to the sheep's wool in Regent's Park (p. 199). While Jesse Oak Taylor speculates that in *Bleak House* Dickens offers the first representation of a carbon footprint (35), Dickens's description may owe a debt to yet another way of measuring air pollution: on the "tops of some houses," Mayhew records, the soot was sometimes so thick that "the impression of [one's] foot" was as distinct "as when snow lies upon the ground" (p. 199). In these examples and others, the variety and creativity of the connections recorded in the turn to veil, sheep, and footprint are, like the chimney-sweep's and watercress girl's lives, inseparable from the wide-ranging and dynamic connections that bind them to broader human and non-human networks.

In the sweep's case, Mayhew traces a history that extends back to the invention of the chimney in 1347 and the use of coal as fuel in the late thirteenth century, before it became ubiquitous around 1600. But it was only by the mid-nineteenth century, he notes, that coal became a truly indispensable player in Britain's internal and worldwide economy. *London Labour* addresses coal not only as a scarce commodity amongst the poor, a source of smoke that they inhaled to provide the sensation of food, a soot-producer, and an item sought by mudlarks and sold on the streets, but also as integral to the back-breaking labour for which the poor nevertheless competed to obtain employment. For "the very poor," he writes, "the importance of coal can scarcely be estimated" (*London Labour* vol. 2, p. 81), but this importance spans the communities with whom he interacts in *London Labour*. He reports that about 3.5 million tons of coal were imported into London annually, excluding the coal that arrived by railway from the north; this quantity of coal, he calculates, produces 900,000 tons of "dust" (pollution) requiring removal from the city (vol. 2, p. 170). *London Labour* accordingly offers a window into the diverse ways in which coal was a vital dimension of the lived experience of the urban poor at mid-century. It also animates coal, rendering it agential and pervasive in the way that smog (not yet coined as such) was pervasive, to the point, as

1 See Pemberton and Herbert, "Rat," for detailed studies of the rat in Mayhew.

Daniel Williams reminds us, that it is fused with humans and sight itself: "my eyes used to feel like two bits of burning coals in my head," one of Mayhew's informants relates when she describes her labour-induced loss of sight (vol. 1, p. 343).

A very different aspect of the ecocritical focus of *London Labour* addresses the economy of recycling that often comprises the experience of the poor in urban environments. From the recycling of dogs' dung (called "pure" and used for treating leather) to the recycling of cigar butts, tea leaves, oyster shells, old shirts and petticoats, and broken crockery, among other things, the urban poor were adept in putting neglected, lost, or rejected items to profitable use. Indeed, the recycling of waste paper (what the working poor simply called "waste"), offers another example of the ways in which print was consumed by the poor: not as reading material but as wrapping for food and other items; the very *Morning Chronicle* pages on which Mayhew celebrates natural cycles may themselves have been sold by weight on the streets, alongside old volumes of Shakespeare, ledgers, copybooks, and, in Mayhew's words, "once perfumed and welcome love-note[s]" (*London Labour* vol. 2, p. 9)—to be used to wrap fish and other items.[1] If these forms of recycling are improvised by the poor to gain an income, Mayhew also applauds the organized work of the public cleansers who, like a "tidy housewife," "silently and efficiently" ensure that London is among the cleanest capitals in Europe (pp. 186–87). The one type of refuse neglected in this tidying is human and other excrement; by Mayhew's calculation, 115,000 tons of excrement were dumped in the Thames each day. He notes that if only that excrement were converted into agricultural fertilizer by adopting the sanitary measures oft-debated in the period, it could yield 246 million pounds of bread per year. This inaction struck Mayhew as an egregious political failure in a city where so many were starving (*London Labour* vol. 2, pp. 161–62). London's inadequate sewage system also resulted in the contamination of the waterways on which the population relied for drinking and was an animated dimension of the public debates related to cholera.

The fact that Mayhew was writing in the period of industrialization that many now associate with the origin of the Anthropocene only makes these foci on coal and sustainable practices more prescient.[2] Indeed, *London Labour* emerges now as an early cry to attend more closely to technological innovations and their implications. As we struggle to shift from an oil-based economy to more sustainable energy options, we, like those in Mayhew's period, confront at once the loss of jobs for vulnerable communities and uncertainty about what the future holds. As Mayhew both documented the old trades and speculated on solutions to the decline of

---

1 See Price for an excellent analysis of these paper economies in relation to broader cultural, historical, and political shifts.

2 See Menely and Taylor for an overview of the debate related to the Anthropocene's origins.

long-established work, he was also in the process of recording a society in transition. In this way, too, we can see parallels with climate change issues today; he was using print to advocate for change in much the same way that many climate change activists seek to galvanize action by documenting current climate issues. Then as now, this approach generated mixed responses but invites questions that remain important. Mayhew was not an environmental activist, but he was alert to ecological issues. *London Labour* addresses not only London labour and poverty, not only "characters," but also an urban ecology inseparable from the rise of industrial modernity. This urban ecology charts the interconnections between city and country, refuse and recycled material, soot and health, animal and human, and, despite the list just offered, *London Labour*'s defiance of these categories. Mayhew's work accordingly provides a rich resource for the reader interested in ecological issues.

"Combustible Materials": Dialogues and Debates

The weekly numbers of *London Labour and the London Poor* appeared in the lead-up to London's Great Exhibition of 1851, the first world's fair. Housed in the grand, purpose-built iron and glass Crystal Palace, designed by Joseph Paxton (1803–65) and erected in Hyde Park, the Great Exhibition was a vast showcase for the planet's "raw materials" and their industrial transformation via machine-driven processes into objects for human use and consumption. Mayhew reported on the event for the *Edinburgh News* and parodied it in a popular serial novel called *1851: or The Adventures of Mr and Mrs Sandboys*. Yet, as several critics have pointed out, we might also compare the structure of *London Labour* to the Great Exhibition in its fascination with cataloguing, gathering, and displaying under "one roof" the peoples of the world and the material things of daily life wrought by human labour.[1] Although the Great Exhibition attracted huge crowds, volumes' worth of press coverage, and much public admiration, it also incited controversy, particularly among the working people whose uncredited labour had helped produce the objects on display and the very building in which they were exhibited.[2] In a similar fashion, some of the working people who were the "raw material" of Mayhew's grand survey were unimpressed with his characterization of them and offered a different account of their experience, returning his gaze in both the "Answers to Correspondents" feature of *London Labour* and in rival publications to Mayhew's (see Appendices B3–5 and D6).

Mayhew's early reviewers were quick to appreciate that he was doing something new with *London Labour*—the *British Quarterly Review* noted that it "has proved an epoch in our social history" (Masson 491)—but the

1 See Schülting; Prasch, "Eating"; Landon; Chase and Levenson; and Joshi for discussions of Mayhew's work in relation to the Great Exhibition.

2 See Leckie, *Open Houses* 65–66.

very innovations of the work lent themselves to challenges and dispute. What was this text? Was it an honest record of a hitherto neglected population living in the heart of London? Or was it a massaged account designed to garner readers and generate entertainment, sometimes at the expense of the very communities it sought to advance? In short, the question of the balance between factual information and journalistic liberty was not always easily determined. *London Labour* also confronted questions of free trade and in doing so elicited predictable responses from journals that supported free trade (the *Economist*) as well the more radical journals, such as the *Northern Star*, that opposed it. In October 1851, the *Eclectic Review* published a 12-page response to *London Labour*: "The revelations of this work should give a new tone and colour to the contemporary history of these times" (see Appendix B1, p. 311). Ominously concluding that "[c]ombustible materials will not for ever accumulate, without an explosion one day taking place" (p. 313), this largely appreciative review dramatizes the material recorded by Mayhew and demonstrates how it could be used to incite fear among middle-class readers. The *Athenaeum* was also inclined to celebrate Mayhew's contribution, but it alerted readers to a controversy that had been stirring over the months preceding the review: the volume "was good ... in most respects" but marred by "a suspicion," likely justified, the reviewer notes, "that the accounts were exaggerated" (see Appendix B2, p. 315).

Mayhew's possibly cavalier approach to facts had already aroused consternation in March 1850 when his sources on ragged schools could not be confirmed. But the question of the accuracy of his data took a deeper hit in the spring of 1851 when, in a public meeting, the Street Traders' Protection Association accused him of "downright falsehood" and "gross misrepresentations" (*Reynolds's Newspaper* 14). The audience concluded that Mayhew's publications were only a "collection of falsehoods" (14) to generate profit for his publication at the street-sellers' expense and to bias middle-class readers against them. Matters were made worse when Mayhew—who did not typically shirk attendance at public meetings—stopped showing up to subsequent meetings and failed to defend himself. It was these meetings and their coverage in *Reynolds's Newspaper*—which included several damning letters from George Martin, the secretary to the Street Traders' Protection Association—that gave rise to the suspicions noted by the *Athenaeum* above. Christopher Anderson suggests that Mayhew's Preface to the first volume of *London Labour*, in which he again underscores his reliance on the testimony of "the people themselves" (p. 47), was his defence (xv). This may be so. It is certainly the account most often recalled in histories of Mayhew, carried forward and referenced by most critics addressing his work. But it also leaves many questions unanswered. How do we determine what is accurate and what is not? Whose voices had authority to make such claims and whose did not? In this case, Mayhew's authority as a prominent journalist gained attention for himself and his project, while history has not remembered the counter-voices as prominently. The three pieces from *Reynolds's Newspaper* included in this edition (Appendices B3–5) attest to this controversy in an effort to offer a fuller picture of the reactions of those who felt that Mayhew had falsely represented them. Their responses prompt us to consider how we approach a writer whose observations may be imperfect and yet who nevertheless merits serious attention.

As we have noted, Mayhew was also often his own worst enemy; where many of his contemporaries were inclined to give him the benefit of the doubt with respect to the controversies his work provoked, he did everything he could to undermine their confidence and tarnish his own reputation. But the work itself has also stood as a testimony to his accomplishment. Since the first of the debates generated by *London Labour*, the text has supplied compelling material for historical fiction, stage plays, and books of poetry, as well as a backbone for new thinking about social history, political economy, and urban studies. If Mayhew's career went into eclipse for almost 100 years, its revival since the 1950s attests to the power of the work he produced. That said, the questions that preoccupied his contemporaries are also questions for us. How do we evaluate it? What counts as knowledge? At what cost? The issue of how to read Mayhew's evidence continues to challenge scholars. Far from only rendering the work unstable, these are opportunities for reading more attentively, with caution and curiosity, being alert to what is there on the page and how that material was shaped to catalyze change and move a complacent public. That Mayhew succeeded in his endeavour to present a fuller picture of the lives of the poor is evident. That he also left us with many questions central to any scholarly pursuit is also part of the legacy that *London Labour and the London Poor* offers.

Henry Mayhew: A Brief Chronology

1812	25 November: Henry Mayhew is born at home in Great Marlborough Street, London, the fifth of twelve children born to Joshua Dorset Joseph Mayhew, a thriving lawyer, and Mary Ann Fenn.
1822	Begins attending Westminster School, where he remains for five years. Attempts to run away on two occasions. Quits school after refusing a caning from the headmaster.
1827–28	Forced by his father to enroll as a trainee midshipman with the East India Company on board the *Marquis of Wellington*. Dismissed from his father's law firm and banished from the family home, he embarks on a career as a journalist and dramatist in London.
1831–39	With his friend Gilbert à Beckett, he launches *Figaro in London*. Mayhew's contributions are published under the pseudonym Ralph Rigmarole. He eventually succeeds à Beckett as editor. The two combine on several other more ephemeral periodicals, such as *The Thief* (1832) and *The Comic Magazine* (1832–33).
1833	11 November–30 December: Imprisoned for debt in Fleet Prison. December: Becomes co-owner and manager with à Beckett of the Fitzroy Theatre, a venue for stage farce, burlesque, and operetta.
1834	16 February: Mayhew's one-act farce, *The Wandering Minstrel*, opens at the Fitzroy Theatre, still under the name of Ralph Rigmarole.
1835	Flees to Paris to avoid creditors.
1838	After a period in Wales, returns to London to resume working as a journalist and dramatist. Also begins to conduct chemistry experiments, with the goal of inventing artificial diamonds.
1841	March: Delivers a series of lectures on *The Intellectualisation of the People* to the Royal Society of British Artists. July: Recruits a coterie of London writers, including Douglas Jerrold, à Beckett, and Thackeray, to launch *Punch, or the London Charivari*, a satirical magazine of London life that became a fixture of literary culture.
1842	Publishes *What to Teach and How to Teach It*, a scholarly treatise on education and pedagogy.
1844	20 April: Marries Jane Jerrold, eldest daughter of Douglas Jerrold, whom he met in Paris in 1835. The couple settle in Parsons Green, a semi-rural suburb, within close distance of Jerrold in Putney. Their daughter, Mary, is born in 1845, their son, Athol, the following year.

1845 Launches the ill-fated *Iron Times*, one of many periodical publications trying to capitalize on the "railway mania," and speculates in railway shares.

1846 16 July: The railway stock bubble bursts, ruining investors and ending the *Iron Times*. Files for bankruptcy. Mayhew's erratic behaviour alienates his *Punch* colleagues, including Jerrold, and he is fired.

December: Serves as editor of the 1847 edition of George Cruikshank's *Comic Almanack*, a role he will return to in 1849 and 1850.

1847 January: begins publication of *The Greatest Plague of Life*, a highly successful comic novel about a lady's servant problems. The work is initially anonymous, before being ascribed to the Brothers Mayhew. Under this name, Mayhew writes collaboratively with his wife Jane and younger brother Augustus.

February: After failing to gain protection from the Bankruptcy Court, flees to Guernsey with Jane and Augustus, to escape his creditors.

1849 September: As a cholera epidemic ravages London, the *Morning Chronicle* prints a series of letters from Mayhew, under the pseudonym "Anti-Zymosis," on the possible causes of the disease and calling for a fully scientific investigation. The *Chronicle* also commissions him to write "A Visit to the Cholera Districts of Bermondsey." He is appointed "Special Correspondent for the Metropolis" for the *Chronicle*'s new "Labour and the Poor Series."

3 December: Calls a public meeting of needlewomen to hear about their working conditions and poverty.

1850 October: Amid controversy, with counterclaims of resignation and being fired, Mayhew leaves the *Morning Chronicle*.

14 December: The first number of the weekly *London Labour and the London Poor* is published, a continuation of his work on the *Morning Chronicle*. Mayhew is joined by his research team from the *Morning Chronicle* and employs his brother Augustus and George Augustus Sala as assistants.

1851 January: Begins serialization of *1851: or The Adventures of Mr and Mrs Sandboys*, a popular parody of the Great Exhibition, with Cruikshank as illustrator.

From May, also covers the Exhibition seriously as correspondent for the *Edinburgh News*.

7 June: The first 26 numbers of *London Labour* are repackaged as *Volume 1: The Street Folk*.

23 August: Begins concurrent serialization of what would become *Volume 2: The Street Folk* and *Volume 3: Those That Will Not Work*.

29 November: Launches *Low Wages*, a new serial detailing Mayhew's critique of "received doctrines of Political Economy."

1852	February: *London Labour* and *Low Wages* come to an abrupt halt when Mayhew is taken to court by the printer, George Woodfall and Son, for unpaid bills. The last number of *London Labour* appears 21 February, ending mid-sentence. With only Volume 1 published, Volumes 2 and 3 are abandoned unfinished.
	March: Delivers lectures in Newcastle and Edinburgh on *The Hidden Life of London* using voices, stories, and illustrations sourced from *London Labour*, the first of several stage series.
1853	24 February–21 July: Imprisoned for debt in Queen's Bench Prison.
	Jane Mayhew in poor health.
	Appeals to the Royal Literary Fund for assistance and is granted £50.
1853–55	Leaves England for Paris with his family, finally settling in Koblenz, Germany.
1855	May: Bogue buys the copyright of *London Labour* for £100, securing the intellectual ownership with plans to revive the series with Mayhew.
1856	January: Returning to London, launches a monthly periodical, *The Great World of London*, together with Bogue, intending to explore all classes of London society. Initially, Mayhew conducts investigations of London's criminal prisons.
	October: Suffers an unspecified health crisis that leaves him unable to speak or work. Retreats to Cornwall for a month.
	17 November: Bogue, his long-time supporter, dies suddenly. Plans for the reissue of *London Labour* and continuation of *Great World* are suspended.
1857	April: First number of *Paved with Gold*, a serial novel by the Brothers Mayhew with Augustus, using the material they had gathered under Bogue for the abortive *London Labour* relaunch. Mayhew abandons the project after the fifth number, leaving Augustus to complete it alone.
	April: Embarks on another lecture tour across Britain, *The Oddities of the London Streets*, using material from *London Labour* and *Great World*. This is followed the same year by another, more elaborately theatrical tour called *Curious Conversazione*, in which Mayhew impersonates his interviewees.
	8 June: Douglas Jerrold, Mayhew's father-in-law, dies.
	September: Another stage show, *Punch on the Platform*, is planned, featuring song and dance routines, written and performed by Mayhew. He suffers a breakdown on stage on opening night in Brighton after spotting his disapproving father in the front row.
1858	20 January: Mayhew's father dies, bequeathing almost nothing to him. His brothers, however, inherit enough to retire in comfort.

1861	January: Copyright of *London Labour* and *The Great World of London* sold by Bogue's executors to Griffin and Bohn for £1000. Volumes 1–3 are published and marketed under Mayhew's name, as is a new Volume 4, the content mainly commissioned from other writers, which follows the next year. Mayhew is not involved.
1861–63	Returns with his family to Germany, settling in Eisenach, Saxony, to research and write his two-volume *German Life and Manners* and a book on the boyhood of Martin Luther.
1863	*The Great World of London* is repackaged by Griffin and sold as *The Criminal Prisons of London*. On returning to London, Henry and Jane Mayhew separate amicably.
1865	Second printing of the four volumes of *London Labour*. March: Launches a one-shilling monthly, *The Shops and Companies of London*. It lasts until the fall.
1866	July: Serves as editor of the *Sunday Times* theatrical review column.
1868	October–November: Imprisoned for debt in Whitecross Street prison. Appeals to the Royal Literary Fund for financial assistance again and is granted £50.
1870	July: Covers Franco-Prussian war with his son Athol for the London evening paper the *Globe and Traveller*. Mistaken as a Prussian spy, he narrowly escapes death by firing squad and is ordered to leave France.
1871	30 November: Griffin sells the copyright of *London Labour* and *Criminal Prisons* to Maxwell publishers for £110. They do not develop the assets, and both go out of print.
1873–87	Lives in a series of rented rooms in lodging houses, primarily in London's Bloomsbury area, where the British Museum is located.
1880	13 June: Delivers a free lecture, *London Wits*, a personal account of London literary society of the past fifty years, at The Star and Garter, Leicester Square. 26 February: Jane Mayhew dies. She requests burial beside her father, with his name on her grave. Mayhew is absent from her funeral.
1887	25 July: Dies of bronchitis at the age of 74, in a rented room at 8 Tavistock Street. Tucked behind Covent Garden in London's theatre district, it was also around the corner from where the offices of *London Labour* had been, in 16 Upper Wellington Street. He is buried in London's Kensal Green Cemetery.

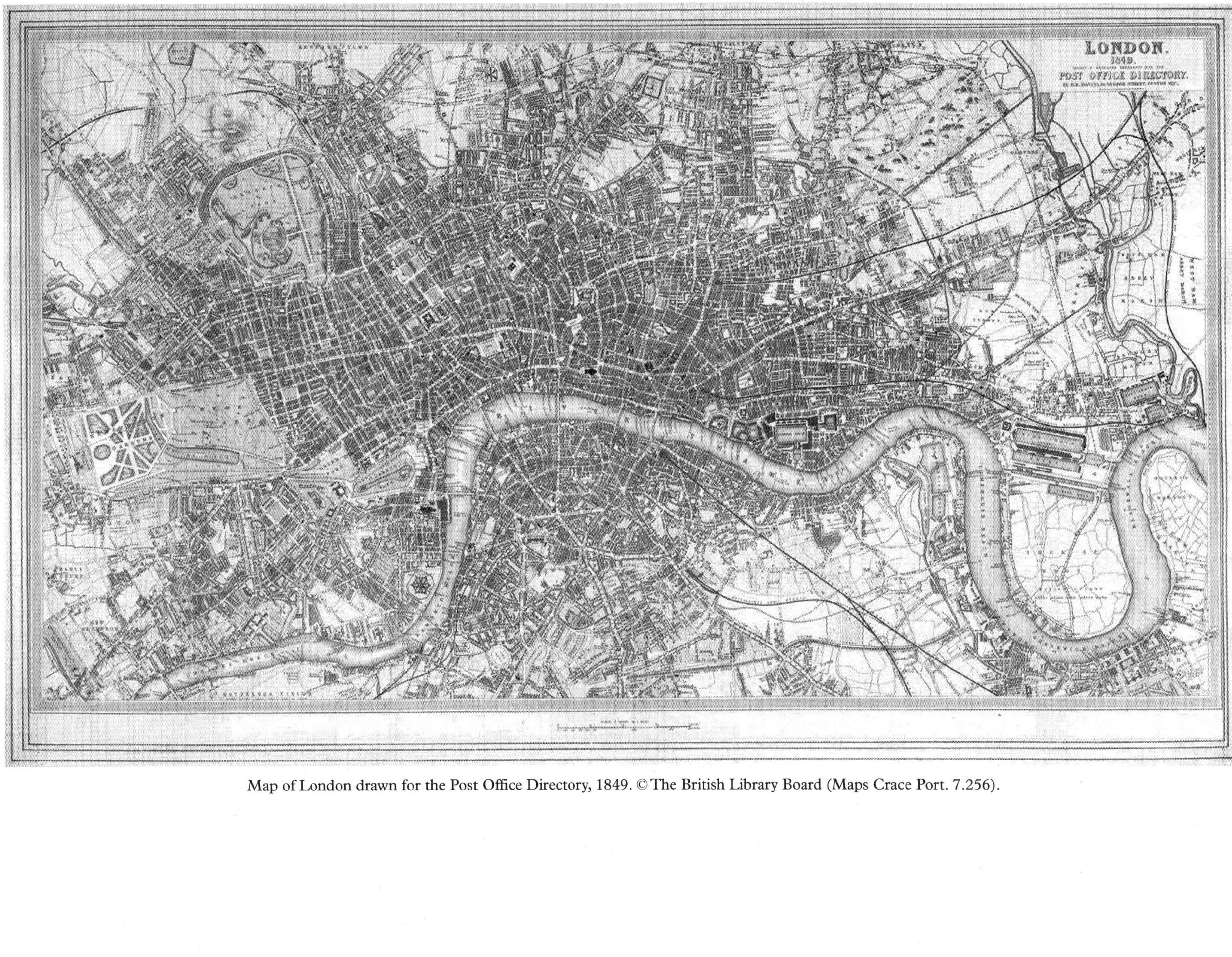

Map of London drawn for the Post Office Directory, 1849. © The British Library Board (Maps Crace Port. 7.256).

A Note on the Text

London Labour and the London Poor has an exceptionally complicated publishing history, as outlined in the Introduction to this volume. For our copy-text we have used the 1968 four-volume Dover Press edition, edited by John D. Rosenberg, an unabridged facsimile reissue of the four volumes published by Griffin, Bohn, and Company in 1861–62. Many of the selections in our abridged edition are excerpted from longer entries; deletions are indicated by ellipses. Minor errors have been silently corrected throughout. We have annotated proper names and many places, historical and literary references, and terms whose meaning may not be readily available to most readers in the dictionary or other sources. The one exception to this rule is the Table of Contents in Appendix A; it does not include any annotations. Some of the cross-references are to selections included in this volume; these are indicated simply by a note such as (see p. 123). Other references are to the Dover Press edition and will appear in the format (*London Labour* vol. 1, p. 23).

Money, Earnings, and the Cost of Living in London Labour and the London Poor

> "I don't know nothing about what I earns during the year, I only know how many pennies goes to a shilling, and two ha'pence goes to a penny, and four fardens goes to a penny. I knows too, how many fardens goes to tuppence—eight. That's as much as I wants to know for the markets." (p. 85)

Money, earnings, and the cost of goods and services were a preoccupation of Mayhew's in *London Labour and the London Poor.* Rarely does Mayhew fail to ask an interviewee how much he or she earns in a day, a week, or per annum. The watercress girl's candid admission above that she knows just enough of the currency system to be able to count to twelve, since twelve pennies equalled a shilling, indicates the money amounts she was accustomed to dealing with in her workplace, Farringdon Market. But it also speaks to the rather complex system of pre-decimalized British currency. Until 1971, British money was divided into pounds (£ or *l.*), shillings (*s.*), and pennies, or pence (*d.*, for denarius, an ancient Roman coin). Twelve pence equalled a shilling, and 20 shillings equalled a pound, thus 240 pence equalled a pound. Pence, shillings, and pounds are the most common denominations in *London Labour*, but there were other coins as well: a guinea was worth 21 shillings, a crown was worth five shillings, a half-crown worth 2s. 6d. Far more common units of currency than these in *London Labour* are halfpennies ("ha-pence") and farthings ("fardens"), worth a quarter of one penny.

The watercress girl is unable to calculate her annual earnings, but the question might well have seemed irrelevant to someone living on a subsistence income. Nevertheless, Mayhew busily set about attempting to calculate the average annual income of people like the watercress girl, factoring things like capital costs and seasonal shifts into his calculations. In "Of Groundsel and Chickweed Sellers," Mayhew estimates, "from the best information I could acquire" that there are 1,000 London street sellers of groundsel (an herb), each person selling on average 18 bunches a day. "We thus have 5,616,000 bunches a year, which, at ½d. each, realise 11,700*l.*—about 4*s.*2*d.* per week per head of sellers of groundsel.... The capital required for groundsel-selling is 4*d.* for a brown wicker-basket; leather strap to sling it from the shoulder 6*d.*" (*London Labour* vol. 1, p. 155).

As many have observed, Mayhew's accounts were not always reliable, but even the most reliable source must be taken with a grain of salt. Calculating the cost of living, not to mention modern equivalents, is difficult.

According to an 1846 article in the *Illustrated London News*, a single rented room for a manual labourer cost between 3s. and 6s. per week. An article by Arthur Morrison published in the *Cornhill Magazine* in April 1901 provided the following tally of a working-class family budget for an average week:[1]

	£	s	d
Rent		7	0
Meat and fish		5	5
Bread and flour		2	1½
Grocery		1	8
Cheese, butter, bacon and eggs		1	11
Greengrocery		1	3
Firing		2	0
Oil and sundries		1	7½
Allowance for clothes		2	0
Club and insurance		1	0
Beer and tobacco		2	9
Balance in hand for contingencies, petty cash, &c.		1	3
[total]	£1	10	0

As Morrison goes on to observe, "these figures will show how narrow is the margin that lies between the workman's plain and healthy livelihood and an unpleasant privation. We have allowed for nothing but reasonable necessaries, and yet very little—almost nothing—remains, wherewith some provision may be made for the evil day of sickness, old age, or lack of work. Yet the provision is often made, as I have said; though it is physically impossible that it should be of a substance to stand a long strain." While the figures noted in this table are different than they would have been in Mayhew's period due to inflation, Mayhew would undoubtedly have concurred with Morrison's conclusions about the "narrow margin" between survival and starvation for the working poor of London.

1 See also Morrison's *A Child of the Jago*.

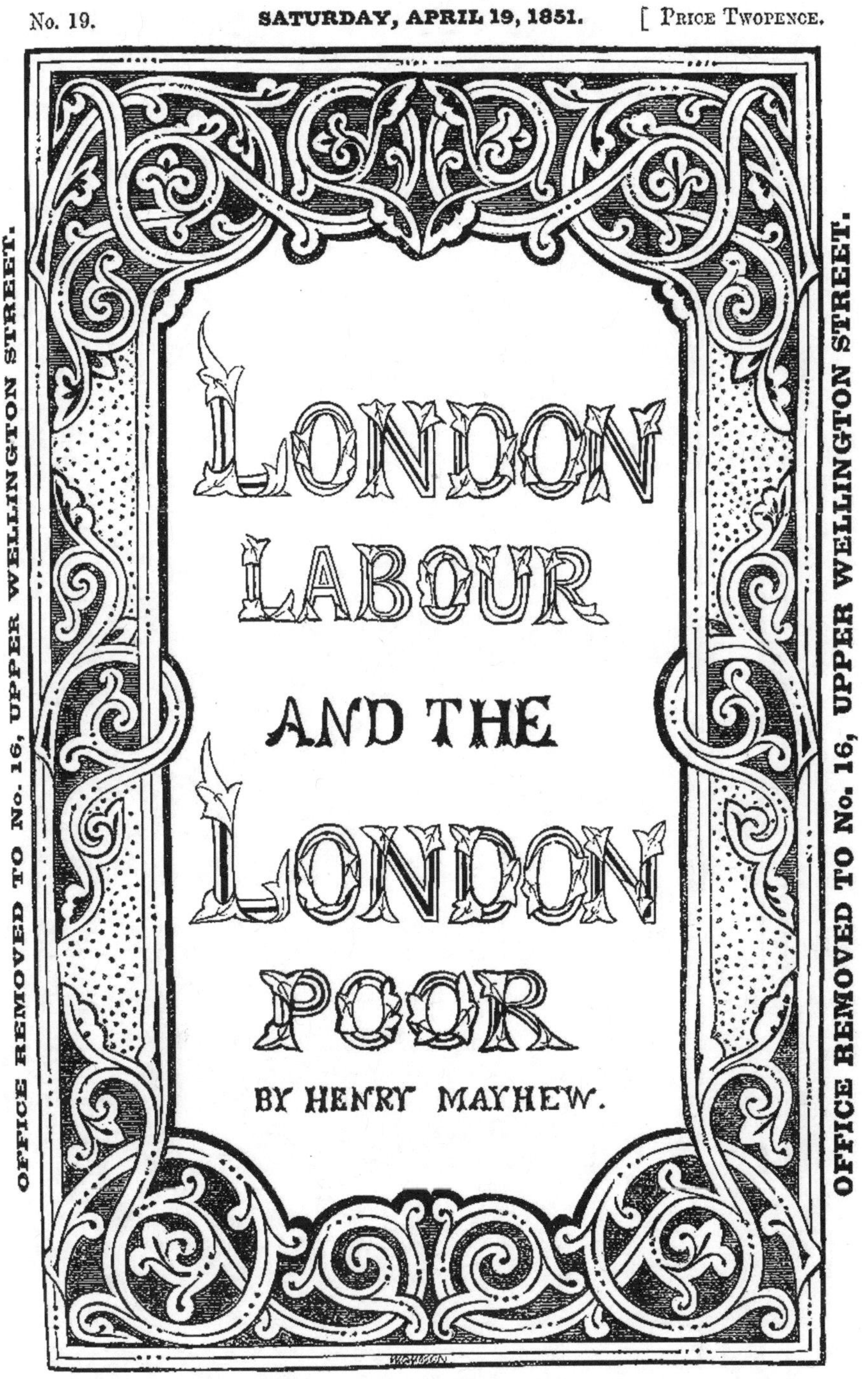
No. 19. SATURDAY, APRIL 19, 1851. [PRICE TWOPENCE.

OFFICE REMOVED TO No. 16, UPPER WELLINGTON STREET.

LONDON LABOUR AND THE LONDON POOR

BY HENRY MAYHEW.

OFFICE REMOVED TO No. 16, UPPER WELLINGTON STREET.

"Title page," *London Labour and the London Poor.*

VOLUME 1.

Preface.[1]

THE present volume is the first of an intended series, which it is hoped will form, when complete, a cyclopædia of the industry, the want, and the vice of the great Metropolis.

It is believed that the book is curious for many reasons:

It surely may be considered curious as being the first attempt to publish the history of a people, from the lips of the people themselves—giving a literal description of their labour, their earnings, their trials, and their sufferings, in their own "unvarnished" language; and to pourtray the condition of their homes and their families by personal observation of the places, and direct communion with the individuals.

It may be considered curious also as being the first commission of inquiry into the state of the people, undertaken by a private individual, and the first "blue book"[2] ever published in twopenny numbers.

It is curious, moreover, as supplying information concerning a large body of persons, of whom the public had less knowledge than of the most distant tribes of the earth—the government population returns not even numbering them among the inhabitants of the kingdom; and as adducing facts so extraordinary, that the traveller in the undiscovered country of the poor must, like Bruce,[3] until his stories are corroborated by after investigators, be content to lie under the imputation of telling such tales, as travellers are generally supposed to delight in.

Be the faults of the present volume what they may, assuredly they are rather short-comings than exaggerations, for in every instance the author and his coadjutors have sought to understate, and most assuredly never to exceed the truth. For the omissions, the author would merely remind the reader of the entire novelty of the task—there being no other similar work in the language by which to guide or check his inquiries. When the following leaves are turned over, and the two or three pages of information derived from books contrasted with the hundreds of pages of facts obtained by positive observation and investigation, surely some allowance will be made for the details which may still be left for others to supply. Within the last two years some thousands of the humbler classes of society

1 Original dates of publication for each entry in this edition have been included when known. Our sources for these dates are from Humpherys, *Henry Mayhew* and *Travels*; Taithe; Anderson; and our own primary research. The Preface was first published on 7 June 1851 in an edition, bound with a "cheap blue cover," of the first 26 numbers of Volume 1 of *London Labour* (Humpherys, *Travels* 76–77).

2 Published records of British parliamentary committees and royal commissions, typically bound in blue.

3 James Bruce (1730–94). The Scottish explorer travelled throughout North Africa, especially Ethiopia, and documented the Blue Nile.

must have been seen and visited with the especial view of noticing their condition and learning their histories; and it is but right that the truthfulness of the poor generally should be made known; for though checks have been usually adopted, the people have been mostly found to be astonishingly correct in their statements,—so much so indeed, that the attempts at deception are certainly the exceptions rather than the rule. Those persons who, from an ignorance of the simplicity of the honest poor, might be inclined to think otherwise, have, in order to be convinced of the justice of the above remarks, only to consult the details given in the present volume, and to perceive the extraordinary agreement in the statements of all the vast number of individuals who have been seen at different times, and who cannot possibly have been supposed to have been acting in concert.

The larger statistics, such as those of the quantities of fish and fruit, &c., sold in London, have been collected from tradesmen connected with the several markets, or from the wholesale merchants belonging to the trade specified—gentlemen to whose courtesy and co-operation I am indebted for much valuable information, and whose names, were I at liberty to publish them, would be an indisputable guarantee for the facts advanced. The other statistics have been obtained in the same manner—the best authorities having been invariably consulted on the subject treated of.

It is right that I should make special mention of the assistance I have received in the compilation of the present volume from Mr. HENRY WOOD and Mr. RICHARD KNIGHT (late of the City Mission),[1] gentlemen who have been engaged with me from nearly the commencement of my inquiries, and to whose hearty co-operation both myself and the public are indebted for a large increase of knowledge. Mr. Wood, indeed, has contributed so large a proportion of the contents of the present volume that he may fairly be considered as one of its authors.

The subject of the Street-Folk will still require another volume, in order to complete it in that comprehensive manner in which I am desirous of executing the modern history of this and every other portion of the people. There still remain—the *Street-Buyers*, the *Street-Finders*, the *Street-Perfumers*, the *Street-Artizans*, and the *Street-Labourers*, to be done, among the several classes of street-people; and the *Street Jews*, the *Street Italians and Foreigners*, and the *Street Mechanics*,[2] to be treated of as varieties of the order. The present volume refers more particularly to the *Street-Sellers*, and includes special accounts of the *Costermongers* and the *Patterers* (the two broadly-marked varieties of street tradesmen), the *Street Irish*, the *Female Street-Sellers*, and the *Children Street-Sellers* of the metropolis.

---

1 Little is known about Henry Wood. Richard Knight worked at the London City Mission, a position that helped him identify informants to interview for this project.

2 At the time, the term "mechanic" referred to a manual labourer or tradesperson.

My earnest hope is that the book may serve to give the rich a more intimate knowledge of the sufferings, and the frequent heroism under those sufferings, of the poor—that it may teach those who are beyond temptation to look with charity on the frailties of their less fortunate brethren—and cause those who are in "high places," and those of whom much is expected, to bestir themselves to improve the condition of a class of people whose misery, ignorance, and vice, amidst all the immense wealth and great knowledge of "the first city in the world," is, to say the very least, a national disgrace to us.

THE STREET-FOLK.

Of Wandering Tribes in General.[1]

OF the thousand millions of human beings that are said to constitute the population of the entire globe, there are—socially, morally, and perhaps even physically considered—but two distinct and broadly marked races, viz., the wanderers and the settlers—the vagabond and the citizen—the nomadic and the civilized tribes. Between these two extremes, however, ethnologists recognize a mediate variety, partaking of the attributes of both. There is not only the race of hunters and manufacturers—those who live by shooting and fishing, and those who live by producing—but, say they, there are also the herdsmen, or those who live by tending and feeding what they consume.

Each of these classes has its peculiar and distinctive physical as well as moral characteristics. "There are in mankind," says Dr. Pritchard,[2] "three principal varieties in the form of the head and other physical characters. Among the rudest tribes of men—the hunters and savage inhabitants of forests, dependent for their supply of food on the accidental produce of the soil and the chase—a form of head is prevalent which is mostly distinguished by the term '*prognathous*,' indicating a prolongation or extension forward of the jaws. A second shape of the head belongs principally to such races as wander with their herds and flocks over vast plains; these nations have broad lozenge-shaped faces (owing to the great development of the cheek bones), and pyramidal skulls. The most civilized races, on the other hand—those who live by the arts of cultivated life,—have a shape of the head which differs from both of those above mentioned. The characteristic form of the skull among these nations may be termed oval or elliptical."

These three forms of head, however, clearly admit of being reduced to two broadly-marked varieties, according as the bones of the face or those of the skull are more highly developed. A greater relative development of the jaws and cheek bones, says the author of the "Natural History of Man," indicates a more ample extension of the organs subservient to sensation and the animal faculties. Such a configuration is adapted to the wandering tribes; whereas, the greater relative development of the bones of the skull—indicating as it does a greater expansion of the brain, and consequently of the intellectual faculties—is especially adapted to the civilized races or settlers, who depend mainly on their knowledge of the powers and properties of things for the necessaries and comforts of life.

1 First published in the weekly serial version of *London Labour*, No. 1, 14 December 1850. Hereafter, in cases where the editors have been unable to verify the serial date of publication for individual entries, no notation has been given.

2 A misspelling of Dr. James Cowles Prichard (1786–1848), physician and ethnologist. His book *The Natural History of Man* (1843) argued for the united origin of the human species.

Moreover it would appear, that not only are all races divisible into wanderers and settlers, but that each civilized or settled tribe has generally some wandering horde intermingled with, and in a measure preying upon, it.

According to Dr. Andrew Smith,[1] who has recently made extensive observations in South Africa, almost every tribe of people who have submitted themselves to social laws, recognizing the rights of property and reciprocal social duties, and thus acquiring wealth and forming themselves into a respectable caste, are surrounded by hordes of vagabonds and outcasts from their own community. Such are the Bushmen and *Sonquas* of the Hottentot race—the term "*sonqua*" meaning literally *pauper*. But a similar condition in society produces similar results in regard to other races; and the Kafirs have their Bushmen as well as the Hottentots—these are called *Fingoes*—a word signifying wanderers, beggars, or outcasts. The Lappes seem to have borne a somewhat similar relation to the Finns; that is to say, they appear to have been a wild and predatory tribe who sought the desert like the Arabian Bedouins, while the Finns cultivated the soil like the industrious Fellahs.[2]

But a phenomenon still more deserving of notice, is the difference of speech between the Bushmen and the Hottentots. The people of some hordes, Dr. Andrew Smith assures us, vary their speech designedly, and adopt new words, with the intent of rendering their ideas unintelligible to all but the members of their own community. For this last custom a peculiar name exists, which is called "*cuze-cat*." This is considered as greatly advantageous in assisting concealment of their designs.

Here, then, we have a series of facts of the utmost social importance. (1) There are two distinct races of men, viz.:—the wandering and the civilized tribes; (2) to each of these tribes a different form of head is peculiar, the wandering races being remarkable for the development of the bones of the face, as the jaws, cheek-bones, &c., and the civilized for the development of those of the head; (3) to each civilized tribe there is generally a wandering horde attached; (4) such wandering hordes have frequently a different language from the more civilized portion of the community, and that adopted with the intent of concealing their designs and exploits from them.

It is curious that no one has as yet applied the above facts to the explanation of certain anomalies in the present state of society among our-

1 Smith (1797 1872) was an English army medical officer and naturalist who specialized in South African zoology, ethnography, and geography.

2 Both Prichard and Smith had published papers that compared and contrasted the groups paired together in these paragraphs. The term "Hottentot," which the writers ascribe to the San indigenous people of South Africa, is now considered a derogatory term, as is the case with "Bushman," a term that originated from the Dutch term "bossiesman," meaning "bandit" or "outlaw." "Sonquas" (a derogatory term for the Khoikhoi people), "Kafirs," and "Fingoes" also refer to indigenous groups in southwestern Africa. "Finns" and "Lappes" referred to groups in northern Scandinavia; "Bedouins" and "Fellahs" to groups in the Middle East. See also p. 87, note 2.

selves. That we, like the Kafirs, Fellahs, and Finns, are surrounded by wandering hordes—the "Sonquas" and the "Fingoes" of this country—paupers, beggars, and outcasts, possessing nothing but what they acquire by depredation from the industrious, provident, and civilized portion of the community;—that the heads of these nomads are remarkable for the greater development of the jaws and cheekbones rather than those of the head;—and that they have a secret language of their own—an English "*cuze-cat*" or "slang" as it is called—for the concealment of their designs: these are points of coincidence so striking that, when placed before the mind, make us marvel that the analogy should have remained thus long unnoticed.

The resemblance once discovered, however, becomes of great service in enabling us to use the moral characteristics of the nomad races of other countries, as a means of comprehending the more readily those of the vagabonds and outcasts of our own. Let us therefore, before entering upon the subject in hand, briefly run over the distinctive, moral, and intellectual features of the wandering tribes in general.

The nomad then is distinguished from the civilized man by his repugnance to regular and continuous labour—by his want of providence in laying up a store for the future—by his inability to perceive consequences ever so slightly removed from immediate apprehension—by his passion for stupefying herbs and roots, and, when possible, for intoxicating fermented liquors—by his extraordinary powers of enduring privation—by his comparative insensibility to pain—by an immoderate love of gaming, frequently risking his own personal liberty upon a single cast—by his love of libidinous dances—by the pleasure he experiences in witnessing the suffering of sentient creatures—by his delight in warfare and all perilous sports—by his desire for vengeance—by the looseness of his notions as to property—by the absence of chastity among his women, and his disregard of female honour—and lastly, by his vague sense of religion—his rude idea of a Creator, and utter absence of all appreciation of the mercy of the Divine Spirit.

Strange to say, despite its privations, its dangers, and its hardships, those who have once adopted the savage and wandering mode of life, rarely abandon it. There are countless examples of white men adopting all the usages of the Indian hunter, but there is scarcely one example of the Indian hunter or trapper adopting the steady and regular habits of civilized life; indeed, the various missionaries who have visited nomad races have found their labours utterly unavailing, so long as a wandering life continued, and have succeeded in bestowing the elements of civilization, only on those compelled by circumstances to adopt a settled habitation.

Costermongers.
The London Street Markets on a Saturday Night.[1]

THE street sellers are to be seen in the greatest numbers at the London street markets on a Saturday night. Here, and in the shops immediately adjoining, the working-classes generally purchase their Sunday's dinner; and after pay-time on Saturday night, or early on Sunday morning, the crowd in the New-cut, and the Brill[2] in particular, is almost impassable. Indeed, the scene in these parts has more of the character of a fair than a market. There are hundreds of stalls, and every stall has its one or two lights; either it is illuminated by the intense white light of the new self-generating gas-lamp, or else it is brightened up by the red smoky flame of the old-fashioned grease lamp. One man shows off his yellow haddock with a candle stuck in a bundle of firewood; his neighbour makes a candlestick of a huge turnip, and the tallow gutters over its sides; whilst the boy shouting "Eight a penny, stunning pears!" has rolled his dip in a thick coat of brown paper, that flares away with the candle. Some stalls are crimson with the fire shining through the holes beneath the baked chestnut stove; others have handsome octohedral lamps, while a few have a candle shining through a sieve: these, with the sparkling ground-glass globes of the tea-dealers' shops, and the butchers' gaslights streaming and fluttering in the wind, like flags of flame, pour forth such a flood of light, that at a distance the atmosphere immediately above the spot is as lurid as if the street were on fire.

The pavement and the road are crowded with purchasers and street-sellers. The housewife in her thick shawl, with the market-basket on her arm, walks slowly on, stopping now to look at the stall of caps, and now to cheapen a bunch of greens. Little boys, holding three or four onions in their hand, creep between the people, wriggling their way through every interstice, and asking for custom in whining tones, as if seeking charity. Then the tumult of the thousand different cries of the eager dealers, all shouting at the top of their voices, at one and the same time, is almost bewildering. "So-old again," roars one. "Chestnuts all 'ot, a penny a score," bawls another. "An 'aypenny a skin, blacking," squeaks a boy. "Buy, buy, buy, buy, buy—bu-u-uy!" cries the butcher. "Half-quire of paper for a penny," bellows the street stationer. "An 'aypenny a lot ing-uns." "Twopence a pound grapes." "Three a penny Yarmouth bloaters." "Who'll buy a bonnet for fourpence?" "Pick 'em out cheap here! three pair for a halfpenny, bootlaces." "Now's your time! beautiful whelks, a penny a lot." "Here's ha'p'orths," shouts the perambulating confectioner. "Come and look at 'em! here's toasters!" bellows one with a Yarmouth

1 First published in the weekly serial version of *London Labour*, No. 1, 14 December 1850.

2 New Cut Market and the Brill were two of London's most popular markets, open Saturday night and Sunday morning. Elsewhere in *London Labour*, Mayhew tallies 300 sellers at each.

bloater stuck on a toasting-fork. "Penny a lot, fine russets," calls the apple woman: and so the Babel goes on.

One man stands with his red-edged mats hanging over his back and chest, like a herald's coat; and the girl with her basket of walnuts lifts her brown-stained fingers to her mouth, as she screams, "Fine warnuts! sixteen a penny, fine war-r-nuts." A bootmaker, to "ensure custom," has illuminated his shop-front with a line of gas, and in its full glare stands a blind beggar, his eyes turned up so as to show only "the whites," and mumbling some begging rhymes, that are drowned in the shrill notes of the bamboo-flute-player next to him. The boy's sharp cry, the woman's cracked voice, the gruff, hoarse shout of the man, are all mingled together. Sometimes an Irishman is heard with his "fine ating apples"; or else the jingling music of an unseen organ breaks out, as the trio of street singers rest between the verses.

Then the sights, as you elbow your way through the crowd, are equally multifarious. Here is a stall glittering with new tin saucepans; there another, bright with its blue and yellow crockery, and sparkling with white glass. Now you come to a row of old shoes arranged along the pavement; now to a stand of gaudy tea-trays; then to a shop with red handkerchiefs and blue checked shirts, fluttering backwards and forwards, and a counter built up outside on the kerb, behind which are boys beseeching custom. At the door of a tea-shop, with its hundred white globes of light, stands a man delivering bills, thanking the public for past favours, and "defying competition." Here, alongside the road, are some half-dozen headless tailors' dummies, dressed in Chesterfields and fustian[1] jackets, each labelled, "Look at the prices," or "Observe the quality." After this is a butcher's shop, crimson and white with meat piled up to the first-floor, in front of which the butcher himself, in his blue coat, walks up and down, sharpening his knife on the steel that hangs to his waist. A little further on stands the clean family, begging; the father with his head down as if in shame, and a box of lucifers held forth in his hand—the boys in newly-washed pinafores, and the tidily got-up mother with a child at her breast. This stall is green and white with bunches of turnips—that red with apples, the next yellow with onions, and another purple with pickling cabbages. One minute you pass a man with an umbrella turned inside up and full of prints; the next, you hear one with a peepshow[2] of Mazeppa,[3] and Paul

1 Commonly worn by workers, the fustian jacket was made from a heavy cotton cloth and became a symbol of the British working class. The chesterfield was a velvet-collared overcoat, usually in grey or black.

2 Picture exhibitions enclosed in boxes or in more elaborate caravans. Customers paid to view slides of famous military battles, murder scenes, or stage plays through small viewing holes fitted with lenses.

3 Ivan Stepanovych Mazepa (1639–1709), often spelled Mazeppa, was a Ukrainian military leader considered a traitor by the Russian Empire. The peepshow was probably an exhibition of the famous 1709 Battle of Poltava between the Swedish and Russian Empires on the Dnieper River, in which Mazepa was defeated.

Jones the pirate,[1] describing the pictures to the boys looking in at the little round windows. Then is heard the sharp snap of the percussion-cap from the crowd of lads firing at the target for nuts; and the moment afterwards, you see either a black man half-clad in white, and shivering in the cold with tracts[2] in his hand, or else you hear the sounds of music from "Frazier's Circus," on the other side of the road, and the man outside the door of the penny concert, beseeching you to "Be in time—be in time!" as Mr. Somebody is just about to sing his favourite song of the "Knife Grinder." Such, indeed, is the riot, the struggle, and the scramble for a living, that the confusion and uproar of the New-cut on Saturday night have a bewildering and saddening effect upon the thoughtful mind.

Each salesman tries his utmost to sell his wares, tempting the passers-by with his bargains. The boy with his stock of herbs offers "a double 'andful of fine parsley for a penny"; the man with the donkey-cart filled with turnips has three lads to shout for him to their utmost, with their "Ho! ho! hi-i-i! What do you think of this here? A penny a bunch—hurrah for free trade! *Here's* your turnips!" Until it is seen and heard, we have no sense of the scramble that is going on throughout London for a living. The same scene takes place at the Brill—the same in Leather-lane—the same in Tottenham-court-road—the same in Whitecross-street; go to whatever corner of the metropolis you please, either on a Saturday night or a Sunday morning, and there is the same shouting and the same struggling to get the penny profit out of the poor man's Sunday's dinner.

Since the above description was written, the New Cut has lost much of its noisy and brilliant glory. In consequence of a New Police regulation,[3] "stands" or "pitches" have been forbidden, and each coster, on a market night, is now obliged, under pain of the lock-up house, to carry his tray, or keep moving with his barrow. The gay stalls have been replaced by deal boards, some sodden with wet fish, others stained purple with blackberries, or brown with walnut-peel; and the bright lamps are almost totally superseded by the dim, guttering candle. Even if the pole under the tray or "shallow" is seen resting on the ground, the policeman on duty is obliged to interfere.

The mob of purchasers has diminished one-half; and instead of the road being filled with customers and trucks, the pavement and kerb-stones are scarcely crowded.

---

1 Paul Jones (1747–92), a Scottish-born merchant sailor who became an American patriot during the War of Independence and was viewed as a traitor to the British.

2 Didactic religious literature distributed to the poor by benevolent societies. These moral stories were often met with skepticism, if not hostility, by their intended readers. They were disseminated widely, however, with their numbers rising from 314,000 printings in 1804 to over 20 million by 1861 (Altick 101).

3 Street selling was technically illegal under old vagrancy laws, but these laws were unenforced unless shopkeepers or local residents complained. Increased police presence on the streets after the Metropolitan Police Act of 1829 meant that even well-established street sellers were required to move their businesses or shut them down altogether.

The Politics of Costermongers.—Policemen.

THE notion of the police is so intimately blended with what may be called the politics of the costermongers that I give them together.

The politics of these people are detailed in a few words—they are nearly all Chartists.[1] "You might say, sir," remarked one of my informants, "that they *all* were Chartists, but as it's better you should rather be under than over the mark, say *nearly* all." Their ignorance, and their being impulsive, makes them a dangerous class. I am assured that in every district where the costermongers are congregated, one or two of the body, more intelligent than the others, have great influence over them; and these leading men are all Chartists, and being industrious and not unprosperous persons, their pecuniary and intellectual superiority cause them to be regarded as oracles. One of these men said to me: "The costers think that working-men know best, and so they have confidence in us. I like to make men discontented, and I will make them discontented while the present system continues, because it's all for the middle and the moneyed classes, and nothing, in the way of rights, for the poor. People fancy when all's quiet that all's stagnating. Propagandism is going on for all that. It's when all's quiet that the seed's a growing. Republicans and Socialists are pressing their doctrines."

The costermongers have very vague notions of an aristocracy; they call the more prosperous of their own body "aristocrats." Their notions of an aristocracy of birth or wealth seem to be formed on their opinion of the rich, or reputed rich salesmen with whom they deal; and the result is anything but favourable to the nobility.

Concerning free-trade, nothing, I am told, can check the costermongers' fervour for a cheap loaf. A Chartist costermonger told me that he knew numbers of costers who were keen Chartists without understanding anything about the six points.

The costermongers frequently attend political meetings, going there in bodies of from six to twelve. Some of them, I learned, could not understand why Chartist leaders exhorted them to peace and quietness, when they might as well fight it out with the police at once. The costers boast, moreover, that they stick more together in any "row" than any other class. It is considered by them a reflection on the character of the thieves that they are seldom true to one another.

It is a matter of marvel to many of this class that people can live without working. The ignorant costers have no knowledge of "property," or "income," and conclude that the non-workers all live out of the taxes.

---

1 Chartism was a working-class movement, prominent in the 1840s, that sought political reform of the electoral system through parliamentary legislation. The *People's Charter*, published by the movement in 1838, laid out six core demands of the movement, including extending the franchise to all men over 21. See the Introduction (p. 19) for further information.

good definition

Of the taxes generally they judge from their knowledge that tobacco, which they account a necessary of life, pays 3*s*. per lb. duty.

As regards the police, the hatred of a costermonger to a "peeler" is intense, and with their opinion of the police, all the more ignorant unite that of the governing power.[1] "Can you wonder at it, sir," said a costermonger to me, "that I hate the police? They drive us about, we must move on, we can't stand here, and we can't pitch there. But if we're cracked up, that is if we're forced to go into the Union (I've known it both at Clerkenwell and the City of London workhouses,) why the parish gives us money to buy a barrow, or a shallow, or to hire them, and leave the house and start for ourselves: and what's the use of that, if the police won't let us sell our goods?—Which is right, the parish or the police?"

To thwart the police in any measure the costermongers readily aid one another. One very common procedure, if the policeman has seized a barrow, is to whip off a wheel, while the officers have gone for assistance; for a large and loaded barrow requires two men to convey it to the green-yard. This is done with great dexterity; and the next step is to dispose of the stock to any passing costers, or to any "standing" in the neighbourhood, and it is honestly accounted for. The policemen, on their return, find an empty, and unwheelable barrow, which they must carry off by main strength, amid the jeers of the populace.

I am assured that in case of a political riot every "coster" would seize his policeman.

Religion of Costermongers.

An intelligent and trustworthy man, until very recently actively engaged in costermongering, computed that not 3 in 100 costermongers had ever been in the interior of a church, or any place of worship, or knew what was meant by Christianity. The same person gave me the following account, which was confirmed by others:

"The costers have no religion at all, and very little notion, or none at all, of what religion or a future state is. Of all things they hate tracts. They hate them because the people leaving them never give them anything, and as they can't read the tract—not one in forty—they're vexed to be bothered with it. And really what is the use of giving people reading before you've taught them to read? Now, they respect the City Missionaries,[2] because they read to them—and the costers will listen to reading when they don't understand it—and because they visit the sick, and sometimes give oranges and such like to them and the children. I've known a City Missionary buy a shilling's worth of oranges of a coster, and give them away to the sick and the children—most of them belonging to the coster-

1 This sentence is as it appears in the original.

2 Connected with the London City Mission founded by David Nasmith (1799–1839) in 1835. See also p. 48, note 1.

mongers—down the court, and that made him respected there. I think the City Missionaries have done good. But I'm satisfied that if the costers had to profess themselves of some religion to-morrow, they would all become Roman Catholics, every one of them. This is the reason:—London costers live very often in the same courts and streets as the poor Irish, and if the Irish are sick, be sure there comes to them the priest, the Sisters of Charity—they *are* good women—and some other ladies. Many a man that's not a Catholic, has rotted and died without any good person near him. Why, I lived a good while in Lambeth, and there wasn't one coster in 100, I'm satisfied, knew so much as the rector's name,—though Mr. Dalton's a very good man. But the reason I was telling you of, sir, is that the costers reckon *that* religion's the best that gives the most in charity, and they think the Catholics do this. I'm not a Catholic myself, but I believe every word of the Bible, and have the greater belief that it's the word of God because it teaches democracy. The Irish in the courts get sadly chaffed by the others about their priests,—but they'll die for the priest. Religion is a regular puzzle to the costers. They see people come out of church and chapel, and as they're mostly well dressed, and there's very few of their own sort among the church-goers, the costers somehow mix up being religious with being respectable, and so they have a queer sort of feeling about it. It's a mystery to them. It's shocking when you come to think of it. They'll listen to any preacher that goes among them; and then a few will say—I've heard it often—'A b—y fool, why don't he let people go to h-ll their own way?' There's another thing that makes the costers think so well of the Catholics. If a Catholic coster—there's only very few of them—is 'cracked up' (penniless), he's often started again, and the others have a notion that it's through some chapel-fund. I don't know whether it is so or not, but I know the cracked-up men are started again, if they're Catholics. It's still the stranger that the regular costermongers, who are nearly all Londoners, should have such respect for the Roman Catholics, when they have such a hatred of the Irish, whom they look upon as intruders and underminers."—"If a missionary came among us with plenty of money," said another costermonger, "he might make us all Christians or Turks, or anything he liked." Neither the Latter-day Saints, nor any similar sect, have made converts among the costermongers.

Language of Costermongers.

THE slang language of the costermongers is not very remarkable for originality of construction; it possesses no humour: but they boast that it is known only to themselves; it is far beyond the Irish, they say, and puzzles the Jews. The *root* of the costermonger tongue, so to speak, is to give the words spelt backward, or rather pronounced rudely backward,—for in my present chapter the language has, I believe, been reduced to orthography for the first time. With this backward pronunciation, which is very arbitrary, are mixed words reducible to no rule and seldom referrable to any origin, thus complicating the mystery of this unwritten tongue; while any syllable is added to a proper slang word, at the discretion of the speaker.

Slang is acquired very rapidly, and some costermongers will converse in it by the hour. The women use it sparingly; the girls more than the women; the men more than the girls; and the boys most of all. The most ignorant of all these classes deal most in slang and boast of their cleverness and proficiency in it. [...]

[...]

Speaking of this language, a costermonger said to me: "The Irish can't tumble to it anyhow; the Jews can tumble better, but we're *their* masters. Some of the young salesmen at Billingsgate[1] understand us,—but only at Billingsgate; and they think they're uncommon clever, but they're not quite up to the mark. The police don't understand us at all. It would be a pity if they did."

I give a few ... phrases:

A doogheno or dabheno?	Is it a good or bad market?
A regular trosseno. .	A regular bad one.
On	No.
Say	Yes.
Tumble to your barrikin	Understand you.
Top o' reeb	Pot of beer.
Doing dab	Doing badly.
Cool him.	Look at him.

The latter phrase is used when one costermonger warns another of the approach of a policeman "who might order him to move on, or be otherwise unpleasant." "Cool" (look) is exclaimed, or "Cool him" (look at him). One costermonger told me as a great joke that a very stout policeman, who was then new to the duty, was when in a violent state of perspiration, much offended by a costermonger saying "Cool him."

Cool the esclop . . .	Look at the police.
Cool the namesclop. .	Look at the policeman.
Cool ta the dillo nemo . .	Look at the old woman;

said of any woman, young or old, who, according to costermonger notions, is "giving herself airs."

This language seems confined, in its general use, to the immediate objects of the costermonger's care; but is, among the more acute members of the fraternity, greatly extended, and is capable of indefinite extension.

1 London fish market formally established in 1699 by an Act of Parliament. an open-air market until 1850, when it was moved indoors.

The costermongers' oaths, I may conclude, are all in the vernacular; nor are any of the common salutes, such as "How d'you do?" or "Good-night" known to their slang.

Kennetseeno	Stinking;
(applied principally to the quality of fish.)	
Flatch kanurd . .	Half-drunk.
Flash it	Show it;
(in cases of bargains offered.)	
On doog	No good.
Cross chap	A thief.
Showfulls	Bad money;
(seldom in the hands of costermongers.)	
I'm on to the deb . .	I'm going to bed.
Do the tightner . .	Go to dinner.
Nommus	Be off.
Tol	Lot, Stock, or Share.

Many costermongers, "but principally—perhaps entirely,"—I was told, "those who had not been regular born and bred to the trade, but had taken to it when cracked up in their own," do not trouble themselves to acquire any knowledge of slang. It is not indispensable for the carrying on of their business; the grand object, however, seems to be, to shield their bargainings at market, or their conversation among themselves touching their day's work and profits, from the knowledge of any Irish or uninitiated fellow-traders.

[...]

[...] The intelligence communicated in this slang is, in a great measure, communicated, as in other slang, as much by the inflection of the voice, the emphasis, the tone, the look, the shrug, the nod, the wink, as by the words spoken.

The Literature of Costermongers.

WE have now had an inkling of the London costermonger's notions upon politics and religion. We have seen the brutified state in which he is allowed by society to remain, though possessing the same faculties and susceptibilities as ourselves—the same power to perceive and admire the forms of truth, beauty, and goodness, as even the very highest in the state. We have witnessed how, instinct with all the elements of manhood and beasthood, the qualities of the beast are principally developed in him, while those of the man are stunted in their growth. It now remains for us to look into some other matters concerning this curious class of people, and, first, of their literature.

It may appear anomalous to speak of the literature of an uneducated body, but even the costermongers have their tastes for books. They are very fond of hearing any one read aloud to them, and listen very attentively. One man often reads the Sunday paper of the beer-shop to them, and on a fine summer's evening a costermonger, or any neighbour who has the advantage of being "a schollard," reads aloud to them in the courts they inhabit. What they love best to listen to—and, indeed, what they are most eager for—are Reynolds's periodicals,[1] especially the "Mysteries of the Court." "They've got tired of Lloyd's blood-stained stories,"[2] said one man, who was in the habit of reading to them, "and I'm satisfied that, of all London, Reynolds is the most popular man among them. They stuck to him in Trafalgar-square, and would again. They all say he's 'a trump,' and Feargus O'Connor's[3] another trump with them."

One intelligent man considered that the spirit of curiosity manifested by costermongers, as regards the information or excitement derived from hearing stories read, augured well for the improvability of the class.

Another intelligent costermonger, who had recently read some of the cheap periodicals to ten or twelve men, women, and boys, all costermongers, gave me an account of the comments made by his auditors. They had assembled, after their day's work or their rounds, for the purpose of hearing my informant read the last number of some of the penny publications.

"The costermongers," said my informant, "are very fond of illustrations. I have known a man, what couldn't read, buy a periodical what had an illustration, a little out of the common way perhaps, just that he might learn from some one, who *could* read, what it was all about. They have all heard of Cruikshank,[4] and they think everything funny is by him—funny scenes in a play and all. His 'Bottle'[5] was very much admired. I heard one man say it was very prime, and showed what 'lush' did, but I saw the same man," added my informant, "drunk three hours afterwards. Look you here, sir," he continued, turning over a periodical, for he had the number with him, "here's a

1 George W.M. Reynolds (1814–79) was an author, journalist, newspaper proprietor, and prominent Chartist. He was well known for his popular penny dreadful series, *The Mysteries of London* (1844–48), and its sequel, *The Mysteries of the Court of London* (1848–56), published in penny weekly numbers. He was also the founder of *Reynolds's Newspaper*. See Appendices B3–5.

2 Edward Lloyd (1815–90) was a publisher of cheap and sensational fiction. His popular penny dreadfuls included James Malcolm Rymer's *Varney the Vampire* (1845) and "The String of Pearls" (1846), in which the character Sweeney Todd debuted. Lloyd also published adaptations of Dickens's novels, which bordered on plagiarism, with titles such as *Oliver Twiss* (1838–39) and *The Penny Pickwick* (1837–39).

3 A prominent Chartist leader, O'Connor (1796?–1855) established the *Northern Star* newspaper in 1837.

4 George Cruikshank (1792–1878), caricaturist and book illustrator.

5 Cruikshank's "The Bottle" (1847) was an eight-part series of illustrations that promoted abstinence from alcohol.

portrait of 'Catherine of Russia.'[1] 'Tell us all about her,' said one man to me last night; 'read it; what was she?' When I had read it," my informant continued, "another man, to whom I showed it, said, 'Don't the cove as did that know a deal?' for they fancy—at least, a many do—that one man writes a whole periodical, or a whole newspaper. Now here," proceeded my friend, "you see's an engraving of a man hung up, burning over a fire, and some costers would go mad if they couldn't learn what he'd been doing, who he was, and all about him. 'But about the picture?' they would say, and this is a very common question put by them whenever they see an engraving.

"Here's one of the passages that took their fancy wonderfully," my informant observed:

'With glowing cheeks, flashing eyes, and palpitating bosom, Venetia Trelawney rushed back into the refreshment-room, where she threw herself into one of the arm-chairs already noticed. But scarcely had she thus sunk down upon the flocculent cushion, when a sharp click, as of some mechanism giving way, met her ears; and at the same instant her wrists were caught in manacles which sprang out of the arms of the treacherous chair, while two steel bands started from the richly-carved back and grasped her shoulders. A shriek burst from her lips—she struggled violently, but all to no purpose: for she was a captive—and powerless!

'We should observe that the manacles and the steel bands which had thus fastened upon her, were covered with velvet, so that they inflicted no positive injury upon her, nor even produced the slightest abrasion of her fair and polished skin.'[2]

"Here all my audience," said the man to me, "broke out with—'Aye! that's the way the harristocrats hooks it. There's nothing o' that sort among us; the rich has all that barrikin[3] to themselves.' 'Yes, that's the b—— way the taxes goes in,' shouted a woman.

"Anything about the police sets them a talking at once. This did when I read it:

'The Ebenezers still continued their fierce struggle, and, from the noise they made, seemed as if they were tearing each other to pieces, to the wild roar of a chorus of profane swearing. The alarm, as Bloomfield had predicted, was soon raised, and some two or three policemen, with their bull's-eyes, and still more effective truncheons, speedily restored order.'

'The blessed crushers is everywhere,' shouted one. 'I wish I'd been there to have had a shy at the eslops,'[4] said another. And then a man sung out: 'O, don't I like the Bobbys?'

1 The periodical can be identified as *Reynolds's Miscellany*, v. 5 no. 124 (23 November 1850), which features a piece entitled "Catherine of Russia" and describes the scandalous coup of Catherine the Great (1729–96) in taking the throne from her husband, Peter III, in 1762.

2 A passage from *The Mysteries of the Court of London*, ch. 35. See p. 61, note 1.

3 Slang for unintelligible language or jargon.

4 Slang for police.

"If there's any foreign language which can't be explained, I've seen the costers," my informant went on, "annoyed at it—quite annoyed. Another time I read part of one of Lloyd's numbers to them—but they like something spicier. One article in them—here it is—finishes in this way:

"The social habits and costumes of the Magyar *noblesse* have almost all the characteristics of the corresponding class in Ireland. This word *noblesse* is one of wide signification in Hungary; and one may with great truth say of this strange nation, that '*qui n'est point noble n'est rien.*'"[1]

'I can't tumble to that barrikin,' said a young fellow; 'it's a jaw-breaker. But if this here—what d'ye call it, you talk about—was like the Irish, why they was a rum lot.' 'Noblesse,' said a man that's considered a clever fellow, from having once learned his letters, though he can't read or write. 'Noblesse! Blessed if I know what he's up to.' Here there was a regular laugh."

From other quarters I learned that some of the costermongers who were able to read, or loved to listen to reading, purchased their literature in a very commercial spirit, frequently buying the periodical which is the largest in size, because when "they've got the reading out of it," as they say, "it's worth a halfpenny for the barrow."

Tracts they will rarely listen to, but if any persevering man *will* read tracts, and state that he does it for their benefit and improvement, they listen without rudeness, though often with evident unwillingness. "Sermons or tracts," said one of their body to me, "gives them the 'orrors." Costermongers purchase, and not unfrequently, the first number of a penny periodical, "to see what it's like."

The tales of robbery and bloodshed, of heroic, eloquent, and gentlemanly highwaymen, or of gipsies turning out to be nobles, now interest the costermongers but little, although they found great delight in such stories a few years back. Works relating to Courts, potentates, or "harristocrats," are the most relished by these rude people.

Of the "Penny Gaff."

In many of the thoroughfares of London there are shops which have been turned into a kind of temporary theatre (admission one penny), where dancing and singing take place every night. Rude pictures of the performers are arranged outside, to give the front a gaudy and attractive look, and at night-time coloured lamps and transparencies are displayed to draw an audience. These places are called by the costers "Penny Gaffs"; and on a Monday night as many as six performances will take place, each one having its two hundred visitors.

---

1 "One who isn't noble is nothing" (French). A passage from *Germania, its Courts, Camps, and People* (1850), by Marie Pauline Rose, the Baroness Blaze de Bury (1813–94), a Scottish-born writer who lived in Paris with her French husband.

[...]

Not wishing to believe in the description which some of the more intelligent of the costermongers had given of these places, it was thought better to visit one of them, so that all exaggeration might be avoided. One of the least offensive of the exhibitions was fixed upon.

The "penny gaff" chosen was situated in a broad street near Smithfield;[1] and for a great distance off, the jingling sound of music was heard, and the gas-light streamed out into the thick night air as from a dark lantern, glittering on the windows of the houses opposite, and lighting up the faces of the mob in the road, as on an illumination night. The front of a large shop had been entirely removed, and the entrance was decorated with paintings of the "comic singers," in their most "humourous" attitudes. On a table against the wall was perched the band, playing what the costers call "dancing tunes" with great effect, for the hole at the money-taker's box was blocked up with hands tendering the penny. The crowd without was so numerous, that a policeman was in attendance to preserve order, and push the boys off the pavement—the music having the effect of drawing them insensibly towards the festooned green-baize curtain.

The shop itself had been turned into a waiting-room, and was crowded even to the top of the stairs leading to the gallery on the first floor. The ceiling of this "lobby" was painted blue, and spotted with whitewash clouds, to represent the heavens; the boards of the trapdoor, and the laths that showed through the holes in the plaster, being all of the same colour. A notice was here posted, over the canvass door leading into the theatre, to the effect that "LADIES AND GENTLEMEN TO THE FRONT PLACES MUST PAY TWOPENCE."

The visitors, with a few exceptions, were all boys and girls, whose ages seemed to vary from eight to twenty years. Some of the girls—though their figures showed them to be mere children—were dressed in showy cotton-velvet polkas, and wore dowdy feathers in their crushed bonnets. They stood laughing and joking with the lads, in an unconcerned, impudent manner, that was almost appalling. Some of them, when tired of waiting, chose their partners, and commenced dancing grotesquely, to the admiration of the lookers-on, who expressed their approbation in obscene terms, that, far from disgusting the poor little women, were received as compliments, and acknowledged with smiles and coarse repartees. The boys clustered together, smoking their pipes, and laughing at each other's anecdotes, or else jingling halfpence in time with the tune, while they whistled an accompaniment to it. Presently one of the performers, with a gilt crown on his well greased locks, descended from the staircase, his fleshings covered by a dingy dressing-gown, and mixed with the mob, shaking hands with old acquaintances. The "comic singer," too, made his appearance among the throng—the huge bow to his cravat, which nearly

---

1 A central London meat market established in the Middle Ages.

covered his waistcoat, and the red end to his nose, exciting neither merriment nor surprise.

To discover the kind of entertainment, a lad near me and my companion was asked "if there was any flash dancing." With a knowing wink the boy answered, "Lots! show their legs and all, prime!" and immediately the boy followed up his information by a request for a "yennep" to get a "tib of occabot."[1] After waiting in the lobby some considerable time, the performance inside was concluded, and the audience came pouring out through the canvass door. As they had to pass singly, I noticed them particularly. Above three-fourths of them were women and girls, the rest consisting chiefly of mere boys—for out of about two hundred persons I counted only eighteen men. Forward they came, bringing an overpowering stench with them, laughing and yelling as they pushed their way through the waiting-room. One woman carrying a sickly child with a bulging forehead, was reeling drunk, the saliva running down her mouth as she stared about her with a heavy fixed eye. Two boys were pushing her from side to side, while the poor infant slept, breathing heavily, as if stupified, through the din. Lads jumping on girls' shoulders, and girls laughing hysterically from being tickled by the youths behind them, every one shouting and jumping, presented a mad scene of frightful enjoyment.

When these had left, a rush for places by those in waiting began, that set at defiance the blows and strugglings of a lady in spangles who endeavoured to preserve order and take the checks. As time was a great object with the proprietor, the entertainment within began directly the first seat was taken, so that the lads without, rendered furious by the rattling of the piano within, made the canvass partition bulge in and out, with the strugglings of those seeking admission, like a sail in a flagging wind.

To form the theatre, the first floor had been removed; the whitewashed beams however still stretched from wall to wall. The lower room had evidently been the warehouse, while the upper apartment had been the sitting-room, for the paper was still on the walls. A gallery, with a canvass front, had been hurriedly built up, and it was so fragile that the boards bent under the weight of those above. The bricks in the warehouse were smeared over with red paint, and had a few black curtains daubed upon them. The coster-youths require no very great scenic embellishment, and indeed the stage—which was about eight feet square—could admit of none. Two jets of gas, like those outside a butcher's shop, were placed on each side of the proscenium, and proved very handy for the gentlemen whose pipes required lighting. The band inside the "theatre" could not compare with the band without. An old grand piano, whose canvass-covered top extended the entire length of the stage, sent forth its wiry notes under the be-ringed fingers of a "professor Wilkinsini," while another professional, with his head resting on his violin, played vigorously, as he stared unconcernedly at the noisy audience.

1 Back slang—words pronounced as though spelled backwards—for "penny and a bit of tobacco." See "Language of the Costermongers," p. 58.

Singing and dancing formed the whole of the hours' performance, and, of the two, the singing was preferred. A young girl, of about fourteen years of age, danced with more energy than grace, and seemed to be well-known to the spectators, who cheered her on by her Christian name. When the dance was concluded, the proprietor of the establishment threw down a penny from the gallery, in the hopes that others might be moved to similar acts of generosity; but no one followed up the offering, so the young lady hunted after the money and departed. The "comic singer," in a battered hat and the huge bow to his cravat, was received with deafening shouts. Several songs were named by the costers, but the "funny gentleman" merely requested them "to hold their jaws," and putting on a "knowing" look, sang a song, the whole point of which consisted in the mere utterance of some filthy word at the end of each stanza. Nothing, however, could have been more successful. The lads stamped their feet with delight; the girls screamed with enjoyment. Once or twice a young shrill laugh would anticipate the fun—as if the words were well known—or the boys would forestall the point by shouting it out before the proper time. When the song was ended the house was in a delirium of applause. The canvass front to the gallery was beaten with sticks, drum-like, and sent down showers of white powder on the heads in the pit. Another song followed, and the actor knowing on what his success depended, lost no opportunity of increasing his laurels. The most obscene thoughts, the most disgusting scenes were coolly described, making a poor child near me wipe away the tears that rolled down her eyes with the enjoyment of the poison. There were three or four of these songs sung in the course of the evening, each one being encored, and then changed. One written about "Pine-apple rock," was the grand treat of the night, and offered greater scope to the rhyming powers of the author than any of the others. In this, not a single chance had been missed; ingenuity had been exerted to its utmost lest an obscene thought should be passed by, and it was absolutely awful to behold the relish with which the young ones jumped to the hideous meaning of the verses.

There was one scene yet to come, that was perfect in its wickedness. A ballet began between a man dressed up as a woman, and a country clown. The most disgusting attitudes were struck, the most immoral acts represented, without one dissenting voice. If there had been any feat of agility, any grimacing, or, in fact, anything with which the laughter of the uneducated classes is usually associated, the applause might have been accounted for; but here were two ruffians degrading themselves each time they stirred a limb, and forcing into the brains of the childish audience before them thoughts that must embitter a lifetime, and descend from father to child like some bodily infirmity.

When I had left, I spoke to a better class costermonger on this saddening subject. "Well, sir, it is frightful," he said, "but the boys *will* have their amusements. If their amusements is bad they don't care; they only wants to laugh, and this here kind of work does it. Give 'em better singing and better dancing, and they'd go, if the price was as cheap as this is. I've seen, when a decent concert was given at a penny, as many as four thousand costers present, behaving themselves as quietly and decently as possible. Their wives and children was with 'em, and no audience was better conducted. It's all stuff talking about them preferring this sort of thing. Give 'em good things at the same price, and I *know* they will like the good, better than the bad."

[...]

Of the Coster-Girls.

THE costermongers, taken as a body, entertain the most imperfect idea of the sanctity of marriage. To their undeveloped minds it merely consists in the fact of a man and woman living together, and sharing the gains they may each earn by selling in the street. The father and mother of the girl look upon it as a convenient means of shifting the support of their child over to another's exertions; and so thoroughly do they believe this to be the end and aim of matrimony, that the expense of a church ceremony is considered as a useless waste of money, and the new pair are received by their companions as cordially as if every form of law and religion had been complied with.

The notions of morality among these people agree strangely, as I have said, with those of many savage tribes—indeed, it would be curious if it were otherwise. They are a part of the nomads of England, neither knowing nor caring for the enjoyments of home. The hearth, which is so sacred a symbol to all civilized races as being the spot where the virtues of each succeeding generation are taught and encouraged, has no charms to them. The tap-room is the father's chief abiding place; whilst to the mother the house is only a better kind of *tent*. She is away at the stall, or hawking her goods from morning till night, while the children are left to play away the day in the court or alley, and pick their morals out of the gutter. So long as the limbs gain strength the parent cares for nothing else. As the young ones grow up, their only notions of wrong are formed by what the policeman will permit them to do. If we, who have known from babyhood the kindly influences of a home, require, before we are thrust out into the world to get a living for ourselves, that our perceptions of good and evil should be quickened and brightened (the same as our perceptions of truth and falsity) by the experience and counsel of those who are wiser and better than ourselves,—if, indeed, it needed a special creation and example to teach the best and strongest of us the law of right, how bitterly must the children of the street-folk require tuition, training, and advice, when from their very cradles (if, indeed, they ever knew such luxuries) they are doomed to witness in their parents, whom they naturally believe to be their superiors, habits of life in which passion is the sole rule of action, and where every appetite of our animal nature is indulged in without the least restraint.

I say thus much because I am anxious to make others feel, as I do myself, that *we* are the culpable parties in these matters. That they poor things should do as they do is but human nature—but that *we* should allow them to remain thus destitute of every blessing vouchsafed to ourselves—that we should willingly share what we enjoy with our brethren at the Antipodes, and yet leave those who are nearer and who, therefore, should be dearer to us, to want even the commonest moral necessaries is a paradox that gives to the zeal of our Christianity a strong savour of the chicanery of Cant.

The costermongers strongly resemble the North American Indians in their conduct to their wives. They can understand that it is the duty of the woman to contribute to the happiness of the man, but cannot feel that there is a reciprocal duty from the man to the woman. The wife is considered as an inexpensive servant, and the disobedience of a wish is punished with blows. She must work early and late, and to the husband must be given the proceeds of her labour. Often when the man is in one of his drunken fits—which sometimes last two or three days continuously—she must by her sole exertions find food for herself and him too. To live in peace with him, there must be no murmuring, no tiring under work, no fancied cause for jealousy—for if there be, she is either beaten into submission or cast adrift to begin life again—as another's leavings.

The story of one coster girl's life may be taken as a type of the many. When quite young she is placed out to nurse with some neighbour, the mother—if a fond one—visiting the child at certain periods of the day, for the purpose of feeding it, or sometimes, knowing the round she has to make, having the infant brought to her at certain places, to be "suckled." As soon as it is old enough to go alone, the court is its play-ground, the gutter its school-room, and under the care of an elder sister the little one passes the day, among children whose mothers like her own are too busy out in the streets helping to get the food, to be able to mind the family at home. When the girl is strong enough, she in her turn is made to assist the mother by keeping guard over the younger children, or, if there be none, she is lent out to carry about a baby, and so made to add to the family income by gaining her sixpence weekly. Her time is from the earliest years fully occupied; indeed, her parents cannot afford to keep her without doing and getting *something*. Very few of the children receive the least education. "The parents," I am told, "never give their minds to learning, for they say, 'What's the use of it? *that* won't yarn a gal a living.'" Everything is sacrificed—as, indeed, under the circumstances it must be—in the struggle to live—aye! and to live *merely*. Mind, heart, soul, are all absorbed in the belly. The rudest form of animal life, physiologists tell us, is simply a locomotive stomach. Verily, it would appear as if our social state had a tendency to make the highest animal sink into the lowest.

At about seven years of age the girls first go into the streets to sell. A shallow-basket is given to them, with about two shillings for stock-money, and they hawk, according to the time of year, either oranges, apples, or violets; some begin their street education with the sale of water-cresses. The money earned by this means is strictly given to the parents. Sometimes—though rarely—a girl who has been unfortunate during the day will not dare to return home at night, and then she will sleep under some dry arch or about some market, until the morrow's gains shall ensure her a safe reception and shelter in her father's room.

The life of the coster-girls is as severe as that of the boys. Between four and five in the morning they have to leave home for the markets, and sell in the streets until about nine. Those that have more kindly parents, return then to breakfast, but many are obliged to earn the morning's meal for themselves. After breakfast, they generally remain in the streets until about ten o'clock at night; many having nothing during all that time but one meal of bread and butter and coffee, to enable them to support the fatigue of walking from street to street with the heavy basket on their heads. In the course of a day, some girls eat as much as a pound of bread, and very seldom get any meat, unless it be on a Sunday.

There are many poor families that, without the aid of these girls, would be forced into the workhouse. They are generally of an affectionate disposition, and some will perform acts of marvellous heroism to keep together the little home. It is not at all unusual for mere children of fifteen to walk their eight or ten miles a day, carrying a basket of nearly two hundred weight on their heads. A journey to Woolwich and back, or to the towns near London, is often undertaken to earn the 1*s*. 6*d*. their parents are anxiously waiting for at home.

Very few of these girls are married to the men they afterwards live with. Their courtship is usually a very short one; for, as one told me, "the life is such a hard one, that a girl is ready to get rid of a *little* of the labour at any price." The coster-lads see the girls at market, and if one of them be pretty, and a boy take a fancy to her, he will make her bargains for her, and carry her basket home. Sometimes a coster working his rounds will feel a liking for a wench selling her goods in the street, and will leave his barrow to go and talk with her. A girl seldom takes up with a lad before she is sixteen, though some of them, when barely fifteen or even fourteen, will pair off. They court for a time, going to raffles and "gaffs" together, and then the affair is arranged. The girl tells her parents "she's going to keep company with so-and-so," packs up what things she has, and goes at once, without a word of remonstrance from either father or mother. A furnished room, at about 4*s*. a week, is taken, and the young couple begin life. The lad goes out as usual with his barrow, and the girl goes out with her basket, often working harder for her lover than she had done for her parents. They go to market together, and at about nine o'clock her day's selling begins. Very often she will take out with her in the morning what food she requires during the day, and never return home until eleven o'clock at night.

The men generally behave very cruelly to the girls they live with. They are as faithful to them as if they were married, but they are jealous in the extreme. To see a man talking to their girl is sufficient to ensure the poor thing a beating. They sometimes ill-treat them horribly—most unmercifully indeed—nevertheless the girls say they cannot help loving them still, and continue working for them, as if they experienced only kindness at their hands. Some of the men are gentler and more considerate in their treatment of them, but by far the larger portion are harsh and merciless. Often when the Saturday night's earnings of the two have been large, the man will take the entire money, and as soon as the Sunday's dinner is over, commence drinking hard, and continue drunk for two or three days together, until the funds are entirely exhausted. The women never gamble; they say, "it gives them no excitement." They prefer, if they have a spare moment in the evening, sitting near the fire making up and patching their clothes. "Ah, sir," said a girl to me, "a neat gown does a deal with a man; he always likes a girl best when everybody else likes her too." On a Sunday they clean their room for the week and go for a treat, if they can persuade their young man to take them out in the afternoon, either to Chalk Farm or Battersea Fields—"where there's plenty of life."

After a girl has once grown accustomed to a street-life, it is almost impossible to wean her from it. The muscular irritability begotten by continued wandering makes her unable to rest for any time in one place, and she soon, if put to any *settled* occupation, gets to crave for the severe exercise she formerly enjoyed. The least restraint will make her sigh after the perfect liberty of the coster's "roving life." As an instance of this I may relate a fact that has occurred within the last six months. A gentleman of high literary repute, struck with the heroic strugglings of a coster Irish girl to maintain her mother, took her to his house, with a view of teaching her the duties of a servant. At first the transition was a painful one to the poor thing. Having travelled barefoot through the streets since a mere child, the pressure of shoes was intolerable to her, and in the evening or whenever a few minutes' rest could be obtained, the boots were taken off, for with them on she could enjoy no ease. The perfect change of life, and the novelty of being in a new place, reconciled her for some time to the loss of her liberty. But no sooner did she hear from her friends, that sprats were again in the market, than, as if there were some magical influence in the fish, she at once requested to be freed from the confinement, and permitted to return to her old calling.

Such is the history of the lower class of girls, though this lower class, I regret to say, constitutes by far the greater portion of the whole. Still I would not for a moment have it inferred that *all* are bad. There are many young girls getting their living, or rather helping to get the living of others in the streets, whose goodness, considering the temptations and hardships besetting such an occupation, approximates to the marvellous. [...]

Of the Homes of the Costermongers.

THE costermongers usually reside in the courts and alleys in the neighbourhood of the different street-markets. They themselves designate the locality where, so to speak, a colony of their people has been established, a "coster district," and the entire metropolis is thus parcelled out, almost as systematically as if for the purposes of registration. These costermonger districts are as follows, and are here placed in the order of the numerical importance of the residents:

The New Cut (Lambeth).	Ratcliffe Highway.
Whitecross-street.	Lisson-grove.
Leather-lane.	Petticoat and Rosemary-lane.
The Brill, Somers' Town.	Marylebone-lane.
Whitechapel.	Oxford-street.
Camberwell.	Rotherhithe.
Walworth.	Deptford.
Peckham.	Dockhead.
Bermondsey.	Greenwich.
The Broadway, Westminster.	Commerical-road (East).
Shoreditch.	Poplar.
Paddington and Edgeware Road.	Limehouse.
Tottenham-court Road.	Bethnal-green.
Drury-lane.	Hackney road.
Old-street Road.	Kingsland.
Clare Market.	Camden Town.

The homes of the costermongers in these places, may be divided into three classes; firstly, those who, by having a regular trade or by prudent economy, are enabled to live in comparative ease and plenty; secondly, those who, from having a large family or by imprudent expenditure, are, as it were, struggling with the world; and thirdly, those who for want of stock-money, or ill success in trade are nearly destitute.

The first home I visited was that of an old woman, who with the assistance of her son and girls, contrived to live in a most praiseworthy and comfortable manner. She and all her family were teetotallers, and may be taken as a fair type of the thriving costermonger.

As I ascended a dark flight of stairs, a savory smell of stew grew stronger at each step I mounted. The woman lived in a large airy room on the first floor ("the drawing-room" as she told me laughing at her own joke), well lighted by a clean window, and I found her laying out the savory smelling dinner looking most temptingly clean. The floor was as white as if it had been newly planed, the coke fire was bright and warm, making the lid of the tin saucepan on it rattle up and down as the steam rushed out. The wall over the fire-place was patched up to the ceiling with little square pictures of saints, and on the mantel-piece, between a row of bright tumblers and wine glasses filled with odds and ends, stood glazed crockeryware images of Prince Albert and M. Jullien.[1] Against the walls, which were papered with

1 Louis-Antoine Jullien (1812–60), French-born conductor and composer known for conducting low-priced Promenade Concerts. The mantelpiece figurines that Mayhew observes were likely cheap glazed earthenware statuettes of celebrities like Jullien, mass produced in Staffordshire potteries after 1840.

"hangings" of four different patterns and colours, were hung several warm shawls, and in the band-box, which stood on the stained chest of drawers, you could tell that the Sunday bonnet was stowed safely away from the dust. A turn-up bedstead thrown back, and covered with a many-coloured patchwork quilt, stood opposite to a long dresser with its mugs and cups dangling from the hooks, and the clean blue plates and dishes ranged in order at the back. There were a few bushel baskets piled up in one corner, "but the apples smelt so," she said, "they left them in a stable at night."

By the fire sat the woman's daughter, a pretty meek-faced gray-eyed girl of sixteen, who "was home nursing" for a cold. "Steve" (her boy) I was informed, was out working. With his help, the woman assured me, she could live very comfortably—"God be praised!" and when he got the barrow he was promised, she gave me to understand, that their riches were to increase past reckoning. Her girl too was to be off at work as soon as sprats came in. "It's on Lord Mayor's-day[1] they comes in," said a neighbour who had rushed up to see the strange gentleman, "they says he has 'em on his table, but I never seed 'em. They never gives us the pieces, no not even the heads," and every one laughed to their utmost. The good old dame was in high spirits, her dark eyes sparkling as she spoke about her "Steve." The daughter in a little time lost her bashfulness, and informed me "that one of the Polish refugees was a-courting Mrs. M ——, who had given him a pair of black eyes."

On taking my leave I was told by the mother that their silver gilt Dutch clock—with its glass face and blackleaded weights—"was the best one in London, and might be relied on with the greatest safety."

As a specimen of the dwellings of the struggling costers, the following may be cited:

The man, a tall, thick-built, almost good-looking fellow, with a large fur cap on his head, lived with his family in a front kitchen, and as there were, with his mother-in-law, five persons, and only one bed, I was somewhat puzzled to know where they could *all* sleep. The barrow standing on the railings over the window, half shut out the light, and when any one passed there was a momentary shadow thrown over the room, and a loud rattling of the iron gratings above that completely prevented all conversation. When I entered, the mother-in-law was reading aloud one of the threepenny papers[2] to her son, who lolled on the bed, that with its curtains nearly filled the room. There was the usual attempt to make the fireside comfortable. The stone sides had been well whitened, and the mantel-

---

1 9 November, a day of festivities and pageantry in which the newly-elected Lord Mayor of London travels to Westminster to swear fealty to the Crown.

2 The 1840s saw the rise of weekly newspapers priced at threepence that catered to the interests of the artisan and working classes. The weeklies reported on the general news alongside sensational reporting on crime, disasters, and exposés of the ruling classes. The paper in this passage might refer to *Lloyd's Weekly Newspaper* (see p. 171, note 1), the *News of the World*, or *Reynolds's Newspaper* (see p. 315, note 2).

piece decorated with its small tin trays, tumblers, and a piece of looking-glass. A cat with a kitten were seated on the hearth-rug in front. "They keeps the varmint away," said the woman, stroking the "puss," "and gives a look of home." By the drawers were piled up four bushel baskets, and in a dark corner near the bed stood a tall measure full of apples that scented the room. Over the head, on a string that stretched from wall to wall, dangled a couple of newly-washed shirts, and by the window were two stone barrels, for lemonade, when the coster visited the fairs and races.

Whilst we were talking, the man's little girl came home. For a poor man's child she was dressed to perfection; her pinafore was clean, her face shone with soap, and her tidy cotton print gown had clearly been newly put on that morning. She brought news that "Janey" was coming home from auntey's, and instantly a pink cotton dress was placed by the mother-in-law before the fire to air. (It appeared that Janey was out at service, and came home once a week to see her parents and take back a clean frock.) Although these people were living, so to speak, in a cellar, still every endeavour had been made to give the home a look of comfort. The window, with its paper-patched panes, had a clean calico blind. The side-table was dressed up with yellow jugs and cups and saucers, and the band-boxes had been stowed away on the flat top of the bedstead. All the chairs, which were old fashioned mahogany ones, had sound backs and bottoms.

Of the third class, or the very poor, I chose the following "type" out of the many others that presented themselves. The family here lived in a small slanting-roofed house, partly stripped of its tiles. More than one half of the small leaden squares of the first-floor window were covered with brown paper, puffing out and crackling in the wind, while through the greater part of the others were thrust out ball-shaped bundles of rags, to keep out the breeze. The panes that did remain were of all shapes and sizes, and at a distance had the appearance of yellow glass, they were so stained with dirt. I opened a door with a number chalked on it, and groped my way up a broken tottering staircase.

It took me some time after I had entered the apartment before I could get accustomed to the smoke, that came pouring into the room from the chimney. The place was filled with it, curling in the light, and making every thing so indistinct that I could with difficulty see the white mugs ranged in the corner-cupboard, not three yards from me. When the wind was in the north, or when it rained, it was always that way, I was told, "but otherwise," said an old dame about sixty, with long grisly hair spreading over her black shawl, "it is pretty good for that."

On a mattrass, on the floor, lay a pale-faced girl—"eighteen years old last twelfth-cake day"[1]—her drawn-up form showing in the patch-work counterpane that covered her. She had just been confined,[2] and the child

1 The twelfth and last night of the Christmas season, usually falling on 5 or 6 January, and celebrated with a feast and cake.

2 She had just given birth. Confinement also referred to the last stages of a woman's pregnancy and early labour.

had died! A little straw, stuffed into an old tick, was all she had to lie upon, and even that had been given up to her by the mother until she was well enough to work again. To shield her from the light of the window, a cloak had been fastened up slantingly across the panes; and on a string that ran along the wall was tied, amongst the bonnets, a clean nightcap—"against the doctor came," as the mother, curtsying, informed me. By the side of the bed, almost hidden in the dark shade, was a pile of sieve baskets, crowned by the flat shallow that the mother "worked" with.

The room was about nine feet square, and furnished a home for three women. The ceiling slanted like that of a garret, and was the colour of old leather, excepting a few rough white patches, where the tenants had rudely mended it. The white light was easily seen through the laths, and in one corner a large patch of the paper looped down from the wall. One night the family had been startled from their sleep by a large mass of mortar—just where the roof bulged in—falling into the room. "We never want rain water," the woman told me, "for we can catch plenty just over the chimney-place."

They had made a carpet out of three or four old mats. They were "obligated to it, for fear of dropping anything through the boards into the donkey stables in the parlour underneath. But we only pay ninepence a week rent," said the old woman, "and mustn't grumble."

The only ornament in the place was on the mantel-piece—an old earthenware sugar-basin, well silvered over, that had been given by the eldest girl when she died, as a remembrance to her mother. Two cracked tea-cups, on their inverted saucers, stood on each side, and dressed up the fire-side into something like tidiness. The chair I sat on was by far the best out of the three in the room, and that had no back, and only half its quantity of straw.

The parish, the old woman told me, allowed her 1*s*. a week and two loaves. But the doctor ordered her girl to take sago and milk, and she was many a time sorely puzzled to get it. The neighbours helped her a good deal, and often sent her part of their unsold greens;—even if it was only the outer leaves of the cabbages, she was thankful for them. Her other girl—a big-boned wench, with a red shawl crossed over her bosom, and her black hair parted on one side—did all she could, and so they lived on. "As long as they kept out of the 'big house' (the workhouse) she would not complain."

I never yet beheld so much destitution borne with so much content. Verily the acted philosophy of the poor is a thing to make those who write and preach about it hide their heads.

THE IRISH STREET-SELLER.

"Sweet Chany! Two a pinny Or-r-ranges—two a pinny!"

[*From a Daguerreotype by* Beard.]

Fig. 2: "The Irish Street-Seller."

Of the Street-Irish.

Of the Street-Irish.[1]

THE Irish street-sellers are both a numerous and peculiar class of people. It therefore behoves me, for the due completeness of this work, to say a few words upon their numbers, earnings, condition, and mode of life.

The number of Irish street-sellers in the metropolis has increased greatly of late years. One gentleman, who had every means of being well-informed, considered that it was not too much to conclude, that, within these five years, the numbers of the poor Irish people who gain a scanty maintenance, or what is rather a substitute for a maintenance, by trading, or begging, or by carrying on the two avocations simultaneously in the streets of London, had been doubled in number.

I found among the English costermongers a general dislike of the Irish. In fact, next to a policeman, a genuine London costermonger hates an Irishman, considering him an intruder. Whether there be any traditional or hereditary ill-feeling between them, originating from a clannish feeling, I cannot ascertain. The costermongers whom I questioned had no knowledge of the feelings or prejudices of their predecessors, but I am inclined to believe that the prejudice is modern, and has originated in the great influx of Irishmen and women, intermixing, more especially during the last five years, with the costermonger's business. An Irish costermonger, however, is no novelty in the streets of London. "From the mention of the costardmonger," says Mr. Charles Knight,[2] "in the old dramatists, he appears to have been frequently an Irishman."

Of the Irish street-sellers, at present, it is computed that there are, including men, women, and children, upwards of 10,000. Assuming the street-sellers attending the London fish and green markets to be, with their families, 30,000 in number, and 7 in every 20 of these to be Irish, we shall have rather more than the total above given. Of this large body three-fourths sell only fruit, and more especially nuts and oranges; indeed, the orange-season is called the "Irishman's harvest." The others deal in fish, fruit, and vegetables, but these are principally men. Some of the most wretched of the street-Irish deal in such trifles as lucifer-matches, water-cresses, &c.

I am informed that the great mass of these people have been connected, in some capacity or other, with the culture of the land in Ireland. The mechanics who have sought the metropolis from the sister kingdom have become mixed with their respective handicrafts in England, some of the Irish—though only a few—taking rank with the English skilled labourers. The greater part of the Irish artizans who have arrived within the last

1 First published in the weekly serial version of *London Labour*, No. 5, 11 January 1851.

2 Knight (1791–1873) was a publisher of low-cost educational periodicals. This quotation is from "Street Noises," a chapter by Knight in *London*, a six-volume series he edited between 1841 and 1844.

five years are to be found among the most degraded of the tailors and shoemakers who work at the East-end for the slop-masters.[1]

A large class of the Irish who were agricultural labourers in their country are to be found among the men working for bricklayers, as well as among the dock-labourers and excavators, &c. Wood chopping is an occupation greatly resorted to by the Irish in London. Many of the Irish, however, who are not regularly employed in their respective callings, resort to the streets when they cannot obtain work otherwise.

The Irish women and girls who sell fruit, &c., in the streets, depend almost entirely on that mode of traffic for their subsistence. They are a class not sufficiently taught to avail themselves of the ordinary resources of women in the humbler walk of life. Unskilled at their needles, working for slop employers, even at the commonest shirt-making, is impossible to them. Their ignorance of household work, moreover (for such description of work is unknown in their wretched cabins in many parts of Ireland), incapacitates them in a great measure for such employments as "charing,"[2] washing, and ironing, as well as from regular domestic employment. Thus there seems to remain to them but one thing to do—as, indeed, was said to me by one of themselves—viz., "to sell for a ha'pinny the three apples which cost a farruthing."

Very few of these women (nor, indeed, of the men, though rather more of them than the women) can read, and they are mostly all wretchedly poor; but the women present two characteristics which distinguish them from the London costerwomen generally—they are chaste, and, unlike the "coster girls," very seldom form any connection without the sanction of the marriage ceremony. They are, moreover, attentive to religious observances.

The majority of the Irish street-sellers of both sexes beg, and often very eloquently, as they carry on their trade; and I was further assured, that, but for this begging, some of them might starve outright.

The greater proportion of the Irish street-sellers are from Leinster and Munster, and a considerable number come from Connaught.

Of the Education, Literature, Amusements, and Politics of the Street-Irish.[3]

THESE several heads have often required from me lengthened notices, but as regards the class I am now describing they may be dismissed briefly enough. The majority of the street-Irish whom I saw were unable to read, but I found those who had no knowledge of reading—(and the same remark applies to the English street-sellers as well)—regret their inability, and say, "I wish I could read, sir; I'd be better off now." On the other hand,

1 Managers of slop-shops, factories producing cheap, ready-made clothing.

2 The cleaning performed by a charwoman in households or workplaces.

3 First published in the weekly serial version of *London Labour*, No. 5, 11 January 1851.

those who had a knowledge of reading and writing, said frequently enough, "Why, yes, sir, I *can* read and write, but it's been no good to me," as if they had been disappointed in their expectations as to the benefits attendant upon scholarship. I am inclined to think, however, that a greater anxiety exists among the poor generally, to have some schooling provided for their children, than was the case a few years back. One Irishman attributed this to the increased number of Roman Catholic schools, "for the more schools there are," he said, "the more people think about schooling their children."

The literature, or reading, of the street-Irish is, I believe, confined to Roman Catholic books, such as the "Lives of the Saints,"[1] published in a cheap form; one, and only one, I found with the "Nation"[2] newspaper. The very poor have no leisure to read. During three days spent in visiting the slop-workers[3] at the East end of the town, not so much as the fragment of a leaf of a book was seen.

The amusements of the street-Irish are not those of the English costermongers—though there are exceptions, of course, to the remark. The Irish fathers and mothers do not allow their daughters, even when they possess the means, to resort to the "penny gaffs" or the "twopenny hops," unaccompanied by them. Some of the men frequent the beer-shops, and are inveterate drinkers and smokers too. I did not hear of any amusements popular among, or much resorted to, by the Irishmen, except dancing parties at one another's houses, where they jig and reel furiously. They frequent raffles also, but the article is often never thrown for, and the evening is spent in dancing.

I may here observe—in reference to the statement that Irish parents will not expose their daughters to the risk of what they consider corrupt influences—that when a young Irishwoman *does* break through the pale of chastity, she often becomes, as I was assured, one of the most violent and depraved of, perhaps, *the* most depraved class.

Of politics, I think, the street-Irish understand nothing, and my own observations in this respect were confirmed by a remark made to me by an Irish gentleman: "Their politics are either a dead letter, or the politics of their priests."

The Homes of the Street-Irish.[4]

In almost all of the poorer districts of London are to be found "nests of Irish"—as they are called—or courts inhabited solely by the Irish costermongers. These people form separate colonies, rarely visiting or mingling

1 A collection of hundreds of biographies of Catholic saints first compiled by Alban Butler (1710–73) in 1759. It went through several editions and has never been out of print.

2 Weekly Irish nationalist newspaper (1842–97).

3 See p. 77, note 1.

4 First published in the weekly serial version of *London Labour*, No. 5, 11 January 1851.

with the English costers. It is curious, on walking through one of these settlements, to notice the manner in which the Irish deal among themselves—street-seller buying of street-seller. Even in some of the smallest courts there may be seen stalls of vegetables, dried herrings, or salt cod, thriving, on the associative principle, by mutual support.

The parts of London that are the most thickly populated with Irish lie about Brook-street, Ratcliff-cross, down both sides of the Commercial-road, and in Rosemary-lane, though nearly all the "coster-districts" cited at p. 47,[1] have their Irish settlements—Cromer-street, Saffron-hill and King-street, Drury-lane, for instance, being thickly peopled with the Irish; but the places I have mentioned above are peculiarly distinguished, by being almost entirely peopled by visitors from the sister isle.

The same system of immigration is pursued in London as in America. As soon as the first settler is thriving in his newly chosen country, a certain portion of his or her earnings are carefully hoarded up, until they are sufficient to pay for the removal of another member of the family to England; then one of the friends left "at home" is sent for; and thus by degrees the entire family is got over, and once more united.

Perhaps there is no quarter of London where the habits and habitations of the Irish can be better seen and studied than in Rosemary-lane, and the little courts and alleys that spring from it on each side. Some of these courts have other courts branching off from them, so that the locality is a perfect labyrinth of "blind alleys"; and when once in the heart of the maze it is difficult to find the path that leads to the main-road. As you walk down "the lane," and peep through the narrow openings between the houses, the place seems like a huge peep-show, with dark holes of gateways to look through, while the court within appears bright with the daylight; and down it are seen rough-headed urchins running with their feet bare through the puddles, and bonnetless girls, huddled in shawls, lolling against the door-posts. Sometimes you see a long narrow alley, with the houses so close together that opposite neighbours are talking from their windows; while the ropes, stretched zig-zag from wall to wall, afford just room enough to dry a blanket or a couple of shirts, that swell out dropsically in the wind.

I visited one of the paved yards round which the Irish live, and found that it had been turned into a complete drying-ground, with shirts, gowns, and petticoats of every description and colour. The buildings at the end were completely hidden by "the things," and the air felt damp and chilly, and smelt of soap-suds. The gutter was filled with dirty gray water emptied from the wash-tubs, and on the top were the thick bubbles floating about under the breath of the boys "playing at boats" with them.

It is the custom with the inhabitants of these courts and alleys to assemble at the entrance with their baskets, and chat and smoke away the morning. Every court entrance has its little group of girls and women,

---

1 See the list of districts in "Of the Homes of the Costermongers," p. 71.

lolling listlessly against the sides, with their heads uncovered, and their luxuriant hair fuzzy as oakum. It is peculiar with the Irish women that—after having been accustomed to their hoods—they seldom wear bonnets, unless on a long journey. Nearly all of them, too, have a thick plaid shawl, which they keep on all the day through, with their hands covered under it. At the mouth of the only thoroughfare deserving of the name of street—for a cart could just go through it—were congregated about thirty men and women, who rented rooms in the houses on each side of the road. Six women, with baskets of dried herrings, were crouching in a line on the kerb-stone with the fish before them; their legs were drawn up so closely to their bodies that the shawl covered the entire figure, and they looked very like the podgy "tombolers"[1] sold by the Italian boys. As all their wares were alike, it was puzzling work to imagine how, without the strongest opposition, they could each obtain a living. The men were dressed in long-tail coats, with one or two brass buttons. One old dame, with a face wrinkled like a dried plum, had her cloak placed over her head like a hood, and the grisly hair hung down in matted hanks about her face, her black eyes shining between the locks like those of a Skye terrier; beside her was another old woman smoking a pipe so short that her nose reached over the bowl.

After looking at the low foreheads and long bulging upper lips of some of the group, it was pleasant to gaze upon the pretty faces of the one or two girls that lolled against the wall. Their black hair, smoothed with grease, and shining almost as if "japanned,"[2] and their large gray eyes with the thick dark fringe of lash, seemed out of place among the hard features of their companions. It was only by looking at the short petticoats and large feet you could assure yourself that they belonged to the same class.

In all the houses that I entered were traces of household care and neatness that I had little expected to have seen. The cupboard fastened in the corner of the room, and stocked with mugs and cups, the mantelpiece with its images, and the walls covered with showy-coloured prints of saints and martyrs, gave an air of comfort that strangely disagreed with the reports of the cabins in "ould Ireland." As the doors to the houses were nearly all of them kept open, I could, even whilst walking along, gain some notion of the furniture of the homes. In one house that I visited there was a family of five persons, living on the ground floor and occupying two rooms. The boards were strewn with red sand, and the front apartment had three beds in it, with the printed curtains drawn closely round. In a dark room, at the back, lived the family itself. It was fitted up as a parlour, and crowded to excess with chairs and tables, the very staircase having pictures fastened against the wooden partition. The fire, although it was

1 "Tombola" is a type of raffle game originating in Italy and is also the name for the barrel from which game tickets are drawn.

2 European "japanning" of furniture was an imitation of Asian lacquer. British manufacturing centres for japanned items were located in Wolverhampton and Bilston.

midday, and a warm autumn morning, served as much for light as for heat, and round it crouched the mother, children, and visitors, bending over the flame as if in the severest winter time. In a room above this were a man and woman lately arrived in England. The woman sat huddled up in a corner smoking, with the husband standing over her in, what appeared at first, a menacing attitude; I was informed, however, that they were only planning for the future. This room was perfectly empty of furniture, and the once white-washed walls were black, excepting the little square patches which showed where the pictures of the former tenants had hung. In another room, I found a home so small and full of furniture, that it was almost a curiosity for domestic management. The bed, with its chintz curtains looped up, filled one end of the apartment, but the mattress of it served as a long bench for the visitors to sit on. The table was so large that it divided the room in two, and if there was one picture there must have been thirty—all of "holy men," with yellow glories round their heads. The window-ledge was dressed out with crockery, and in a tumbler were placed the beads. The old dame herself was as curious as her room. Her shawl was fastened over her large frilled cap. She had a little "button" of a nose, with the nostrils entering her face like bullet holes. She wore over her gown an old pilot coat, well-stained with fish slime, and her petticoats being short, she had very much the appearance of a Dutch fisherman or stage smuggler.

Her story was affecting—made more so, perhaps, by the emotional manner in which she related it. Nine years ago "the father" of the district—"the Blissed Lady guard him!"—had found her late at night, rolling in the gutter, and the boys pelting her with orange-peel and mud. She was drunk—"the Lorrud pass by her"—and when she came to, she found herself in the chapel, lying before the sanctuary, "under the shadow of the holy cross." Watching over her was the "good father," trying to bring back her consciousness. He spoke to her of her wickedness, and before she left she took the pledge of temperance. From that time she prospered, and the 1*s*. 6*d*. the "father" gave her "had God's blissin' in it," for she became the best dressed woman in the court, and in less than three years had 15*l*. in the savings' bank, "the father—Heaven chirish him"—keeping her book for her, as he did for other poor people. She also joined "the Association of the Blissed Lady,"[1] (and bought herself the dress of the order "a beautiful grane vilvit, which she had now, and which same cost her 30*s*."), and then she was secure against want in old age and sickness. But after nine years' prudence and comfort, a brother of hers returned home from the army, with a pension of 1*s*. a day. He was wild, and persuaded her to break her pledge, and in a short time he got all her savings from her and spent every penny. She couldn't shake him off, "for he was the only kin she had on airth," and "she must love her own flish and bones." Then began her

1 Likely a reference to the Guild of St. Joseph and Our Blessed Lady, a London Catholic religious order and temperance society.

misery. "It plased God to visit her ould limbs with aches and throubles, and her hips swole with the cowld," so that she was at last forced into a hospital, and all that was left of her store was "aten up by sufferin's." This, she assured me, all came about by the "good father's" leaving that parish for another one, but now he had returned to them again, and, with his help and God's blessing, she would yet prosper once more.

Whilst I was in the room, the father entered, and "old Norah," half-divided between joy at seeing him and shame at "being again a beggar," laughed and wept at the same time. She stood wiping her eyes with the shawl, and groaning out blessings on "his rivirince's hid," begging of him not "to scould her for she was a wake woman." The renegade brother was had in to receive a lecture from "his rivirince." A more sottish idiotic face it would be difficult to imagine. He stood with his hands hanging down like the paws of a dog begging, and his two small eyes stared in the face of the priest, as he censured him, without the least expression even of consciousness. Old Norah stood by, groaning like a bagpipe, and writhing while the father spoke to her "own brother," as though every reproach were meant for her.

The one thing that struck me during my visit to this neighbourhood, was the apparent listlessness and lazy appearance of the people. The boys at play were the only beings who seemed to have any life in their actions. The women in their plaid shawls strolled along the pavements, stopping each friend for a chat, or joining some circle, and leaning against the wall as though utterly deficient in energy. The men smoked, with their hands in their pockets, listening to the old crones talking, and only now and then grunting out a reply when a question was directly put to them. And yet it is curious that these people, who here seemed as inactive as negroes, will perform the severest bodily labour, undertaking tasks that the English are almost unfitted for.

[...]

Street-Sellers of Green Stuff.
Watercress Girl.[1]

THE little watercress girl who gave me the following statement, although only eight years of age, had entirely lost all childish ways, and was, indeed, in thoughts and manner, a woman. There was something cruelly pathetic in hearing this infant, so young that her features had scarcely formed themselves, talking of the bitterest struggles of life, with the calm earnestness of one who had endured them all. I did not know how to talk with her. At first I treated her as a child, speaking on childish subjects; so that I might, by being familiar with her, remove all shyness, and get her to narrate her life freely. I asked her about her toys and her games with

1 First published in the weekly serial version of *London Labour*, No. 7, 25 January 1851.

her companions; but the look of amazement that answered me soon put an end to any attempt at fun on my part. I then talked to her about the parks, and whether she ever went to them. "The parks!" she replied in wonder, "where are they?" I explained to her, telling her that they were large open places with green grass and tall trees, where beautiful carriages drove about, and people walked for pleasure, and children played. Her eyes brightened up a little as I spoke; and she asked, half doubtingly, "Would they let such as me go there—just to look?" All her knowledge seemed to begin and end with watercresses, and what they fetched. She knew no more of London than that part she had seen on her rounds, and believed that no quarter of the town was handsomer or pleasanter than it was at Farringdon-market[1] or at Clerkenwell, where she lived. Her little face, pale and thin with privation, was wrinkled where the dimples ought to have been, and she would sigh frequently. When some hot dinner was offered to her, she would not touch it, because, if she eat too much, "it made her sick," she said; "and she wasn't used to meat, only on a Sunday."

The poor child, although the weather was severe, was dressed in a thin cotton gown, with a threadbare shawl wrapped round her shoulders. She wore no covering to her head, and the long rusty hair stood out in all directions. When she walked she shuffled along, for fear that the large carpet slippers that served her for shoes should slip off her feet.

"I go about the streets with water-creases, crying, 'Four bunches a penny, water-creases.' I am just eight years old—that's all, and I've a big sister, and a brother and a sister younger than I am. On and off, I've been very near a twelvemonth in the streets. Before that, I had to take care of a baby for my aunt. No, it wasn't heavy—it was only two months old; but I minded it for ever such a time—till it could walk. It was a very nice little baby, not a very pretty one; but, if I touched it under the chin, it would laugh. Before I had the baby, I used to help mother, who was in the fur trade;[2] and, if there was any slits in the fur, I'd sew them up. My mother learned me to needle-work and to knit when I was about five. I used to go to school, too; but I wasn't there long. I've forgot all about it now, it's such a time ago; and mother took me away because the master whacked me, though the missus use'n't to never touch me. I didn't like him at all. What do you think? he hit me three times, ever so hard, across the face with his cane, and made me go dancing down stairs; and when mother saw the marks on my cheek, she went to blow him up, but she couldn't see him—he was afraid. That's why I left school.

"The creases is so bad now, that I haven't been out with 'em for three days. They're so cold, people won't buy 'em; for when I goes up to them,

1 Meat and produce market established in 1826 in the wake of street clearances underway to widen thoroughfares in the city.

2 Fur sewing and pulling were common forms of employment for women, who worked in their homes and were paid by the piece.

they say, 'They'll freeze our bellies.' Besides, in the market, they won't sell a ha'penny handful now—they're ris to a penny and tuppence. In summer there's lots, and 'most as cheap as dirt; but I have to be down at Farringdon-market between four and five, or else I can't get any creases, because everyone almost—especially the Irish—is selling them, and they're picked up so quick. Some of the saleswomen—we never calls 'em ladies—is very kind to us children, and some of them altogether spiteful. The good one will give you a bunch for nothing, when they're cheap; but the others, cruel ones, if you try to bate them a farden less than they ask you, will say, 'Go along with you, you're no good.' I used to go down to market along with another girl, as must be about fourteen, 'cos she does her back hair up. When we've bought a lot, we sits down on a door-step, and ties up the bunches. We never goes home to breakfast till we've sold out; but, if it's very late, then I buys a penn'orth of pudden, which is very nice with gravy. I don't know hardly one of the people, as goes to Farringdon, to talk to; they never speaks to me, so I don't speak to them. We children never play down there, 'cos we're thinking of our living. No; people never pities me in the street—excepting one gentleman, and he says, says he, 'What do you do out so soon in the morning?' but he gave me nothink—he only walked away.

"It's very cold before winter comes on reg'lar—specially getting up of a morning. I gets up in the dark by the light of the lamp in the court. When the snow is on the ground, there's no creases. I bears the cold—you must; so I puts my hands under my shawl, though it hurts 'em to take hold of the creases, especially when we takes 'em to the pump to wash 'em. No; I never see any children crying—it's no use.

"Sometimes I make a great deal of money. One day I took 1*s.* 6*d.*, and the creases cost 6*d.*; but it isn't often I get such luck as that. I oftener makes 3*d.* or 4*d.* than 1*s.*; and then I'm at work, crying, 'Creases, four bunches a penny, creases!' from six in the morning to about ten. What do you mean by mechanics?—I don't know what they are. The shops buys most of me. Some of 'em says, 'Oh! I ain't a-goin' to give a penny for these'; and they want 'em at the same price as I buys 'em at.

"I always give mother my money, she's so very good to me. She don't often beat me; but, when she do, she don't play with me. She's very poor, and goes out cleaning rooms sometimes, now she don't work at the fur. I ain't got no father, he's a father-in-law. No; mother ain't married again—he's a father-in-law. He grinds scissors, and he's very good to me. No; I dont mean by that that he says kind things to me, for he never hardly speaks. When I gets home, after selling creases, I stops at home. I puts the room to rights: mother don't make me do it, I does it myself. I cleans the chairs, though there's only two to clean. I takes a tub and scrubbing-brush and flannel, and scrubs the floor—that's what I do three or four times a week.

"I don't have no dinner. Mother gives me two slices of bread-and-butter and a cup of tea for breakfast, and then I go till tea, and has the same. We has meat of a Sunday, and, of course, I should like to have it every day. Mother has just the same to eat as we has, but she takes more tea—three cups, sometimes. No; I never has no sweet-stuff; I never buy none—I don't like it. Sometimes we has a game of 'honey-pots' with the girls in the court, but not often. Me and Carry H—— carries the little 'uns. We plays, too, at 'kiss-in-the-ring.' I knows a good many games, but I don't play at 'em, 'cos going out with creases tires me. On a Friday night, too, I goes to a Jew's house till eleven o'clock on Saturday night. All I has to do is to snuff the candles and poke the fire. You see they keep their Sabbath then, and they won't touch anything; so they gives me my wittals and 1½*d.*, and I does it for 'em. I have a reg'lar good lot to eat. Supper of Friday night, and tea after that, and fried fish of a Saturday morning, and meat for dinner, and tea, and supper, and I like it very well.

"Oh, yes; I've got some toys at home. I've a fire-place, and a box of toys, and a knife and fork, and two little chairs. The Jews gave 'em to me where I go to on a Friday, and that's why I said they was very kind to me. I never had no doll; but I misses little sister—she's only two years old. We don't sleep in the same room; for father and mother sleeps with little sister in the one pair, and me and brother and other sister sleeps in the top room. I always goes to bed at seven, 'cos I has to be up so early.

"I am a capital hand at bargaining—but only at buying watercreases. They can't take me in. If the woman tries to give me a small handful of creases, I says, 'I ain't a goin' to have that for a ha'porth,' and I go to the next basket, and so on, all round. I know the quantities very well. For a penny I ought to have a full market hand, or as much as I could carry in my arms at one time, without spilling. For 3*d.* I has a lap full, enough to earn about a shilling; and for 6*d.* I gets as many as crams my basket. I can't read or write, but I knows how many pennies goes to a shilling, why, twelve, of course, but I don't know how many ha'pence there is, though there's two to a penny. When I've bought 3*d.* of creases, I ties 'em up into as many little bundles as I can. They must look biggish, or the people won't buy them, some puffs them out as much as they'll go. All my money I earns I puts in a club and draws it out to buy clothes with. It's better than spending it in sweet-stuff, for them as has a living to earn. Besides it's like a child to care for sugar-sticks, and not like one who's got a living and vittals to earn. I aint a child, and I shan't be a woman till I'm twenty, but I'm past eight, I am. I don't know nothing about what I earns during the year, I only know how many pennies goes to a shilling, and two ha'pence goes to a penny, and four fardens goes to a penny. I knows, too, how many fardens goes to tuppence—eight. That's as much as I wants to know for the markets."

The market returns I have obtained show the following result of the quantity vended in the streets, and of the receipts by the cress-sellers:—

A Table Showing the Quantity of Watercresses Sold Wholesale throughout the Year in London, with the Proportion Retailed in the Streets.

Market.	Quantity sold wholesale.	Proportion retailed in the Streets.
Covent Garden	1,578,000 bunches	one-eighth.
Farringdon .	12,960,000 "	one-half.
Borough . .	180,000 "	one-half.
Spitalfields .	180,000 "	one-half.
Portman . .	60,000 "	one-third.
Total . .	14,958,000 "	

From this sale the street cress-sellers receive:—

	Bunches.		Receipts
Farringdon .	6,480,000	1/2d. per bunch	£13,500
Covent Garden	16,450	"	34
Borough . .	90,000	"	187
Spitalfields .	90,000	"	187
Portman . .	20,000	"	41
			£13,949

The discrepancy in the quantity sold in the respective markets is to be accounted for by the fact, that Farringdon is the water-cress market to which are conveyed the qualities, large-leaved and big-stalked, that suit the street-folk. Of this description of cress they purchase one-half of all that is sold in Farringdon; of the finer, and smaller, and brown-leaved cress sold there, they purchase hardly any. At Covent Garden only the finer sorts of cress are in demand, and, consequently, the itinerants buy only an eighth in that market, and they are not encouraged there. They purchase half the quantity in the Borough, and the same in Spitalfields, and a third at Portman. I have before mentioned that 500 might be taken as the number supported by the sale of "creases"; that is, 500 families, or at least 1,000 individuals. The total amount received is nearly 14,000*l.*, and this apportioned among 1,000 street-sellers, gives a weekly receipt of 5*s.* 5*d.*, with a profit of 3*s.* 3*d.* per individual.

The discrepancy is further accounted for because the other market salesmen buy cresses at Farringdon; but I have given under the head of Farringdon *all* that is sold to those other markets to be disposed to the street-sellers, and the returns from the other markets are of the cresses carried *direct* there, apart from any purchases at Farringdon.

Of the Street-Sellers of Stationery, Literature, and the Fine Arts.

Of the Street-Sellers of Stationery, Literature, and the Fine Arts.[1]

WE now come to a class of street-folk wholly distinct from any before treated of. As yet we have been dealing principally with the uneducated portion of the street-people—men whom, for the most part, are allowed to remain in nearly the same primitive and brutish state as the savage—creatures with nothing but their appetites, instincts, and passions to move them, and made up of the same crude combination of virtue and vice—the same generosity combined with the same predatory tendencies as the Bedouins of the desert—the same love of revenge and disregard of pain, and often the same gratitude and susceptibility to kindness as the Red Indian—and, furthermore, the same insensibility to female honour and abuse of female weakness, and the same utter ignorance of the Divine nature of the Godhead as marks either Bosjesman, Carib, or Thug.[2]

The costers and many other of the street-sellers before described, however, are bad—not so much from their own perversity as from our selfishness. That they partake of the natural evil of human nature is not their fault but ours,—who would be like them if we had not been taught by others better than ourselves to controul the bad and cherish the good principles of our hearts.

The street-sellers of stationery, literature, and the fine arts, however, differ from all before treated of in the *general*, though far from universal, education of the sect. They constitute principally the class of street-orators, known in these days as "patterers," and formerly termed "mountebanks,"—people who, in the words of Strutt,[3] strive to "help off their wares by pompous speeches, in which little regard is paid either to truth or propriety." To patter, is a slang term, meaning to speak. To indulge in this kind of oral puffery, of course, requires a certain exercise of the intellect, and it is the consciousness of their mental superiority which makes the patterers look down upon the costermongers as an inferior body, with whom they object either to be classed or to associate. The scorn of some of the "patterers" for the mere costers is as profound as the contempt of the pickpocket for the pure beggar. Those who have not witnessed this pride of class among even the most degraded, can form no adequate idea

1 First published in the weekly serial version of *London Labour*, No. 11, 22 February 1851.

2 Bosjesman: variation of the South African 'Bushman'. Carib: term for the Kalina people, indigenous peoples from northern coastal South America who had been construed as cannibals by Columbus. Thug: the Indian "Thuggee," presented as a cult of professional criminals who robbed and strangled travellers. See also p. 51, note 2.

3 Joseph Strutt (1749–1802), the author of *Glig-Gamena Angel-Deod; or, the Sports and Pastimes of the People of England* (1801).

of the arrogance with which the skilled man, no matter how base the art, looks upon the unskilled. "We are the haristocracy of the streets," was said to me by one of the street-folks, who told penny fortunes with a bottle. "People don't pay us for what we gives 'em, but only to hear us talk. We live like yourself, sir, by the hexercise of our hintellects—we by talking, and you by writing."

[...]

The costers, we have seen, are mostly hereditary wanderers—having been as it were born to frequent the public thoroughfares; some few of the itinerant dealers in fish, fruit, and vegetables, have it is true been driven by want of employment to adopt street-selling as a means of living, but these are, so to speak, the aliens rather than the natives of the streets. The patterers, on the other hand, have for the most part neither been born and bred nor driven to a street life—but have rather *taken* to it from a natural love of what they call "roving." This propensity to lapse from a civilized into a nomad state—to pass from a settler into a wanderer—is a peculiar characteristic of the pattering tribe. The tendency however is by no means extraordinary; for ethnology teaches us, that whereas many abandon the habits of civilized life to adopt those of a nomadic state of existence, but few of the wandering tribes give up vagabondising and betake themselves to settled occupations. The innate "love of a roving life," which many of the street-people themselves speak of as the cause of their originally taking to the streets, appears to be accompanied by several peculiar characteristics; among the most marked of these are an indomitable "self-will" or hatred of the least restraint or controul—an innate aversion to every species of law or government, whether political, moral, or domestic—a stubborn, contradictory nature—an incapability of continuous labour, or remaining long in the same place occupied with the same object, or attending to the same subject—an unusual predilection for amusements, and especially for what partakes of the ludicrous—together with a great relish of all that is ingenious, and so finding extreme delight in tricks and frauds of every kind. There are two patterers now in the streets (brothers)—well-educated and respectably connected—who candidly confess they prefer that kind of life to any other, and would not leave it if they could.

Nor are the patterers less remarkable than the costermongers for their utter absence of all religious feeling. There is, however, this distinction between the two classes—that whereas the creedlessness of the one is but the consequence of brutish ignorance, that of the other is the result of natural perversity and educated scepticism—as the street-patterers include many men of respectable connections, and even classical attainments. Among them, may be found the son of a military officer, a clergyman, a man brought up to the profession of medicine, two Grecians of the

Blue-coat School,[1] clerks, shopmen, and a class who have been educated to no especial calling—some of the latter being the natural sons of gentlemen and noblemen—and who, when deprived of the support of their parents or friends, have taken to the streets for bread. Many of the younger and smarter men, I am assured, reside with women of the town, though they may not be dependent for their livelihood on the wages got by the infamy of these women. Not a few of the patterers, too, in their dress and appearance, present but little difference to that of the "gent." Some wear a moustache, while others indulge in a Henri-Quatre beard. The patterers are, moreover, as a body, not distinguished by that good and friendly feeling one to another which is remarkable among costermongers. If an absence of heartiness and good fellowship be characteristic of an aristocracy—as some political philosophers contend—then the patterers may indeed be said to be the aristocrats of the streets.

The patterers or oratorical street-sellers include among their class many itinerant traders, other than the wandering "paper-workers"—as those vending the several varieties of street-literature are generally denominated. The Cheap Jacks, or oratorical hucksters of hardware at fairs and other places, are among the most celebrated and humorous of this class. The commercial arts and jests of some of these people, display considerable cleverness. Many of their jokes, it is true, are traditional—and as purely a matter of parrotry as the witticisms of the "funny gentlemen" on the stage, but their ready adaptation of accidental circumstances to the purposes of their business, betrays a modicum of wit far beyond that which falls to the share of ordinary "low comedians." The street-vendors of cough drops—infallible cures for the toothache and other ailments—also belong to the pattering class. These are, as was before stated, the remains of the obsolete mountebanks of England and the *saltimbanque* of France—a class of *al fresco* orators who derived their names from the *bench*—the street pulpit, rostrum, or platform—that they ascended, in order the better to deliver their harangues. The street jugglers, actors, and showmen, as well as the street-sellers of grease-removing compositions, corn-salve, razor-paste, plating-balls, waterproof blacking, rat poisons, sovereigns sold for wagers, and a multiplicity of similar street-trickeries—such as oratorical begging—are other ingenious and wordy members of the same chattering, jabbering, or "pattering" fraternity. These will all be spoken of under the head of the different things they respectively sell or do. For the present we have only to deal with that portion of the "pattering" body who are engaged in the street sale of literature—or the "paper-workers" as they call themselves. The latter include the "running patter-

1 A Blue Coat School was a charity school, the oldest and most famous of which was Christ's Hospital, located on Newgate Street in London. The pupils, distinguished by their dark blue coats and yellow stockings, would have been recognizable sights in the city. Grecians were the distinguished head boys of the school, destined for Oxford or Cambridge, whose duties included giving speeches before distinguished company.

ers," or "death-hunters"; being men (no women) engaged in vending last dying speeches and confessions—in hawking "second editions" of newspapers—or else in "working," that is to say, in getting rid of what are technically termed "cocks"; which, in polite language, means accounts of fabulous duels between ladies of fashion—of apochryphal elopements, or fictitious love-letters of sporting noblemen and certain young milliners not a hundred miles from the spot—"cooked" assassinations and sudden deaths of eminent individuals—pretended jealous affrays between Her Majesty and the Prince Consort (but these papers are now never worked)—or awful tragedies, including mendacious murders, impossible robberies, and delusive suicides.

The sellers of these choice articles, however, belong more particularly to that order or species of the pattering genus known as "running patterers," or "flying stationers," from the fact of their being continually on the move while describing the attractions of the "papers" they have to sell. Contradistinguished from them, however, are the "standing patterers," or those for whose less startling announcements a crowd is necessary, in order that the audience may have time to swallow the many marvels worked by their wares. The standing patterers require, therefore, what they term a "pitch," that is to say a fixed locality, where they can hold forth to a gaping multitude for, at least, some few minutes continuously. They are mainly such street-sellers as deal in nostrums and the different kinds of street "wonders." Occasionally, however, the running patterer (who is especially literary) transmigrates into a standing one, betaking himself to "board work," as it is termed in street technology, and stopping at the corners of thoroughfares with a large pictorial placard raised upon a pole, and glowing with a highly-coloured exaggeration of the interesting terrors of the pamphlet he has for sale. This is either "The Life of Calcraft, the Hangman,"[1] "The Diabolical Practices of Dr. —— on his Patients when in a state of Mesmerism," or "The Secret Doings at the White House, Soho,"[2] and other similar attractively-repulsive details. Akin to this "board work" is the practice of what is called "strawing," or selling straws in the street, and giving away with them something that is either really or fictionally forbidden to be sold,—as indecent papers, political songs, and the like. This practice, however, is now seldom resorted to, while the sale of "secret papers" is rarely carried on in public. It is true, there are three or four patterers who live chiefly by professing to dispose of "sealed packets" of obscene drawings and cards for gentlemen; but this is generally a trick adopted to extort money from old debauchees, young libertines, and people of degraded or diseased tastes; for the packets, on

1 William Calcraft (1800–79), a famous hangman who carried out approximately 450 executions over 45 years. Several fake biographies and pamphlets capitalized on Calcraft's fame throughout his career, and he eventually wrote his own autobiography, *Life and Recollections of Calcraft the Hangman*, c. 1880.

2 A notorious brothel in Soho Square from 1778–1801, famous for its lavish rooms with dark, baroque special effects.

being opened, seldom contain anything but an odd number of some defunct periodical. There is, however, a large traffic in such secret papers carried on in what is called "the public-house trade," that is to say, by itinerant "paper-workers" (mostly women), who never make their appearance in the streets, but obtain a livelihood by "busking," as it is technically termed, or, in other words, by offering their goods for sale only at the bars and in the tap-rooms and parlours of taverns. The excessive indulgence of one appetite is often accompanied by the disease of a second; the drunkard, of course, is super-eminently a sensualist, and is therefore easily taken by anything that tends to stimulate his exhausted desires: so sure is it that one form of bestiality is a necessary concomitant of another. There is another species of patterer, who, though usually included among the standing patterers, belongs rather to an intermediate class, viz., those who neither stand nor "*run*," as they descant upon what they sell; but those walk at so slow a rate that, though never stationary, they can hardly be said to move. These are the reciters of dialogues, litanies, and the various street "squibs" upon passing events; they also include the public propounders of conundrums, and the "hundred and fifty popular song" enumerators—such as are represented in the engraving here given. Closely connected with them are the "chaunters," or those who do not cry, but (if one may so far stretch the English language) *sing* the contents of the "papers" they vend.

These traffickers constitute the principal street-sellers of literature, or "paper-workers," of the "pattering" class. In addition to them there are many others vending "papers" in the public thoroughfares, who are mere traders resorting to no other acts for the disposal of their goods than a simple cry or exposition of them; and many of these are but poor, humble, struggling, and inoffensive dealers. They do not puff or represent what they have to sell as what it is not—(allowing them a fair commercial latitude). They are not of the "enterprising" class of street tradesmen. Among these are the street-sellers of stationery—such as note-paper, envelopes, pens, ink, pencils, sealing-wax, and wafers. Belonging to the same class, too, are the street-vendors of almanacs, pocket-books, memorandum and account-books. Then there are the sellers of odd numbers of periodicals and broadsheets, and those who vend either playing cards, conversation cards, stenographic cards, and (at Epsom, Ascot, &c.[1]) racing cards. Besides these, again, there are the vendors of illustrated cards, such as those embellished with engravings of the Crystal Palace,[2] Views of the Houses of Parliament, as well as the gelatine poetry cards[3]—all of whom, with the exception of the racing-card sellers (who belong generally to the pattering tribe), partake of the usual characteristics of the street-selling class.

1 Horse racecourses in Surrey and Ascot, respectively.

2 Designed by Joseph Paxton (1803–65), a massive, innovative, and much-debated modular building constructed of glass and iron to house the Great Exhibition. See p. 116, note 1.

3 Cards varnished with a thin sheet of gelatin.

After these may be enumerated the vendors of old engravings out of inverted umbrellas, and the hawkers of coloured pictures in frames. Then there are the old book-stalls and barrows, and "the pinners-up," as they are termed, or sellers of old songs pinned against the wall, as well as the vendors of manuscript music. Moreover, appertaining to the same class, there are the vendors of playbills and "books of the performance" outside the theatre; and lastly, the pretended sellers of tracts—such as the Lascars[1] and others, who use this kind of street traffic as a cloak for the more profitable trade of begging. The street-sellers of images, although strictly comprised within those who vend fine art productions in the public thoroughfares will be treated of under the head of THE STREET ITALIANS, to which class they mostly belong.

Of the Death and Fire Hunters.[2]

I have described the particular business of the running patterer,[3] who is known by another and a very expressive cognomen—as a "Death Hunter." This title refers not only to his vending accounts of all the murders that become topics of public conversation, but to his being a "murderer" on his own account, as in the sale of "cocks"[4] mentioned incidentally in this narrative. If the truth be saleable, a running patterer prefers selling the truth, for then—as one man told me—he can "go the same round comfortably another day." If there be no truths for sale—no stories of criminals' lives and loves to be condensed from the diffusive biographies in the newspapers—no "helegy" for a great man gone—no prophecy and no crim. con.[5]—the death hunter invents, or rather announces, them. He puts some one to death for the occasion, which is called "a cock." The paper he sells may give the dreadful details, or it may be a religious tract, "brought out in mistake," should the vendor be questioned on the subject; or else the poor fellow puts on a bewildered look and murmurs, "O, it's shocking to be done this way—but I can't read." The patterers pass along so rapidly that this detection rarely happens.

One man told me that in the last eight or ten years, he, either singly or with his "mob," had twice put the Duke of Wellington to death, once by a

1 Sailors from India, Southeast Asia, and the Arab world. They were most commonly Bengali Muslims working for the British East India Company and employed on European ships (see p. 253, note 2). Lascars whose contracts did not guarantee them passage back to India were not entitled to relief under the Poor Laws, and many took to begging when stranded in London. See Appendix C2d.

2 First published in the weekly serial version of *London Labour*, No. 11, 22 February 1851.

3 Sellers of newspapers and other printed works who advertised their wares while moving from location to location. See also "Of the Street-Sellers of Stationery, Literature, and the Fine Arts," p. 87.

4 See "Of 'Cocks,' etc.," p. 102.

5 Short for "criminal conversation," the tort of adultery that enabled a husband to sue his wife's lover for monetary damages.

fall from his horse, and the other time by a "sudden and mysterious" death, without any condescension to particulars. He had twice performed the same mortal office for Louis Phillipe,[1] before that potentate's departure from France; each death was by the hands of an assassin; "one was stabbing, and the other a shot from a distance." He once thought of poisoning the Pope, but was afraid of the street Irish. He broke Prince Albert's leg, or arm, (he was not sure which), when his royal highness was out with his harriers. He never had much to say about the Queen; "it wouldn't go down," he thought, and perhaps nothing had lately been said. "Stop, there, sir," said another patterer, of whom I inquired as to the correctness of those statements, (after my constant custom in sifting each subject thoroughly,) "stop, stop, sir. I *have* had to say about the Queen lately. In coorse, nothing can be said against her, and nothing ought to; that's true enough, but the last time she was confined, I cried her *accouchement* (the word was pronounced as spelt to a merely English reader, or rather more broadly) of *three*![2] Lord love you, sir, it would have been no use crying *one*; people's so used to that; but a Bobby came up and he stops me, and said it was some impudence about the Queen's *coachman*! Why look at it, says I, fat-head—I knew I was safe—and see if there's anything in it about the Queen or her coachman! And he looked, and in coorse there was nothing. I forget just now what the paper *was* about." My first-mentioned informant had apprehended Feargus O'Connor[3] on a charge of high treason. He assassinated Louis Napoleon, "from a *fourth* edition of the *Times*," which "did well." He caused Marshal Haynau[4] to die of the assault by the draymen. He made Rush[5] hang himself in prison. He killed Jane Wilbred, and put Mrs. Sloane to death; and he announced the discovery that Jane Wilbred was Mrs. Sloane's daughter.[6]

---

1 Phillipe (1773–1850) was a French monarch from 1830 to 1848, when the French Revolution of 1848 forced him into exile in Britain.

2 The patterer, here, is claiming that the last time the Queen was secluded from the public during pregnancy (confinement), he announced that she had given birth ("accouchement") to three babies.

3 See p. 61, note 3.

4 Field Marshall Lieutenant Julius Jacob von Haynau (1786–1853) was an Austrian general infamous for his ruthlessness.

5 In 1848, tenant farmer James Bloomfield Rush (d. 1849) killed his landlord Isaac Jermy and Jermy's son, after many disputes over their land. Rush garnered much public interest by representing himself at trial, but was ultimately hanged. Emily Sandford was hired as a governess by James Bloomfield Rush and became his mistress, giving birth to a child in 1848 who died soon after. She was considered an unwitting accomplice in the double murder, which came to be known as the "Murders at Stanfield Hall." Sandford at first attempted to provide an alibi for Rush during his trial but later rescinded it, which led to a dramatic cross-examination by an angered Rush, and to much public sympathy for Sandford.

6 The case of Jane Wilbred, who was starved and abused as a servant for Mr. and Mrs. Sloane, was widely reported in the newspapers in 1850. The Sloanes were sentenced to two years in prison, and donations poured in for Wilbred, who became a political symbol of the cruel mistreatment of the poor.

This informant did not represent that he had originated these little pieces of intelligence, only that he had been a party to their sale, and a party to originating one or two. Another patterer and of a higher order of genius—told me that all which was stated was undoubtedly correct, "but me and my mates, sir," he said, "did Haynau in another style. A splendid slum, sir! Capital! We assassinated him—mysterious. Then about Rush. His hanging hisself in prison was a fake, I know; but we've had him lately. His ghost appeared—as is shown in the Australian papers—to Emily Sandford, and threatened her; and took her by the neck, and there's the red marks of his fingers to be seen on her neck to this day!" The same informant was so loud in his praise of the "Ass-sass-sination" of Haynau that I give the account. I have little doubt it was his own writing. It is confused in passages, and has a blending of the "I" and the "we":—

"We have just received upon undisputed authority, that, that savage and unmanly tyrant, that enemy to civil and religious liberty, the inhuman Haynau has at last finished his career of guilt by the hand of an assassin, the term assassin I have no doubt will greet harshly upon the ears of some of our readers, yet never the less I am compelled to use it although I would gladly say the *average* of outraged innocence, which would be a name more suitable to one who has been the means of ridden the world of such a despicable monster."

[My informant complained bitterly, and not without reason, of the printer. "Average," for instance (which I have *italicised*), should be "avenger." The "average of outraged innocence!"]

"It appears by the Columns of the Corour le Constituonal of Brussels," runs the paper, "that the evening before last, three men one of which is supposed to be the miscreant, Haynau entered a Cafe in the Neighbourhood of Brussels kept by a man in the name of Priduex, and after partaking of some refreshments which were ordered by his two companions they desired to be shown to their chambers, during their stay in the public or Travellers Room, they spoke but little and seemed to be very cautious as to joining in the conversations which was passing briskly round the festive board, which to use the landlord's own words was rather strange, as his Cafe was mostly frequented by a set of jovial fellows, M. Priduex goes on to state that after the three strangers had retired to rest some time a tall and rather noble looking man enveloped in a large cloak entered and asked for a bed, and after calling for some wine he took up a paper and appeared to be reading it very attentively, in due time he was shown to bed and all passed on without any appearance of anything wrong until about 6 o'clock in the morning, when the landlord and his family, were roused by a noise over head and cries of murder, and upon going up stairs to ascertain the cause, he discovered the person who was [known] to be Marshal Haynau, lying on his bed with his throat cut in a frightful manner, and his two companions standing by his bed side bewailing his loss. On the table was discovered a card, on which was written these words 'Monster, I am avenged at last.' Suspicion went upon the tall stranger, who was not anywhere to be found, the Garde arms instantly were on the alert, and are now in active persuit of him but up to the time of our going to press nothing further has transpired."

It is very easy to stigmatise the death-hunter when he sets off all the attractions of a real or pretended murder,—when he displays on a board, as does the standing patterer, "illustrations" of "the 'dentical pick-axe" of Manning,[1] or the stable of Good,—or when he invents or embellishes atrocities which excite the public mind. He does, however, but follow in the path of those who are looked up to as "the press,"—as the "fourth estate." The conductors of the *Lady's Newspaper*[2] sent an artist to Paris to give drawings of the scene of the murder by the Duc de Praslin,[3]—to "illustrate" the bloodstains in the duchess's bed-chamber. The *Illustrated London News*[4] is prompt in depicting the locality of any atrocity over which the curious in crime may gloat. The *Observer*,[5] in costly advertisements, boasts of its 20 columns (sometimes with a supplement) of details of some vulgar and mercenary bloodshed,—the details being written in a most honest deprecation of the morbid and savage tastes to which the writer is pandering. Other weekly papers have engravings—and only concerning murder—of any wretch whom vice has made notorious. Many weekly papers had expensive telegraphic despatches of Rush's having been hung at Norwich, which event, happily for the interest of Sunday newspapers, took place in Norwich at noon on a Saturday. [I may here remark, that the patterers laugh at telegraphs and express trains for rapidity of communication, boasting that the press strives in vain to rival *them*,—as at a "hanging match," for instance, the patterer has the full particulars, dying speech, and confession included—if a confession be feasible—ready for his customers the moment the drop falls, and while the criminal may still be struggling, at the very scene of the hanging. At a distance he sells it before the hanging. "If the *Times* was cross-examined about it," observed one patterer, "he must confess he's outdone, though he's a rich *Times*, and we is poor fellows." But to resume—]

A penny-a-liner[6] is reported, and without contradiction, to have made a large sum by having hurried to Jersey in Manning's business, and by

1 In 1849, Swiss immigrant Maria Manning (1821–49) and her husband Frederick (d. 1849) murdered Patrick O'Connor, a customs officer and money lender who was also Maria's lover. The Mannings attempted to flee with O'Connor's money but were discovered and found guilty. Their hanging—the first of a married couple since 1700—attracted a remarkably large crowd, including Charles Dickens.

2 *The Lady's Newspaper and Pictorial Times*, founded in 1847, was one of the first newspapers written for women.

3 Charles Laure Hugues Théobold, duc de Choiseul-Praslin (1805–47). French politician and nobleman who was suspected in his wife's brutal murder in 1847 and committed suicide awaiting trial. This scandal is considered one of the causes of the 1848 French Revolution.

4 The first illustrated weekly news magazine in the world, founded in 1842 by Herbert Ingram (1811–60).

5 Founded in 1791; the first Sunday newspaper in the world.

6 A writer who is paid by the line.

being allowed to accompany the officers when they conducted that paltry tool of a vindictive woman from Jersey to Southampton by steamer, and from Southampton to London by "special engine," as beseemed the popularity of so distinguished a rascal and homicide; and next morning the daily papers, in all the typographical honour of "leads" and "a good place," gave details of this fellow's—this Manning's—conversation, looks, and demeanour. Until the "respectable" press become a more healthful public instructor, we have no right to blame the death-hunter, who is but an imitator—a follower—and that for a meal. So strong has this morbid feeling about criminals become, that an earl's daughter, who had "an order" to see Bedlam, would not leave the place until she had obtained Oxford's autograph for her album![1] The rich vulgar are but the poor vulgar—without an excuse for their vulgarity.

"Next to murders, fires are tidy browns," I was told by a patterer experienced both in "murders" and "fires." The burning of the old Houses of Parliament was very popular among street-sellers, and for the reason which ensures popularity to a commercial people; it was a source of profit, and was certainly made the most of. It was the work of incendiaries,—of ministers, to get rid of perplexing papers,—of government officers with troublesome accounts to balance,—of a sporting lord, for a heavy wager,—of a conspiracy of builders,—and of "a unsuspected party." The older "hands" with whom I conversed on the subject, all agreed in stating that they "did well" on the fire. One man said, "No, sir, it wasn't only the working people that bought of me, but merchants and their clerks. I s'pose they took the papers home with 'em for their wives and families, which is a cheap way of doing, as a newspaper costs 3*d.* at least. But stop, sir,—stop; there wasn't no threepennies then,—nothing under 6*d.*, if they wasn't more; I can't just say, but it was better for us when newspapers was high. I never heard no sorrow expressed,—not in the least. Some said it was a good job, and they wished the ministers was in it." The burning of the Royal Exchange was not quite so beneficial to the street-sellers, but "was uncommon tidy." The fire at the Tower, however, was almost as great a source of profit as that of the Houses of Parliament, and the following statement shows the profit reaped.[2]

My informant had been a gentleman's servant, his last place being with a gentleman in Russell-square, who went to the East Indies, and his servant was out of a situation so long that he "parted with everything." When he was at the height of his distress, he went to see the fire at the

1 Edward Oxford (1822–1900) attempted to assassinate Queen Victoria and Prince Albert in 1840. He was found not guilty of treason by reason of insanity, and was sent to Bethlem Royal Hospital, the psychiatric institution also known as Bedlam.

2 The Palace of Westminster, which housed the British parliament, was mostly destroyed by a chimney fire in 1834. The Royal Exchange, London's centre of commerce, was rebuilt after the Great Fire of London in 1666. That building was then destroyed by fire in January 1838. A fire at the Tower of London in 1841 destroyed its Grand Armoury and almost burned the crown jewels.

Tower, as he "had nothing better to do." He remained out some hours, and before he reached his lodging, men passed him, crying the full and true particulars of the fire. "I bought one," said the man, "and changed my last shilling. It was a sudden impulse, for I saw people buy keenly. I never read it, but only looked at the printer's name. I went to him at the Dials,[1] and bought some, and so I went into the paper trade. I made 6*s.* or 7*s.* some days, while the Tower lasted; and 3*s.* and 4*s.* other days, when the first polish was off. I sold them mostly at 1*d.* a piece at first. It was good money then. The Tower was good, or middling good, for from 14 to 20 days. There was at least 100 men working nothing but the Tower. There's no great chance of any more great buildings being burnt; worse luck. People don't care much about private fires. A man in this street don't heed so much who's burnt to death in the next. But the foundation-stone of the new Royal Exchange—fire led to that—was pretty fair, and portraits of Halbert[2] went off, so that it was for two or three days as good as the Tower. Fires is our best friends next to murders, if they're *good* fires. [...]

After the burning of York Minster by Jonathan Martin,[3] I was told by an old hand, the (street) destruction of the best known public buildings in the country was tried; such as Canterbury Cathedral, Dover Castle, the Brighton Pavilion, Edinburgh Castle, or Holyrood House—all known to "travelling" patterers—but the success was not sufficiently encouraging. It was no use, I was told, firing such places as Hampton Court[4] or Windsor Castle, for unless people *saw* the reflection of a great fire, they wouldn't buy.

Of Political Litanies, Dialogues, Etc.[5]

To "work a litany" in the streets is considered one of the higher exercises of professional skill on the part of the patterer. In working this, a clever patterer—who will not scruple to introduce anything out of his head which may strike him as suitable to his audience—is very particular in his choice of a mate, frequently changing his ordinary partner, who may be good "at a noise" or a ballad, but not have sufficient acuteness or intelligence to patter politics as if he understood what he was speaking about. I am told that there are not twelve patterers in London whom a critical professor of street elocution will admit to be capable of 'working a catechism' or a litany. "Why, sir," said one patterer, "I've gone out with a mate to work a litany, and he's humped it in no time." To 'hump,' in street parlance, is equivalent to 'botch,' in more genteel colloquialism. "And when a

1 Seven Dials, at the time a poor and working-class neighbourhood of narrow streets near Covent Garden in central London.

2 Prince Albert.

3 Jonathan Martin (1782–1838) set fire to York Minster in 1829, causing significant damage. He was tried and declared not guilty on the grounds of insanity.

4 See p. 164, note 2.

5 First published in the weekly serial version of *London Labour*, No. 12, 1 March 1851.

thing's humped," my informant continued, "you can only 'call a go.'" To 'call a go,' signifies to remove to another spot, or adopt some other patter, or, in short, to resort to some change or other in consequence of a failure.

An elderly man, not now in the street trade, but who had "pattered off a few papers" some years ago, told me that he had heard three or four old hands—"now all dead, for they're a short-lived people"—talk of the profits gained and the risk ran by giving Hone's[1] parodies on the Catechism, Litany, St. Athanasius' Creed, &c. in the streets, after the three consecutive trials and the three acquittals of Hone had made the parodies famous and Hone popular. To work them in the streets was difficult, "for though," said my informant, "there was no new police in them days, there was plenty of officers and constables ready to pull the fellows up, and though Hone was acquitted, a beak[2] that wanted to please the high dons, would find some way of stopping them that sold Hone's things in the street, and so next to nothing could be done that way, but a little was done." The greatest source of profit, I learned from the reminiscences of the same man, was in the parlours and tap-rooms of public-houses, where the patterers or reciters were well paid "for going through their catechisms," and sometimes, that there might be no interruption, the door was locked, and even the landlord and his servants excluded. The charge was usually 2*d.* a copy, but 1*d.* was not refused.

During Queen Caroline's trial[3] there were the like interruptions and hindrances to similar performances; and the interruptions continued during the passing of the Catholic Emancipation Bill[4] until about the era of the Reform Bill,[5] and then the hindrance was but occasional. "And perhaps it was our own fault, sir," said one patterer, "that we was then molested at all in the dialogues and catechisms and things; but we was uncommon bold, and what plenty called sarcy, at that time: we was so."

---

1 William Hone (1780–1842) published three parodies in 1817: *The Late John Wilkes's Catechism of a Ministerial Member*, *The Political Litany Diligently Revised to Be Said or Sung until the Appointed Change Come*, and *The Sinecurists' Creed or Belief, as the Same Can or May Be Said.* He was put on trial for blasphemy, with a separate trial for each parody, and was subsequently acquitted in each trial. Though the government apparently intended to make an example of Hone, he framed his parodies as attacking the government, not religion, and presented himself as standing for the freedom of the press, which led to his public popularity.

2 Magistrate.

3 Queen Caroline (1768–1821), the estranged wife of George IV (r. 1820–30), who separated from her in 1796 while still Prince of Wales. In 1820, the newly ascended king spurred the cabinet to prepare a bill to end the marriage and strip the queen of her title. This dramatic event led to public support for the queen, as well as the circulation of accounts of the proceedings, obscene prints, and caricatures.

4 Passed through Parliament in April 1829, the Catholic Emancipation Act dictated, among other things, that Catholics could sit as MPs and were eligible for most public offices.

5 The Representation of the People Act 1832 (commonly known as the first Reform Act), which increased the franchise and redistributed the electoral system.

Thus this branch of a street profession continued to be followed, half surreptitiously, until after the subsidence of the political ferment consequent on the establishment of a new franchise and the partial abolition of an old one. The calling, however, has never been popular among street purchasers, and I believe that it is sometimes followed by a street-patterer as much from the promptings of the pride of art as from the hope of gain.

The street-papers in the dialogue form have not been copied nor derived from popular productions—but even in the case of Political Litanies and Anti-Corn-law Catechisms and Dialogues are the work of street authors.

One intelligent man told me, that properly to work a political litany, which referred to ecclesiastical matters, he "made himself up," as well as limited means would permit, as a bishop! and "did stunning, until he was afraid of being stunned on skilly."[1] Of the late papers on the subject of the Pope, I cite the one which was certainly the best of all that appeared, and concerning which indignant remonstrances were addressed to some of the newspapers. The "good child" in the patter, was a tall bulky man; the examiner (also the author), was rather diminutive:—

"*The old English Bull John v. the Pope's Bull of Rome.*

"My good Child as it is necessary at this very important crisis; when, that good pious and very reasonable old gentleman Pope Pi-ass the nineth[2] has promised to favor us with his presence, and the pleasures of Popery—and trampled on the rights and privilages which, we, as Englishmen, and Protestants, have engaged for these last three hundred years—Since Bluff, king Hal. began to take a dislike to the broad brimmed hat of the venerable Cardinal Wolsey, and proclaimed himself an heretic; It is necessary I say, for you, and all of you, to be perfect in your Lessons so as you may be able to verbly chastize this saucy prelate, his newly made Car-

1 Slang for being sent to prison, where one would have to eat skilly, a thin gruel made of water and oatmeal.

2 Both litanies quoted here refer to the history of Catholicism in England. They satirize the Papal Aggression of the fall of 1850, in which Pope Pius IX proclaimed a territorial hierarchy in England for the Roman Catholic Church. The term "Pusyites" refers to the Oxford Movement, which challenged the doctrines established in the English Reformation and argued for the inclusion of some older Christian traditions in Anglican theology. The litany's speakers appeal to various figures to protect them from the encroachment of Catholicism, including Lord John Russell, the prime minister (referred to here as "Jack Russell" and "Johnny"), the Duke of Wellington ("Nosey"; "Arthur"), and John Cumming, a hostile anti-Catholic preacher. Other references abound in both litanies to Henry VIII (r. 1509–47) ("Bluff, king Hal"; "Harry the stout"); Nicholas Wiseman (1802–65) (the "Wiseman of Westminster"), whom the pope had appointed as the first cardinal-archbishop of Westminster in September 1850; St. Barnabas, Pimlico, the first church established in the doctrines of the Oxford Movement; and the execution of Catholics at Smithfield in the sixteenth century.

dinal Foolishman, and the whole host of Puseites and protect our beloved Queen, our Church, and our Constitution.

"Q. Now my boy can you tell me what is your Name?

"A. B—— Protestant.

"Q. How came you by that name?

"A. At the time of Harry the stout, when Popery was in a galloping consumption the people protested against the surpremacy and instalence of the Pope; and his Colleges had struck deep at the hallow tree of superstition I gained the name of Protestant, and proud am I, and ever shall be to stick to it till the day of my death.

"*Let us say.*

"From all Cardinals whether wise or foolish. Oh! Queen Spare us.

"*Spare us, Oh Queen.*

"From the pleasure of the Rack, and the friendship of the kind hearted officers of the Inquisition. Oh! Johnny hear us.

"*Oh! Russell hear us.*

"From the comforts of being frisled like a devil'd kidney. Oh! Nosey save us.

"*Hear us Oh Arthur.*

"From such saucy Prelates, as Pope Pi-ass. Oh! Cumming's save us.

"*Save us good Cumming.*

"And let us have no more Burnings in Smithfield,[1] no more warm drinks in the shape of boiled oil, or, molten lead, and send the whole host of Pusyites along with the Pope, Cardinals to the top of mount Vesuvius there to dine off of hot lava, so that we may live in peace & shout long live our Queen and No Popery!"

For some pitches the foregoing was sufficient, for a street auditory "hates too long a patter"; but where a favourable opportunity offered, easily tested by the pecuniary beginnings, the "Lesson of the Day" was given in addition, and was inserted after the second "Answer" in the foregoing parody, so preceding the "Let us say":

1 See p. 64, note 1.

"The Lesson of the Day.

"You seem an intelligent lad, so I think you are quite capable of Reading with me the Lessons for this day's service.

"Now the Lesson for the day is taken from all parts of the Book of Martyrs, beginning at just where you like.

"It was about the year 1835, that a certain renagade of the name of Pussy—I beg his pardon, I mean Pusey, like a snake who stung his master commenced crawling step by step, from the master; he was bound to serve to worship a puppet, arrayed in a spangle and tincel of a romish showman.

"And the pestelance that he shed around spread rapidly through the minds of many unworthy members of our established Church; even up to the present year, 1850, inasmuch that St Barnabus, of Pimlico, unable to see the truth by the aid of his occulars, mounted four pounds of long sixes in the mid-day, that he might see through the fog of his own folly, by which he was surrounded.

"And Pope Pi-ass the nineth taking advantage of the hubub, did create unto himself a Cardinal in the person of one Wiseman of Westminster.

"And Cardinal broadbrim claimed four counties in England as his dioces, and his master the Pope claimed as many more as his sees, but the people of England could not see that, so they declared aloud they would see them blowed first.

"So when Jack Russell heard of his most impudent intentions, he sent him a Letter saying it was the intention of the people of England never again to submit to their infamous mumerys for the burnings in Smithfield was still fresh in their memory.

"And behold great meetings were held in different parts of England where the Pope was burnt in effigy, like unto a Yarmouth Bloater, as a token of respect for him and his followers.

"And the citizens of London were stanch to a man, and assembled together in the Guildhall of our mighty City and shouted with stentarian lungs, long live the Queen and down with the Pope, the sound of which might have been heard even unto the vatican of Rome.

"And when his holyness the Pope heard that his power was set at naught, his nose became blue even as a bilberry with rage and declared Russell and Cummings or any who joined in the No Popery cry, should ever name the felisity of kissing his pious great toe.

"Thus Endeth the Lesson."

In the course of my inquiries touching this subject I had more than once occasion to observe that an acute patterer had always a reason, or an excuse for anything. One quick-witted Irishman, whom I knew to be a Roman Catholic, was "working" a "patter against the Pope," (not the one I have given), and on my speaking to him on the subject, and saying that I supposed he did it for a living, he replied: "That's it then, sir. You're right, sir, yes. I work it just as a Catholic lawyer would plead against a Catholic paper for a libel on Protestants—though in his heart he knew the paper was right—and a Protestant lawyer would defend the libel hammer and tongs. Bless you, sir, you'll not find much more honour that way among us (laughing) than among them lawyers; not much." The readiness with which the sharpest of those men plead the doings not only of tradesmen, but of the learned and sacred professions, to justify themselves, is remarkable.

[...]

Of "Cocks," Etc.[1]

THESE "literary forgeries," if so they may be called, have already been alluded to under the head of the "Death and Fire Hunters," but it is necessary to give a short account of a few of the best and longest known of those stereotyped; no new cocks, except for an occasion, have been printed for some years.

One of the stereotyped cocks is, the "Married Man Caught in a Trap." One man had known it sold "for years and years," and it served, he said, when there was any police report in the papers about sweethearts in coal-cellars, &c. The illustration embraces two compartments. In one a severe-looking female is assaulting a man, whose hat has been knocked off by the contents of a water-jug, which a very stout woman is pouring on his head from a window. In the other compartment, as if from an adjoining room, two women look on encouragingly. The subject matter, however, is in no accordance with the title or the embellishment. It is a love-letter from John S—n to his most "adorable Mary." He expresses the ardour of his passion, and then twits his adored with something beyond a flirtation with Robert E—, a "decoyer of female innocence." Placably overlooking this, however, John S—n continues:—

> "My dearest angel consent to my request, and keep me no longer in suspense—nothing, on my part, shall ever be wanting to make you happy and comfortable. My apprenticeship will expire in four months from hence, when I intend to open a shop in the small ware line, and your abilities in dress-making and self-adjusting stay-maker, and the assistance of a few female mechanics, we shall be able to realize an independency."

"Many a turn in seductions talked about in the papers and not talked about nowhere," said one man, "has that slum served for, besides other things, such as love-letters, and confessions of a certain lady in this neighbourhood."

Another old cock is headed, "Extraordinary and Funny Doings in this Neighbourhood." The illustration is a young lady, in an evening dress, sitting with an open letter in her hand, on a sort of garden-seat, in what appears to be a churchyard. After a smart song, enforcing the ever-neg-

1 First published in the weekly serial version of *London Labour*, No. 12, 1 March 1851.

lected advice that people should "look at home and mind their own business," are two letters, the first from R.G.; the answer from S.H.M. The gentleman's epistle commences:—

"Madam,

"The love and tenderness I have hitherto expressed for / you is false, and I now feel that my indifference towards / you increases every day, and the more I see you the more / you appear ridiculous in my eyes and contemptible— / I feel inclined & in every respect disposed & determined / to hate you. Believe me, I never had any inclination / to offer you my hand."

The lady responds in a similar strain, and the twain appear very angry, until a foot-note offers an explanation: "By reading every other line of the above letters the true meaning will be found."

Of this class of cocks I need cite no other specimens, but pass on to one of another species—the "Cruel and Inhuman Murder Committed on the Body of Capt. Lawson."[1] The illustration is a lady, wearing a coronet, stabbing a gentleman, in full dress, through the top button of his waistcoat. The narrative commences:—

"WITH surprise we have learned that this neighbourhood for a length of time was amazingly alarmed this day by a crowd of people carrying the body of Mr. James Lawless, to a doctor while streams of blood besmeared the way in such a manner that the cries of Murder re-echoed the sound of numerous voices. It appears that the cause of alarm, originated through a court-ship attended with a solemn promise of marriage between him and miss Lucy Guard, a handsome young Lady of refined feelings with the intercourse of a superior enlightened mind she lived with her aunt who spared neither pain nor cost to improve the talents of miss G. those seven years past, since the death of her mother in Ludgate Hill, London, and bore a most excellent character until she got entangled by the delumps alcurement[2] of Mr. L."

The writer then deplores Miss Guard's fall from virtue, and her desertion by her betrayer, "on account of her fortune being small." Capt. Lawson, or Mr. James Lawless, next woos a wealthy City maiden, and the banns are published. What follows seems to me to be a rather intricate detail:—

"We find that the intended bride learned that Miss Guard, held certain promissory letters of his, and that she was determined to enter an action against him for a breach of promise,[3] which moved clouded Eclipse over the extacy of the variable miss Lawless who knew that Miss G had Letters of his sufficient to substantiate her claims in a court."

---

1 The story circulated in a broadsheet published by the Catnach Press, owned by James Catnach (1792–1841), who operated in Seven Dials in London. Catnach broadsheets, printed on cheap paper, were affordably priced and played an important role in the development of early-nineteenth-century London street literature.

2 As in original text. Meaning uncertain.

3 Because a marriage engagement was considered a legally binding contract, a woman could sue a man for damages if he failed to honour—or "breached"—his promise of marriage.

Lawson visits Miss Guard to wheedle her out of his letters, but "she drew a large carving-knife and stabbed him under the left breast." At the latest account the man was left without hope of recovery, while "the valiant victress" was "ordered to submit to judicial decorum in the nineteenth year of her age." The murders and other atrocities for which this "cock" has been sponsor, are—I was informed emphatically—a thundering lot!

I conclude with another cock, which may be called a narrative "on a subject," as we have "ballads on a subject" (afterwards to be described), but with this difference, that the narrative is fictitious, and the ballad must be founded on a real event, however embellished. The highest newspaper style, I was told, was aimed at. Part of the production reads as if it had done service during the Revolution of February, 1848.

"Express from Paris. Supposed Death of LOUIS NAPOLEON. We stop the press to announce, That Luis Napoleon has been assasinated, by some it is said he is shot dead, by others that he is only wounded in the right arm.

"We have most important intelligence from Paris. That capital is in a state of insurrection. The vivacious people, who have herefore defeated the goverment by paving-stones, have again taken up those missiles. On Tuesday the Ministers forbade the reform banquet, and the prefect of police published a proclamation warning the people to respect the laws, which he declared were violated, and he meant to enforce them. But the people dispised the proclamation and rejected his authority. They assembled in great multitudes round the Chambers of Deputies, and forced their way over the walls. They were attacked by the troops and dispersed, but, re-assembled in various quarters. They showed their hatred of M. Guizot[1] by demolishing his windows and attempting to force an entrance into his hotel, but were again repulced by the troops. All the military in Paris, and all the National Guard, have been summoned to arms, and every preparation made on the part of the government to put down the people.

"The latter have raised barricades in various places, and have unpaved the streets, overturned omnibusses, and made preparations for a vigorous assault, or a protracted resistance. Five o'Clock—At this momont the Rue St. Honore is blockaded by a detachment of dragoons, who fill the market-place near the Rue des Petits Champs, and are charging the people sword in hand, carriages full of people are being taken to the hospitals.

"In fact the maddest excitement reigns throughout the capital.

"Half past Six.—During the above we have instituted enquiries at the Foreign office, they have not received any inteligence of the above report,

1 François Guizot (1787–1874) was a French historian and politician who served in high-ranking positions during the July Monarchy (1830–48). Guizot supported constitutional monarchy, opposed expansion of the political franchise to all landowners, and banned political meetings, making him an object of hatred from the left. Guizot resigned as prime minister on 23 February 1848, and the monarchy collapsed the next day, leading to the establishment of the French Second Republic.

if it has come, it must have been by pigeon express. We have not given the above in our columns with a view of its authenticity, any further information as soon as obtained shall be immediately announced to the public."

Of "Strawing."[1]

I have already alluded to "strawing," which can hardly be described as quackery. It is rather a piece of mountebankery. Many a quack—confining the term to its most common signification, that of a "quack doctor"—has faith in the excellence of his own nostrums, and so proffers that which he believes to be curative: the strawer, however, sells what he *knows* is not what he represents it.

The strawer offers to *sell* any passer by in the streets a straw and to *give* the purchaser a paper which he *dares not* sell. Accordingly as he judges of the character of his audience, so he intimates that the paper is political, libellous, irreligious, or indecent.

I am told that as far back as twenty-five or twenty-six years, straws were sold, but only in the country, with leaves from the *Republican*, a periodical published by Carlile,[2] then of Fleet-street, which had been prosecuted by the government; but it seems that the trade died away, and was little or hardly known again until the time of the trial of Queen Caroline,[3] and then but sparingly. The straw sale reached its highest commercial pitch at the era of the Reform Bill.[4] The most successful trader in the article is remembered among the patterers as "Jack Straw," who was oft enough represented to me as the original strawer. If I inquired further, the answer was: "He was the first in my time." This Jack Straw was, I am told, a fine-looking man, a natural son of Henry Hunt,[5] the blacking manufacturer. He was described to me as an inveterate drunkard and a very reckless fellow. One old hand was certain that this man was Hunt's son, as he himself had "worked" with him, and was sometimes sent by him when he was "in trouble," or in any strait, to 32, Broadwall, Blackfriars, for assistance, which was usually rendered. (This was the place where Hunt's "Matchless Blacking" and "Roasted Corn" were vended.) Jack Straw's principal "pitch" was at Hyde Park Corner, "where," said the man whom I have mentioned as working with him, "he used to come it very strong against Old Nosey,[6] the Hyde Park bully as he called him. To my knowledge he's made 10*s*., and he's made 15*s*. on a night. O, it didn't matter to him what he sold with his straws, religion or anything. There was no three-

1 First published in the weekly serial version of *London Labour*, No. 12, 1 March 1851.

2 Richard Carlile (1790–1843) was a London-based radical journalist who founded the *Republican*, which replaced *Sherwin's Political Register* when it was shut down by the government in 1819.

3 See p. 98, note 3.

4 See p. 98, note 5.

5 Hunt (1773–1835) was a political radical known for his oration skills.

6 Nickname for the Duke of Wellington.

pennies (threepenny newspapers)[1] then, and he had had a gentleman's education, and knew what to say, and so the straws went off like smoke." The articles which this man "durst not sell" were done up in paper, so that no one could very well peruse them on the spot, as a sort of stealth was implied. On my asking Jack Straw's coworker if he had ever drank with him, "Drank with him!" he answered, "Yes, many a time. I've gone out and pattered, or chaunted, or anything, to get money to buy him two glasses of brandy—and good brandy was very dear then—before he could start, for he was all of a tremble until he had his medicine. If I couldn't get brandy, it was the best rum, 'cause he had all the tastes of a gentleman. Ah! he's been dead some years, sir, but where he died I don't know. I only heard of his death. He was a nice kindly fellow."

The *ruse* in respect of strawing is not remarkable for its originality. It was an old smuggler's trick to *sell* a sack and *give* the keg of contraband spirit placed within it and padded out with straw so as to resemble a sack of corn. The hawkers, prior to 1826, when Mr. Huskisson introduced changes into the Silk Laws, *gave* "real Ingy handkerchiefs" (sham) to a customer,[2] and *sold* him a knot of tape for about 4*s*. The price of a true Bandana, then prohibited, and sold openly in the draper's shops, was about 8*s*. The East India Company[3] imported about a million of Bandanas yearly; they were sold by auction for exportation to Hamburgh, &c., at about 4*s*. each, and were nearly all smuggled back again to England, and disposed of as I have stated.

It is not possible to give anything like statistics as to the money realised by strawing. A well-informed man calculated that when the trade was at its best, or from 1832 to 1836, there might be generally fifty working it in the country and twenty in London; they did not confine themselves, however, to strawing, but resorted to it only on favourable opportunities. Now there are none in London—their numbers diminished gradually—and very rarely any in the country.

Of the Sham Indecent Street-Trade.[4]

THIS is one of those callings which are at once repulsive and ludicrous; repulsive, when it is considered under what pretences the papers are sold, and ludicrous, when the disappointment of the gulled purchaser is contemplated.

I have mentioned that one of the allurements held out by the strawer was that his paper—the words used by Jack Straw—could "not be admit-

1 See p. 72, note 2.

2 Legislation passed in 1825 and 1826 eliminated the prohibition on silk imports and reduced duties on raw and wrought silk. The importation of raw silk into London by the East India (Ingy) Company (see p. 253, note 2) made silk handkerchiefs and other clothing more affordable for the middle classes.

3 See p. 253, note 2.

4 First published in the weekly serial version of *London Labour*, No. 12, 1 March 1851.

ted into families." Those following the "sham indecent trade" for a time followed his example, and professed to sell straws and give away papers; but the London police became very observant of the sale of straws—more especially under the pretences alluded to—and it has, for the last ten years, been rarely pursued in the streets.

The plan now adopted is to sell the sealed packet itself, which the "patter" of the street-seller leads his auditors to believe to be some improper or scandalous publication. The packet is some coloured paper, in which is placed a portion of an old newspaper, a Christmas carol, a religious tract, or a slop-tailor's puff[1] (given away in the streets for the behoof of another class of gulls). The enclosed paper is, however, never indecent.

From a man who had, not long ago, been in this trade, I had the following account. He was very anxious that nothing should be said which would lead to a knowledge that he was my informant. After having expressed his sorrow that he had ever been driven to this trade from distress, he proceeded to justify himself. He argued—and he was not an ignorant man—that there was neither common sense nor common justice in interfering with a man like him, who, "to earn a crust, pretended to sell what *shopkeepers*, that must pay church and all sorts of rates, sold without being molested." The word "shopkeepers" was uttered with a bitter emphasis. There are, or were, he continued, shops—for he seemed to know them all—and some of them had been carried on for years, in which shameless publications were not only sold, but exposed in the windows;[2] and why should he be considered a greater offender than a shopkeeper, and be knocked about by the police? There are, or lately were, he said, such shops in the Strand, Fleet-street, a court off Ludgate-hill, Holborn, Drury-lane, Wych-street, the courts near Drury-lane Theatre, Haymarket, High-street, Bloomsbury, St. Martin's-court, May's buildings, and elsewhere, to say nothing of Holywell-street![3] Yet *he* must be interfered with!

[I may here remark, that I met with no street-sellers who did not disbelieve, or affect to disbelieve, that they were really meddled with by the police for obstructing the thoroughfare. They either hint, or plainly state, that they are removed solely to please the shop-keepers. Such was the reiterated opinion, real or pretended, of my present informant.]

I took a statement from this man, but do not care to dwell upon the subject. The trade, in the form I have described, had been carried on, he thought, for the last six years. At one time, 20 men followed it; at present, he believed there were only 6, and they worked only at intervals, and as opportunities offered: some going out, for instance, to sell almanacs or memorandum books, and, when they met with a favourable chance, offering their sealed packets. My informant's customers were principally boys,

---

1 A misleading, exaggerated advertisement for an inferior tailor. (See p. 77, note 1.)

2 The display of obscene books for sale was illegal under the 1824 Vagrancy Act.

3 A well-known street in London's bookselling district notorious for its "indecent" trade in pornography.

young men, and old gentlemen; but old gentlemen chiefly when the trade was new. This street-seller's "great gun," as he called it, was to make up packets, as closely resembling as he could accomplish it, those which were displayed in the windows of any of the shops I have alluded to. He would then station himself at some little distance from one of those shops, and, if possible, so as to encounter those who had stopped to study the contents of the window, and would represent—broadly enough, he admitted, when he dared—that he could sell for 6*d.* what was charged 5*s.*, or 2*s.* 6*d.*, or whatever price he had seen announced, "in that very neighbourhood." He sometimes ventured, also, to mutter something, unintelligibly, about the public being imposed upon! On one occasion, he took 6*s.* in the street in about two hours. On another evening he took 4*s.* 8*d.* in the street and was called aside by two old gentlemen, each of whom told him to come to an address given (at the West-end), and ask for such and such initials. To one he sold two packets for 2*s.*; to the other, five packets, each 1*s.*—or 11*s.* 8*d.* in one evening. The packets were in different coloured papers, and had the impressions of a large seal on red wax at the back; and he assured the old gents., as he called them, one of whom, he thought, was "silly," that they were all different. "And very likely," he said, chucklingly, "they were different; for they were made out of a lot of missionary tracts and old newspapers that I got dirt cheap at a 'waste' shop. I should like to have seen the old gent.'s face, as he opened his 5*s.* worth, one after another!" This trade, however, among old gentlemen, was prosperous for barely a month: "It got blown then, sir, and they wouldn't buy any more, except a very odd one."

This man—and he believed it was the same with all the others in the trade—never visited the public-houses, for a packet would soon have been opened and torn there, which, he said, people was ashamed to do in the public streets. As well as he could recollect, he had never sold a single packet to a girl or a woman. Drunken women of the town had occasionally made loud comments on his calling, and offered to purchase; but on such occasions, fearful of a disturbance, he always hurried away.

I have said that the straw trade is now confined to the country, and I give a specimen of the article vended there, by the patterer in the sham indecent trade. It was purchased of a man, who sold it folded in the form of a letter, and is addressed, "On Royal Service. By Express. Private. To Her Royal Highness, Victoria, Princess Royal. Kensington Palace, London. Entered at Stationer's Hall." The man who sold it had a wisp of straw round his neck, and introduced his wares with the following patter:

"I am well aware that many persons here present will say what an absurd idea—the idea of selling straws for a halfpenny each, when there are so many lying about the street; but the reason is simply this: I am not allowed by the authorities to sell these papers, so I give them away and sell my straws. There are a variety of figures in these papers for gentlemen; some in the bed, some on the bed, some under the bed." The following is a copy of the document thus sold:—

"Bachelors or Maidens, Husbands and Wives,
Will love each other and lead happy lives;
If both these Letters to read are inclined,
Secrets worth knowing therein they will find.

"Dated from the Duchy of Coburg.

"My Dearest Victoria,

Hiᵹhuessəs' ɐnsʍeɹ, Ibəᵹ ləaʌe ʇosnbscɹiqe ɯyseʅf pleᵖgəsof aɟɟeoʇıou—ɐuxıouslyɐwɐıʇıug ʎonr royal-ɹoʎaʅqɹipe aud fntnrəsovərəign, ʌeɹy mɐnʎaud ʅıʌiug snrəd ou mʎpɹinoeʅy qouour, tɥaʇI ʍiʅl aʍaɹdʇo ɯy ɯeʇo ʇhɐt euvıepstɐtıon oɟqeınᵹtɥy hnsqaud, rəsʇas-ɯohɹisʇeudoɯ; aud ʍhənʇhou ɥast dəiᵹnədʇo əxɥalt bəudep kueəs, ʇo ɟaʌonr ɯʎsnit, aqoʌe ɐnyoʇɥer dɹınce oɟ aʅl ɥeırsʇo ɐbɹıʇısɥdıadəm—I ıɯpʅoɹeʇhəe ou uʎ amıɐbʅe oɟ Eugʅaup'sdɹınoessəs—ɐnd tɥə ɯosʇ ʌıɹʇuons quɹyɥıɯsəʅɟ ʍıʇhıu tɥy oʍndoʍnʎ dlnmɐᵹe! Mosʇ əɥɐruıug uoʇes, audʍıʇh ɟlnʇʇeɹiug ʍiugswısɥes ʇo ʍɥo ʅıke ɐbɪrpoɟ perɐdıse, ısoalʅınᵹtɥeəto ʅısʇeu ʇo hıs ɔoɯe ʇo ɯyʅougınᵹ aɹaɯs—ıt ıs oulʎtɥʎ peɐr Aʅqərt, ɐmıaqlə Vıɔʇoɹıɐ, theɯosʇ duɹe ɐnp sɗoʇləss oɟ vırᵹius, fntnrıʇʎ,audɔoutınne ʇo prəaɯoɟ loʌə ɐnptɥeə! Wʎ sqaʅlqe əncɥanʇep wıtɥtɥe mosʇ bəantıfnl vısıousoɟ mənt oɟ ʇhɐt qalmʎsʅeəd I hɐvəbəen ʅonᵹ ʍɐntıuᵹ, I *nom* sʅeəpʅess ɔouch,aud resınınᵹ ɯysouʅ ʇo tɥeenjoʎ-wonnps—Ʇɥenʍiʅl I dləasɐnʇʅʎ rədose ɯysəʅɟ ou ɯʎ bntɔoɯe ɐnp ponr tɥy ɥeɐlınᵹ belsɐmınʇo ɯʎ sɯaɹtıng ʌənʅysɐmɐrıtɐn, pass uoʇaʍaʎ ɟroɯ ʇɥyɐdoɹiug ɐlqeɹʇ; iugʅovə! Ʇhənɥasʇeu ɯy ᵹloɹıonsəhərnb—ʇhou həa-wɥoʅeqopy ıs qeınᵹcousnmepın tɥeɟuɹnɐsə oɟ eʌeɹlɐsʇ-tɐlısəd ʍıʇhʌɐrıəd aud ɔoufʅıotınᵹ eɯoʇıous, aud mʎ ɟusəto po ʇhəıɹoɟfıcə; əʌəɹʎ oueoɟ ɯy ɯeɯbərsɐrə ʇɐn-fırə, ɯyɟeəʇ sʇuɯbʅes—ʎeɐ, mʎ ɐrɯs audɯy ləgs ɹe-ɯy sənsəsʍaudər, ɯy ɥaırsʇauds ou eup, mʎ ɥeɐd ısou əlɐsdtɥeə ıu ɯyaɹms—Mʎ qosomɥeɐvəs, ɯy ɥearʇpɐnʇs, tɥylovəlʎ forɯ, audʅoug for ʇhəhɐpdy ɥonr wɥeuɪ sɥall royɐlɥıᵹhuess—ɯy sʍeeʇestauᵹeʅ, oɥ! ɥow I po apore doʍnʇo tɥe pəʅıᵹhʇfuʅtɐsk oɟ ʍrıʇıuᵹa loʌe ʅətʇeɹto ʇhʎ —— nəvərpip I eujoʎgɹeɐtər qlıss, ʇhauwɥeuI sɐʇ

"Your adored Lover,

"ALBERT,

"Prince of Coburg."

On the back of this page is the following cool initiation of the purchaser into the mysteries of the epistle:

"Directions for the purchasers to understand the *Royal Love Letters*, and showing them how to practise the art of Secret Letter Writing:—

"Proceed to lay open 'Albert's Letter' by the side of 'Victoria's,' and having done so, then look carefully down them until you have come to a word at the left hand corner, near the end of each Letter, having two marks thus — —, when you must commence with that word, and read from left to right after you have turned them bottom upwards before a looking glass so that you may peruse the copy reflected therein. But you must notice, throughout all the words every other letter is upside down, also every other word single; but the next two words being purposely joined together, therefore they are double; and in addition to those letters placed upside down; makes it more mysterious in the reading. The reader is recommended to copy each word in writing, when he will be able to read the letters forward, and after a little practice he can soon learn to form all his words in the same curious manner, when he wants to write a 'secret letter.'

"Be sure when holding it up side down before a looking-glass, that the light of a candle, is placed between then by the reflection it will show much plainer, and be sooner discovered.

"If you intend to practise a *Joke* and make it answer the purpose of a Valentine, write what you think necessary on the adjoining *blank page*; then post it, with the superscription filled up in this manner:—After the word To, *write the name and address of the party* also place the word FROM *before* VICTORIA'S name: then the address on the outside of this letter will read somewhat after the following fashion:—To Mr. or Mrs. so and so, (with the number if any,) in such and such a street: at the same time your letter will appear as if it came from Royalty.

"N.B. You must first buy both the letters, as the other letter is an answer to this one; and because, without the reader has got both letters, he will not have the secrets perfect."

Notwithstanding the injunction to buy *both* letters, and the seeming necessity of having both to understand the "directions," the patterer was selling only the one I have given.

[...]

Of the Low Lodging-houses of London.[1]

THE patterers, as a class, usually frequent the low lodging-houses. I shall therefore now proceed to give some further information touching the

1 First published in the weekly serial version of *London Labour*, No. 13, 8 March 1851.

abodes of these people—reminding the reader that I am treating of patterers in general, and not of any particular order, as the "paper workers."

In applying the epithet "low" to these places, I do but adopt the word commonly applied, either in consequence of the small charge for lodging, or from the character of their frequenters. To some of these domiciles, however, as will be shown, the epithet, in an opprobrious sense, is unsuited.

[...]

[...] I was told by a trustworthy man that not long ago he was compelled to sleep in one of the lowest (as regards cheapness) of the lodging-houses. All was dilapidation, filth, and noisomeness. In the morning he drew, for purposes of ablution, a basinfull of water from a pailfull kept in the room. In the water were floating alive, or apparently alive, bugs and lice, which my informant was convinced had fallen from the ceiling, shaken off by the tread of some one walking in the rickety apartments above!

"Ah, sir," said another man with whom I conversed on the subject, "if you had lived in the lodging-houses, you would say what a vast difference a penny made,—it's often all in all. It's 4*d.* in the Mint House you've been asking me about; you've sleep and comfort there, and I've seen people kneel down and say their prayers afore they went to bed. Not so many, though. Two or three in a week at nights, perhaps. And it's wholesome and sweet enough there, and large separate beds; but in other places there's nothing to smell or feel but bugs. When daylight comes in the summer—and it's often either as hot as hell or as cold as icicles in those places; but in summer, as soon as its light, if you turn down the coverlet, you'll see them a-going it like Cheapside when it's throngest." The poor man seemed to shudder at the recollection.

One informant counted for me 180 of these low lodging-houses; and it is reasonable to say that there are, in London, at least 200 of them. The average number of beds in each was computed for me, by persons cognizant of such matters, from long and often woful experience, at 52 single or 24 double beds, where the house might be confined to single men or single women lodgers, or to married or pretendedly married couples, or to both classes. In either case, we may calculate the number that can be, and generally are, accommodated at 50 per house; for children usually sleep with their parents, and 50 may be the lowest computation. We have thus no fewer than 10,000 persons domiciled, more or less permanently, in the low lodging-houses of London—a number more than doubling the population of many a parliamentary borough.

The proprietors of these lodging-houses mostly have been, I am assured, vagrants, or, to use the civiller and commoner word, "travellers" themselves, and therefore sojourners, on all necessary occasions, in such places. In four cases out of five I believe this to be the case. [...]

[...]

Some of the lodging-houses present no appearance differing from that of ordinary houses; except, perhaps, that their exterior is dirtier. Some of the older houses have long flat windows on the ground-floor, in which there is rather more paper, or other substitutes, than glass. "The windows there, sir," remarked one man, "are not to let the light in, but to keep the cold out."

In the abodes in question there seems to have become tacitly established an arrangement as to what character of lodgers shall resort thither; the thieves, the prostitutes, and the better class of street-sellers or traders, usually resorting to the houses where they will meet the same class of persons. The patterers reside chiefly in Westminster and Whitechapel.

Some of the lodging-houses are of the worst class of low brothels, and some may even be described as brothels for children.

On many of the houses is a rude sign, "Lodgings for Travellers, 3*d.* a night. Boiling water always ready," or the same intimation may be painted on a window-shutter, where a shutter is in existence. A few of the better order of these housekeepers post up small bills, inviting the attention of "travellers," by laudations of the cleanliness, good beds, abundant water, and "gas all night," to be met with. The same parties also give address-cards to travellers, who can recommend one another.

The beds are of flock,[1] and as regards the mere washing of the rug, sheet, and blanket, which constitute the bed-furniture, are in better order than they were a few years back; for the visitations of the cholera alarmed even the reckless class of vagrants, and those whose avocations relate to vagrants. In perhaps a tenth of the low lodging-houses of London, a family may have a room to themselves, with the use of the kitchen, at so much a week—generally 2*s.* 6*d.* for a couple without family, and 3*s.* 6*d.* where there are children. To let out "beds" by the night is however the general rule.

[...]

Of the Filth, Dishonesty, and Immorality of Low Lodging-houses.[2]

In my former and my present inquiries, I received many statements on this subject. Some details, given by coarse men and boys in the grossest language, are too gross to be more than alluded to, but the full truth must be manifested, if not detailed. It was remarked when my prior account appeared, that the records of gross profligacy on the part of some of the

1 Mattresses stuffed with "flock," the coarse shearings of wool, cotton, or other cloth.

2 First published in the weekly serial version of *London Labour*, No. 13, 8 March 1851.

most licentious of the rich (such as the late Marquis of Hertford[1] and other worthies of the same depraved habits) were equalled, or nearly equalled, by the account of the orgies of the lowest lodging-houses. Sin, in any rank of life, shows the same features.

And first, as to the want of cleanliness, comfort, and decency: "Why, sir," said one man, who had filled a commercial situation of no little importance, but had, through intemperance, been reduced to utter want, "I myself have slept in the top room of a house not far from Drury-lane, and you could study the stars, if you were so minded, through the holes left by the slates having been blown off the roof. It was a fine summer's night, and the openings in the roof were then rather an advantage, for they admitted air, and the room wasn't so foul as it might have been without them. I never went there again, but you may judge what thoughts went through a man's mind—a man who had seen prosperous days—as he lay in a place like that, without being able to sleep, watching the sky."

The same man told me (and I received abundant corroboration of his statement, besides that incidental mention of the subject occurs elsewhere), that he had scraped together a handful of bugs from the bed-clothes, and crushed them under a candlestick, and had done that many a time, when he could only resort to the lowest places. He had slept in rooms so crammed with sleepers—he believed there were 30 where 12 would have been a proper number—that their breaths in the dead of night and in the unventilated chamber, rose (I use his own words) "in one foul, choking steam of stench." This was the case most frequently a day or two prior to Greenwich Fair or Epsom Races,[2] when the congregation of the wandering classes, who are the supporters of the low lodging-houses, was the thickest. It was not only that two or even three persons jammed themselves into a bed not too large for one full-sized man; but between the beds—and their partition one from another admitted little more than the passage of a lodger—were placed shakes-down, or temporary accommodation for nightly slumber. In the better lodging-houses the shake-downs are small palliasses[3] or mattresses; in the worst, they are bundles of rags of any kind; but loose straw is used only in the country for shake-downs. One informant saw a traveller, who had arrived late, eye his shake-down in one of the worst houses with anything but a pleased expression of countenance; and a surly deputy, observing this, told the customer he had his choice, "which," the deputy added, "it's not all men as has, or I shouldn't

1 Presumably a reference to the third Marquess of Hertford, Francis Charles Seymour-Conway (1777–1842), whose scandalous behaviour included being in an open marriage, hiring prostitutes, and, reportedly, engaging in a ménage with a married woman and three of her daughters.

2 Greenwich Fair was held every Easter and Whitsun (the seventh Sunday after Easter) in the village of Greenwich, whose mass crowds were associated with debauchery and licentiousness. For Epsom Races, see p. 91, note 1.

3 Thin pads filled with straw.

have been waiting here on you. But you has your choice, I tell you;—sleep there on that shake-down, or turn out and be d——; that's fair." At some of the busiest periods, numbers sleep on the kitchen floor, all huddled together, men and women (when indecencies are common enough), and without bedding or anything but their scanty clothes to soften the hardness of the stone or brick floor. A penny is saved to the lodger by this means. More than 200 have been accommodated in this way in a large house. The Irish, at harvest-time, very often resort to this mode of passing the night.

I heard from several parties, of the surprise, and even fear or horror, with which a decent mechanic—more especially if he were accompanied by his wife—regarded one of these foul dens, when destitution had driven him there for the first time in his life. Sometimes such a man was seen to leave the place abruptly, though perhaps he had pre-paid his last halfpenny for the refreshment of a night's repose. Sometimes he was seized with sickness. I heard also from some educated persons who had "seen better days," of the disgust with themselves and with the world, which they felt on first entering such places. "And I have some reason to believe," said one man, "that a person, once well off, who has sunk into the very depths of poverty, often makes his first appearance in one of the worst of those places. Perhaps it is because he keeps away from them as long as he can, and then, in a sort of desperation fit, goes into the cheapest he meets with; or if he knows it's a vile place, he very likely says to himself—I did—'I may as well know the worst at once.'"

[...]

I have now to speak of the habitual violation of all the injunctions of law, of all the obligations of morality, and of all the restraints of decency, seen continually in the vilest of the lodging-houses. I need but cite a few facts, for to detail minutely might be to disgust. In some of these lodging-houses, the proprietor—or, I am told, it might be more correct to say, the proprietress, as there are more women than men engaged in the nefarious traffic carried on in these houses—are "fences," or receivers of stolen goods in a small way. *Their* "fencing," unless as the very exception, does not extend to any plate, or jewellery, or articles of value, but is chiefly confined to provisions, and most of all to those which are of ready sale to the lodgers.

Of very ready sale are "fish got from the gate" (stolen from Billingsgate);[1] "sawney" (thieved bacon), and "flesh found in Leadenhall" (butcher's-meat stolen from that market). I was told by one of the most respectable tradesmen in Leadenhall-market, that it was infested—but not now to so great an extent as it was—with lads and young men, known there as "finders." They carry bags round their necks, and pick up bones,

1 See p. 59, note 1.

or offal, or pieces of string, or bits of papers, or "anything, sir, please, that a poor lad, that has neither father nor mother, and is werry hungry, can make a ha'penny by to get him a bit of bread, please, sir." This is often but a cover for stealing pieces of meat, and the finders, with their proximate market for disposal of their meat in the lowest lodging-houses in Whitechapel, go boldly about their work, for the butchers, if the "finder" be detected, "won't," I was told by a sharp youth who then was at a low lodging-house in Keate-street, "go bothering theirselves to a beak,[1] but gives you a scruff of the neck and a kick and lets you go. But some of them kicks werry hard." The tone and manner of this boy—and it is a common case enough with the "prigs"—showed that he regarded hard kicking merely as one of the inconveniences to which his business-pursuits were unavoidably subjected; just as a struggling housekeeper might complain of the unwelcome calls of the tax-gatherers. These depredations are more frequent in Leadenhall-market than in any of the others, on account of its vicinity to Whitechapel. Even the Whitechapel meat-market is less the scene of prey, for it is a series of shops, while Leadenhall presents many stalls, and the finders seem loath to enter shops without some plausible pretext.

[...]

The licentiousness of the frequenters, and more especially of the juvenile frequenters, of the low lodging-houses, must be even more briefly alluded to. In some of these establishments, men and women, boys and girls,—but perhaps in no case, or in very rare cases, unless they are themselves consenting parties, herd together promiscuously. The information which I have given from a reverend informant indicates the nature of the proceedings, when the sexes are herded indiscriminately, and it is impossible to present to the reader, in full particularity, the records of the vice practised.

Boys have boastfully carried on loud conversations, and from distant parts of the room, of their triumphs over the virtue of girls, and girls have laughed at and encouraged the recital. Three, four, five, six, and even more boys and girls have been packed, head and feet, into one small bed; some of them perhaps never met before. On such occasions any clothing seems often enough to be regarded as merely an incumbrance. Sometimes there are loud quarrels and revilings from the jealousy of boys and girls, and more especially of girls whose "chaps" have deserted or been inveigled from them. At others, there is an amicable interchange of partners, and next day a resumption of their former companionship. One girl, then fifteen or sixteen, who had been leading this vicious kind of life for nearly three years, and had been repeatedly in prison, and twice in hospitals—and who expressed a strong desire to "get out of the life" by emigration—

1 See p. 98, note 2.

said: "Whatever that's bad and wicked, that any one can fancy could be done in such places among boys and girls that's never been taught, or won't be taught, better, *is* done, and night after night." In these haunts of low iniquity, or rather in the room into which the children are put, there are seldom persons above twenty. The younger lodgers in such places live by thieving and pocket-picking, or by prostitution. The charge for a night's lodging is generally 2*d.*, but smaller children have often been admitted for 1*d.* If a boy or girl resort to one of these dens at night without the means of defraying the charge for accommodation, the "mot of the ken" (mistress of the house) will pack them off, telling them plainly that it will be no use their returning until they have stolen something worth 2*d.* If a boy or girl do not return in the evening, and have not been heard to express their intention of going elsewhere, the first conclusion arrived at by their mates is that they have "got into trouble" (prison).

The indiscriminate admixture of the sexes among adults, in many of these places, is another evil. Even in some houses considered of the better sort, men and women, husbands and wives, old and young, strangers and acquaintances, sleep in the same apartment, and if they choose, in the same bed. Any remonstrance at some act of gross depravity, or impropriety on the part of a woman not so utterly hardened as the others, is met with abuse and derision. One man who described these scenes to me, and had long witnessed them, said that almost the only women who ever hid their faces or manifested dislike of the proceedings they could not but notice (as far as he saw), were poor Irishwomen, generally those who live by begging: "But for all that," the man added, "an Irishman or Irishwoman of that sort will sleep anywhere, in any mess, to save a halfpenny, though they may have often a few shillings, or a good many, hidden about them."

There is no provision for purposes of decency in some of the places I have been describing, into which the sexes are herded indiscriminately; but to this matter I can only allude. A policeman, whose duty sometimes called him to enter one of those houses at night, told me that he never entered it without feeling sick.

There are now fewer of such filthy receptacles than there were. Some have been pulled down—especially for the building of Commercial-street, in Whitechapel, and of New Oxford-street—and some have fallen into fresh and improved management. Of those of the worst class, however, there may now be at least thirty in London; while the low lodgings of all descriptions, good or bad, are more frequented than they were a few years back. A few new lodging-houses, perhaps half a dozen, have been recently opened, in expectation of a great influx of "travellers" and vagrants at the opening of the Great Exhibition.[1]

1 The Great Exhibition of the Works of Industry of All Nations, housed in the Crystal Palace (see p. 91, note 2) in London's Hyde Park and running from May to October 1851, was the first international exhibition to showcase modern technologies, innovations, and design. See the Introduction (p. 33) for further information.

Of Street "Ballads on a Subject."[1]

THERE is a class of ballads which may with perfect propriety be called *street* ballads, as they are written by street authors for street singing (or chaunting) and street sale. These effusions, however, are known in the trade by a title appropriate enough—"Ballads on a Subject." The most successful workers in this branch of the profession, are the men I have already described among the patterers and chaunters.

The "Ballads on a Subject" are always on a political, criminal, or exciting public event, or one that has interested the public, and the celerity with which one of them is written, and then sung in the streets, is in the spirit of "these railroad times."[2] After any great event, "a ballad on the subject" is often enough written, printed, and sung in the street, in little more than an hour. Such was the case with a song "in honour," it was announced, "of Lord John Russell's resignation."[3] Of course there is no time for either the correction of the rhymes or of the press; but this is regarded as of little consequence—while an early "start" with a new topic is of great consequence, I am assured; "yes, indeed, both for the sake of meals and rents." If, however, the songs were ever so carefully revised, their sale would not be greater.

I need not treat this branch of our street literature at any great length, as specimens of the "Ballad on a Subject" will be found in many of the preceding statements of paper-workers.

It will have struck the reader that all the street lays[4] quoted as popular have a sort of burthen or jingle at the end of each verse. I was corrected, however, by a street chaunter for speaking of this burthen as a jingle. "It's a chorus, sir," he said. "In a proper ballad on a subject, there's often twelve verses, none of them under eight lines,—and there's a four-line chorus to every verse; and, if it's the right sort, it'll sell the ballad." I was told, on all hands, that it was not the words that ever "made a ballad, but the subject; and, more than the subject,—the chorus; and, far more than either,—*the tune*!" Indeed, many of the street-singers of ballads on a subject have as supreme a contempt for words as can be felt by any modern composer. To select a tune for a ballad, however, is a matter of deep deliberation. To adapt the ballad to a tune too common or popular is injudicious; for then, I was told, any one can sing it—boys and all. To select a more elaborate and less-known air, however appropriate, may not be pleasing to some of the members of "the school" of ballad-singers, who may feel it to be beyond their vocal powers; neither may it be relished by

---

1 First published in the weekly serial version of *London Labour*, No. 14, 15 March 1851.

2 The 1840s saw a massive expansion of railroads in Britain. By the end of the decade, a near comprehensive network of railway lines connected the country.

3 Refers to the prime minister, John Russell (1792–1878) (see also p. 199, note 2), who would not actually resign until 1853.

4 From French "lai," a short lyric or narrative poem meant to be sung.

the critical in street song, whose approving criticism induces them to purchase as well as to admire.

The license enjoyed by the court jesters, and, in some respects, by the minstrels of old, is certainly enjoyed, undiminished, by the street-writers and singers of ballads on a subject. They are unsparing satirists, who, with a rare impartiality, lash all classes and all creeds, as well as any individual. One man, upon whose information I can rely, told me that, eleven years ago, he himself had "worked," in town and country, 23 different songs at the same period and on the same subject—the marriage of the Queen. They all "sold,"—but the most profitable was one "as sung by Prince Albert in character." It was to the air of the "Dusty Miller";[1] and "it was good," said the ballad-man, "because we could easily dress up to the character given to Albert." I quote a verse:

"Here I am in rags
  From the land of All-dirt,
To marry England's Queen,
  And my name it is Prince Albert."

"And what's more, sir," continued my informant, "not very long after the honeymoon, the Duchess of L——— drove up in her carriage to the printer's, and bought all the songs in honour of Victoria's wedding, and gave a sovereign for them and wouldn't take the change. It was a duchess. Why I'm sure about it—though I can't say whether it were the Duchess of L—— or S——; for didn't the printer, like an honest man, when he'd stopped the price of the papers, hand over to us chaps the balance to drink, and *didn't* we drink it! There can't be a mistake about *that*."

Of street ballads on political subjects, or upon themes which have interested the whole general public, I need not cite additional instances. There are, however, other subjects, which, though not regarded as of great interest by the whole body of the people are still eventful among certain classes, and for them the street author and ballad-singer cater.

I first give a specimen of a ballad on a Theatrical Subject. The best I find, in a large collection of these street effusions, is entitled "Jenny Lind and Poet B."[2] After describing how Mr. Bunn "flew to Sweden" and engaged Miss Lind, the poet proceeds,—the tune being "Lucy Long":[3]

"After Jenny sign'd the paper,
She repented what she'd done,

1 To the tune of "The Dusty Miller," a popular song likely originating in seventeenth-century Scotland.

2 A song about Swedish opera singer Jenny Lind (1820–87), who first appeared on the British stage in 1845.

3 "Jenny Lind and Poet B" was sung to the tune of "Lucy Long," a popular minstrel song originating in America in the 1840s and found in *Lloyd's Song Book*, published in London in 1846.

And said she must have been a cake,
To be tempted by A. Bunn.
The English tongue she must decline,
It was such awkward stuff,
And we find 'mongst our darling dames,
That one tongue's quite enough.

CHORUS.

So take your time Miss Jenny,
Oh, take your time Miss Lind,
You're only to raise your voice,
John Bull,[1] will raise the wind.

Says Alfred in the public eye,
My name you shan't degrade,
So birds that can and won't sing
Why in course they must be made
This put Miss Jenny's pipe out,
Says Bunn your tricks I see,
Altho' you are a Nightingale,
You shan't play larks with me.

The Poet said he'd seek the law,
No chance away he'd throw;
Says Jenny if you think I'll come,
You'll find it is no go!
When a bird-catcher named "Lummy
With independence big,
Pounced down upon the Nightingale,
And with her hopp'd the twig!"

I am inclined to think—though I know it to be an unusual case—that in this theatrical ballad the street poet was what is tenderly called a "plagiarist." I was assured by a chaunter that it was written by a street author,—but probably the chaunter was himself in error or forgetfulness.

Next, there is the Ballad on a Civic Subject. In the old times the Lord Mayor had his laureate. This writer, known as "poet to the City of London," eulogised all lord mayors, and glorified all civic pageants. That of the 9th November,[2] especially, "lived in Settle's numbers, one day

1 A symbolic character, representing England, created by Dr. John Arbuthnot (1667–1735) in 1712.

2 See p. 72, note 1.

more,"—but Elkanah Settle[1] was the last of such scribes. After his death, the city eschewed a poet. The office has now descended to the street bard, who annually celebrates the great ceremony. I cite two stanzas and the chorus from the latest of these civic Odes:

"Now Farncombe's out and Musgrove's in,[2]
And grand is his position,
Because he will be made a king,
At the Hyde Park Exhibition;[3]
A feast he'll order at Guildhall,
For hypocrites and sinners,
And he has sent Jack Forester[4] to Rome,
To invite the Pope to dinner!

A day like this we never saw,
The truth I am confessing,
Batty's astonishing menagerie,
Is in the great procession;
There's lions, tigers, bears and wolves,
To please each smiling feature,
And elephants in harness drawing
Drury Lane Theatre!

CHORUS.

It is not as it used to be,
Cut on so gay and thrifty,
The funny Lord Mayor's Show to see,
In eighteen hundred and fifty."

There is, beside the descriptions of ballads above cited, the Ballad Local. One of these is headed the "Queer Doings in Leather-lane," and is on a subject concerning which street-sellers generally express themselves strongly—Sunday trading. The endeavour to stop street trading (generally) in Leather-lane, with its injurious results to the shopkeepers, has been already mentioned. The ballad on this local subject presents a personality now, happily, almost confined to the street writers:

"A rummy saintly lot is there,
A domineering crew,

1 Settle (1648–1724) a dramatist, was London's "city poet" from 1691 until at least 1708. His duties included producing the pageants performed for the Lord Mayor's show.

2 In 1850, Sir John Musgrove (1793–1881), 1st Baronet, succeeded Thomas Farncombe (1779–1865) as Lord Mayor of London.

3 See p. 116, note 1.

4 Unknown.

A Butcher, and a Baker,
   And an Undertaker too,
Besides a cove who deals in wood,
   And makes his bundles small,
And looks as black on Sunday
   As the Undertaker's pall.

CHORUS.

You must not buy, you must not sell,
   Oh! is it not a shame?
It is a shocking place to dwell,
   About sweet Leather Lane.

The Butcher does not like to hear
   His neighbours holloa, buy!
Although he on the Sunday
   Sells a little on the sly;
And the Coffin Maker struts along
   Just like the great Lord Mayor,
To bury folks on Sundays,
   Instead of going to prayers."

[...]

Of the Experience of a Street Author, or Poet.[1]

I have already mentioned the present number of street authors, as I most frequently heard them styled, though they write only verses.[2] I called upon one on the recommendation of a neighbouring tradesman, of whom I made some inquiries. He could not tell me the number of the house in the court where the man lived, but said I had only to inquire for the Tinker, or the Poet, and any one would tell me.

I found the poor poet, who bears a good character, on a sick bed; he was suffering, and had long been suffering, from abscesses. He was apparently about forty-five, with the sunken eyes, hollow cheeks, and, not pale but thick and rather sallow complexion, which indicate ill-health and scant food. He spoke quietly, and expressed resignation. His room was not very small, and was furnished in the way usual among the very poor, but there were a few old pictures over the mantel-piece. His eldest boy, a lad of thirteen or fourteen, was making dog-chains; at which he earned a shilling or two, sometimes 2*s*. 6*d*., by sale in the streets.

---

1 First published in the weekly serial version of *London Labour*, No. 14, 15 March 1851.

2 Discussed in previous selections entitled "Of Street 'Ballads on a Subject'" (included in this edition, p. 117) and "Of the Street Poets and Authors."

"I was born at Newcastle-under-Lyme," the man said, "but was brought to London when, I believe, I was only three months old. I was very fond of reading poems, in my youth, as soon as I could read and understand almost. Yes, very likely, sir; perhaps it was that put it into my head to write them afterwards. I was taught wire-working, and jobbing, and was brought up to hawking wire-work in the streets, and all over England and Wales. It was never a very good trade—just a living. Many and many a weary mile we've travelled together,—I mean, my wife and I have: and we've sometimes been benighted, and had to wander or rest about until morning. It wasn't that we hadn't money to pay for a lodging, but we couldn't get one. We lost count of the days sometimes in wild parts; but if we did lose count, or thought we had, I could always tell when it was Sunday morning by the look of nature; there was a mystery and a beauty about it as told me. I was very fond of Goldsmith's poetry always. I can repeat 'Edwin and Emma' now. No, sir; I never read the 'Vicar of Wakefield.' I found 'Edwin and Emma'[1] in a book called the 'Speaker.'[2] I often thought of it in travelling through some parts of the country.

"Above fourteen years ago I tried to make a shilling or two by selling my verses. I'd written plenty before, but made nothing by them. Indeed I never tried. The first song I ever sold was to a concert-room manager. The next I sold had great success. It was called the 'Demon of the Sea,' and was to the tune of 'The Brave Old Oak.'[3] Do I remember how it began? Yes, sir, I remember every word of it. It began:

Unfurl the sails
We've easy gales;
And helmsman steer aright,
Hoist the grim death's head—
The Pirate's head—
For a vessel heaves in sight!

That song was written for a concert-room, but it was soon in the streets, and ran a whole winter. I got only 1*s*. for it. Then I wrote the 'Pirate of the Isles,' and other ballads of that sort. The concert-rooms pay no better than the printers for the streets.

"Perhaps the best thing I ever wrote was the 'Husband's Dream.' I'm very sorry indeed that I can't offer you copies of some of my ballads, but

1 Oliver Goldsmith (1728–74). Irish author known for his poetry, plays, and his 1766 novel *The Vicar of Wakefield*. "Edwin and Emma" is a 1760 ballad by David Mallet (1705–65). Mayhew's interviewee is possibly confusing "Edwin and Emma" with "The Hermit, or Edwin and Angelina," a ballad appearing in the *Vicar of Wakefield*.

2 Published in 1774 by Unitarian minister William Enfield (1741–97), the *Speaker* was a popular collection of excerpts from famous literary works for the study of elocution—the art of public speaking.

3 A popular song from the 1830s for voice and piano. The text is from a poem by Henry Fothergill Chorley (1808–72); the music is by composer Edward J. Loder (1809–65).

I haven't a single copy myself of any of them, not one, and I dare say I've written a thousand in my time, and most of them were printed. I believe 10,000 were sold of the 'Husband's Dream.' It begins:

O Dermot, you look healthy now,
  Your dress is neat and clean;
I never see you drunk about,
  Then tell me where you've been.

Your wife and family—are they well?
  You once did use them strange:
O, are you kinder to them grown,
  How came this happy change?

"Then Dermot tells how he dreamed of his wife's sudden death, and his children's misery as they cried about her dead body, while he was drunk in bed, and as he calls out in his misery, he wakes, and finds his wife by his side. The ballad ends:

I pressed her to my throbbing heart,
  Whilst joyous tears did stream;
And ever since, I've heaven blest,
  For sending me that dream.

"Dermot turned teetotaller. The teetotallers were very much pleased with that song. The printer once sent me 5*s*. on account of it.

"I have written all sorts of things—ballads on a subject, and copies of verses, and anything ordered of me, or on anything I thought would be accepted, but now I can't get about. I've been asked to write indecent songs, but I refused. One man offered me 5*s*. for six such songs.—'Why, that's less than the common price,' said I, 'instead of something over to pay for the wickedness.'—All those sort of songs come now to the streets, I believe all do, from the concert-rooms. I can imitate any poetry. I don't recollect any poet I've imitated. No, sir, not Scott[1] or Moore,[2] that I know of, but if they've written popular songs, then I dare say I have imitated them. Writing poetry is no comfort to me in my sickness. It might if I could write just what I please. The printers like hanging subjects best, and I don't. But when any of them sends to order a copy of verses for a 'Sorrowful Lamentation' of course I must supply them. I don't think much of what I've done that way. If I'd my own fancy, I'd keep writing acrostics, such as one I wrote on our rector." "God bless him," interrupted the wife,

---

1 Sir Walter Scott (1771–1832), celebrated and influential Scottish poet, novelist, and literary critic.

2 Thomas Moore (1779–1852), a well-known Irish poet famous for the *Irish Melodies* (1808–34) and his oriental romance *Lalla Rookh* (1817).

"he's a good man." "That he is," said the poet, "but he's never seen what I wrote about him, and perhaps never will." He then desired his wife to reach him his big Bible, and out of it he handed me a piece of paper, with the following lines written on it, in a small neat hand enough:

" C elestial blessings hover round his head,
H undreds of poor, by his kindness were fed,
A nd precepts taught which he himself obeyed.
M an, erring man, brought to the fold of God,
P reaching pardon through a Saviour's blood.
N o lukewarm priest, but firm to Heaven's cause;
E xamples showed how much he loved its laws.
Y outh and age, he to their wants attends,
S teward of Christ—the poor man's sterling friend."[1]

"There would be some comfort, sir," he continued, "if one could go on writing at will like that. As it is, I sometimes write verses all over a slate, and rub them out again. Live hard! yes, indeed, we do live hard. I hardly know the taste of meat. We live on bread and butter, and tea; no, not any fish. As you see, sir, I work at tinning. I put new bottoms into old tin tea-pots, and such like. Here's my sort of bench, by my poor bit of a bed. In the best weeks I earn 4*s.* by tinning, never higher. In bad weeks I earn only 1*s.* by it, and sometimes not that,—and there are more shilling than four shilling weeks by three to one. As to my poetry, a good week is 3*s.*, and a poor week is 1*s.*—and sometimes I make nothing at all that way. So I leave you to judge, sir, whether we live hard; for the comings in, and what we have from the parish, must keep six of us—myself, my wife, and four children. It's a long, hard struggle." "Yes, indeed," said the wife, "it's just as you've heard my husband tell, sir. We've 2*s.* a week and four loaves of bread from the parish, and the rent's 2*s.* 6*d.*, and the landlord every week has 2*s.*,—and 6*d.* he has done for him in tinning work. Oh, we do live hard, indeed."

As I was taking my leave, the poor man expressed a desire that I would take a copy of an epitaph which he had written for himself. "If ever," he said, "I am rich enough to provide for a tomb-stone, or my family is rich enough to give me one, this shall be my epitaph" [I copied it from a blank page in his Bible:]

"Stranger, pause, a moment stay,
Tread lightly o'er this mound of clay.
Here lies J—— H——, in hopes to rise,
And meet his Saviour in the skies.
Christ his refuge, Heaven his home,
Where pain and sorrow never come.

1 The acrostic refers to William Weldon Champneys (1807–75), a popular evangelical Anglican clergyman who served in Whitechapel. Church attendance in his parish increased dramatically under his leadership, and he established schools and campaigned for protective legislation for dock workers.

His journey's done, his trouble's past,
With God he sleeps in peace at last."

Of the Street Booksellers.[1]

THE course of my inquiry now leads me to consider one of the oldest, and certainly not least important of the street traffics—that of the book-stalls. Of these there are now about twenty in the London streets, but in this number I include only those which are *properly* street-stalls. Many book-stalls, as in such a locality as the London-road, are appendages to shops, being merely a display of wares outside the bookseller's premises; and with these I do not now intend to deal.

The men in this trade I found generally to be intelligent. They have been, for the most part, engaged in some minor department of the book-selling or newspaper trade, in the regular way, and are unconnected with the street-sellers in other lines, of whose pursuits, habits, and characters, they seem to know nothing.

The street book-stalls are most frequent in the thoroughfares which are well-frequented, but which, as one man in the trade expressed himself, are not so "shoppy" as others—such as the City-road, the New-road, and the Old Kent-road. "If there's what you might call a recess," observed another street book-stall-keeper, "*that's* the place for us; and you'll often see us along with flower-stands and pinners-up." The stalls themselves do not present any very smart appearance; they are usually of plain deal.[2] If the stock of books be sufficiently ample, they are disposed on the surface of the stall, "fronts up," as I heard it described, with the titles, when lettered on the back, like as they are presented in a library. If the "front" be unlettered, as is often the case with the older books, a piece of paper is attached, and on it is inscribed the title and the price. Sometimes the description is exceeding curt, as, "Poetry," "French," "Religious," "Latin" (I saw an odd volume, in Spanish, of Don Quixote, marked "Latin," but it was at a shop-seller's stall), "Pamphlets," and such like; or where it seems to have been thought necessary to give a somewhat fuller appellation, such titles are written out as "Locke's Understanding," "Watts's Mind," or "Pope's Rape."[3] If the stock be rather scant, the side of the book is then shown, and is either covered with white paper, on which the title and price are written, or "brushed," or else a piece of paper is attached, with the necessary announcement.

Sometimes these announcements are striking enough, as where a number of works of the same size have been bound together (which used to be the case, I am told, more frequently than it is now); or where there

1 First published in the weekly serial version of *London Labour*, No. 15, 22 March 1851.

2 Planks sawn from inexpensive wood.

3 *An Essay Concerning Human Understanding* (1689) by John Locke (1632–1704); *The Improvement of the Mind* (1741) by Isaac Watts (1674–1743); "The Rape of the Lock" (1712), a poem by Alexander Pope (1688–1744).

has been a series of stories in one volume. One such announcement was, "Smollett's Peregrine Pickle Captain Kyd Pirate Prairie Rob of the Bowl Bamfyeld Moore Carew 2*s*." Alongside this miscellaneous volume was, "Wilberforce's Practical View of Christianity, 1*s*."; "Fenelon's Aventures de Télémaque, plates, 9*d*."; "Arres, de Predestinatione, 1*s*." (the last-mentioned work, which, at the first glance, seems as if it were an odd mixture of French and Latin, was a Latin quarto[1]); "Coronis ad Collationem Hagiensem, &c. &c., Gulielmo Amesio." Another work, on another stall, had the following description: "Lord Mount Edgecumbe's Opera What is Currency Watts's Scripture History Thoughts on Taxation only 1*s*. 3*d*." Another was, "Knickerbocker Bacon 1*s*." As a rule, however, the correctness with which the work is described is rather remarkable.

At some few of the street-stalls, and at many of the shop-stalls, are boxes, containing works marked, "All 1*d*.," or 2*d*., 3*d*., or 4*d*. Among these are old Court-Guides,[2] Parliamentary Companions,[3] Railway Plans, and a variety of sermons, and theological, as well as educational and political pamphlets. To show the character of the publications thus offered—not, perhaps, as a rule, but generally enough, for sale—I copied down the titles of some at 1*d*. and 2*d*.[4]

"*All these at* 1*d*.—'Letters to the Right Honourable Lord John Russell, on State Education, by Edward Baines, jun.'; 'A Pastoral Letter to the Clergy and Members of the Protestant Episcopal Church in the United States of America'; 'A Letter to the Protestant Dissenters of England and Wales, by the Rev. Robert Ainslie'; 'Friendly Advice to Conservatives'; 'Elementary Thoughts on the Principles of Currency and Wealth, and on the Means of Diminishing the Burthens of the People, by J.D. Basset, Esq., price 2*s*. 6*d*.'" The others were each published at 1*s*.

"*All these at* 2*d*.—'Poems, by Eleanor Tatlock, 1811, 2 vols., 9*s*.'; 'Two Sermons, on the Fall and Final Restoration of the Jews, by the Rev. John Stuart'; 'Thoughts and Feelings, by Arthur Brooke, 1820'; 'The Amours of Philander and Sylvia, being the third and last part of Love-letters between a Nobleman and his Sister.[5] Volume the Second. The Seventh Edition. London.'"

---

1 Blanksheet paper of various dimensions folded twice to produce four leaves, and thus eight pages of text. Multiple quartos could be sewn together to produce a book or pamphlet.

2 Directories of London nobility and the fashionable elite, containing their names, addresses, country estates, rank, and occupation. Some also listed upscale London hotels, coffee houses, and clubs.

3 Annual directories containing names, biographies, and addresses of members of Parliament.

4 The following list of titles demonstrates the range of publications available in London's street bookstalls—from political treatises to sermons to poetry and novels—and is a snapshot of the kinds of subjects that caught Mayhew's eye.

5 A three-volume epistolary novel by Aphra Behn (1640?–89), published between 1684 and 1687. While not a "cock" in the sense that it is not street literature, the novel is loosely based on scandalous true events.

[...]

Of the Experience of a Street Bookseller.[1]

I now give a statement, furnished to me by an experienced man, as to the nature of his trade, and the class of his customers. Most readers will remember having seen an account in the life of some poor scholar, having read—and occasionally, in spite of the remonstrances of the stall-keeper—some work which he was too needy to purchase, and even of his having read it through at intervals. That something of this kind is still to be met with will be found from the following account:

"My customers, sir, are of all sorts," my informant said. "They're gentlemen on their way from the City,[2] that have to pass along here by the City-road. Bankers' clerks, very likely, or insurance-office clerks, or such like. They're fairish customers, but they often screw me. Why only last month a gentleman I know very well by sight, and I see him pass in his brougham in bad weather, took up an old Latin book—if I remember right it was an odd volume of a French edition of Horace—and though it was marked only 8*d.*, it was long before he would consent to give more than 6*d.* And I should never have got my price if I hadn't heard him say quite hastily, when he took up the book, 'The very thing I've long been looking for!' Mechanics are capital customers for scientific or trade books, such as suit their business; and so they often are for geography and history, and some for poetry; but *they're* not so screwy. I know a many such who are rare ones for searching into knowledge. Women buy very little of me in comparison to men; sometimes an odd novel, in one volume, when its cheap, such as 'The Pilot,' or 'The Spy,' or 'The Farmer of Inglewood Forest,' or 'The Monk.'[3] No doubt some buy 'The Monk,' not knowing exactly what sort of a book it is, but just because it's a romance; but some young men buy it, I know, because they have learned what sort it's like. Old three vol. novels won't sell at all, if they're ever so cheap. Boys very seldom buy of me, unless it's a work about pigeons, or something that way.

"I can't say that odd vols. of Annual Registers[4] are anything but a bad sale, but odd vols. of old Mags. (magazines), a year or half-year bound together, are capital. Old London Mags., or Ladies', or Oxford and Cambridges, or Town and Countrys, or Universals, or Monthly Reviews, or

---

1 First published in the weekly serial version of *London Labour,* No. 15, 22 March 1851.

2 Historic financial district covering just over one square mile in central London, originating in the Roman period.

3 Two American adventure novels by James Fenimore Cooper, *The Pilot* (1823) and *The Spy* (1821); and two Gothic novels, Elizabeth Helme's *The Farmer of Inglewood Forest* (1796) and Matthew Gregory Lewis's *The Monk* (1796). All four of these novels were frequently reprinted throughout the nineteenth century.

4 *The Annual Register: A View of the History, Politics, and Literature of the Year,* a periodical founded in 1758 by Robert Dodsley and Edmund Burke.

THE STREET-STATIONER.

[From a Daguerreotype by BEARD.]

Fig. 3: "The Street-Stationer."

Humourists, or Ramblers, or Europeans,[1] or any of any sort, that's from 40 to 100 years old, no matter what they are, go off rapidly at from 1*s.* 6*d.* to 3*s.* 6*d.* each, according to size, and binding, and condition. Odd numbers of Mags. are good for little at a stall. The old Mags. in vols. are a sort of reading a great many are very fond of. Lives of the Princess Charlotte are a ready penny enough. So are Queen Carolines,[2] but not so good. Dictionaries of all kinds are nearly as selling as the old Mags., and so are good Latin books. French are only middling; not so well as you might think."

My informant then gave me a similar account to what I had previously received concerning English classics, and proceeded: "Old religious books, they're a fair trade enough, but they're not so plentiful on the stalls now, and if they're black-letter[3] they don't find their way from the auctions or anywhere to any places but the shops or to private purchasers. Mrs. Rowe's 'Knowledge of the Heart'[4] goes off, if old. Bibles, and Prayer-books, and Hymn-books, are very bad." [This may be accounted for by the cheapness of these publications, when new, and by the facilities afforded to obtain them gratuitously.] "Annuals[5] are dull in going off; very much so, though one might expect different. I can hardly sell 'Keepsakes'[6] at all. Children's books, such as are out one year at 2*s.* 6*d.* apiece, very nicely got up, sell finely next year at the stalls for from 6*d.* to 10*d.* Genteel people buy them of us for presents at holiday times. They'll give an extra penny quite cheerfully if there's 'Price 2*s.* 6*d.*' or 'Price 3*s.* 6*d.*' lettered on the back or part of the title-page. School-books in good condition don't stay long on hand, especially Pinnock's.[7] There's not a few people who stand and read and read for half an hour or an hour at a time. It's very trying to the temper when they take up room that way, and prevent others

---

1 A variety of literary and general interest periodicals published between 1732 and 1826.

2 Biographies of Princess Charlotte Augusta (1796–1817) and her mother Queen Caroline of Brunswick. Charlotte's death in childbirth and her popularity with the public led her to be widely commemorated. For Queen Caroline, see p. 98, note 3.

3 Gothic script typeface.

4 Most likely Elizabeth Singer Rowe's *Devout Exercises of the Heart* (1737), a popular and frequently reprinted devotional text.

5 Annuals were decorative, elaborately bound, and engraved books of literature generally given as gifts. They were popular from the 1820s to the 1840s with middle-class readers. Though sometimes dismissed as sentimental, annuals generally paid well and attracted contributors. In addition, they often provided employment for women, as both editors and contributors.

6 *The Keepsake* (1827–56), established by engraver Charles Heath, was the longest running literary annual. This publication included contributions by several famous authors including Mary Shelley (1797–1851), Harriet Beecher Stowe (1811–96), Sir Walter Scott, and William Wordsworth (1770–1850).

7 William Pinnock (1782–1843) was a writer, publisher, and compiler of educational texts including *Pinnock's Catechisms*, a series of short catechistic manuals for children on a variety of subjects.

seeing the works, and never lay out a penny theirselves. But they seem quite lost in a book. Well, I'm sure I don't know what they are. Some seem very poor, judging by their dress, and some seem shabby genteels. I can't help telling them, when I see them going, that I'm much obliged, and I hope that perhaps next time they'll manage to say 'thank ye,' for they don't open their lips once in twenty times. I know a man in the trade that goes dancing mad when he has customers of this sort, who aren't customers. I dare say, one day with another, I earn 3*s.* the year through; wet days are greatly against us, for if we have a cover people won't stop to look at a stall. Perhaps the rest of my trade earn the same." This man told me that he was not unfrequently asked, and by respectable people, for indecent works, but he recommended them to go to Holywell-street[1] themselves. He believed that some of his fellow-traders *did* supply such works, but to no great extent.

An elderly man, who had known the street book-trade for many years, but was not concerned in it when I saw him, told me that he was satisfied he had sold old books, old plays often, to Charles Lamb,[2] whom he described as a stuttering man, who, when a book suited him, sometimes laid down the price, and smiled and nodded, and then walked away with it in his pocket or under his arm, without a word having been exchanged. When we came to speak of dates, I found that my informant—who had only conjectured that this was Lamb—was unquestionably mistaken. One of the best customers he ever had for anything old or curious, and in Italian, if he remembered rightly, as well as in English, was the late Rev. Mr. Scott, who was chaplain on board the Victory, at the time of Nelson's death at Trafalgar.[3] "He had a living in Yorkshire, I believe it was," said the man, "and used to come up every now and then to town. I was always glad to see his white head and rosy face, and to have a little talk with him about books and trade, though it wasn't always easy to catch what he said, for he spoke quick, and not very distinct. But he was a pleasant old gentleman, and talked to a poor man as politely as he might to an admiral. He was very well known in my trade, as I was then employed."

The same man once sold to a gentleman, he told me, and he believed it was somewhere about twenty-five years ago, if not more, a Spanish or Portuguese work, but what it was he did not know. It was marked 1*s.* 9*d.*, being a good-sized book, but the stall-keeper was tired of having had it a long time, so that he gladly would have taken 9*d.* for it. The gentleman in question handed him half-a-crown, and, as he had not the change, the purchaser said: "O, don't mind; it's worth far more than half-a-crown to me." When this liberal customer had walked away, a gentleman who had

---

1 See p. 107, note 3.

2 Lamb (1775–1834) was most known for his essays, written under the pseudonym Elia, for the *London Magazine* (1820–33).

3 Alexander John Scott (1768–1840) was a naval chaplain who was notably present at the death of Lord Nelson at Trafalgar, 21 October 1805.

been standing at the stall all the time, and who was an occasional buyer, said, "Do you know him?" and, on receiving an answer in the negative, he rejoined, "That's Southey."[1]

[...]

Of the Street-sellers of Engravings, Etc., in Umbrellas, Etc.[2]

THE sale of "prints," "pictures," and "engravings"—I heard them designated by each term—in umbrellas in the streets, has been known, as far as I could learn from the street-folk for some fifteen years, and has been general from ten to twelve years. In this traffic the umbrella is inverted and the "stock" is disposed within its expanse. Sometimes narrow tapes are attached from rib to rib of the umbrella, and within these tapes are placed the pictures, one resting upon another. Sometimes a few pins are used to attach the larger prints to the cotton of the umbrella, the smaller ones being "fitted in at the side" of the bigger. "Pins is best, sir, in my opinion," said a little old man, who used to have a "print umbrella" in the New Cut;[3] "for the public has a more unbrokener display. I used werry fine pins, though they's dearer, for people as has a penny to spare likes to see things nice, and big pins makes big holes in the pictures."

This trade is most pursued on still summer evenings, and the use of an inverted umbrella seems so far appropriate that it can only be so used, in the street, in *dry* weather. "I used to keep a sharp look-out, sir," said the same informant, "for wind or rain, and many's the time them devils o' boys—God forgive me, they's on'y poor children—but they *is* devils—has come up to me and has said—one in particler, standin' afore the rest: 'It'll thunder in five minutes, old bloke, so hup with yer humbereller, and go 'ome; hup with it jist as it is; it'll show stunnin; and sell as yer goes.' O, they're a shocking torment, sir; nobody can feel it like people in the streets,—shocking."

The engravings thus sold are of all descriptions. Some have evidently been the frontispieces of sixpenny or lower-priced works. These works sometimes fall into hands of the "waste collectors," and any "illustrations" are extracted from the letter-press and are disposed of by the collectors, by the gross or dozen, to those warehousemen who supply the small shopkeepers and the street-sellers. Sometimes, I was informed, a number of engravings, which had for a while appeared as "frontispieces" were issued for sale separately. Many of these were and are found in the "street umbrellas"; more especially the portraits of popular actors and actresses. "Mr. J.P. Kemble, as Hamlet"—"Mr. Fawcett, as Captain Copp"—"Mr.

1 Robert Southey (1774–1843), Romantic poet and writer who held the post of Poet Laureate from 1813 to his death.

2 First published in the weekly serial version of *London Labour*, No. 16, 29 March 1851.

3 See p. 53, note 2.

now cite some of the titles of this street-sale: "Le Petit Tambour. Sujet d'un Grand Rondeau pour le Piano Forte. Composé par L. Zerbini," (MS.) "Di Tanti Palpiti. The Celebrated Cavatina, by Rossini, &c." "Twenty Short Lessons, or Preludes in the most Convenient Keys for the Harp. Composed and Respectfully Dedicated to Lady Ann Collins. By John Baptist Meyer. Price *5s.*" "An Cota Caol (given in the ancient Irish character.) The Slender Coat," (MS.) "Cailin beog chruite na mbo (also in Irish). The Pretty Girl Milking the Cow," (MS.)

There are now no persons regularly employed in preparing MS. music for the streets. But occasionally a person skilled in music writing will, when he or she, I was told, had nothing better in hand, do a little for the street sale, disposing of the MSS. to any street-stationer or bookseller. If four persons are this way employed, receiving *4s.* a week each, the year through—which I am assured is the extent—we find upwards of *40l.* thus earned, and about twice that sum taken by the street retailers.

OF THE CAPITAL AND INCOME OF THE STREET-SELLERS OF STATIONERY, LITERATURE, AND THE FINE ARTS.

I now proceed to give a summary of the capital, and income of the above classes. I will first however, endeavour to give a summary of the number of individuals belonging to the class.

This appears to be made up (so far as I am able to ascertain) of the following items:—120 sellers of stationery; 20 sellers of pocket-books and diaries; 50 sellers of almanacks and memorandum-books; 12 sellers of account-books; 31 card-sellers; 6 secret papers-sellers; 250 sellers of songs and ballads; 90 running patterers; 20 standing patterers; 8 sellers of "cocks" (principally elopements); 15 selling conundrums, "comic exhibitions," &c.; 200 selling play-bills and books for the play; 40 back-number-sellers; 4 waste paper-sellers at Billingsgate; 40 sellers of tracts and pamphlets; 12 newsvenders, &c., at steam-boat piers; 2 book auctioneers; 70 book-stall keepers and book barrow-men; 16 sellers of guide-books; 30 sellers of song-books and children's books; 40 dealers in pictures in frames; 30 vendors of engravings in umbrellas, and 4 sellers of manuscript music—making altogether a total of 1,110. Many of the above street-trades are, however, only temporary. As, for instance, the street-sale of playing-cards, continues only fourteen days in the year; pocket-books and diaries, four weeks; others, again, are not regularly pursued from day to day, as the sale of prints and engravings in umbrellas, which affords employment for but twelve weeks out of the fifty-two, and conundrums for two months. One trade, however, (namely, that of "Comic Exhibition Papers," gelatine and engraved cards of the Exhibition) is entirely now in the streets. In the broad-sheet trade, again, the "running patterers" work what are called "cocks," when there are no incidents happening to incite the public mind. Hence, making due allowances for such variations, we may fairly assume that the street-sellers belonging to this class number at least 1,000. The following statistics will show the whole amount of capital, and the gross income of this branch of street traffic:

CAPITAL OR VALUE OF THE STOCK-IN-TRADE OF THE STREET-SELLERS OF STATIONERY, LITERATURE AND THE FINE ARTS.

	£	s.	d.
Street-sellers of Stationery.			
40 stalls, *4s.* each; 80 boxes, *3s. 6d.* each; and stock-money for 120 sellers, *10s.* each	82	0	0
Street-sellers of Pocket-books and Diaries.			
Stock-money for 20 vendors, *10s.* each	10	0	0
Street-sellers of Almanacks and Memorandum-books.			
Stock-money for 50 vendors, *1s.* per head	2	10	0
Street-sellers of Account-books.			
12 baskets, *3s.* each; 12 waterproof bags, *2s. 6d.* each; stock-money for 12 sellers, *15s.* each	12	6	0
Street-sellers of Cards.			
Stock-money for 20 sellers, *1s. 6d.* each	2	5	0
Street-seller of Stenographic-cards.			
Stock-money for 1 seller . . .	0	1	6
Street-sellers of Long-songs.			
20 poles to which songs are attached, *2d.* each; stock-money for 20 sellers, *1s.* each	1	3	4
Street-sellers of Wall-songs ("Pinners-up.")			
30 canvass frames, to which songs are hung, *2s.* each; stock-money for 30 sellers, *1s.* each	4	10	0
Street-sellers of Ballads ("Chaunters.")			
2 fiddles, *7s.* each; stock-money for 200 chaunters, *1s.* each . . .	10	14	0
Street-sellers of "Dialogues," "Litanies," &c. ("Standing Patterers.")			
20 boards with appendages "for pictures," *5s. 6d.* each; 20 paintings for boards, *3s. 6d.* each; stock-money for 20 vendors, *1s.* each . .	10	0	0
Street-sellers of Executions, &c. ("Running Patterers.")			
Stock-money for 90 sellers, *1s.* each	4	10	0
Street-sellers of "Cocks."			
Stock-money for 8 sellers, *1s.* each	0	8	0
Street-sellers of Conundrums and Nuts to Crack.			
Stock-money for 15 sellers, *1s.* each	0	15	0

Fig. 4–5: "Of the Capital and Income of the Street-Sellers of Stationery, Literature, and the Fine Arts."

Street-sellers of Exhibition Papers, Magical Delusions, &c.

Stock-money for 15 sellers, 1*s.* each 0 15 0

Street-sellers of Secret Papers.

Stock-money for 6 vendors, 1*s.* each 0 6 0

Street-sellers of Play-bills and Books of the Play.

Stock-money for 200 vendors, 2*s.* each 20 0 0

Street-sellers of Back Numbers.

Stock-money for 40 sellers, 5*s.* each 10 0 0

Street-sellers of Waste-paper at Billingsgate.

Stock-money for 4 sellers, 5*s.* each 1 0 0

Street-sellers of Tracts and Pamphlets.

Stock-money for 40 sellers, 6*d.* each 1 0 0

Street-sellers of Newspapers (Second Edition).

Stock-money for 20 sellers, 2*s.* 6*d.* each 2 10 0

Street-sellers of Newspapers, &c., on board Steam-boats.

Stock-money for 12 sellers, 5*s.* each 3 0 0

Street-sellers of Books by Auction.

Stock-money for 2 sellers, 2*l.* each; 2 barrows, 1*l.* each; 2 boards, for barrows, 3*s.* each 6 6 0

Street-sellers of Books on Stalls and Barrows.

20 stalls, 4*s.* each; 50 barrows, 1*l.* each; 50 boards, for barrows, 3*s.* each; stock-money, for 70 sellers, 2*l.* each 201 10 0

Street-sellers of Guide-books.

Stock-money, for 16 sellers, 5*s.* each 4 0 0

Street-sellers of Song Books and Children's Books.

Stock-money, for 30 vendors, 1*s.* each 1 10 0

Street-sellers of Pictures in Frames.

40 stalls, 2*s.* 6*d.* each; stock-money, for 40 sellers, 5*s.* each . . 15 0 0

Street-sellers of Engravings in Umbrellas.

Umbrellas, 2*s.* 6*d.* each; stock-money, for 30 sellers, 2*s.* each . . 3 0 0

Street-sellers of Manuscript-music.

Stock-money, for 4 sellers, 1*s.* 6*d.* each 0 6 0

TOTAL CAPITAL INVESTED IN THE STREET-SALE OF STATIONERY, LITERATURE, AND THE FINE ARTS 411 5 10

INCOME, OR AVERAGE ANNUAL "TAKINGS," OF THE STREET-SELLERS OF STATIONERY, LITERATURE, AND THE FINE ARTS.

Street-sellers of Stationery.

There are 120 vendors of stationery, who sell altogether during the year, 224,640 quires of writing paper at 3*d.* per quire; 149,760 doz. envelopes, at 1½*d.* per doz.; 37,440 doz. pens, at 3*d.* per doz.; 24,960 bottles of ink, at 1*d.* each; 112,320 black lead pencils, at 1*d.* each; 24,960 pennyworths of wafers, and 49,920 sticks of sealing-wax, at ½*d.* per stick; amounting altogether to £4,992

Street-sellers of Pocket-books and Diaries.

During the year 1,440 pocket-books, at 6*d.* each, and 960 diaries, at 6*d.* each, are sold in the streets by 20 vendors; amounting to £60

Street-sellers of Almanacks and Memorandum-books.

There are sold during the year, in the streets of London, 280,800 memorandum-books, at 1*d.* each, and 4,800 almanacks at 1*d.* each, among 50 vendors, altogether amounting to . . . £1,190

Street-sellers of Account-books.

There are now 12 itinerants vending account-books in various parts of the metropolis, each of whom sells daily, upon an average, 4 account-books, at 1*s.* 9*d.* each; the number sold during the year is therefore 14,976, and the sum expended thereon amounts to . . £1,310

Street-sellers of "Gelatine," "Engraved," and "Playing-cards."

There are 20 street-sellers vending gelatine and engraved cards during the day, and 30 selling playing-cards (for 14 days) at night. These vendors get rid of, among them, in the course of the year, 43,200 gelatine, and 14,400 engraved cards, at 1*d.* each, and 3,360 packs of playing-cards, at 3*d.* per pack; so that the money spent in the streets on the sale of engraved, gelatine, and playing-cards, during the year, amounts to £282

Street-seller of Stenographic Cards.

There is only 1 individual "working" stenographic cards in the streets of London, and the number he sells in the course of the year is 7,448 cards, at 1*d.* each, amounting to £31 4

Street-sellers of Long Songs.

I am assured, that if 20 persons were selling long songs in the street last summer (during a period of 12 weeks), it was "the outside;" as long songs are now "for fairs and races, and country work." Calculating that each cleared 9*s.* in a week, and to clear that took 15*s.*, we find there is expended in long songs in the streets annually . . £180

Street-sellers of Wall Songs ("Pinners-up.")

On fine summer days, the wall song-sellers (of whom there are 30) take 2*s.* on an average. On short wintry days they may not take half so much, and on very foggy or rainy days they take nothing at all. Reckoning that each wall song-man now takes 10*s.* 6*d.* weekly (7*s.* being the profit), we find there is expended yearly in London streets, in the ballads of the pinners-up £810

Street-sellers of Ballads ("Chaunters.")

There are now 200 chaunters, who also sell the ballads they sing; the average takings of each are 3*s.* per day; altogether amounting to . . . £4,680

Street-sellers of Executions, &c. ("Running Patterers.")

Some represent their average weekly earnings at 12*s.* 6*d.* the year through; some at 10*s.* 6*d.*; and others at less than half of 12*s.* 6*d.* Reckoning, however, that only 9*s.* weekly is an average profit per individual, and that 14*s.* be taken to realise that profit, we find there is expended yearly, on executions, fires, deaths, &c., in London . . . £3,276

Street-sellers of Dialogues, Litanies, &c. (Standing Patterers.)

If 20 standing patterers clear 10*s.* weekly, each, the year through, and take 15*s.* weekly, we find there is yearly expended in the standing patter of London streets £780

Street-sellers of "Cocks" (Elopements, Love Letters, &c.

There are now 8 men who sell nothing but "Cocks," each of whom dispose daily of 6 dozen copies at ½*d.* per copy, or altogether, during the year, 179,712 copies, amounting to £374 8*s.*

Street-sellers of Conundrums—"Nuts to Crack," &c.

From the best information I could acquire, it appears that fifteen men may be computed as working conundrums for two months throughout the twelve, and clearing 10*s.* 6*d.* weekly, per individual. The cost of the "Nuts to Crack" (when new) is 5*d.* a dozen to the seller; but old "Nuts" often answer the purpose of the street-seller, and may be had for about half the price; the cost of the "Nut-crackers" is 2*s.* to 2*s.* 6*d.* It may be calculated, then, that to realize the 10*s.* 6*d.* above-mentioned 15*s.* must be taken. This shows the street expenditure in "Nuts to Crack" and "Nut-crackers" to be yearly . . . £90 .

Street-sellers of Exhibition Papers, Magical Delusions, &c.

This trade is carried on only for a short time in the winter, as regards the magical portion; and I am informed that, including the "Comic Exhibitions," it extends to about half of the sum taken for conundrums; or to about £45

Street-sellers of Secret Papers.

Supposing that 6 men last year each cleared 6*s.* weekly, we find expended yearly in the streets on this rubbish £93

Street-sellers of Play-bills and Books.

Taking the profits at 3*s.* a week, at cent. per cent. on the outlay, and reckoning 200 sellers, including those at the saloons, concert-rooms, &c., there is expended yearly on the sale of play-bills purchased in the streets of London £3,120

Street-sellers of Back Numbers.

There are now 40 vendors in the streets of London, each selling upon an average 3 dozen copies daily, at ½*d.* each, or during the year 336,960 odd numbers. Hence, the sum expended annually in the streets for back numbers of periodicals amounts to upwards of £700

Street-sellers of Waste-paper at Billingsgate.

There are 4 individuals selling waste-paper at Billingsgate, one of whom informed me that from 70 to 100 pounds weight of "waste"—about three-fourths being newspapers—is supplied to Billingsgate market and its visitants. The average price is not less than 2½*d.* a pound, or from that to 3*d.* A single paper is 1*d.* Reckoning that 85 pounds of waste-paper are sold a day, at 2½*d.* per pound, we find that the annual expenditure in waste-paper at Billingsgate is upwards of £275

Street-sellers of Tracts and Pamphlets.

From the information I obtained from one of this class of street-sellers, I find there are 40 individuals gaining a livelihood in selling tracts and pamphlets in the streets, full one half are men of colour, the other half consists of old and infirm men, and young boys, the average takings of each is about 1*s.* a day, the year through; the annual street expenditure in the sale of tracts and pamphlets is thus upwards of £620

Street-sellers of Newspapers (Second Edition.)

There are 20 who are engaged in the street sale of newspapers, second edition, each of whom take weekly (for a period of 6 weeks in the year) 1*l.* 5*s.*; so that, adopting the calculation of my informant, and giving a profit of 150 per cent., the yearly expenditure in the streets, in second editions, amounts to £150

Street-sellers of Newspapers, &c., at Steam-Boat Piers.

I am informed that the average earnings of these traders, altogether, may be taken at 15*s.* weekly; calculating that twelve carry on the trade the year through, we find that (assuming each man to sell at thirty-three per cent. profit—though in the case of old works it will be often cent. per cent.), the sum expended annually in steam-boat papers is upwards of . £1,500

Street-sellers of Books (by Auction).

There are at present only 2 street-sellers of books by auction in London, whose clear weekly earnings are 10*s.* 6*d.* each. Calculating their profits at 250*l.* per cent., their weekly receipts will amount to 35*s.* each per week; giving a yearly expenditure of £91

Street-sellers of Books on Stalls and Barrows.

The number of book-stalls and barrows in the streets of the metropolis is 70. The proprietors of these sell weekly upon an average 42 volumes each. The number of volumes annually sold in the streets is thus 1,375,920, and reckoning each volume sold to average 9*d.*, we find that the yearly expenditure in the sale of books in the street amounts to £5,733

Street-sellers of Guide-books.

The street-sellers of guide-books to public places of amusement, are 16 in number, the profit of each is 4*s.* weekly, at 25 per cent., hence the takings must be 20*s.*; thus making the annual expenditure in the street-sale of such books amount to £832

Street-sale of Song-books and Chidren's books.

There are 30 street-sellers who vend children's books and song-books, and dispose of, among them, 2 dozen each daily, or during the year 224,640 books, at 1*d.* each; hence the sum yearly expended in the street-sale of children's books and song-books is £936

Street-sellers of Pictures in Frames.

If we calculate 40 persons selling pictures in frames, and each taking 10*s.* weekly; we find the annual amount spent in the streets in the sale of these articles is £1,040

Street-sellers of Prints and Engravings in Umbrellas.

The street-sale of prints and engravings in umbrellas lasts only 12 weeks. There are 30 individuals who gain a livelihood in the sale of these articles during that period. The average takings of each seller is 12*s.* weekly; so that the annual street-expenditure upon prints and engravings is £216

Street-sellers of Manuscript Music.

There are only 4 sellers of manuscript music in the streets, who take on an average 4*s.* each weekly; hence we find the annual expenditure in this article amounts in round numbers to . . . £40

TOTAL SUM EXPENDED YEARLY IN THE STREETS ON STATIONERY, LITERATURE, AND THE FINE ARTS . . . . £33,446 12*s.*

AN EPITOME OF THE PATTERING CLASS.

I wish, before passing to the next subject—the street-sellers of manufactured articles (of one of whom the engraving here given furnishes a well-known specimen)—I wish, I say, as I find some mistakes have occurred on the subject, to give the public a general view of the patterers, as well as to offer some few observations concerning the means of improving the habits of street-people in general.

The patterers consist of three distinct classes; viz., those who sell something, and patter to help off their goods; those who exhibit something, and patter to help off the show; and those who do nothing but patter, with a view to elicit alms. Under the head of "Patterers who sell" may be classed

Paper Workers,	Dealers in Razor Paste,
Quack Doctors,	" French Polish,
Cheap Jacks,	" Plating Balls,
Grease Removers,	" CandleShades,
Wager Patterers,	" Rat Poisons, &
Ring Sellers,	" Blacking,
Dealers in Corn Salve,	Book Auctioneers.

The second class of patterers includes jugglers, showmen, clowns, and fortune-tellers; beside several exhibitors who invite public notice to the wonders of the telescope or microscope.

The third and last class of patterers are those who neither sell nor amuse, but only victimise those who get into their clutches. These (to use their own words) "do it on the bounce." Their general resort is an inferior public-house, sometimes a brothel, or a coffee-shop. One of the tricks of these worthies is to group together at a window, and if a well-dressed person pass by, to salute him with the contents of a flour-bag. One of their pals—better dressed than the rest—immediately walks out, declares it was purely accidental, and invites the gentleman in "to be brushed." Probably he consents, and still more probably, if he be "good-natured," he is plied with liquor, drugged with snuff for the occasion, and left in some obscure court, utterly stupified. When he awakes, he finds that his watch, purse, &c., are gone.

"A casual observer, or even a stranger, may be induced to contract a wayside acquaintance with the parties to whom I allude," says one of the pattering class, from whom I have received much valuable information; "and if he be a visitor of fairs and races, that acquaintance, though slight, may sometimes prove expensive.

Young, as Iago"—"Mr. Liston, as Paul Pry"—"Mrs. Siddons, as Lady Macbeth"—"Miss O'Neil, as Belvidera," &c., &c.[1] In the course of an inquiry into the subject nearly a year and a half ago, I learned from one "umbrella man" that, six or seven years previously, he used to sell more portraits of "Mr. Edmund Kean, as Richard III.,"[2] than of anything else. Engravings, too, which had first been admired in the "Annuals"—when half-a-guinea was the price of the "Literary Souvenir," the "Forget-me-not," "Friendship's Offering," the "Bijou," &c., &c.[3]—are frequently found in these umbrellas; and amongst them are not unfrequently seen portraits of the aristocratic beauties of the day, from "waste" "Flowers of Loveliness"[4] and old "Court Magazines,"[5] which "go off very fair." The majority of these street-sold "engravings" are "coloured," in which state the street-sellers prefer them, thinking them much more saleable, though the information I received hardly bears out their opinion.

[...]

Of the "Screevers," or Writers of Begging-Letters and Petitions.[6]

"SCREEVING"—that is to say, *writing* false or exaggerated accounts of afflictions and privations, is a necessary corollary to "Pattering," or making pompous *orations* in public—and I here subjoin a brief description of the "business"—for although the "screevers," "economically" considered, belong properly to the class who will *not work*, yet as they are intimately connected with the street-trade of begging I have thought it best to say a few words on the subject here, reserving a more comprehensive and scientific view of the subject till such time as I come to treat of the *professional* beggar, under the head of those who are *able* but *unwilling* to labour for their livelihood, in contradistinction to the involuntary beggars, who belong more properly to those who are *willing* but *unable* to work. The subjoined information has been obtained from one who has had many opportunities of making himself acquainted with the habits and tricks of

---

1 All referring to famous actors of the early- to mid-Victorian stage, among them John Philip Kemble (1757–1823), his sister Sarah Siddons (1755–1831), John Liston (c. 1776–1846), and John Fawcett (1768–1837).

2 Edmund Kean (1789–1833). British actor best known for playing Shakespeare's villains.

3 Titles of popular annuals; see p. 129, note 5.

4 *Flowers of Loveliness; Twelve Groups of Female Figures, Emblematic of Flowers* (1836) was a book of illustrations and poems designed by E.T. Parris, Esq. (1793–1873), "with poetical illustrations" by the Countess of Blessington (1789–1849).

5 Originally *La Belle Assemblée* (1806–37), *The Court Magazine and Monthly Critic* was a women's magazine that included many fashion plates, as well as stories, poetry, and articles.

6 First published in the weekly serial version of *London Labour*, No. 16, 29 March 1851.

the class here treated of,—indeed, at one part of his life he himself belonged to the "profession."

"In England and Wales the number of vagrants committed to prison annually amounts to 19,621; and as many are not imprisoned more than a dozen times during their lives, and a few never at all, the number of tramps and beggars may be estimated, at the very lowest, at 22,000 throughout England and Wales. The returns from Scotland are indeterminate. Of this wretched class many are aged and infirm; others are destitute orphans; while not a few are persons whose distress is real, and who suffer from temporary causes.

"With this excusable class, however, I have not now to do. Of professional beggars there are two kinds—those who 'do it on the *blob*' (by word of mouth), and those who do it by '*screeving*,' that is, by petitions and letters, setting forth imaginary cases of distress.

"Of these documents there are two sorts, 'slums' (letters) and 'fakements' (petitions). These are seldom written by the persons who present or send them, but are the production of a class of whom the public little imagine either the number or turpitude. I mean the 'professional begging-letter writers.'

"Persons who write begging-letters for others sometimes, though seldom, beg themselves. They are in many cases well supported by the fraternity for whom they write. A professional of this kind is called by the 'cadgers,' 'their man of business.' Their histories vary as much as their abilities; generally speaking they have been clerks, teachers, shopmen, reduced gentlemen, or the illegitimate sons of members of the aristocracy; while others, after having received a liberal education, have broken away from parental control, and commenced the 'profession' in early life, and will probably pursue it to their graves.

"I shall take a cursory view of the various pretences set forth in these begging documents," says my informant, "and describe some of the scenes connected with their preparation. The documents themselves are mournful catalogues of all the ills that flesh is heir to.

"I address myself first to that class of petitions which represent losses by sea, or perhaps shipwreck itself. These documents are very seldom carried by one person, unless indeed he is really an old sailor; and, to the credit of the navy be it spoken, this is very seldom the case. When the imposition under notice has to be carried out, it is, for the most part, conducted by half-a-dozen worthless men, dressed in the garb of seamen (and known as turnpike sailors), one of their number having really been at sea and therefore able to reply to any nautical inquiries which suspicion may throw out. This person mostly carries the document; and is, of course, the spokesman of the company. Generally speaking, the gang have a subscription-book, sometimes only a fly-leaf or two to the document, to receive the names of contributors.

"It may not be out of place here, to give a specimen—drawn from memory—of one of those specious but deceitful 'fakements' upon which the 'swells,' (especially those who have 'been in the service,') 'come down with a *couter*' (sovereign) if they 'granny the mauley' (perceive the signature) of a brother officer or friend. The document is generally as follows—

"'These are to Certify, to all whom it may concern, that the THUNDERER, Captain Johnson, was returning on her homeward-bound passage from China, laden with tea, fruit, &c., and having beside, twenty passengers, chiefly ladies, and a crew of thirty hands, exclusive of the captain and other officers. That the said vessel encountered a tremendous gale off the banks of Newfoundland, and was dismasted, and finally wrecked at midnight on' (such a day, including the hour, latitude, and other particulars). 'That the above-named vessel speedily foundered, and only the second mate and four of the crew (the bearers of this certificate) escaped a watery grave. These, after floating several days on broken pieces of the ship, were providentially discovered, and humanely picked up by the brig INVINCIBLE, Captain Smith, and landed in this town and harbour of Portsmouth, in the county of Hants. That we, the Master of Customs, and two of her Majesty's Justices of the Peace for the said harbour and county, do hereby grant and afford to the said' (here follows the names of the unfortunate mariners) 'this our vouchment of the truth of the said wreck, and their connection therewith, and do empower them to present and use this certificate for twenty-eight days from the date hereof, to enable them to get such temporal aid as may be adequate to reaching their respective homes, or any sea-port where they may be re-engaged. And this certificate further showeth, that they are not to be interrupted in the said journey by any constabulary or other official authority; provided, that is to say, that no breach of the peace or other cognizable offence be committed by the said Petitioners,

'As witness our hands,

John Harris, M.C.	£1	0	0
James Flood, J.P.	1	0	0
Capt. W. Hope, R.N., J.P. . .	1	10	0

'Given at Portsmouth, this 10th day of October, 1850.

'GOD SAVE THE QUEEN.'

Rev. W. Wilkins	£1	0	0
An Officer's Widow . . .	0	10	0
An Old Sailor	0	5	0
A Friend	0	2	6'

[...]

"But the most expert and least suspected dodge is referring to some dignified person in the country; a person however who exists nowhere but in imagination. Suppose (says my informant) I am a beggar, I apply to you for relief. Perhaps I state that I am in prospect of lucrative employment, if I could get enough money to clothe myself. You plead the number of impositions; I consent to that fact, but offer you references as to the truth of my statement. I refer you to the Hon. and Rev. Mr. Erskine, at Cheltenham (any name or place will do). You promise to write, and tell me to call in a few days; meanwhile, I assume the name of the gentleman to whom I have referred you, and write forthwith to the post-master of the town in question, requesting that any letter coming there directed to the Hon. and Rev. Mr. Erskine, may be forwarded to my present address. I thus discover what you have written, frame a flattering reply, and address it to you. I send it (under cover) to a pal of mine at Cheltenham, or elsewhere, who posts it; I call half an hour after you receive it, and, being satisfied, you give me a donation, and perhaps introduce me to some of your friends. Thus I raise a handsome sum, and the fraud is probably never found out.

"One of the London lurkers, who has good means of forming a calculation on the subject, assures me that the average earnings of 'lurkers' in London alone (including those who write for them), cannot be less than 6,000*l.* per annum.

"Two of the class were lately apprehended, at the instance of the Duke of Wellington; on their persons was found fifteen sovereigns, one five-pound note, a silver watch with gold guard, and two gold watches with a ribbon attached to each; their subscription book showed that they had collected 620*l.* during the current year.

"A man named M'Kensie—who was transported at the last Bristol Assizes—had just received a cheque for 100*l.* from a nobleman lately deceased.

"Most of the 'professionals' of this class include a copy of the 'Court Guide'[1] among their stock in trade. In this all the persons known to be charitable, have the mark ⊕ set against their names. I have been furnished with a list of such persons, accompanied with comments, from the note-book of 'an old stager' 'thirty years on the monkery,' and, as he adds, 'never quodded[2] but twice.'

"The late Queen Dowager.[3]
Hon. Wm. Ashley.
The Bishop of Norwich.

---

1 See p. 126, note 2.

2 That is, from the notebook of an old hand who has been an itinerant seller in the country (monkery) for 30 years, and imprisoned (quodded) only twice.

3 The list reads as a who's who of the charitable elite, including everyone from the widow of a monarch (Queen Dowager) to politicians (Ashley, Talfourd, Norton, Peel, Breadalbane, Manners); clergymen (Bishop of Norwich, Holland, Sinclair, Pott); writers (Dickens, Rogers, Ponsonby); philanthropists (Burdett-Coutts); and various members of the English nobility.

Serjeant Talfourd.
Charles Dickins.
Samuel Rogers, the Poet.
Samuel Warren (Author of 'Extracts from the Diary of a Physician').
Hon. G.C. Norton, the 'beak' (magistrate), but good for all that.
Rev. E. Holland, Hyde-park-gardens.
The late Sir Robert Peel.
Countess of Essex (only good to sickness, or distressed authorship).
Marquess of Bredalbane (good on anything religious).
The Editor of the 'Sun.'
Madame Celeste.
Marquess of Blandford.
Duke of Portland.
Duke of Devonshire.
Lord George Bentinck (deceased; God A'mighty wouldn't let him live; he was too good for this world).
Lord Skelmersdale.
Lord John Manners.
Lord Lyttleton.
Mrs. Elder, Exeter.
Lady Emily Ponsonby (a devilish pretty wench).
Miss Burdett Coutts.
F. Stewart, Esq., Bath.
Mrs. Groves, Salisbury.
Mrs. Mitchell, Dorchester.
Mrs. Taggart, Bayswater (her husband is a Unitarian minister, not so good as *she*, but he'll stand a 'bob' if you look straight at him and keep to one story).

Archdeacon Sinclair, at Kensington (but not so good as Archdeacon Pott, as was there afore him; he *was* a good man; he couldn't refuse a dog, much more a Christian; but he had a butler, a regular 'knark,' who was a b— and a half, *good weight*).

Lady Cottenham used to be good, but she is 'coopered' (spoilt) now, without you has a 'slum,' any one as she knows, and then she won't stand above a 'bull' (five shillings)."

Of the Street-Sellers of Manufactured Articles.
The Crippled Street-Seller of Nut-Meg-Graters.[1]

I now give an example of one of the classes *driven* to the streets by utter inability to labour. I have already spoken of the sterling independence of some of these men possessing the strongest claims to our sympathy and charity, and yet preferring to *sell* rather than *beg*. As I said before, many ingrained beggars certainly use the street *trade* as a cloak for alms-seeking,

1 First published in the weekly serial version of *London Labour*, No. 17, 5 April 1851.

THE STREET-SELLER OF NUTMEG-GRATERS.

[*From a Daguerreotype by* BEARD.]

Fig 6: "The Street-Seller of Nutmeg-Graters."

but as certainly many more, with every title to our assistance, use it as a means of redemption from beggary. That the nutmeg-grater seller is a noble example of the latter class, I have not the least doubt. I have made all due inquiries to satisfy myself as to his worthiness, and I feel convinced that when the reader looks at the portrait here given, and observes how utterly helpless the poor fellow is, and then reads the following plain unvarnished tale,[1] he will marvel like me, not only at the fortitude which could sustain him under all his heavy afflictions, but at the resignation (not to say philosophy) with which he bears them every one.[2] His struggles to earn his own living (notwithstanding his physical incapacity even to put the victuals to his mouth after he has earned them), are instances of a nobility of pride that are I believe without a parallel. The poor creature's legs and arms are completely withered; indeed he is scarcely more than head and trunk. His thigh is hardly thicker than a child's wrist. His hands are bent inward from contraction of the sinews, the fingers being curled up and almost as thin as the claws of a bird's foot. He is unable even to stand, and cannot move from place to place but on his knees, which are shod with leather caps, like the heels of a clog, strapped round the joint; the soles of his boots are on the *upper* leathers, that being the part always turned towards the ground while he is crawling along. His countenance is rather handsome than otherwise; the intelligence indicated by his ample forehead is fully borne out by the testimony as to his sagacity in his business, and the mild expression of his eye by the statements as to his feeling for all others in affliction.

"I sell nutmeg-graters and funnels," said the cripple to me; "I sell them at 1*d.* and 1½*d.* a piece. I get mine of the man in whose house I live. He is a tinman, and makes for the street-trade and shops and all. I pay 7*d.* a dozen for them, and I get 12*d.* or 18*d.* a dozen, if I can when I sell them, but I mostly get only a penny a piece—it's quite a chance if I have a customer at 1½*d.* [...] On a wet day when I can't get out, I often go without food. I may have a bit of bread and butter give me, but that's all—then I lie a-bed. I feel miserable enough when I see the rain come down of a week day, I can tell you. Ah, it *is* very miserable indeed lying in bed all day, and in a lonely room, without perhaps a person to come near one—helpless as I am—and hear the rain beat against the windows, and all that without nothing to put in your lips. I've done *that* over and over again where I lived before; but where I am now I'm more comfortable like. My breakfast is mostly bread and butter and tea; and my supper, bread and

1 A reference to *Othello*, 1.3.91–94: "And therefore little shall I grace my cause / In speaking for myself. Yet, by your gracious patience, / I will a round unvarnished tale deliver / Of my whole course of love."

2 The nutmeg-grater seller's name was Charles Alloway. Following the publication of this article, Alloway wrote three letters to Mayhew's readers, which were published in the "Answers to Correspondents," a supplementary text published on the wrapping papers of the serial (see Appendix D).

butter and tea with a bit of fish, or a small bit of meat. What my landlord and landlady has I share with them. I never break my fast from the time I go out in the morning till I come home—unless it is a halfpenny orange I buy in the street; I do that when I feel faint. I have only been selling in the streets since this last winter. I was in the workhouse with a fever all the summer. I was destitute afterwards, and obliged to begin selling in the streets. The Guardians[1] gave me 5*s.* to get stock. I had always dealt in tin ware, so I knew where to go to buy my things. It's very hard work indeed is street-selling for such as me. I can't walk no distance. I suffer a great deal of pains in my back and knees. Sometimes I go in a barrow, when I'm travelling any great way. When I go only a short way I crawl along on my knees and toes. The most I've ever crawled is two miles. When I get home afterwards, I'm in great pain. My knees swell dreadfully, and they're all covered with blisters, and my toes ache awful. I've corns all on top of them.

"Often after I've been walking, my limbs and back ache so badly that I can get no sleep. Across my lines it feels as if I'd got some great weight, and my knees are in a heat, and throb, and feel as if a knife was running into them. When I go up-stairs I have to crawl upon the back of my hands and my knees. I can't lift nothing to my mouth. The sinews of my hands is all contracted. I am obliged to have things held to my lips or me to drink, like a child. I *can* use a knife and fork by leaning my arm on the table and then stooping my head to it. I can't wash nor undress myself. Sometimes I think of my helplessness a great deal. The thoughts of it used to throw me into fits at one time—very bad. It's the Almighty's will that I am so, and I must abide by it. People says, as they passes me in the streets, 'Poor fellow, it's a shocking thing'; but very seldom they does any more than pity me; some lays out a half-penny or a penny with me, but the most of 'em goes on about their business. Persons looks at me a good bit when I go into a strange place. I *do* feel it very much, that I haven't the power to get my living or to do a thing for myself, but I never begged for nothing. I'd sooner starve than I'd do that. [...] Often when I couldn't afford to pay a boy, I've not had my boots off for four or five nights and days, nor my clothes neither. Give me the world I couldn't take them off myself, and then my feet has swollen to that degree that I've been nearly mad with pain, and I've been shivering and faint, but still I was obliged to go out with my things; if I hadn't I should have starved. Such as I am can't afford to be ill—it's only rich folks as can lay up, not we; for us to take to our beds is to go without food altogether. When I was without never a boy, I used to tie the wet towel round the back of one of the chairs, and wash myself by rubbing my face up against it. I've been two days without a bit of anything passing between my lips. I couldn't go and beg for victuals—

1 Elected board of representatives from the local parishes, usually farmers and tradesmen, who made up each Poor Law Union. Poor Law Unions were geographical areas demarcating areas of relief distribution introduced under the New Poor Law of 1834. See Introduction, p. 20 for further information.

I'd rather go without. Then I used to feel faint, and my head used to ache dreadful. I used then to drink a plenty of water. The women sex is mostly more kinder to me than the men. Some of the men fancies, as I goes along, that I can walk. They often says to me, 'Why, the sole of your boot is as muddy as mine'; and one on 'em is, because I always rests myself on that foot—the other sole, you see, is as clean as when it was first made. The women never seem frightened on me. My trade is to sell brooms and brushes, and all kinds of cutlery and tin-ware. I learnt it myself. I never was brought up to nothing, because I couldn't use my hands. Mother was a cook in a nobleman's family when I were born. They say as I was a love-child. I was not brought up by mother, but by one of her fellow-servants. Mother's intellects was so weak, that she couldn't have me with her. She used to fret a great deal about me, so her fellow-servant took me when she got married. After I were born, mother married a farmer in middling circumstances. They tell me as my mother was frightened afore I was born. I never knew my father. He went over to Buonos Ayres, and kept an hotel there—I've heard mother say as much. No mother couldn't love a child more than mine did me, but her feelings was such she couldn't bear to see me. I never went to mother's to live, but was brought up by the fellow-servant as I've told you of. Mother allowed her 30*l.* a-year. I was with her till two years back. She was always very kind to me—treated me like one of her own. Mother used to come and see me about once a-year—sometimes not so often: she was very kind to me then. Oh, yes; I used to like to see her very much. Whatever I wished for she'd let me have; if I wrote to her, she always sent me what I wanted. I was very comfortably then. Mother died four years ago; and when I lost her I fell into a fit—I was told of it all of a sudden. She and the party as I was brought up with was the only friends as I had in the world—the only persons as cared anything about a creature like me. I was in a fit for hours, and when I came to, I thought what would become of me: I knew I could do nothing for myself, and the only friend as I had as could keep me was gone. The person as brought me up was very good, and said, while she'd got a home I should never want; but, two years after mother's death, she was seized with the cholera, and then I hadn't a friend left in the world. When she died I felt ready to kill myself; I was all alone then, and what could I do—cripple as I was? She thought her sons and daughters as I'd been brought up with—like brothers and sisters—would look after me; but it was not in their power—they was only hard-working people. My mother used to allow so much a year for my schooling, and I can read and write pretty well." (He wrote his name in my presence kneeling at the table; holding the pen almost as one might fancy a bird would, and placing the paper sideways instead of straight before him.) "While mother was alive, I was always foraging about to learn something unbeknown to her. I wanted to do so, in case mother should leave me without the means of getting a living. I used to buy old bedsteads, and take them to a man, and get him to repair them, and then I'd put the sacking on myself; I can hold a hammer somehow in my right hand. I used to polish them on my knees. I made a bench to my height out of two old chairs. I used to know what I should get for the bedsteads, and so could tell what I could afford to give the man to do up the parts as I couldn't manage. It was so I got to learn something like a business for myself. When the person died as had brought me up, I *could* do a little; I had then got the means. Before her death I had opened a kind of shop for things in the general line; I sold tin-ware, and brass-work, and candlesticks, and fire-irons, and all old furniture, and gown-prints[1] as well. I went into the tally business,[2] and that ruined me altogether. I couldn't get my money in; there's a good deal owing to me now. Me and a boy used to manage the whole. I used to make all my account-books and everything. My lodgers didn't pay me my rent, so I had to move from the house, and live on what stock I had. In my new lodging I went on as well as I could for a little while; but about eighteen months ago I could hold on no longer. Then I borrowed a little, and went hawking tin-ware and brushes in the country. I sold baking-dishes, Dutch ovens, roasting-jacks, skewers and gridirons, teapots, and saucepans, and combs. I used to exchange sometimes for old clothes. I had a barrow and a boy with me; I used to keep him, and give him 1*s*. a week. I managed to get just a living that way. When the winter came on I gave it up; it was too cold. After that I was took bad with a fever; my stock had been all gone a little while before, and the boy had left because I couldn't keep him, and I had to do all for myself. All my friends was dead, and I had no one to help me, so I was obligated to lay about all night in my things, for I couldn't get them off alone; and that and want of food brought on a fever. Then I was took into the workhouse, and there I stopped all the summer, as I told you. I can't say they treated me bad, but they certainly didn't use me well. If I could have worked after I got better, I could have had tea; but 'cause I couldn't do nothing, they gave me that beastly gruel morning and night. I had meat three times a week. They would have kept me there till now, but I would die in the streets rather than be a pauper. So I told them, if they would give me the means of getting a stock, I would try and get a living for myself. After refusing many times to let me have 10*s*., they agreed to give me 5*s*. Then I came out, but I had no home, and so I crawled about till I met with the people where I am now, and they let me sit up there till I got a room of my own. Then some of my friends collected for me about 15*s*. altogether, and I did pretty well for a little while. I went to live close by the Blackfriars-road, but the people where I lodged treated me very bad. There was a number of girls of the town in the same street, but they was too fond of their selves and their drink to give nothing. They

1 Material used for making dresses.

2 Also called the "tally trade," an informal installment system in which essentials such as household goods, clothes, or coal were sold on credit. The "tallyman" usually went door to door with samples of his wares and returned later to collect installments on the debt.

used to buy things of me and never pay me. They never made game of me, nor played me any tricks, and if they saw the boys doing it they would protect me. They never offered to give me no victuals; indeed, I shouldn't have liked to have eaten the food they got. After that I couldn't pay my lodgings, and the parties where I lodged turned me out, and I had to crawl about the streets for four days and nights. This was only a month back. I was fit to die with pain all that time. If I could get a penny I used to go into a coffee-shop for half-a-pint of coffee, and sit there till they drove me out, and then I'd crawl about till it was time for me to go out selling. Oh! dreadful, dreadful, it was to be all them hours—day and night—on my knees. I couldn't get along at all, I was forced to sit down every minute, and then I used to fall asleep with my things in my hand, and be woke up by the police to be pushed about and druv on by them. It seemed like as if I was walking on the bare bones of my knees. The pain in them was like the cramp, only much worse. At last I could bear it no longer, so I went afore Mr. Secker,[1] the magistrate, at Union Hall, and told him I was destitute, and that the parties where I had been living kept my bed and the few things I had, for 2*s.* 6*d.* rent, that I owed them. He said he couldn't believe that anybody would force me to crawl about the streets, for four days and nights, cripple as I was, for such a sum. One of the officers told him I was a honest and striving man, and the magistrate sent the officer, with the money, to get my things, but the landlady wouldn't give them till the officer compelled her, and then she chucked my bed out into the middle of the street. A neighbour took it in for me and took care of it till I found out the tinman who had before let me sit up in his house. I should have gone to him at first, but he lived farther than I could walk. I am stopping with him now, and he is very kind to me. I have still some relations living, and they are well to do, but, being a cripple, they despise me. My aunt, my mother's sister, is married to a builder, in Petersham, near Richmond, and they are rich people—having some houses of their own besides a good business. I have got a boy to wheel me down on a barrow to them, and asked assistance of them, but they will have nothing to do with me. They won't look at me for my affliction. Six months ago they gave me half-a-crown. I had no lodgings nor victuals then; and *that* I shouldn't have had from them had I not said I was starving and must go to the parish. This winter I went to them, and they shut the door in my face. After leaving my aunt's, I went down to Ham Common, where my father-in-law lives, and there his daughter's husband sent for a policeman to drive me away from the place. I told the husband I had no money nor food; but he advised me to go begging, and said I shouldn't have a penny of them. My father-in-law was ill up-stairs at the time, but I don't think he would have treated me a bit better—and all this they do because the Almighty has made me a cripple. I can,

1 Isaac Onslow Secker (1799–1861), barrister and police magistrate. He was a stipendiary police magistrate whose duties included distributing financial relief to the poor and resolving disputes.

indeed, solemnly say, that there is nothing else against me, and that I strive hard and crawl about till my limbs ache enough to drive me mad, to get an honest livelihood. With a couple of pounds I could, I think, manage to shift very well for myself. I'd get a stock, and go into the country with a barrow, and buy old metal, and exchange tin ware for old clothes, and, with that, I'm almost sure I could get a decent living. I'm accounted a very good dealer."

In answer to my inquiries concerning the character of this man, I received the following written communication:

"I have known C—— A—— twelve years; the last six years he has dealt with me for tinware. I have found him honest in all his dealings with me, sober and industrious.

"C—— H——, Tinman."

From the writer of the above testimonial I received the following account of the poor cripple:—

"He is a man of generous a disposition, and very sensitive for the afflictions of others. One day while passing down the Borough he saw a man afflicted with St. Vitus's dance[1] shaking from head to foot, and leaning on the arm of a woman who appeared to be his wife." The cripple told my informant that he should never forget what he felt when he beheld that poor man. "I thought," he said, "what a blessing it is I am not like him." Nor is the cripple, I am told, less independent than he is generous. In all his sufferings and privations he never pleads poverty to others; but bears up under the trials of life with the greatest patience and fortitude. When in better circumstances he was more independent than at present, having since, through illness and poverty, been much humbled.

"His privations have been great," adds my informant. "Only two months back, being in a state of utter destitution and quite worn out with fatigue, he called at the house of a person (where my informant occupied a room) about ten o'clock at night, and begged them to let him rest himself for a short while, but the inhuman landlady and her son laid hold of the wretched man, the one taking him by the arms and the other by the legs, and literally hurled him into the street. The next morning," my informant continued, "I saw the poor creature leaning against a lamp-post, shivering with the cold, and my heart bled for him; and since that he has been living with me."

1 Now referred to as "Sydenham's chorea" and understood to result from childhood infection from the bacteria streptococcus. Symptoms can include gait disturbance, speech abnormality, psychiatric disorder, or the involuntary muscle contractions that gave it its association with St. Vitus, the patron saint of dancers.

Of the Street-Sellers of Poison for Rats.[1]

THE number of Vermin-Destroyers and Rat-Catchers who ply their avocation in London has of late years become greatly diminished. One cause which I heard assigned for this was that many ruinous old buildings and old streets had been removed,[2] and whole colonies of rats had been thereby extirpated. Another was that the race of rat-catchers had become distrusted, and had either sought some other mode of subsistence, or had resorted to other fields for the exercise of their professional labours.

The rat-catcher's dress is usually a velveteen jacket, strong corduroy trowsers, and laced boots. Round his shoulder he wears an oil-skin belt, on which are painted the figures of huge rats, with fierce-looking eyes and formidable whiskers. His hat is usually glazed and sometimes painted after the manner of his belt. Occasionally—and in the country far more than in town—he carries in his hand an iron cage in which are ferrets, while two or three crop-eared rough terriers dog his footsteps. Sometimes a tamed rat runs about his shoulders and arms, or nestles in his bosom or in the large pockets of his coat. When a rat-catcher is thus accompanied, there is generally a strong aromatic odour about him, far from agreeable; this is owing to his clothes being rubbed with oil of thyme and oil of aniseed, mixed together. This composition is said to be so attractive to the sense of the rats (when used by a man who understands its due apportionment and proper application) that the vermin have left their holes and crawled to the master of the powerful spell. I heard of one man (not a rat-catcher professionally) who had in this way tamed a rat so effectually that the animal would eat out of his mouth, crawl upon his shoulder to be fed, and then "smuggle into his bosom" (the words of my informant) "and sleep there for hours." The rat-catchers have many wonderful stories of the sagacity of the rat, and though in reciting their own feats, these men may not be the most trustworthy of narrators, any work on natural history will avouch that rats *are* sagacious, may be trained to be very docile, and are naturally animals of great resources in all straits and difficulties.

One great source of the rat-catcher's employment and emolument thirty years ago, or even to a later period, is now comparatively a nonentity. At that time the rat-catcher or killer sometimes received a yearly or quarterly stipend to keep a London granary clear of rats. I was told by a man who has for twenty-eight years been employed about London granaries, that he had never known a rat-catcher employed in one except about twenty or twenty-two years ago, and that was in a granary by the river-

1 First published in the weekly serial version of *London Labour*, No. 24, 24 May 1851.

2 The sanitary movement in the 1840s brought on metropolitan improvement efforts, often referred to as slum clearances, that involved removing many old unsanitary buildings in crowded and impoverished neighbourhoods. These efforts, though framed as city improvement, had high social costs and displaced many of the London poor.

side. The professional man, he told me, certainly poisoned many rats, "which stunk so," continued my informant—but then all evil odours in old buildings are attributed to dead rats—"that it was enough to infect the corn. He poisoned two fine cats as well. But I believe he was a young hand and a bungler." The rats, after these measures had been taken, seem to have deserted the place for three weeks or a month, when they returned in as great numbers as ever; nor were their ravages and annoyances checked until the drains were altered and rebuilt.[1] It is in the better disposition of the drains of a corn-magazine, I am assured, that the great check upon the inroads of these "varmint" is attained—by strong mason work and by such a series and arrangement of grates, as defy even the perseverance of a rat. Otherwise the hordes which prey upon the garbage in the common sewers, are certain to find their way into the granary along the drains and channels communicating with those sewers, and will increase rapidly despite the measures of the rat-catcher.

The same man told me that he had been five or six times applied to by rat-catchers, and with liberal offers of beer, to allow them to try and capture the black rats in the granary. One of these traders declared that he wanted them "for a gent as vas curous in them there hinteresting warmint"; But from the representations of the other applicants, my informant was convinced that they were wanted for rat-hunts, the Dog Billy[2] being backed for 100*l.* to kill so many rats in so many minutes. "You see, sir," the corn merchant's man continued, "ours is an old concern, and there's black rats in it, great big fellows; some of 'em must be old, for they're as white about the muzzle as is the Duke of Wellington, and they have the character of being very strong and very fierce. One of the catchers asked me if I knew what a stunning big black rat would weigh, as if I weighed rats! I always told them that I cared nothing about rat-hunts and that I knew our people wouldn't like to be bothered; and they was gentlemen that didn't admire sporting characters."

The black rat, I may observe, or the English rat, is now comparatively scarce, while the brown, or Hanoverian, rat is abundant. This brown rat seems to have become largely domiciled in England about the period of the establishment of the Hanoverian dynasty; whence its name. "A Hanover rat" was a term of reproach applied by the Jacobites to the successful party.

The rat-catchers are also rat-killers. They destroy the animals sometimes by giving them what is called in the trade "an alluring poison." Every professional destroyer, or capturer, of rats will pretend that as to

---

1 The newly formed Metropolitan Commission of Sewers (1847) surveyed the city's sewers and drains in response to cholera outbreaks and other public health issues. Its commissioners ensured that older rotted and leaking wooden drains were rebuilt and repaired with sturdier materials including stone, brick, or piping.

2 A record-setting bull terrier from the 1820s famous in ratting circles and widely covered in sporting publications for his feats of killing one hundred rats in short time frames. See p. 219, note 1.

poison he has his own particular method—his secret—his discovery. But there is no doubt that arsenic is the basis of all their poisons. Its being inodorous, and easily reducible to a soft fine powder, renders it the best adapted for mixing with anything of which rats are fond—toasted cheese, or bacon, or fried liver, or tallow, or oatmeal. Much as the poisoner may be able to tempt the animal's appetite, he must, and does, proceed cautiously. If the bait be placed in an unwonted spot, it is often untouched. If it be placed where rats have been accustomed to find their food, it is often devoured. But even then it is frequently accounted best to leave the bait unpoisoned for the first night; so that a hungry animal may attack it greedily the second. With oatmeal it is usual to mix for the first and even second nights a portion of pounded white sugar. If this be eaten it accustoms the jealous pest to the degree of sweetness communicated by arsenic. The "oatmeal poison" is, I am told, the most effectual; but even when mixed only with sugar it is often refused; as "rats is often better up to a dodge nor Kirstians" (Christians).

Another mode of killing rats is for the professional destroyer to slip a ferret into the rats' haunts wherever it is practicable. The ferret soon dislodges them, and as they emerge for safety they are seized by terriers, who, after watching the holes often a long time, and very patiently, and almost breathlessly, throttle them silently, excepting the short squeak, or half-squeak, of the rat, who, by a "good dog," is seized unerringly by the part of the back where the terrier's gripe and shake is speedy death; if the rat still move, or shows signs of life, the well-trained rat-killer's dog cracks the vermin's skull between his teeth.

If the rats have to be taken alive, they are either trapped, so as not to injure them for a rat-hunt (or the procedure in the pit would be accounted "foul"), or if driven out of their holes by ferrets, they can only run into some cask, or other contrivance, where they can be secured for the "sportsman's" purposes. Although any visible injury to the body of the rat will prevent its reception into a pit, the creatures' teeth are often drawn, and with all the cruelty of a rough awkwardness, by means of pinchers, so that they may be unable to bite the puppies being trained for the pit on the rats. If the vermin be not truly seized by the dog, the victim will twist round and inflict a tremendous bite on his worrier, generally on the lip. This often causes the terrier to drop his prey with a yell, and if a puppy he may not forget the lesson from the sharp nip of the rat. To prevent this it is that the rat-catchers play the dentist on their unfortunate captives.

I heard many accounts of the "dodges" practised by, or imputed to, the rat-catchers: that it was not a very unusual thing to deposit here and there a dead rat, when those vermin were to be poisoned on any premises; it is then concluded that the good poison has done its good work, and the dead animal supplies an ocular demonstration of professional skill. These men, also, I am informed, let loose live rats in buildings adapted for the purpose, and afterwards apply for employment to destroy them.

I am informed that the principal scene of the rat-catcher's labours in London is at the mews, and in private stables, coach-houses, and outbuildings. It is probable that the gentlemen's servants connected with such places like the excitement of rat-hunting, and so encourage the profession which supplies them with that gratification. In these places such labours are often necessary as well as popular; for I was informed by a coachman, then living with his family in a West End mews, and long acquainted with the mews in different parts of town, that the drainage was often very defective, and sanitary regulations—except, perhaps, as regarded the horses—little cared for. Hence rats abounded, and were with difficulty dislodged from their secure retreats in the ill-constructed drains and kennels.

The great sale of the rat-catchers is to the shops supplying "private parties" with rats for the amusement of seeing them killed by dogs. With some "fast" men, one of these shopkeepers told me, it was a favourite pastime in their own rooms on the Sunday mornings. It is, however, somewhat costly if carried on extensively, as the retail charge from the shops is 6*d.* per rat. The price from the catcher to the dealer is from 2*s.* 6*d.* to 7*s.* the dozen. Rats, it appears, are sometimes scarce, and then the shopkeeper must buy, "to keep up his connection," at enhanced cost. One large bird-seller, who sold also plain and fancy rats, white mice, and live hedgehogs, told me that he had, last winter, been compelled to give 7*s.* a dozen for his vermin and sell them at 6*d.* each.

The grand consumption of rats, however, is in Bunhill-row, at a public-house kept by a pugilist. A rat-seller told me that from 200 to 500 rats were killed there weekly, the weekly average being, however, only the former number; while at Easter and other holidays, it is not uncommon to see bills posted announcing the destruction of 500 rats on the same day and in a given time, admittance 6*d.* Dogs are matched at these and similar places, as to which kills the greatest number of these animals in the shortest time. I am told that there are forty such places in London, but in some only the holiday times are celebrated in this small imitation of the beast combats of the ancients. There is, too, a frequent abandonment of the trade in consequence of its "not paying," and perhaps it may be fair to estimate that the average consumption of this vermin-game does not exceed, in each of these places, 20 a week, or 1040 in a year; giving an aggregate—over and above those consumed in private sport—of 52,000 rats in a year, or 1000 a week in public amusement alone.

To show the nature of the sport of rat-catching, I print the following bill, of which I procured two copies. The words and type are precisely the same in each, but one bill is printed on good and the other on very indifferent paper, as if for distribution among distinct classes. The concluding announcement, as to the precise moment at which killing will commence, reads supremely businesslike:—

RATTING FOR THE MILLION !

A SPORTING GENTLEMAN, Who is a Staunch Supporter of the destruction of these VERMIN

WILL GIVE A

GOLD REPEATER

WATCH,[1]

TO BE KILLED FOR BY

DOGS Under 13 3/4*lbs. Wt.*

15 *RATS EACH*!

TO COME OFF AT JEMMY MASSEY'S,[2]

KING'S HEAD,

COMPTON ST., SOHO,

On Tuesday, May 20, 1851.

☞ To be Killed in a Large Wire Pit. A chalk Circle to be drawn in the centre for the Second.— Any Man touching Dog or Rats, or acting in any way unfair his dog will be disqualified.

TO GO TO SCALE AT Half past 7 KILLING TO COMMENCE At Half past 8 PRECISELY.

[...]

1 A type of watch meant for use in the dark that audibly repeats back the time when a button is pressed.

2 Jemmy Massey (1824–63) was a well-known prizefighter and proprietor of the King's Head on Old Compton Street in the 1850s, where he hosted both boxing and ratting events.

VOLUME 2.

The STREET-FOLK.

Book the Second.

Introduction.[1]

In commencing a new volume I would devote a few pages to the consideration of the import of the facts already collected concerning the London Street-Folk, not only as regards the street-people themselves, but also in connection with the general society of which they form so large a proportion.

The precise extent of the proportion which the Street-Traders bear to the rest of the Metropolitan Population is the first point to be evolved; for the want, the ignorance, and the vice of a street-life being in a direct ratio to the numbers, it becomes of capital importance that we should know how many are seeking to pick up a livelihood in the public thoroughfares. This is the more essential because the Government returns never *have* given us, and probably never *will* give us, any correct information respecting it. The Census of 1841[2] set down the "Hawkers, Hucksters, and Pedlars" of the Metropolis as numbering 2045; and from the inquiries I have made among the street-sellers as to the means taken to obtain a full account of their numbers for the next population return, the Census of 1851 appears likely to be about as correct in its statements concerning the Street-Traders and Performers as the one which preceded it.

[...]

The gross amount of trade done by the London Street-Sellers in the course of the year is so large that the mind is at first unable to comprehend how, without reckless extravagance, want can be in any way associated with the class. After the most cautious calculation, the results having been checked and re-checked in a variety of ways, so that

1 First published in the weekly serial version of *London Labour*, Vol. 2, No. 1, 14 June 1851. The rest of the numbers for Volume 2 reverted to the numbering system of Volume 1, so the next number of Volume 2 was 28, published 21 June 1851.

2 The United Kingdom Census of 1841 was the first to be centralized under the Registrar General, rather than undertaken by local authorities. It was also the first to record information about every member of every household on a single day (6 June 1841). The census documented each person's name, age, sex, occupation, and whether they were born in the country. The census makers documented 850 classes of occupation, including "Hawkers, Hucksters and Pedlars."

the conclusion arrived at might be somewhat near and certainly not beyond the truth, it appears that the "*takings*" of the London Street-Sellers cannot be said to be less than 2,500,000*l.* per annum. But vast as this sum may seem, and especially when considered as only a portion of the annual expenditure of the Metropolitan Poor, still, when we come to spread the gross yearly receipts over 40,000 people, we find that the individual takings are but 62*l.* per annum, which (allowing the rate of profit to be in all cases even 50 per cent., though I am convinced it is often much less) gives to each street-trader an annual income of 20*l.* 13*s.* 4*d.*, or within a fraction of 8*s.* a week, all the year round. And when we come to deduct from this the loss by perishable articles, the keep of donkeys, the wear and tear, or hire, of barrows—the cost of stalls and baskets, together with the interest on stock-money (generally at the rate of 4*s.* a week—and often 1*s.* a day—for 1*l.*, or 1040*l.* per cent, per annum), we may with safety assert that the average gain or clear income of the Metropolitan Street-Sellers is rather under than over 7*s.* 6*d.* a week. Some of the more expert street-traders may clear 10*s.* or even 15*s.* weekly throughout the year, while the weekly profit of the less expert, the old people, and the children, may be said to be 3*s.* 6*d.* These incomes, however, are the average of the gross yearly profits rather than the regular weekly gains; the consequence is, that though they might be sufficient to keep the majority of the street-sellers in comparative comfort, were they constant and capable of being relied upon, from week to week—but being variable and uncertain, and rising sometimes from nothing in the winter to 1*l.* a week in the summer, when street commodities are plentiful and cheap, and the poorer classes have money wherewith to purchase them—and fluctuating moreover, even at the best of times, according as the weather is wet or fine, and the traffic of the streets consequently diminished or augmented—it is but natural that the people subject to such alternations should lack the prudence and temperance of those whose incomes are more regular and uniform.

To place the above facts clearly before the reader the following table has been prepared. The first column states the titles of the several classes of street-sellers; the second, the number of individuals belonging to each of these classes; the third, the value of their respective capitals or stock in trade; the fourth, the gross amount of trade done by them respectively every year; the fifth, the average yearly takings of each class; and the sixth, their average weekly gains. This gives us, as it were, a bird's-eye view of the earnings and pecuniary condition of the various kinds of street-sellers already treated of. It is here cited, as indeed all the statistics in this work are, as an approximation to the truth rather than a definite and accurate result.

DESCRIPTION OF CLASS.	Number of Persons in each Class.	Gross amount of capital, or stock in trade belonging to each class.	Gross amount of trade annually done by each class.		Average yearly receipts per head.	Average weekly gains.
COSTERMONGERS[a].			£			
Street-Sellers of Wet Fish			1,177,200			
" " Dry fish			127,000			
" " Shell Fish			156,600			
				1,460,800		
" " Green Fruit			332,400			
" " Dry Fruit	30,000[b]	£25,000	1,000		£60	8s.
" " Vegetables			292,200			
				625,600		
" " Game, Poultry, Rabbits, &c.				80,000		
" " Flowers, Roots, &c.				14,800		
				2,181,200		
STREET-SELLERS OF GREEN STUFF.						
Watercresses[c]	1,000	87		13,900	13	3s. 6d.
Chickweed, Groundsell, and Plantain[d]	1,000	42		14,000	14	5s.
Turf-Cutters and Sellers	40	20		570	14	5s. 6d.
STREET-SELLERS OF EATABLES AND DRINKABLES	4,000	9,000		203,100	50	10s.
STREET-SELLERS OF STATIONERY, LITERATURE, AND THE FINE ARTS	1,000	400		33,400	30	8s.
STREET-SELLERS OF MANUFACTURED ARTICLES of Metal, Crockery and Glass, Textile, Chemical, or Miscellaneous Substances	4,000	2,800		188,200	47	10s.
	41,040	£37,529		£2,634,370	£60	8s.

[a] The definition of a Costermonger strictly includes only such individuals as confine themselves to the sale of the produce of the Green and Fruit Markets: the term is here restricted to that signification.

[b] This number includes Men, Women, and Children.

[c] The Watercress trade is carried on in the streets, principally by old people and children. The chief mart to which the street-sellers of cresses resort is Farringdon-market, a place which but few or none of the regular Costermongers attend.

[d] The Chickweed and Groundsell Sellers and the Turf-Cutters' traffic has but little expense connected with it, and their trade is therefore nearly all profit.

Fig. 7: Unnamed table.

Now, according to the above estimate, it would appear that the gross annual receipts of the entire body of street-sellers (for there are many besides those above specified—as for instance, the vendors of second-hand articles, &c.) may be estimated in round numbers at 3,000,000*l.* sterling, and their clear income at about 1,000,000*l.* per annum. Hence, we are enabled to perceive the importance of the apparently insignificant traffic of the streets; for were the street-traders to be prohibited from pursuing their calling, and so forced to apply for relief at the several metropolitan unions, the poor-rates[1] would be at the least doubled. The total sum expended in the relief of the London poor, during 1848, was 725,000*l.*,

1 Property taxes used to pay for poor relief, collected under the Poor Law.

but this we see is hardly three-fourths of the income of the street-traders. Those, therefore, who would put an end to the commerce of our streets, should reflect whether they would like to do so at the cost of doubling the present poor-rates and of reducing one-fortieth part of the entire metropolitan population from a state of comparative independence to absolute pauperism.

However unsatisfactory it may be to the aristocratic pride of the wealthy commercial classes, it cannot be denied that a very important element of the trade of this vast capital—this marvellous centre of the commerce of the world—I cite the stereotype phrases of civic eloquence, for they are at least truths—it is still undeniable, I say, that a large proportion of the commerce of the capital of Great Britain is in the hands of the Street-Folk. This simple enunciation might appear a mere platitude were it not that the street-sellers are a *proscribed class.* They are driven from stations to which long possession might have been thought to give them a quasi legal right; driven from them at the capricious desire of the shopkeepers, some of whom have had bitter reason, by the diminution of their own business, to repent their interference. They are bandied about at the will of a police-officer. They must "move on"[1] and not obstruct a thoroughfare which may be crammed and blocked with the carriages of the wealthy until to cross the road on foot is a danger. They are, in fine, a body numbering thousands, who are allowed to live in the prosecution of the most ancient of all trades, sale or barter in the open air, *by sufferance alone.* They are classed as unauthorized or illegal and intrusive traders, though they *"turn over" millions in a year.*

[...]

[...] To revile the street-people is stark folly. Their ignorance is no demerit to them, even as it is no merit to us to know the little that we do. If we really wish the people better, let us, I say again, do for them what others have done for us, and without which (humiliating as it may be to our pride) we should most assuredly have been as they are. It is the continued forgetfulness of this truth—a truth which our wretched self-conceit is constantly driving from our minds—that prevents our stirring to improve the condition of these poor people; though, if we knew but the whole of the facts concerning them, and their sufferings and feelings, our very fears alone for the safety of the state would be sufficient to make us do something in their behalf. I am quite satisfied, from all I have seen, that there are thousands in this great metropolis ready to rush forth, on the least evidence of a rising of the people, to commit the most savage and revolting excesses—men who have no knowledge of the government of the

---

1 Mayhew also discusses the ways in which police compel poor people to "move on" in "The Politics of Costermongers.—Policemen" (p. 57) and "Language of Costermongers" (p. 59).

country but as an armed despotism, preventing their earning their living, and who hate all law, because it is made to appear to them merely as an organised tyranny—men, too, who have neither religious nor moral principles to restrain the exercise of their grossest passions when once roused, and men who, from our very neglect of them, are necessarily and essentially the dangerous classes, whose existence we either rail at or deplore.

[...]

That there is every day a greater difficulty for working men to live by their labour—either from the paucity of work, or from the scanty remuneration given for it—surely no one will be disposed to question when every one is crying out that the country is over-populated. Such being the case, it is evident that the number of mechanics in the streets must be daily augmenting, for, as I have before said, street-trading is the last shift of an unemployed artizan to keep himself and his family from the "Union."[1] The workman out of work, sooner than starve or go to the parish for relief, takes to making up and vending on his own account the articles of his craft, whilst the underpaid workman, sooner than continue toiling from morning till midnight for a bare subsistence, resorts to the easier trade of buying and selling. Again, even among the less industrious of the working classes, the general decline in wages has tended, and is continually tending, to make their labour more and more irksome to them. There is a cant abroad at the present day, that there is a special pleasure in industry, and hence we are taught to regard all those who object to work as appertaining to the class of natural vagabonds; but where is the man among us that loves labour? for work or labour is merely that which is irksome to perform, and which every man requires a certain amount of remuneration to induce him to perform. If men really loved work they would pay to be allowed to do it rather than require to be paid for doing it. That occupation which is agreeable to us we call amusement, and that and that only which is disagreeable we term labour, or drudgery, according to the intensity of its irksomeness. Hence as the amount of remuneration given by way of inducement to a man to go through a certain amount of work becomes reduced, so does the stimulus to work become weakened, and this, through the decline of wages, is what is daily taking place among us. Our operatives[2] are continually ceasing to be producers, and passing from the creators of wealth into the exchangers or distributors of it; becoming mere tradesmen, subsisting on the labour of other people rather than their own, and so adding to the very non-producers, the great number of whom is the main cause of the poverty of those who make all our riches. To teach a people the difficulty of living by labour is to inculcate the most dangerous of all lessons, and this is what

1 The workhouse.

2 Manual labourers.

we are daily doing. Our trading classes are increasing at a most enormous rate, and so giving rise to that exceeding competition, and consequently, to that continual reduction of prices—all of which must ultimately fall upon the working man. This appears to me to be the main cause of the increase of the London street people, and one for which I candidly confess I see no remedy.

Of the Street-Sellers of Second-Hand Articles.
Of the Street-Sellers of Petticoat and Rosemary-Lanes.[1]

IMMEDIATELY connected with the trade of the central mart for old clothes are the adjoining streets of Petticoat-lane, and those of the not very distant Rosemary-lane. In these localities is a second-hand garment-seller at almost every step, but the whole stock of these traders, decent, frowsy, half-rotten, or smart and good habilments, has first passed through the channel of the Exchange.[2] The men who sell these goods have all bought them at the Exchange—the exceptions being insignificant—so that this street-sale is but an extension of the trade of the central mart, with the addition that the wares have been made ready for use.

A cursory observation might lead an inexperienced person to the conclusion, that these old clothes traders who are standing by the bundles of gowns, or lines of coats, hanging from their door-posts, or in the place from which the window has been removed, or at the sides of their houses, or piled in the street before them, are drowsy people, for they seem to sit among their property, lost in thought, or caring only for the fumes of a pipe. But let any one indicate, even by an approving glance, the likelihood of his becoming a customer, and see if there be any lack of diligence in business. Some, indeed, pertinaciously invite attention to their wares; some (and often well-dressed women) leave their premises a few yards to accost a stranger pointing to a "good dresscoat" or "an excellent frock" (coat). I am told that this practice is less pursued than it was, and it seems that the solicitations are now addressed chiefly to strangers. These strangers, persons happening to be passing, or visitors from curiosity, are at once recognised; for as in all not very extended localities, where the inhabitants pursue a similar calling, they are, as regards their knowledge of one another, as the members of one family. Thus a stranger is as easily recognised as he would be in a little rustic hamlet where a strange face is not seen once a quarter. Indeed so narrow are some of the streets and alleys in this quarter, and so little is there of privacy, owing to the removal, in warm weather, even of the casements, that the room is commanded in

1 First published in the weekly serial version of *London Labour*, No. 28, 21 June 1851.

2 Market in Houndsditch where used clothing was purchased by street vendors for resale. Elsewhere in *London Labour*, Mayhew described the Old Clothes Exchange as the largest of the London markets, and the most "picturesque," "novel," and "animated" (*London Labour* vol. 2, p. 27).

all its domestic details; and as among these details there is generally a further display of goods similar to the articles outside, the jammed-up places really look like a great family house with merely a sort of channel, dignified by the name of a street, between the right and left suites of apartments.

In one off-street, where on a Sunday there is a considerable demand for Jewish sweet-meats by Christian boys, and a little sly, and perhaps not very successful gambling on the part of the ingenuous youth to possess themselves of these confectionaries at the easiest rate, there are some mounds of builders' rubbish upon which, if an inquisitive person ascended, he could command the details of the upper rooms, probably the bed chambers—if in their crowded apartments these traders can find spaces for beds.

It must not be supposed that old clothes are more than the great staple of the traffic of this district. Wherever persons are assembled there are certain to be purveyors of provisions and of cool or hot drinks for warm or cold weather. The interior of the Old Clothes Exchange has its oyster-stall, its fountain of ginger-beer, its coffee-house, and ale-house, and a troop of peripatetic traders, boys principally, carrying trays. Outside the walls of the Exchange this trade is still thicker. A Jew boy thrusts a tin of highly-glazed cakes and pastry under the people's noses here; and on the other side a basket of oranges regales the same sense by its proximity. At the next step the thoroughfare is interrupted by a gaudy-looking ginger-beer, lemonade, raspberryade, and nectar fountain; "a halfpenny a glass, a halfpenny a glass, sparkling lemonade!" shouts the vendor as you pass. The fountain and the glasses glitter in the sun, the varnish of the wood-work shines, the lemonade really does sparkle, and all looks clean—except the owner. Close by is a brawny young Irishman, his red beard unshorn for perhaps ten days, and his neck, where it had been exposed to the weather, a far deeper red than his beard, and he is carrying a small basket of nuts, and selling them as gravely as if they were articles suited to his strength. A little lower is the cry, in a woman's voice, "Fish, fried fish! Ha'penny; fish, fried fish!" and so monotonously and mechanically is it ejaculated that one might think the seller's life was passed in uttering these few words, even as a rook's is in crying "Caw, caw." Here I saw a poor Irishwoman who had a child on her back buy a piece of this fish (which may be had "hot" or "cold"), and tear out a piece with her teeth, and this with all the eagerness and relish of appetite or hunger; first eating the brown outside and then *sucking* the bone. I never saw fish look firmer or whiter. That fried fish is to be procured is manifest to more senses than one, for you can hear the sound of its being fried, and smell the fumes from the oil. In an open window opposite frizzle on an old tray, small pieces of thinly-cut meat, with a mixture of onions, kept hot by being placed over an old pan containing charcoal. In another room a mess of batter is smoking over a grate. "Penny a lot, oysters," resounds from different parts. Some of the sellers command two streets by establishing their stalls or tubs at a corner. Lads pass, carrying sweet-stuff on trays. I observed one very dark-eyed Hebrew boy chewing the hard-bake he vended—if it were not a substitute—with an expression of great enjoyment. Heaped-up trays of fresh-looking sponge-cakes are carried in tempting pyramids. Youths have stocks of large hard-looking biscuits, and walk about crying, "Ha'penny biscuits, ha'penny; three a penny, biscuits"; these, with a morsel of cheese, often supply a dinner or a luncheon. Dates and figs, as dry as they are cheap, constitute the stock in trade of other street-sellers. "Coker-nuts"[1] are sold in pieces and entire; the Jew boy, when he invites to the purchase of an entire nut, shaking it at the ear of the customer. I was told by a costermonger that these juveniles had a way of drumming with their fingers on the shell so as to satisfy a "green" customer that the nut offered was a sound one.

[...]

But Petticoat-lane is essentially the old clothes district. Embracing the streets and alleys adjacent to Petticoat-lane, and including the rows of old boots and shoes on the ground, there is perhaps between two and three miles of old clothes. Petticoat-lane proper is long and narrow, and to look down it is to look down a vista of many coloured garments, alike on the sides and on the ground. The effect sometimes is very striking, from the variety of hues, and the constant flitting, or gathering, of the crowd into little groups of bargainers. Gowns of every shade and every pattern are hanging up, but none, perhaps, look either bright or white; it is a vista of dinginess, but many coloured dinginess, as regards female attire. Dress coats, frock coats, great coats, livery and game-keepers' coats, paletots, tunics, trowsers, knee-breeches, waistcoats, capes, pilot coats, working jackets, plaids, hats, dressing gowns, shirts, Guernsey frocks,[2] are all displayed. The predominant colours are black and blue, but there is every colour; the light drab of some aristocratic livery; the dull brown-green of velveteen; the deep blue of a pilot jacket; the variegated figures of the shawl dressing-gown; the glossy black of the restored garments; the shine of newly turpentined black satin waistcoats; the scarlet and green of some flaming tartan; these things—mixed with the hues of the women's garments, spotted and striped—certainly present a scene which cannot be beheld in any other part of the greatest city of the world, nor in any other portion of the world itself.

The ground has also its array of colours. It is covered with lines of boots and shoes, their shining black relieved here and there by the admixture of females' boots, with drab, green, plum or lavender-coloured "legs," as the upper part of the boot is always called in the trade. There is, too, an admixture of men's "button-boots" with drab cloth legs; and of a few red, yellow, and russet coloured slippers; and of children's coloured morocco

1 Coconuts.

2 Heavy wool sweaters commonly worn by seamen.

boots and shoes. Handkerchiefs, sometimes of a gaudy orange pattern, are heaped on a chair. Lace and muslins occupy small stands or are spread on the ground. Black and drab and straw hats are hung up, or piled one upon another and kept from falling by means of strings; while, incessantly threading their way through all this intricacy, is a mass of people, some of whose dresses speak of a recent purchase in the lane.

[...]

On one of my visits to Petticoat-lane I saw two foreign Jews—from Smyrna I was informed. An old street-seller told me he believed it was their first visit to the district. But, new as the scene might be to them, they looked on impassively at all they saw. They wore the handsome and peculiar dresses of their country. A glance was cast after them by the Petticoat-lane people, but that was all. In the Strand they would have attracted considerable attention; not a few heads would have been turned back to gaze after them; but it seems that only to those who may possibly be customers is any notice paid in Petticoat-lane.

Of the Street-Sellers of Live Animals.
Of the Street-Sellers of Live Birds.[1]

THE bird-*sellers* in the streets are also the bird-*catchers* in the fields, plains, heaths, and woods, which still surround the metropolis; and in compliance with established precedent it may be proper that I should give an account of the catching, before I proceed to any further statement of the procedures subsequent thereunto. The bird-catchers are precisely what I have described them in my introductory remarks.[2] An intelligent man, versed in every part of the bird business, and well acquainted with the character of all engaged in it, said they might be represented as of "the fancy," in a small way, and always glad to run after, and full of admiration of, fighting men. The bird-catcher's life is one essentially vagrant; a few gipsies pursue it, and they mix little in street-trades, except as regards tinkering; and the mass, not gipsies, who become bird-catchers, rarely leave it for any other avocation. They "catch" unto old age. During last winter two men died in the parish of Clerkenwell, both turned seventy, and both bird-catchers—a profession they had followed from the age of six.

The mode of catching I will briefly describe. It is principally effected by means of nets. A bird-net is about twelve yards square; it is spread flat upon the ground, to which it is secured by four "stars." These are iron pins, which are inserted in the field, and hold the net, but so that the two "wings," or

1 First published in the weekly serial version of *London Labour*, No. 30, 5 July 1851.

2 This section of Volume 2 begins with an introduction, "Of the Street-Sellers of Live Animals" (not included in this edition), in which Mayhew outlines the characteristics of bird-catchers.

"flaps," which are indeed the sides of the nets, are not confined by the stars. In the middle of the net is a cage with a fine wire roof, widely worked, containing the "call-bird." This bird is trained to sing loudly and cheerily, great care being bestowed upon its tuition, and its song attracts the wild birds. Sometimes a few stuffed birds are spread about the cage as if a flock were already assembling there. The bird-catcher lies flat and motionless on the ground, 20 or 30 yards distant from the edge of the net. As soon as he considers that a sufficiency of birds have congregated around his decoy, he rapidly draws towards him a line, called the "pull-line," of which he has kept hold. This is so looped and run within the edges of the net, that on being smartly pulled, the two wings of the net collapse and fly together, the stars still keeping their hold, and the net encircles the cage of the call-bird, and incloses in its folds all the wild birds allured round it. In fact it then resembles a great cage of net-work. The captives are secured in cages—the call-bird continuing to sing as if in mockery of their struggles—or in hampers proper for the purpose, which are carried on the man's back to London.

The use of the call-bird as a means of decoy is very ancient. Sometimes—and more especially in the dark, as in the taking of nightingales—the bird-catcher imitates the notes of the birds to be captured. A small instrument has also been used for the purpose, and to this Chaucer, although figuratively, alludes: "So, the birde is begyled with the merry voice of the foulers' whistel, when it is closed in your nette."[1]

Sometimes, in the pride of the season, a bird-catcher engages a costermonger's poney or donkey cart, and perhaps his boy, the better to convey the birds to town. The net and its apparatus cost 1*l.* The call-bird, if he have a good wild note—goldfinches and linnets being principally so used—is worth 10*s.* at the least.

The bird-catcher's life has many, and to the constitution of some minds, irresistible charms. There is the excitement of "sport"—not the headlong excitement of the chase, where the blood is stirred by motion and exercise—but still sport surpassing that of the angler, who plies his finest art to capture one fish at a time, while the bird-catcher despises an individual capture, but seeks to ensnare a flock at one twitch of a line. There is, moreover, the attraction of idleness, at least for intervals, and sometimes long intervals—perhaps the great charm of fishing—and basking in the lazy sunshine, to watch the progress of the snares. Birds, however, and more especially linnets, are caught in the winter, when it is not quite such holiday work. A bird-dealer (not a street-seller) told me that the greatest number of birds he had ever heard of as having been caught at one pull was nearly 200. My informant happened to be present on the occasion. "Pulls" of 50, 100, and 150 are not very unfrequent when the young broods are all on the wing.

---

1 This passage, from Thomas Usk's (d. 1388) *The Testament of Love* (Ch. 3, line 241), was often mistakenly attributed to Geoffrey Chaucer (c. 1343–1400).

[...]

The *Linnet* is the cheapest and among the most numerous of what may be called the London-caught birds, for it is caught in the nearer suburbs, such as Holloway. The linnet, however,—the brown linnet being the species—is not easily reared, and for some time ill brooks confinement. About one-half of those birds die after having been caged a few days. The other evening a bird-catcher supplied 26 fine linnets to a shopkeeper in Pentonville, and next morning ten were dead. But in some of those bird shops, and bird chambers connected with the shops, the heat at the time the new broods are caught and caged, is excessive; and the atmosphere, from the crowded and compulsory fellowship of pigeons, and all descriptions of small birds, with white rats, hedgehogs, guinea-pigs, and other creatures, is often very foul; so that the wonder is, not that so many die, but that so many survive.

[...]

The buyers of singing-birds are eminently the working people, along with the class of tradesmen whose means and disposition are of the same character as those of the artisan. Grooms and coachmen are frequently fond of birds; many are kept in the several mews, and often the larger singing-birds, such as blackbirds and thrushes. The fondness of a whole body of artificers for any particular bird, animal, or flower, is remarkable. No better instance need be cited than that of the Spitalfields weavers.[1] In the days of their prosperity they were the cultivators of choice tulips, afterwards, though not in so full a degree, of dahlias, and their pigeons were the best "fliers" in England. These things were accomplished with little cost, comparatively, for the weavers were engaged in tasks, grateful and natural to their tastes and habitudes; and what was expense in the garden or aviary of the rich, was an exercise of skill and industry on the part of the silk-weaver. The humanising and even refining influence of such pursuits is very great, and as regards these pure pleasures it is not seldom that the refinement which can appreciate them has proceeded not to but *from* the artisans. The operatives have often been in the van of those who have led the public taste from delighting in the cruelty and barbarity of bear and bull-baiting and of cock-fighting—among the worst of all possible schools, and very influential those schools were—to the delight in some of the most beautiful works of nature. It is easy to picture the difference of mood between a man going home from a dog-fight at night, or going home from a visit to his flowers, or from an examination to satisfy himself that his birds were "all right." The families of the two men felt the difference. Many of the rich appear to remain mere savages in their tastes and sports. Battues, lion and hippopotamus hunting, &c.,—all are mere civilized barbarisms. When shall we learn, as Wordsworth says,

1 See p. 274, note 1.

"Never to blend our pleasure or our pride
With sorrow of the meanest thing that feels."

But the change in Spitalfields is great. Since the prevalence of low wages the weaver's garden has disappeared, and his pigeon-cote, even if its timbers have not rotted away, is no longer stocked with carriers, dragoons, horsemen, jacobins, monks, poulters, turtles, tumblers, fantails, and the many varieties of what is in itself a variety—the fancy-pigeon. A thrush, or a linnet, may still sing to the clatter of the loom, but that is all. The culture of the tulip, the dahlia, and (sometimes) of the fuchsia, was attended, as I have said, with small cost, still it *was* cost, and the weaver, as wages grew lower, could not afford either the outlay or the loss of time. To cultivate flowers, or rear doves, so as to make them a means of subsistence, requires a man's whole time, and to such things the Spitalfields man did not devote his time, but his leisure.

The readers who have perused this work from its first appearance will have noticed how frequently I have had to comment on the always realized indication of good conduct, and of a superior taste and generally a superior intelligence, when I have found the rooms of working people contain flowers and birds. I could adduce many instances. I have seen and heard birds in the rooms of tailors, shoemakers, coopers, cabinet-makers, hatters, dressmakers, curriers, and street-sellers,—all people of the best class. One of the most striking, indeed, was the room of a street-confectioner. His family attended to the sale of the sweets, and he was greatly occupied at home in their manufacture, and worked away at his peppermint-rock, in the very heart of one of the thickliest populated parts of London, surrounded by the song of thrushes, linnets, and goldfinches, all kept, not for profit, but because he "loved" to have them about him. I have seldom met a man who impressed me more favourably.

[...]

Of the Street-Buyers.
Of the "Rag-and-Bottle," and the "Marine-Store," Shops.[1]

THE principal purchasers of any refuse or worn-out articles are the proprietors of the rag-and-bottle-shops. Some of these men make a good deal of money, and not unfrequently unite with the business the letting out of vans for the conveyance of furniture, or for pleasure excursions, to such places as Hampton Court.[2] The stench in these shops is positively sickening. Here in

1 First published in the weekly serial version of *London Labour*, spanning No. 32, 19 July 1851, and No. 33, 26 July 1851.

2 Royal palace and pleasure gardens southwest of London on the Thames River. Construction began during the reign of King Henry VIII (1509–47); in the Victorian period it became a free public attraction and a popular destination for day trippers from London.

a small apartment may be a pile of rags, a sack-full of bones, the many varieties of grease and "kitchen-stuff," corrupting an atmosphere which, even without such accompaniments, would be too close. The windows are often crowded with bottles, which exclude the light; while the floor and shelves are thick with grease and dirt. The inmates seem unconscious of this foulness,—and one comparatively wealthy man, who showed me his horses, the stable being like a drawing-room compared to his shop, in speaking of the many deaths among his children, could not conjecture to what cause it could be owing. This indifference to dirt and stench is the more remarkable, as many of the shopkeepers have been gentlemen's servants, and were therefore once accustomed to cleanliness and order. The door-posts and windows of the rag-and-bottle-shops are often closely placarded, and the front of the house is sometimes one glaring colour, blue or red; so that the place may be at once recognised, even by the illiterate, as the "red house," or the "blue house." If these men are not exactly street-buyers, they are street-billers, continually distributing hand-bills, but more especially before Christmas. The more aristocratic, however, now send round cards, and to the following purport:—

No. — No. —

THE —— HOUSE IS ——'S

RAG, BOTTLE, AND KITCHEN STUFF WAREHOUSE,

—— STREET, —— TOWN,

Where you can obtain Gold and Silver to any amount.

ESTABLISHED ——.

THE HIGHEST PRICE GIVEN

For all the undermentioned articles, viz:—

Wax and Sperm Pieces[1]	Old Copper, Brass, Pewter, &c.
Kitchen Stuff, &c.	Lead, Iron, Zinc, Steel, &c., &c.
Wine & Beer Bottles	Old Horse Hair, Mattresses, &c.
Eau de Cologne, Soda Water	Old Books, Waste paper, &c.
Doctors' Bottles, &c.	All kinds of Coloured Rags
White Linen Rags	
Bones, Phials, & Broken Flint Glass	

The utmost value given for all kinds of Wearing Apparel.

Furniture and Lumber of every description bought, and full value given at his Miscellaneous Warehouse.

Articles sent for.

1 A waxy liquid called spermaceti sourced from the head of sperm whales was used for items like candles, lamp oil, and soap. Derivatives from processing were sold as solids that could later be melted down. Consumer demand for this product in the eighteenth and nineteenth centuries devastated the sperm whale population.

Some content themselves with sending hand-bills to the houses in their neighbourhood, which many of the cheap printers keep in type, so that an alteration in the name and address is all which is necessary for any customer.

I heard that suspicions were entertained that it was to some of these traders that the facilities with which servants could dispose of their pilferings might be attributed, and that a stray silver spoon might enhance the weight and price of kitchen-stuff. It is not pertaining to my present subject to enter into the consideration of such a matter; and I might not have alluded to it, had not I found the regular street-buyers fond of expressing an opinion of the indifferent honesty of this body of traders; but my readers may have remarked how readily the street-people have, on several occasions, justified (as they seem to think) their own delinquencies by quoting what they declared were as great and as frequent delinquencies on the part of shopkeepers: "I know very well," said an intelligent street-seller on one occasion, "that two wrongs can never make a right; but tricks that shopkeepers practise to grow rich upon we must practise, just as they do, to live at all. As long as they give short weight and short measure, the streets can't help doing the same."

The *rag-and-bottle* and *the marine-store shops* are in many instances but different names for the same description of business. The chief distinction appears to be this: the marine-store shopkeepers (proper) do not meddle with what is a very principal object of traffic with the rag-and-bottle man, the purchase of dripping,[1] as well as of every kind of refuse in the way of fat or grease. The marine-store man, too, is more miscellaneous in his wares than his contemporary of the rag-and-bottle-store, as the former will purchase any of the smaller articles of household furniture, old tea-caddies, knife-boxes, fire-irons, books, pictures, draughts and backgammon boards, bird-cages, Dutch clocks, cups and saucers, tools and brushes. The-rag-and-bottle tradesman will readily purchase any of these things to be disposed of as old metal or waste-paper,[2] but his brother tradesman buys them to be re-sold and re-used for the purposes for which they were originally manufactured. When furniture, however, is the staple of one of these second-hand storehouses, the proprietor is a furniture-broker, and not a marine-store dealer. If, again, the dealer in these stores confine his business to the purchase of old metals, for instance, he is classed as an old metal dealer, collecting it or buying it of collectors, for sale to iron-founders, coppersmiths, brass-founders, and plumbers. In perhaps the majority of instances there is little or no distinction between the establishments I have spoken of. The *dolly* business[3] is common to both, but most common to the marine-store dealer, and of it I shall speak afterwards.

---

1 Melted fat from roasted meat, sold in its congealed form.

2 See "Of the Street-Buyers of Waste (Paper)," p. 169.

3 A pawn system used by the very poor. The name came from black wooden dolls in white clothing that hung above the doors of the Rag-and-Bottle and Marine shops.

These shops are exceedingly numerous. Perhaps in the poorer and smaller streets they are more numerous even than the chandlers'[1] or the beer-sellers' places. At the corner of a small street, both in town and the nearer suburbs, will frequently be found the chandler's shop, for the sale of small quantities of cheese, bacon, groceries, &c., to the poor. Lower down may be seen the beer-seller's; and in the same street there is certain to be one rag-and-bottle or marine-store shop, very often two, and not unfrequently another in some adjacent court.

I was referred to the owner of a marine-store shop, as to a respectable man, keeping a store of the best class. Here the counter, or table, or whatever it is to be called, for it was somewhat nondescript, by an ingenious contrivance could be pushed out into the street, so that in bad weather the goods which were at other times exposed in the street could be drawn inside without trouble. The glass frames of the window were removable, and were placed on one side in the shop, for in the summer an open casement seemed to be preferred. This is one of the remaining old trade customs still seen in London; for previously to the great fire in 1666,[2] and the subsequent rebuilding of the city, shops with open casements, and protected from the weather by overhanging eaves, or by a sloping wooden roof, were general.

The house I visited was an old one, and abounded in closets and recesses. The fire-place, which apparently had been large, was removed, and the space was occupied with a mass of old iron of every kind; all this was destined for the furnace of the iron-founder, wrought iron being preferred for several of the requirements of that trade. A chest or range of very old drawers, with defaced or worn-out labels—once a grocer's or a chemist's—was stuffed, in every drawer, with old horseshoe nails (valuable for steel manufacturers), and horse and donkey shoes; brass knobs; glass stoppers; small bottles (among them a number of the cheap cast "hartshorn bottles"[3]); broken pieces of brass and copper; small tools (such as shoemakers' and harness-makers' awls), punches, gimlets, plane-irons, hammer heads, &c.; odd dominoes, dice, and backgammon-men; lock escutcheons, keys, and the smaller sort of locks, especially padlocks; in fine, any small thing which could be stowed away in such a place.

In one corner of the shop had been thrown, the evening before, a mass of old iron, then just bought. It consisted of a number of screws of different lengths and substance; of broken bars and rails; of the odds and ends of the cogged wheels of machinery, broken up or worn out; of odd-looking spikes, and rings, and links; all heaped together and scarcely distinguish-

1 Originally a purveyor of candles, but expanded to include other goods.

2 The Great Fire of London began on the night of 2 September 1666 in a bake house. Four days later, it had devastated much of the property inside the ancient walls of the City of London.

3 Smelling salts, composed of a crystalline solid extracted from the horns of a hart, or deer.

able. These things had all to be assorted; some to be sold for re-use in their then form; the others to be sold that they might be melted and cast into other forms. The floor was intricate with hampers of bottles; heaps of old boots and shoes; old desks and work-boxes; pictures (all modern) with and without frames; waste-paper, the most of it of quarto,[1] and some larger sized, soiled or torn, and strung closely together in weights of from 2 to 7 lbs.; and a fire-proof safe, stuffed with old fringes, tassels, and other upholstery goods, worn and discoloured. The miscellaneous wares were carried out into the street, and ranged by the door-posts as well as in front of the house. In some small out houses in the yard were piles of old iron and tin pans, and of the broken or separate parts of harness.

From the proprietor of this establishment I had the following account:—

"I've been in the business more than a dozen years. Before that, I was an auctioneer's, and then a furniture broker's, porter. I wasn't brought up to any regular trade, but just to jobbing about, and a bad trade it is, as all trades is that ain't regular employ for a man. I had some money when my father died—he kept a chandler's shop—and I bought a marine." [An elliptical form of speech among these traders.] "I gave 10*l.* for the stock, and 5*l.* for entrance and good-will, and agreed to pay what rents and rates was due. It was a smallish stock then, for the business had been neglected, but I have no reason to be sorry for my bargain, though it might have been better. There's lots taken in about good-wills, but perhaps not so many in my way of business, because we're rather 'fly to a dodge.' It's a confined sort of life, but there's no help for that. Why, as to my way of trade, you'd be surprised, what different sorts of people come to my shop. I don't mean the regular hands; but the chance comers. I've had men dressed like gentlemen—and no doubt they was respectable when they was sober—bring two or three books, or a nice cigar case, or anythink that don't show in their pockets, and say, when as drunk as blazes, 'Give me what you can for this; I want it sold for a particular purpose.' That particular purpose was more drink, I should say; and I've known the same men come back in less than a week, and buy what they'd sold me at a little extra, and be glad if I had it by me still. O, we sees a deal of things in this way of life. Yes, poor people run to such as me. I've known them come with such things as teapots, and old hair mattresses, and flock beds,[2] and *then* I'm sure they're hard up—reduced for a meal. I don't like buying big things like mattresses, though I do purchase 'em sometimes. Some of these sellers are as keen as Jews at a bargain; others seem only anxious to get rid of the things and have hold of some bit of money anyhow. Yes, sir, I've known their hands tremble to receive the money, and mostly the women's. They haven't been used to it, I know, when that's the case. Perhaps they comes to sell to me what the pawns won't take in, and what they would-

---

1 See p. 126, note 1.

2 See p. 112, note 1.

n't like to be seen selling to any of the men that goes about buying things in the street.

"Why, I've bought everythink; at sales by auction there's often 'lots' made up of different things, and they goes for very little. I buy of people, too, that come to me, and of the regular hands that supply such shops as mine. I sell retail, and I sell to hawkers. I sell to anybody, for gentlemen'll come into my shop to buy anythink that's took their fancy in passing. Yes, I've bought old oil paintings. I've heard of some being bought by people in my way as have turned out stunners, and was sold for a hundred pounds or more, and cost, perhaps, half-a-crown or only a shilling. I never experienced such a thing myself. There's a good deal of gammon about it. Well, it's hardly possible to say anything about a scale of prices. I give 2*d.* for an old tin or metal teapot, or an old saucepan, and sometimes, two days after I've bought such a thing, I've sold it for 3*d.* to the man or woman I've bought it of. I'll sell cheaper to them than to anybody else, because they come to me in two ways—both as sellers and buyers. For pictures I've given from 3*d.* to 1*s.* I fancy they're among the last things some sorts of poor people, which is a bit fanciful, parts with. I've bought them of hawkers, but often I refuse them, as they've given more than I could get. Pictures requires a judge. Some brought to me was published by newspapers and them sort of people. Waste-paper I buy as it comes. I can't read very much, and don't understand about books. I take the backs off and weighs them, and gives 1*d.*, and 1½*d.*, and 2*d.* a pound, and there's an end. I sell them at about ¼*d.* a pound profit, or sometimes less, to men as we calls 'waste' men. It's a poor part of our business, but the books and paper takes up little room, and then it's clean and can be stowed anywhere, and is a sure sale. Well, the people as sells 'waste' to me is not such as can read, I think; I don't know what they is; perhaps they're such as obtains possession of the books and whatnot after the death of old folks, and gets them out of the way as quick as they can. I know nothink about what they are. Last week, a man in black—he didn't seem rich—came into my shop and looked at some old books, and said 'Have you any black lead?' He didn't speak plain, and I could hardly catch him. I said, 'No, sir, I don't sell black lead, but you'll get it at No. 27,' but he answered, 'Not black lead, but black letter,'[1] speaking very pointed. I said, 'No,' and I haven't a notion what he meant. [...]"

[...]

Of the Street-Buyers of Waste (Paper).[2]

BEYOND all others the street-purchase of waste paper is the most curious of any in the hands of the class I now treat of. Some may have formed the

1 See p. 129, note 3.

2 First published in the weekly serial version of *London Labour*, No. 33, 26 July 1851.

notion that waste paper is merely that which is soiled or torn, or old numbers of newspapers, or other periodical publications; but this is merely a portion of the trade, as the subsequent account will show.

The men engaged in this business have not unfrequently an apartment, or a large closet, or recess, for the reception of their purchases of paper. They collect their paper street by street, calling upon every publisher, coffee-shop keeper, printer, or publican (but rarely on a publican), who may be a seller of "waste." I heard the refuse paper called nothing but "waste" after the general elliptical fashion. Attorneys' offices are often visited by these buyers, as are the offices of public men, such as tax or rate collectors, generally.

One man told me that until about ten years ago, and while he was a youth, he was employed by a relation in the trade to carry out waste paper sold to, or ordered by cheesemongers, &c., but that he never "collected," or bought paper himself. At last he thought he would start on his own account, and the first person he called upon, he said, was a rich landlady, not far from Hungerford-market,[1] whom he saw sometimes at her bar, and who was always very civil. He took an opportunity to ask her if she "happened to have any waste in the house, or would have any in a week or so?" Seeing the landlady look surprised and not very well pleased at what certainly appeared an impertinent inquiry, he hastened to explain that he meant old newspapers, or anything that way, which he would be glad to buy at so much a pound. The landlady however took in but one daily and one weekly paper (both sent into the country when a day or so old), and having had no dealings with men of my informant's avocation, could not understand his object in putting such questions.

Every kind of paper is purchased by the "waste-men." One of these dealers said to me: "I've often in my time 'cleared out' a lawyer's office. I've bought old briefs, and other law papers, and 'forms' that weren't the regular forms then, and any d——d thing they had in my line. You'll excuse me, sir, but I couldn't help thinking what a lot of misery was caused, perhaps, by the cwts. of waste I've bought at such places. If my father hadn't got mixed up with law he wouldn't have been ruined, and his children wouldn't have had such a hard fight of it; so I hate law. All that happened when I was a child, and I never understood the rights or the wrongs of it, and don't like to think of people that's so foolish. I gave 1½*d.* a pound for all I bought at the lawyers, and done pretty well with it, but very likely that's the only good turn such paper ever did any one—unless it were the lawyers themselves."

The waste-dealers do not confine their purchases to the tradesmen I have mentioned. They buy of any one, and sometimes act as middlemen or brokers. For instance, many small stationers and newsvendors, sometimes tobacconists in no extensive way of trade, sometimes chandlers, announce by a bill in their windows, "Waste Paper Bought and Sold in

---

1 Produce market at Charing Cross, first built in 1682 and revitalized in 1833.

any Quantity," while more frequently perhaps the trade is carried on, as an understood part of these small shopmen's business, without any announcement. Thus the shop-buyers have much miscellaneous waste brought to them, and perhaps for only some particular kind have they a demand by their retail customers. The regular itinerant waste dealer then calls and "clears out everything" the "everything" being not an unmeaning word. One man, who "did largely in waste," at my request endeavoured to enumerate all the kinds of paper he had purchased as waste, and the packages of paper he showed me, ready for delivery to his customers on the following day, confirmed all he said as he opened them and showed me of what they were composed. He had dealt, he said—and he took great pains and great interest in the inquiry, as one very curious, and was a respectable and intelligent man—in "books on *every* subject" [I give his own words] "on which a book can be written." After a little consideration he added: "Well, perhaps *every* subject is a wide range; but if there are any exceptions, it's on subjects not known to a busy man like me, who is occupied from morning till night every week day. The only worldly labour I do on a Sunday is to take my family's dinner to the bakehouse, bring it home after chapel, and read *Lloyd's Weekly*.[1] I've had Bibles—the backs are taken off in the waste trade, or it wouldn't be fair weight—Testaments, Prayer-books, Companions to the Altar, and Sermons and religious works. Yes, I've had the Roman Catholic books, as is used in their public worship—at least so I suppose, for I never was in a Roman Catholic chapel. Well, it's hard to say about proportions, but in my opinion, as far as it's good for anything, I've not had *them* in anything like the proportion that I've had Prayer-books, and Watts' and Wesley's hymns.[2] More shame; but you see, sir, perhaps a godly old man dies, and those that follow him care nothing for hymn-books, and so they come to such as me, for they're so cheap now they're not to be sold second-hand at all, I fancy. I've dealt in tragedies and comedies, old and new, cut and uncut[3]—they're best uncut, for you can make them into sheets then—and farces, and books of the opera. I've had scientific and medical works of every possible kind, and histories, and travels, and lives, and memoirs. I needn't go through them—everything, from a needle to an anchor, as the saying is. Poetry, ay, many a hundred weight; Latin and Greek (sometimes), and French, and other foreign languages. Well now, sir, as you mention it, I think I never *did* have a Hebrew

1 *Lloyd's Weekly Newspaper*, founded in 1842, was one of the earliest newspapers distributed for leisurely Sunday reading. For more about Lloyd, see p. 61, note 2.

2 The popular religious hymns of Isaac Watts (1674–1748) and Charles Wesley (1707–88) circulated under various titles in the nineteenth century. Watts is credited with approximately 750 hymns, including "Joy to the World." Wesley, an early Methodist leader, wrote more than six thousand hymns.

3 Book pages were made up of larger sheets, folded into three, typically, making sixteen pages per sheet before being sewn together. If not trimmed, books were then sold uncut, with the pages to be cut by the reader. If left uncut, the pages could be taken apart and unfolded back into sheets.

work; I think not, and I know the Hebrew letters when I see them. Black letter,[1] not once in a couple of years; no, nor in three or four years, when I think of it. I have met with it, but I always take anything I've got that way to Mr. ——, the bookseller, who uses a poor man well. Don't you think, sir, I'm complaining of poverty; though I have been very poor, when I was recovering from cholera at the first break-out of it, and I'm anything but rich now. Pamphlets I've had by the ton, in my time; I think we should both be tired if I could go through all they were about. Very many were religious, more's the pity. I've heard of a page round a quarter of cheese, though, touching a man's heart."

In corroboration of my informant's statement, I may mention that in the course of my inquiry into the condition of the fancy cabinet-makers of the metropolis, one elderly and very intelligent man, a first-rate artisan in skill, told me he had been so reduced in the world by the underselling of slop-masters[2] (called "butchers" or "slaughterers," by the workmen in the trade), that though in his youth he could take in the *News* and *Examiner* papers[3] (each he believed 9*d.* at that time, but was not certain), he could afford, and enjoyed, no reading when I saw him last autumn, beyond the book-leaves in which he received his quarter of cheese, his small piece of bacon or fresh meat, or his saveloys; and his wife schemed to go to the shops who "wrapped up their things from books," in order that he might have something to read after his day's work.

My informant went on with his specification: "Missionary papers of all kinds. Parliamentary papers, but not so often new ones, very largely. Railway prospectuses, with plans to some of them, nice engravings; and the same with other joint-stock companies. Children's copy-books, and cyphering-books. Old account-books of every kind. A good many years ago, I had some that must have belonged to a West End perfumer, there was such French items for Lady this, or the Honourable Captain that. I remember there was an Hon. Capt. G., and almost at every second page was '100 tooth-picks, 3*s.* 6*d.*' I think it was 3*s.* 6*d.*; in arranging this sort of waste one now and then gives a glance to it. Dictionaries of every sort, I've had, but not so commonly. Music books, lots of them. Manuscripts, but only if they're rather old; well, 20 or 30 years or so: I call that old. Letters on every possible subject, but not, in my experience, any very modern ones. An old man dies, you see, and his papers are sold off, letters and all; that's the way; get rid of all the old rubbish, as soon as the old boy's pointing his toes to the sky. What's old letters worth, when the writers are dead and buried? why, perhaps 1½*d.* a pound, and it's a rattling big letter that will weigh half-an-ounce. O, it's a queer trade, but there's many worse."

1 See p. 129, note 3.

2 See p. 77, note 1.

3 The *Examiner* (1808–86) was a weekly paper known for publishing radical views and authors such as John Stuart Mill (1806–73) and Charles Dickens (1812–70). The *News* is unknown.

[...]

The purchasers of the waste-paper from the collectors are cheesemongers, buttermen, butchers, fishmongers, poulterers, pork and sausage-sellers, sweet-stuff-sellers, tobacconists, chandlers—and indeed all who sell provisions or such luxuries as I have mentioned in retail. Some of the wholesale provision houses buy very largely and sell the waste again to their customers, who pay more for it by such a medium of purchase, but they have it thus on credit. Any retail trader in provisions at all "in a large way," will readily buy six or seven cwt. at a time. The price given by them varies from 1¼*d.* to 3½*d.* the pound, but it is very rarely either so low or so high. The average price may be taken at 18*s.* the cwt., which is not quite 2*d.* a pound, and at this rate I learn from the best-informed parties there are twelve tons sold weekly, or 1624 tons yearly (1,397,760 lbs.), at the cost of 11,232*l.* One man in the trade was confident the value of the waste paper sold could not be less than 12,000*l.* in a year.

There are about 60 men in this trade, nearly 50 of whom live entirely, as it was described to me, "by their waste," and bring up their families upon it. The others unite some other avocation with it. The earnings of the regular collectors vary from 15*s.* weekly to 35*s.* accordingly as they meet with a supply on favourable terms, or, as they call it, "a good pull in a lot of waste." They usually reside in a private room with a recess, or a second room, in which they sort, pack, and keep their paper.

[...]

Of the Street-Finders or Collectors.
Of the Sewer-Hunters.[1]

SOME few years ago, the main sewers, having their outlets on the river side, were completely open, so that any person desirous of exploring their dark and uninviting recesses might enter at the river side, and wander away, provided he could withstand the combination of villanous stenches which met him at every step, for many miles, in any direction. At that time it was a thing of very frequent occurrence, especially at the spring tides, for the water to rush into the sewers, pouring through them like a torrent, and then to burst up through the gratings into the streets, flooding all the low-lying districts in the vicinity of the river, till the streets of Shadwell and Wapping resembled a Dutch town, intersected by a series of muddy canals. Of late, however, to remedy this defect, the Commissioners have had a strong brick wall built within the entrance to the several sewers.[2] In each of these brick walls there is an opening covered by a strong iron door,

1 First published in the weekly serial version of *London Labour*, likely in No. 35, 9 August 1851.

2 See p. 149, note 1.

which hangs from the top and is so arranged that when the tide is low the rush of the water and other filth on the inner side, forces it back and allows the contents of the sewer to pass into the river, whilst when the tide rises the door is forced so close against the wall by the pressure of the water outside that none can by any possibility enter, and thus the river neighbourhoods are secured from the deluges which were heretofore of such frequent occurrence.

Were it not a notorious fact, it might perhaps be thought impossible, that men could be found who, for the chance of obtaining a living of some sort or other, would, day after day, and year after year, continue to travel through these underground channels for the offscouring of the city; but such is the case even at the present moment. In former times, however, this custom prevailed much more than now, for in those days the sewers were entirely open and presented no obstacle to any one desirous of entering them. Many wondrous tales are still told among the people of men having lost their way in the sewers, and of having wandered among the filthy passages—their lights extinguished by the noisome vapours—till, faint and overpowered, they dropped down and died on the spot. Other stories are told of sewer-hunters beset by myriads of enormous rats, and slaying thousands of them in their struggle for life, till at length the swarms of the savage things overpowered them, and in a few days afterwards their skeletons were discovered picked to the very bones. Since the iron doors, however, have been placed on the main sewers a prohibition has been issued against entering them, and a reward of 5*l.* offered to any person giving information so as to lead to the conviction of any offender. Nevertheless many still travel through these foul labyrinths, in search of such valuables as may have found their way down the drains.

The persons who are in the habit of searching the sewers, call themselves "shore-men" or "shore-workers." They belong, in a certain degree, to the same class as the "mud-larks," that is to say, they travel through the mud along shore in the neighbourhood of ship-building and ship-breaking yards, for the purpose of picking up copper nails, bolts, iron, and old rope. The shore-men, however, do not collect the lumps of coal and wood they meet with on their way, but leave them as the proper perquisites of the mud-larks. The sewer-hunters were formerly, and indeed are still, called by the name of "Toshers," the articles which they pick up in the course of their wanderings along shore being known among themselves by the general term "tosh," a word more particularly applied by them to anything made of copper. These "Toshers" may be seen, especially on the Surrey side of the Thames, habited in long greasy velveteen coats, furnished with pockets of vast capacity, and their nether limbs encased in dirty canvas trowsers, and any old slops of shoes, that may be fit only for wading through the mud. They carry a bag on their back, and in their hand a pole seven or eight feet long, on one end of which there is a large iron hoe. The uses of this instrument are various; with it they try the ground wherever it appears unsafe, before venturing on it, and, when assured of its safety, walk forward steadying their footsteps with the staff. Should they, as often happens, even to the most experienced, sink in some quagmire, they immediately throw out the long pole armed with the hoe, which is always held uppermost for this purpose, and with it seizing hold of any object within their reach, are thereby enabled to draw themselves out; without the pole, however, their danger would be greater, for the more they struggled to extricate themselves from such places, the deeper they would sink; and even with it, they might perish, I am told, in some part, if there were nobody at hand to render them assistance. [...]

[...]

I found one of these men, from whom I derived much information, and who is really an active intelligent man, in a court off Rosemary-lane. Access is gained to this court through a dark narrow entrance, scarcely wider than a doorway, running beneath the first floor of one of the houses in the adjoining street. The court itself is about 50 yards long, and not more than three yards wide, surrounded by lofty wooden houses, with jutting abutments in many of the upper stories that almost exclude the light, and give them the appearance of being about to tumble down upon the heads of the intruders. This court is densely inhabited; every room has its own family, more or less in number; and in many of them, I am assured, there are two families residing, the better to enable the one to whom the room is let to pay the rent. At the time of my visit, which was in the evening, after the inmates had returned from their various employments, some quarrel had arisen among them. The court was so thronged with the friends of the contending individuals and spectators of the fight that I was obliged to stand at the entrance, unable to force my way through the dense multitude, while labourers and street-folk with shaggy heads, and women with dirty caps and fuzzy hair, thronged every window above, and peered down anxiously at the affray. There must have been some hundreds of people collected there, and yet all were inhabitants of this very court, for the noise of the quarrel had not yet reached the street. On wondering at the number, my informant, when the noise had ceased, explained the matter as follows: "You see, sir, there's more than 30 houses in this here court, and there's not less than eight rooms in every house; now there's nine or ten people in some of the rooms, I knows, but just say four in every room, and calculate what that there comes to." I did, and found it, to my surprise, to be 960. "Well," continued my informant, chuckling and rubbing his hands in evident delight at the result, "you may as well just tack a couple a hundred on to the tail o' them for make-weight, as we're not werry pertikler about a hundred or two one way or the other in these here places."

In this court, up three flights of narrow stairs that creaked and trembled at every footstep, and in an ill-furnished garret, dwelt the shore-worker—a man who, had he been careful, according to his own account at least, might have money in the bank and be the proprietor of the house in which he lived. The sewer-hunters, like the street-people, are all known by some peculiar nickname, derived chiefly from some personal characteristic. It would be a waste of time to inquire for them by their right names, even if you were acquainted with them, for none else would know them, and no intelligence concerning them could be obtained; while under the title of Lanky Bill, Long Tom, One-eyed George, Short-armed Jack, they are known to every one.

My informant, who is also dignified with a title, or as he calls it a "handle to his name," gave me the following account of himself: "I was born in Birmingham, but afore I recollects anythink, we came to London. The first thing I remembers is being down on the shore at Cuckold's P'int,[1] when the tide was out and up to my knees in mud, and a gitting down deeper and deeper every minute till I was picked up by one of the shore-workers. I used to git down there every day, to look at the ships and boats a sailing up and down; I'd niver be tired a looking at them at that time. At last father 'prenticed me to a blacksmith in Bermondsey, *and then I couldn't git down to the river when I liked, so I got to hate the forge and the fire, and blowing the bellows, and couldn't stand the confinement no how,—at last I cuts and runs.*[2] After some time they gits me back ag'in, but I cuts ag'in. I was determined not to stand it. I wouldn't go home for fear I'd be sent back, so I goes down to Cuckold's P'int and there I sits near half the day, when who should I see but the old un as had picked me up out of the mud when I was a sinking. I tells him all about it, and he takes me home along with hisself, and gits me a bag and an o, and takes me out next day, and shows me what to do, and shows me the dangerous places, and the places what are safe, and how to rake in the mud for rope, and bones, and iron, and that's the way I comed to be a shore-worker. Lor' bless you, I've worked Cuckold's P'int for more nor twenty year. I know places where you'd go over head and ears in the mud, and jist alongside on 'em you may walk as safe as you can on this floor. But it don't do for a stranger to try it, he'd wery soon git in, and it's not so easy to git out agin, I can tell you. I stay'd with the old un a long time, and we used to git lots o' tin, specially when we'd go to work the sewers. I liked that well enough. I could git into small places where the old un couldn't, and when I'd got near the grating in the street, I'd search about in the bottom of the sewer; I'd put down my arm to my shoulder in the mud and bring up shillings and half-crowns, and lots of coppers, and plenty other things. I once found a silver jug as big as a quart pot, and often found spoons and knives and forks and every thing you can think of. Bless your heart the smells nothink; it's a roughish smell at first, but nothink near so bad as you thinks, 'cause, you see,

1 Located on the south bank of the River Thames, its name comes from the placement of a horned post at the location, likely associated with the Horn Fair at Charlton. The horns symbolize the cuckold, the husband of an adulterous wife.

2 Italicized in original.

there's sich lots o' water always a coming down the sewer, and the air gits in from the gratings, and that helps to sweeten it a bit. There's some places, 'specially in the old sewers, where they say there's foul air, and they tells me the foul air 'ill cause instantious death, but I niver met with anythink of the kind, and I think if there was sich a thing I should know somethink about it, for I've worked the sewers, off and on, for twenty year. When we comes to a narrow-place as we don't know, we takes the candle out of the lantern and fastens it on the hend of the o, and then runs it up the sewer, and if the light stays in, we knows as there a'n't no danger. We used to go up the city sewer at Blackfriars-bridge, but that's stopped up now; it's boarded across inside. The city wouldn't let us up if they knew it, 'cause of the danger, they say, but they don't care if we hav'n't got nothink to eat nor a place to put our heads in, while there's plenty of money lying there and good for nobody. If you was caught up it and brought afore the Lord Mayor, he'd give you fourteen days on it, as safe as the bellows, so a good many on us now is afraid to wenture in. We don't wenture as we used to, but still it's done at times. There's a many places as I knows on where the bricks has fallen down, and that there's dangerous; it's so delaberated that if you touches it with your head or with the hend of the o, it 'ill all come down atop o' you. I've often seed as many as a hundred rats at once, and they're woppers in the sewers, I can tell you; them there water rats, too, is far more ferociouser than any other rats, and they'd think nothink of tackling a man, if they found they couldn't get away no how, but if they can why they runs by and gits out o' the road. I knows a chap as the rats tackled in the sewers; they bit him hawfully: you must ha' heard on it; it was him as the watermen went in arter when they heard him a shouting as they was a rowin' by. Only for the watermen the rats would ha' done for him, safe enough. Do you recollect hearing on the man as was found in the sewers about twelve year ago?—oh you must—the rats eat every bit of him, and left nothink but his bones. I knowed him well, he was a rig'lar shore-worker.

"The rats is wery dangerous, that's sartain, but we always goes three or four on us together, and the varmint's too wide awake to tackle us then, for they know they'd git off second best. You can go a long way in the sewers if you like; I don't know how far. I niver was at the end on them myself, for a cove can't stop in longer than six or seven hour, 'cause of the tide; you must be out before that's up. There's a many branches on ivery side, but we don't go into all; we go where we know, and where we're always sure to find somethink. I know a place now where there's more than two or three hundred weight of metal all rusted together, and plenty of money among it too; but it's too heavy to carry it out, so it 'ill stop there I s'pose till the world comes to an end. I often brought out a piece of metal half a hundred in weight, and took it under the harch of the bridge, and broke it up with a large stone to pick out the money. I've found sovereigns and half sovereigns over and over ag'in, and three on us has often cleared a couple of pound apiece in one day out of the sewers. But we no sooner got the money than the publican had it. I only wish I'd back all the money I've guv to the publican, and I wouldn't care how the wind blew for the rest of my life. I never thought about taking a hammer along with me into the sewer, no; I never thought I'd want it. You can't go in every day, the tides don't answer, and they're so pertikler now, far more pertikler than formerly; if you was known to touch the traps, you'd git hauled up afore the beak. It's done for all that, and though there *is* so many eyes about. The 'Johnnys'[1] on the water are always on the look out, and if they sees any on us about, we has to cut our lucky. We shore-workers sometimes does very well other ways. When we hears of a fire anywheres, we goes and watches where they shoots the rubbish, and then we goes and sifts it over, and washes it afterwards, then all the metal sinks to the bottom. The way we does it is this here: we takes a barrel cut in half, and fills it with water, and then we shovels in the siftings, and stirs 'em round and round and round with a stick; then we throws out that water and puts in some fresh, and stirs that there round ag'in; arter some time the water gets clear, and every thing heavy's fell to the bottom, and then we sees what it is and picks it out. I've made from a pound to thirty shilling a day, at that there work on lead alone. The time the Parliament Houses was burnt, the rubbish was shot in Hyde Park, and Long J— and I goes to work it, and while we were at it, we didn't make less nor three pounds apiece a day; we found sovereigns and half sovereigns, and lots of silver half melted away, and jewellery, such as rings, and stones, and brooches; but we never got half paid for them. I found two sets of bracelets for a lady's arms, and took 'em to a jeweller, and he tried them jist where the 'great' heat had melted the catch away, and found they was only metal double plated, or else he said as how he'd give us thirty pounds for them; howsomever, we takes them down to a Jew in Petticoat-lane, who used to buy things of us, and he gives us 7*l.* 10*s.* for 'em. We found so many things, that at last Long J— and I got to quarrel about the 'whacking'; there was cheatin' a goin' on; it wasn't all fair and above board as it ought to be, so we gits to fightin', and kicks up sich a jolly row, that they wouldn't let us work no more, and takes and buries the whole on the rubbish. There's plenty o' things under the ground along with it now, if anybody could git at them. There was jist two loads o' rubbish shot at one time in Bishop Bonner's-fields, which I worked by myself, and what do you think I made out of that there?—why I made 3*l.* 5*s.* The rubbish was got out of a cellar, what hadn't been stirred for fifty year or more, so I thinks there ought to be somethink in it, and I keeps my eye on it, and watches where it's shot; then I turns to work, and the first thing I gits hold on is a chain, which I takes to be copper; it was so dirty, but it turned out to be all solid gold, and I gets 1*l.* 5*s.* for it from the Jew; arter that I finds lots o' coppers, and silver money, and many things besides. *The reason I likes this sort of life is, 'cause I can sit down when I likes, and nobody can't order me about. When I'm*

1 Police officers.

hard up, I knows as how I must work, and then I goes at it like sticks a breaking;[1] and tho' the times isn't as they was, I can go now and pick up my four or five bob a day, where another wouldn't know how to get a brass farden."

There is a strange tale in existence among the shore-workers, of a race of wild hogs inhabiting the sewers in the neighbourhood of Hampstead. The story runs, that a sow in young, by some accident got down the sewer through an opening, and, wandering away from the spot, littered and reared her offspring in the drain, feeding on the offal and garbage washed into it continually. Here, it is alleged, the breed multiplied exceedingly, and have become almost as ferocious as they are numerous. This story, apocryphal as it seems, has nevertheless its believers, and it is ingeniously argued, that the reason why none of the subterranean animals have been able to make their way to the light of day is, that they could only do so by reaching the mouth of the sewer at the river-side, while, in order to arrive at that point, they must necessarily encounter the Fleet ditch,[2] which runs towards the river with great rapidity, and as it is the obstinate nature of a pig to swim *against* the stream, the wild hogs of the sewers invariably work their way back to their original quarters, and are thus never to be seen. What seems strange in the matter is, that the inhabitants of Hampstead never have been known to see any of these animals pass beneath the gratings, nor to have been disturbed by their gruntings. The reader of course can believe as much of the story as he pleases, and it is right to inform him that the sewer-hunters themselves have never yet encountered any of the fabulous monsters of the Hampstead sewers.

Of the Mud-Larks.[3]

THERE is another class[4] who may be termed river-finders, although their occupation is connected only with the shore; they are commonly known by the name of "mud-larks," from being compelled, in order to obtain the articles they seek, to wade sometimes up to their middle through the mud left on the shore by the retiring tide. These poor creatures are certainly about the most deplorable in their appearance of any I have met with in the course of my inquiries. They may be seen of all ages, from mere childhood to positive decrepitude, crawling among the barges at the various wharfs along the river; it cannot be said that they are clad in rags, for they

1 Italicized in original.

2 The Fleet River, once a major river, was by the nineteenth century a subterranean river flowing from waters at Hampstead Heath to the River Thames. The Fleet Ditch, as the lower part of the river was known, was a sewer surrounded by housing of the poor and prisons, and covered by new construction.

3 First published in the weekly serial version of *London Labour*, likely in No. 35, 9 August 1851.

4 Mayhew also published articles on other scavengers, such as purefinders (collectors of dog dung), bone grubbers (collectors of animal bones), etc.

THE MUD-LARK.

[*From a Daguerreotype by* BEARD.]

Fig. 8: "The Mud-Lark."

are scarcely half covered by the tattered indescribable things that serve them for clothing; their bodies are grimed with the foul soil of the river, and their torn garments stiffened up like boards with dirt of every possible description.

Among the mud-larks may be seen many old women, and it is indeed pitiable to behold them, especially during the winter, bent nearly double with age and infirmity, paddling and groping among the wet mud for small pieces of coal, chips of wood, or any sort of refuse washed up by the tide. These women always have with them an old basket or an old tin kettle, in which they put whatever they chance to find. It usually takes them a whole tide to fill this receptacle, but when filled, it is as much as the feeble old creatures are able to carry home.

The mud-larks generally live in some court or alley in the neighbourhood of the river, and, as the tide recedes, crowds of boys and little girls, some old men, and many old women, may be observed loitering about the various stairs, watching eagerly for the opportunity to commence their labours. When the tide is sufficiently low they scatter themselves along the shore, separating from each other, and soon disappear among the craft lying about in every direction. This is the case on both sides of the river, as high up as there is anything to be found, extending as far as Vauxhall-bridge, and as low down as Woolwich. The mud-larks themselves, however, know only those who reside near them, and whom they are accustomed to meet in their daily pursuits; indeed, with but few exceptions, these people are dull, and apparently stupid; this is observable particularly among the boys and girls, who, when engaged in searching the mud, hold but little converse one with another. The men and women may be passed and repassed, but they notice no one; they never speak, but with a stolid look of wretchedness they plash their way through the mire, their bodies bent down while they peer anxiously about, and occasionally stoop to pick up some paltry treasure that falls in their way.

The mud-larks collect whatever they happen to find, such as coals, bits of old-iron, rope, bones, and copper nails that drop from ships while lying or repairing along shore. Copper nails are the most valuable of all the articles they find, but these they seldom obtain, as they are always driven from the neighbourhood of a ship while being new-sheathed. Sometimes the younger and bolder mud-larks venture on sweeping some empty coal-barge, and one little fellow with whom I spoke, having been lately caught in the act of so doing, had to undergo for the offence seven days' imprisonment in the House of Correction: this, he says, he liked much better than mud-larking, for while he staid there he wore a coat and shoes and stockings, and though he had not over much to eat, he certainly was never afraid of going to bed without anything at all—as he often had to do when at liberty. He thought he would try it on again in the winter, he told me, saying, it would be so comfortable to have clothes and shoes and stockings then, and not be obliged to go into the cold wet mud of a morning.

[...]

At one of the stairs in the neighbourhood of the pool, I collected about a dozen of these unfortunate children; there was not one of them over twelve years of age, and many of them were but six. It would be almost impossible to describe the wretched group, so motley was their appearance, so extraordinary their dress, and so stolid and inexpressive their countenances. Some carried baskets, filled with the produce of their morning's work, and others old tin kettles with iron handles. Some, for want of these articles, had old hats filled with the bones and coals they had picked up; and others, more needy still, had actually taken the caps from their own heads, and filled them with what they had happened to find. The muddy slush was dripping from their clothes and utensils, and forming a puddle in which they stood. There did not appear to be among the whole group as many filthy cotton rags to their backs as, when stitched together, would have been sufficient to form the material of one shirt. There were the remnants of one or two jackets among them, but so begrimed and tattered that it would have been difficult to have determined either the original material or make of the garment. [...]

[...]

[...] There was a painful uniformity in the stories of all the children: they were either the children of the very poor, who, by their own improvidence or some overwhelming calamity, had been reduced to the extremity of distress, or else they were orphans, and compelled from utter destitution to seek for the means of appeasing their hunger in the mud of the river. That the majority of this class are ignorant, and without even the rudiments of education, and that many of them from time to time are committed to prison for petty thefts, cannot be wondered at. Nor can it even excite our astonishment that, once within the walls of a prison, and finding how much more comfortable it is than their previous condition, they should return to it repeatedly. As for the females growing up under such circumstances, the worst may be anticipated of them; and in proof of this I have found, upon inquiry, that very many of the unfortunate creatures who swell the tide of prostitution in Ratcliff-highway, and other low neighbourhoods in the East of London, have originally been mud-larks; and only remained at that occupation till such time as they were capable of adopting the more easy and more lucrative life of the prostitute.

As to the numbers and earnings of the mud-larks, the following calculations fall short of, rather than exceed, the truth. From Execution Dock[1] to the lower part of Limehouse Hole,[2] there are 14 stairs or landing-places, by which the mud-larks descend to the shore in order to pursue

1 Site along the Thames where pirates, traitors, and anyone convicted of a crime at sea were executed by hanging.

2 East London area along the Thames known for ship-building and dock-related industry since the seventeenth century.

their employment. There are about as many on the opposite side of the water similarly frequented.

At King James' Stairs, in Wapping Wall,[1] which is nearly a central position, from 40 to 50 mud-larks go down daily to the river; the mud-larks "using" the other stairs are not so numerous. If, therefore, we reckon the number of stairs on both sides of the river at 28, and the average number of mud-larks frequenting them at 10 each, we shall have a total of 280. Each mud-lark, it has been shown, earns on an average 3*d.* a day, or 1*s.* 6*d.* per week; so that the annual earnings of each will be 3*l.* 18*s.*, or say 4*l.*, a year, and hence the gross earnings of the 280 will amount to rather more than 1000*l.* per annum.

[...]

As an illustration of the doctrines I have endeavoured to enforce throughout this publication, I cite the following history of one of the above class. It may serve to teach those who are still sceptical as to the degrading influence of circumstances upon the poor, that many of the humbler classes, if placed in the same easy position as ourselves, would become, perhaps, quite as "respectable" members of society.

The lad of whom I speak was discovered by me now nearly two years ago "mud-larking" on the banks of the river near the docks. He was a quick, intelligent little fellow, and had been at the business, he told me, about three years. He had taken to mud-larking, he said, because his clothes were too bad for him to look for anything better. He worked every day, with 20 or 30 boys, who might all be seen at daybreak with their trowsers tucked up, groping about, and picking out the pieces of coal from the mud on the banks of the Thames. He went into the river up to his knees, and in searching the mud he often ran pieces of glass and long nails into his feet. When this was the case, he went home and dressed the wounds, but returned to the river-side directly, "for should the tide come up," he added, "without my having found something, why I must starve till next low tide." In the very cold weather he and his other shoeless companions used to stand in the hot water that ran down the river side from some of the steam-factories,[2] to warm their frozen feet.

At first he found it difficult to keep his footing in the mud, and he had known many beginners fall in. He came to my house, at my request, the morning after my first meeting with him. It was the depth of winter, and the poor little fellow was nearly destitute of clothing. His trousers were worn away up to his knees, he had no shirt, and his legs and feet (which were bare) were covered with chilblains. On being questioned by me he gave the following account of his life:—

1 King James's Stairs were one in a network of staircases and causeways that provided safe access to and from the Thames. Wapping Wall, a street in the East End of London, was the location of dockland industries such as warehousing.

2 A factory powered by a steam engine. Coal-powered steam engines replaced water power in British industry during the nineteenth century.

He was fourteen years old. He had two sisters, one fifteen and the other twelve years of age. His father had been dead nine years. The man had been a coal-whipper,[1] and, from getting his work from one of the publican employers[2] in those days, had become a confirmed drunkard. When he married he held a situation in a warehouse, where his wife managed the first year to save 4*l.* 10*s.* out of her husband's earnings; but from the day he took to coal-whipping she had never saved one halfpenny, indeed she and her children were often left to starve. The man (whilst in a state of intoxication) had fallen between two barges, and the injuries he received had been so severe that he had lingered in a helpless state for three years before his death. After her husband's decease the poor woman's neighbours subscribed 1*l.* 5*s.* for her; with this sum she opened a greengrocer's shop, and got on very well for five years.

When the boy was nine years old his mother sent him to the Red Lion school at Green-bank, near Old Gravel-lane, Ratcliffe-highway; she paid 1*d.* a week for his learning. He remained there for a year; then the potato-rot came, and his mother lost upon all she bought. About the same time two of her customers died 30*s.* in her debt; this loss, together with the potato-disease, completely ruined her, and the whole family had been in the greatest poverty from that period. Then she was obliged to take all her children from their school, that they might help to keep themselves as best they could. Her eldest girl sold fish in the streets, and the boy went to the river-side to "pick up" his living. The change, however, was so great that shortly afterwards the little fellow lay ill eighteen weeks with the ague. As soon as the boy recovered his mother and his two sisters were "taken bad" with a fever. The poor woman went into the "Great House,"[3] and the children were taken to the Fever Hospital.[4] When the mother returned home she was too weak to work, and all she had to depend on was what her boy brought from the river. They had nothing to eat and no money until the

---

1 As Mayhew describes elsewhere, coal-whippers worked in gangs to unload coal from ships' holds using a basket and pulley system. Coal-whipping was an exhausting, filthy, and poorly paid form of temporary employment. See "The Coal-Heavers," p. 263.

2 Coal-whippers were hired by the owners of Thames riverfront pubs (publicans), who acted as middle men between ship owners and coal merchants. Publicans paid the coal-whippers directly, on condition that they used part of their meagre earnings to buy alcohol from the publican, further impoverishing workers and their families. The more alcohol a job-seeker pledged to purchase, the more likely he was to obtain employment. Chronic alcoholism and many workplace accidents and fatalities led to the 1843 Coal Whippers Act, which attempted to end this practice. See "The Coal-Heavers," p. 265.

3 Used here as slang for workhouse, but the term also referred to the opulent mansions of landowners.

4 Charitable hospital providing medical treatment for those who could not afford to hire doctors and physicians privately. Upwards of two dozen such hospitals were established in London by the middle of the nineteenth century.

little fellow had been down to the shore and picked up some coals, selling them for a trifle. "And hard enough he had to work for what he got, poor boy," said his mother to me on a future occasion, sobbing; "still he never complained, but was quite proud when he brought home enough for us to get a bit of meat with; and when he has sometimes seen me down-hearted, he has clung round my neck, and assured me that one day God would see us cared for if I would put my trust in Him." As soon as his mother was well enough she sold fruit in the streets, or went out washing when she could get a day's work.

The lad suffered much from the pieces of broken glass in the mud. Some little time before I met with him he had run a copper nail into his foot. This lamed him for three months, and his mother was obliged to carry him on her back every morning to the doctor. As soon, however, as he could "hobble" (to use his mother's own words) he went back to the river, and often returned (after many hours' hard work in the mud) with only a few pieces of coal, not enough to sell even to get them a bit of bread. One evening, as he was warming his feet in the water that ran from a steam factory, he heard some boys talking about the Ragged School[1] in High-street, Wapping.

"They was saying what they used to learn there," added the boy. "They asked me to come along with them for it was great fun. They told me that all the boys used to be laughing and making game of the master. They said they used to put out the gas and chuck the slates all about. They told me, too, that there was a good fire there, so I went to have a warm and see what it was like. When I got there the master was very kind to me. They used to give us tea-parties, and to keep us quiet they used to show us the magic lantern.[2] I soon got to like going there, and went every night for six months. There was about 40 or 50 boys in the school. The most of them was thieves, and they used to go thieving the coals out of barges along shore, and cutting the ropes off ships, and going and selling it at the rag-shops.[3] They used to get ¾*d.* a lb. for the rope when dry, and ½*d.* when wet. Some used to steal pudding out of shops and hand it to those outside, and the last boy it was handed to would go off with it. They used to steal bacon and bread sometimes as well. About half of the boys at the school was thieves. Some had work to do at ironmongers, lead-factories, engineers, soap-boilers, and so on, and some had no work to do and was good boys still. After we came out of school at nine o'clock at night, some of the bad boys would go a thieving, perhaps half-a-dozen and from that to eight

1 Charitable schools run by volunteers for destitute children in poor districts of London, such as Wapping. Ragged schools accepted children who were excluded from more established schools for being too dirty, ill-clothed, or undisciplined.

2 An early form of image projector using hand-painted pictures on glass slides. First developed in Europe in the seventeenth century, they were used for both entertainment and educational purposes by the nineteenth century.

3 See "Of the 'Rag-and-Bottle,' and the 'Marine-Store,' Shops," p. 164.

would go out in a gang together. There was one big boy of the name of C——; he was 18 years old, and is in prison now for stealing bacon; I think he is in the House of Correction. [...]

[...]

"[...] While waiting outside the school-doors, before they opened, we used to plan up where we would go thieving after school was over. I was taken up once for thieving coals myself, but I was let go again."

I was so much struck with the boy's truthfulness of manner, that I asked him, *would* he really lead a different life, if he saw a means of so doing? He assured me he would, and begged me earnestly to try him. Upon his leaving me, 2*s*. were given him for his trouble. This small sum (I afterwards learned) kept the family for more than a fortnight. The girl laid it out in sprats (it being then winter-time); these she sold in the streets.

I mentioned the fact to a literary friend, who interested himself in the boy's welfare; and eventually succeeded in procuring him a situation at an eminent printer's. The subjoined letter will show how the lad conducted himself while there.

"Whitefriars, April 22, 1850.

"Messrs. Bradbury and Evans[1] beg to say that the boy J.C. has conducted himself in a very satisfactory manner since he has been in their employment."

The same literary friend took the girl into his service. She is in a situation still, though not in the same family.

The boy now holds a good situation at one of the daily newspaper offices. So well has he behaved himself, that, a few weeks since, his wages were increased from 6*s*. to 9*s*. per week. His mother (owing to the boy's exertions) has now a little shop, and is doing well.

This simple story requires no comments, and is narrated here in the hope that it may teach many to know how often the poor boys reared in the gutter are thieves, merely because society forbids them being honest lads.

Of the London Dustmen, Nightmen, Sweeps, and Scavengers.[2]

THESE men constitute a large body, and are a class who, all things considered, do their work silently and efficiently. Almost without the cogni-

1 London printing and publishing house established in 1830 and associated with Charles Dickens and William Makepeace Thackeray (1811–63).

2 A shorter version of this selection was published in the *Morning Chronicle*, 1 October 1849. An expanded version was published in the weekly serial of *London Labour*, likely in No. 35, 9 August 1851.

sance of the mass of the people, the refuse is removed from our streets and houses; and London, as if in the care of a tidy housewife, is *always* being cleaned. Great as are the faults and absurdities of many parts of our system of public cleansing, nevertheless, when compared with the state of things in any continental capital, the superiority of the metropolis of Great Britain is indisputable.

In all this matter there is little merit to be attributed to the workmen, except that they may be well drilled; for the majority of them are as much machines, apart from their animation, as are the cane and whalebone made to cleanse the chimney, or the clumsy-looking machine which, in its progress, is a vehicular scavenger, sweeping as it goes.

These public cleansers are to be thus classified:—

1. Dustmen, or those who empty and remove the collection of ashes, bones, vegetables, &c., deposited in the dust-bins, or other refuse receptacles throughout the metropolis.
2. Nightmen, or those who remove the contents of the cesspools.
3. Sweeps, or those who remove the soot from the chimneys.
4. Scavengers, or those who remove the dirt from the streets, roads, and markets.

[...]

The removal of the refuse of a large town is, perhaps, one of the most important of social operations. Not only is it necessary for the wellbeing of a vast aggregation of people that the ordure should be removed from both within and around their dwellings as soon as it is generated, but nature, ever working in a circle and reproducing in the same ratio as she destroys, has made this same ordure not only the cause of present disease when allowed to remain within the city, but the means of future health and sustenance when removed to the fields.

In a leading article in the *Morning Chronicle*, written about two years since,[1] I said—

"That man gets his bones from the rocks and his muscles from the atmosphere, is beyond all doubt. The iron in his blood and the lime in his teeth were originally in the soil. But these could not be in his body unless they had previously formed part of his food. And yet we can neither live on air nor on stones. We cannot grow fat upon lime, and iron is positively indigestible in our stomachs. It is by means of the vegetable creation alone that we are enabled to convert the mineral into flesh and blood. The only apparent use of herbs and plants is to change the inorganic earth, air, and water, into organic substances fitted for the nutrition of animals. The little lichen, which, by means of the oxalic acid that it secretes, decomposes the rocks to which it clings, and fits their lime for 'assimilation' with higher

1 See p. 186, note 2.

organisms, is, as it were, but the primitive bone-maker of the world. By what subtle transmutation inorganic nature is changed into organic, and dead inert matter quickened with life, is far beyond us even to conjecture. Suffice it that an express apparatus is required for the process—a special mechanism to convert the '*crust* of the earth,' as it is called, into food for man and beast.

"Now, in Nature everything moves in a circle—perpetually changing, and yet ever returning to the point whence it started. Our bodies are continually decomposing and recomposing—indeed, the very process of breathing is but one of decomposition. As animals live on vegetables, even so is the refuse of the animal the vegetable's food. The carbonic acid which comes from our lungs, and which is poison for us to inhale, is not only the vital air of plants, but positively their nutriment. With the same wondrous economy that marks all creation, it has been ordained that what is unfitted for the support of the superior organisms, is of all substances the best adapted to give strength and vigour to the inferior. That which we excrete as pollution to our system, they secrete as nourishment to theirs. Plants are not only Nature's scavengers but Nature's purifiers. They remove the filth from the earth, as well as disinfect the atmosphere, and fit it to be breathed by a higher order of beings. Without the vegetable creation the animal could neither have been nor be. Plants not only fitted the earth originally for the residence of man and the brute, but to this day they continue to render it habitable to us. For this end their nature has been made the very antithesis to ours. The process by which we live is the process by which they are destroyed. That which supports respiration in us produces putrefaction in them. What our lungs throw off, their lungs absorb—what our bodies reject, their roots imbibe.

"Hence, in order that the balance of waste and supply should be maintained—that the principle of universal compensation should be kept up, and that what is rejected by us should go to the sustenance of plants, Nature has given us several instinctive motives to remove our refuse from us. She has not only constituted that which we egest the most loathsome of all things to our senses and imagination, but she has rendered its effluvium highly pernicious to our health—sulphuretted hydrogen being at once the most deleterious and offensive of all gases. Consequently, as in all other cases where the great law of Nature has to be enforced by special sanctions, a double motive has been given us to do that which it is necessary for us to do, and thus it has been made not only advantageous to us to remove our refuse to the fields, but positively detrimental to our health, and disgusting to our senses, to keep it in the neighbourhood of our houses.

"In every well-regulated State, therefore, an effective and rapid means for carrying off the ordure of the people to a locality where it may be fruitful instead of destructive, becomes a most important consideration. Both the health and the wealth of the nation depend upon it. If to make two blades of wheat grow where one grew before is to confer a benefit on the world, surely to remove that which will enable us at once to do this, and to purify the very air which we breathe, as well as the water which we drink, must be a still greater boon to society. It is, in fact, to give the community not only a double amount of food, but a double amount of health to enjoy it. We are now beginning to understand this. Up to the present time we have only thought of removing our refuse—the idea of using it never entered our minds. It was not until science taught us the dependence of one order of creation upon another, that we began to see that what appeared worse than worthless to us was Nature's capital—*wealth set aside for future production*."

In connection with this part of the subject, viz., the use of human refuse, I would here draw attention to those erroneous notions, as to the multiplication of the people, which teach us to look upon the increases of the population beyond certain limits as the greatest possible evil that can befall a community. Population, it is said, multiplies itself in a geometrical ratio, whereas the produce of the land is increased only in arithmetical proportion; that is to say, while the people are augumented after the rate of—

2	4	8	16	32	64

the quantity of food for them can be extended only in the following degrees:—

2	4	6	8	10	12

The cause of this is said to be that, after a certain stage in the cultivation of the soil, the increase of the produce from land is not in proportion to the increase of labour devoted to it; that is to say, doubling the labour does not double the crop; and hence it is asserted that the human race increasing at a quicker rate than the food, insufficient sustenance must be the necessary lot of a portion of the people in every densely-populated community.

That men of intelligence and education should have been persuaded by so plausible a doctrine at the time of its first promulgation may be readily conceived, for then the notions concerning organic chemistry were vague in the extreme, and the great universal law of Waste and Supply remained to be fully developed; but that men pretending to the least scientific knowledge should in these days be found advocating the Population Theory is only another of the many proofs of the indisposition of even the strongest minds to abandon their pet prejudices. Assuredly Malthus and Liebig are incompatible.[1] If the new notions as to the chemistry of vege-

1 Thomas Malthus's (1766–1834) controversial theory that population increased geometrically whereas food increased arithmetically (thus leading to food shortages) was contested by Justus von Liebig (1803–73), the German founder of organic chemistry, who advocated using waste as fertilizer to enhance food supplies. Mayhew draws liberally on Liebig's *Chemistry in its Application to Agriculture and Physiology* (1840) in this selection.

tation be true, then must the old notions as to population be utterly unfounded. If what we excrete plants secrete—if what we exhale they inspire—if our refuse is their food—then it follows that to increase the population is to increase the quantity of manure, while to increase the manure is to augment the food of plants, and consequently the plants themselves. If the plants nourish us, we at least nourish them. It seems never to have occurred to the economists that plants themselves required sustenance, and consequently they never troubled themselves to inquire whence they derived the elements of their growth. Had they done this they would never have even expected that a double quantity of mere labour upon the soil should have doubled the produce; but they would rather have seen that it was utterly impossible for the produce to be doubled without the food in the soil being doubled likewise; that is to say, they would have perceived that plants could not, whatever the labour exerted upon their cultivation, extract the elements of their organization from the earth and air, unless those elements previously existed in the land and atmosphere in which they grew, and that such elements, moreover, could not exist there without some organic being to egest them.

This doctrine of the universal Compensation extending throughout the material world, and more especially through the animal and vegetable kingdom, is, perhaps, one of the grandest and most consoling that science has yet revealed to us, making each mutually dependent on the other, and so contributing each to the other's support. Moreover it is the more comforting, as enabling us almost to demonstrate the falsity of a creed which is opposed to every generous impulse of our nature, and which is utterly irreconcilable with the attributes of the Creator.

[...]

Of the Dustmen of London.[1]

DUST and rubbish accumulate in houses from a variety of causes, but principally from the residuum of fires, the white ash and cinders, or small fragments of unconsumed coke, giving rise to by far the greater quantity. Some notion of the vast amount of this refuse annually produced in London may be formed from the fact that the consumption of coal in the metropolis is, according to the official returns, 3,500,000 tons per annum, which is at the rate of a little more than 11 tons per house; the poorer families, it is true, do not burn more than 2 tons in the course of the year, but then many such families reside in the same house, and hence the average will appear in no way excessive. Now the ashes and cinders arising from this enormous consumption of coal would, it is evident, if allowed to lie scattered about in such a place as London, render, ere long, not only the back streets, but even the important thoroughfares, filthy and impassable.

1 First published in the weekly serial version of *London Labour*, No. 36, 16 August 1851.

Upon the Officers of the various parishes, therefore, has devolved the duty of seeing that the refuse of the fuel consumed throughout London is removed almost as fast as produced; this they do by entering into an agreement for the clearance of the "dust-bins" of the parishioners as often as required, with some person who possesses all necessary appliances for the purpose—such as horses, carts, baskets, and shovels, together with a plot of waste ground whereon to deposit the refuse. The persons with whom this agreement is made are called "dust-contractors," and are generally men of considerable wealth.

The collection of "dust," is now, more properly speaking, the removal of it. The collection of an article implies the voluntary seeking after it, and this the dustmen can hardly be said to do; for though they parade the streets shouting for the dust as they go, they do so rather to fulfil a certain duty they have undertaken to perform than in any expectation of profit to be derived from the sale of the article.

Formerly the custom was otherwise; but then, as will be seen hereafter, the residuum of the London fuel was far more valuable. Not many years ago it was the practice for the various master dustmen to send in their tenders to the vestry, on a certain day appointed for the purpose, offering to pay a considerable sum yearly to the parish authorities for liberty to collect the dust from the several houses. The sum formerly paid to the parish of Shadwell, for instance, though not a very extensive one, amounted to between 400*l.* or 500*l.* per annum; but then there was an immense demand for the article, and the contractors were unable to furnish a sufficient supply from London; ships were frequently freighted with it from other parts, especially from Newcastle and the northern ports, and at that time it formed an article of considerable international commerce—the price being from 15*s.* to 1*l.* per chaldron. Of late years, however, the demand has fallen off greatly, while the supply has been progressively increasing, owing to the extension of the metropolis, so that the Contractors have not only declined paying anything for liberty to collect it, but now stipulate to receive a certain sum for the removal of it. It need hardly be stated that the parishes always employ the man who requires the least money for the performance of what has now become a matter of duty rather than an object of desire. Some idea may be formed of the change which has taken place in this business, from the fact, that the aforesaid parish of Shadwell, which formerly received the sum of 450*l.* per annum for liberty to collect the dust, now pays the Contractor the sum of 240*l.* per annum for its removal.

[…]

Computing the London dust-contractors at 90, and the inhabited houses at 300,000, it follows that each contractor would have 3333 houses to remove the refuse from. Now it has been calculated that the ashes and cinders alone from each house average about three loads per annum, so that each contractor would have, in round numbers, 10,000 loads of dust to remove in the course of the year. I find, from inquiries, that every two dustmen carry to the yard about five loads a day, or about 1500 loads in the course of the year, so that at this rate, there must be between six and seven carts, and twelve and fourteen collectors employed by each master. But this is exclusive of the men employed in the yards. In one yard that I visited there were fourteen people busily employed. Six of these were women, who were occupied in sifting, and they were attended by three men who shovelled the dust into their sieves, and the foreman, who was hard at work loosening and dragging down the dust from the heap, ready for the "fillers-in." Besides these there were two carts and four men engaged in conveying the sifted dust to the barges alongside the wharf. At a larger dust-yard, that formerly stood on the banks of the Regent's-canal, I am informed that there were sometimes as many as 127 people at work. It is but a small yard, which has not 30 to 40 labourers connected with it; and the lesser dust-yards have generally from four to eight sifters, and six or seven carts. There are, therefore, employed in a medium-sized yard twelve collectors or cartmen, six sifters, and three fillers-in, besides the foreman or forewoman, making altogether 22 persons; so that, computing the contractors at 90, and allowing 20 men to be employed by each, there would be 1800 men thus occupied in the metropolis, which appears to be very near the truth.

[...]

The next part of the subject is—what becomes of this vast quantity of dust—to what use it is applied.

The dust thus collected is used for two purposes, (1) as a manure for land of a peculiar quality; and (2) for making bricks. [...]

But during the operation of sifting the dust, many things are found which are useless for either manure or brick-making, such as oyster shells, old bricks, old boots and shoes, old tin kettles, old rags and bones, &c. These are used for various purposes.

The bricks, &c., are sold for sinking beneath foundations, where a thick layer of concrete is spread over them. Many old bricks, too, are used in making new roads, especially where the land is low and marshy. The old tin goes to form the japanned[1] fastenings for the corners of trunks, as well as to other persons, who re-manufacture it into a variety of articles. The old shoes are sold to the London shoemakers, who use them as stuffing between the in-sole and the outer one; but by far the greater quantity is sold to the manufacturers of Prussian blue,[2] that substance being formed

1 See p. 80, note 2.

2 The first truly synthetic pigment, discovered in the early eighteenth century. The deep blue colour was created by heating a mixture of processed animal matter—often blood, but also hooves, horns, or other parts—with an alkali, with other compounds added once the mixture cooled.

out of refuse animal matter. The rags and bones are of course disposed of at the usual places—the marine-store shops.[1]

A dust-heap, therefore, may be briefly said to be composed of the following things, which are severally applied to the following uses:—

1. "Soil," or fine dust, sold to brickmakers for making bricks, and to farmers for manure, especially for clover.

2. "Brieze," or cinders, sold to brickmakers, for burning bricks.

3. Rags, bones, and old metal, sold to marine-store dealers.

4. Old tin and iron vessels, sold for "clamps" to trunks, &c., and for making copperas.

5. Old bricks and oyster shells, sold to builders, for sinking foundations, and forming roads.

6. Old boots and shoes, sold to Prussian-blue manufacturers.

7. Money and jewellery, kept, or sold to Jews.

The dust-yards, or places where the dust is collected and sifted, are generally situated in the suburbs, and they may be found all round London, sometimes occupying open spaces adjoining back streets and lanes, and surrounded by the low mean houses of the poor; frequently, however, they cover a large extent of ground in the fields, and there the dust is piled up to a great height in a conical heap, and having much the appearance of a volcanic mountain. The reason why the dust-heaps are confined principally to the suburbs is, that more space is to be found in the outskirts than in a thickly-peopled and central locality. Moreover, the fear of indictments for nuisance[2] has had considerable influence in the matter, for it was not unusual for the yards in former times, to be located within the boundaries of the city. They are now, however, scattered round London, and always placed as near as possible to the river, or to some canal communicating therewith. In St. George's, Shadwell, Ratcliffe, Limehouse, Poplar, and Blackwall, on the north side of the Thames, and in Redriffe, Bermondsey, and Rotherhithe, on the south, they are to be found near the Thames. The object of this is, that by far the greater quantity of the soil or ashes is conveyed in sailing-barges, holding from 70 to 100 tons each, to Feversham, Sittingbourne, and other places in Kent, which are the great brick-making manufactories for London. These barges come up invariably loaded with bricks, and take home in return a cargo of soil. [...]

[...]

A visit to any of the large metropolitan dust-yards is far from uninteresting. Near the centre of the yard rises the highest heap, composed of

---

1 See "Of the 'Rag-and-Bottle,' and the 'Marine-Store,' Shops," p. 164.

2 1846 legislation allowed magistrates to order the cleansing, repair, or removal of "nuisances" such as slum houses, cesspools, manure, and garbage. The proximity of urban dust-yards to living quarters, workplaces, and water sources led to numerous reports, complaints, and indictments.

what is called the "soil," or finer portion of the dust used for manure. Around this heap are numerous lesser heaps, consisting of the mixed dust and rubbish carted in and shot down previous to sifting. Among these heaps are many women and old men with sieves made of iron, all busily engaged in separating the "brieze" from the "soil." There is likewise another large heap in some other part of the yard, composed of the cinders or "brieze" waiting to be shipped off to the brickfields. The whole yard seems alive, some sifting and others shovelling the sifted soil on to the heap, while every now and then the dust-carts return to discharge their loads, and proceed again on their rounds for a fresh supply. Cocks and hens keep up a continual scratching and cackling among the heaps, and numerous pigs seem to find great delight in rooting incessantly about after the garbage and offal collected from the houses and markets.

In a dust-yard lately visited the sifters formed a curious sight; they were almost up to their middle in dust, ranged in a semi-circle in front of that part of the heap which was being "worked"; each had before her a small mound of soil which had fallen through her sieve and formed a sort of embankment, behind which she stood. The appearance of the entire group at their work was most peculiar. Their coarse dirty cotton gowns were tucked up behind them, their arms were bared above their elbows, their black bonnets crushed and battered like those of fish-women; over their gowns they wore a strong leathern apron, extending from their necks to the extremities of their petticoats, while over this, again, was another leathern apron, shorter, thickly padded, and fastened by a stout string or strap round the waist. In the process of their work they pushed the sieve from them and drew it back again with apparent violence, striking it against the outer leathern apron with such force that it produced each time a hollow sound, like a blow on the tenor drum. All the women present were middle aged, with the exception of one who was very old—68 years of age she told me—and had been at the business from a girl. She was the daughter of a dustman, the wife, or woman of a dustman, and the mother of several young dustmen—sons and grandsons—all at work at the dust-yards at the east end of the metropolis.

[...]

The manner in which the dust is collected is very simple. The "filler" and the "carrier" perambulate the streets with a heavily-built high box cart, which is coated with a thick crust of filth, and drawn by a clumsy-looking horse. These men used, before the passing of the late Street Act, to ring a dull-sounding bell so as to give notice to housekeepers of their approach, but now they merely cry, in a hoarse unmusical voice, "Dust oy-eh!" Two men accompany the cart, which is furnished with a short ladder and two shovels and baskets. These baskets one of the men fills from the dust-bin, and then helps them alternately, as fast as they are filled, upon the shoulder of the other man, who carries them one by one to the cart, which is placed immediately alongside the pavement in front of the house where they are at work. The carrier mounts up the side of the cart by means of the ladder, discharges into it the contents of the basket on his shoulder, and then returns below for the other basket which his mate has filled for him in the interim. This process is pursued till all is cleared away, and repeated at different houses till the cart is fully loaded; then the men make the best of their way to the dust-yard, where they shoot the contents of the cart on to the heap, and again proceed on their regular rounds.

The dustmen, in their appearance, very much resemble the waggoners of the coal-merchants. They generally wear knee-breeches, with ancle boots or gaiters, short dirty smockfrocks or coarse gray jackets, and fantail hats. In one particular, however, they are at first sight distinguishable from the coal-merchants' men, for the latter are invariably black from coal dust, while the dustmen, on the contrary, are gray with ashes.

In their personal appearance the dustmen are mostly tall stalwart fellows; there is nothing sickly-looking about them, and yet a considerable part of their time is passed in the yards and in the midst of effluvia most offensive, and, if we believe "zymotic theorists,"[1] as unhealthy to those unaccustomed to them; nevertheless, the children, who may be said to be reared in the yard and to have inhaled the stench of the dust-heap with their first breath, are healthy and strong. It is said, moreover, that during the plague in London the dustmen were the persons who carted away the dead, and it remains a tradition among the class to the present day, that not one of them died of the plague, even during its greatest ravages. In Paris, too, it is well known, that, during the cholera of 1849, the quarter of Belleville, where the night-soil and refuse of the city is deposited, escaped the freest from the pestilence; and in London the dustmen boast that, during both the recent visitations of the cholera, they were altogether exempt from the disease. "Look at that fellow, sir!" said one of the dust-contractors to me, pointing to his son, who was a stout red-cheeked young man of about twenty. "Do you see anything ailing about him? Well, he has been in the yard since he was born. There stands my house just at the gate, so you see he hadn't far to travel, and when quite a child he used to play and root away here among the dust all his time. I don't think he ever had a day's illness in his life. The people about the yard are all used to the smell and don't complain about it. It's all stuff and nonsense, all this talk about dust-yards being unhealthy. I've never done anything else all my days and I don't think I look very ill. I shouldn't wonder now but what I'd be set down as being fresh from the sea-side by those very fellows that write all this trash about a matter that they don't know just *that* about";

1 Followers of the work of Justus von Liebig (1803–73) and William Farr (1807–83), who believed that disease was caused by the introduction of zymotic, or infectious materials—causing fermentation and decomposition—into the body. Here, Mayhew undermines these relatively new (1839) theories, as he explains how individuals spending their time in heaps of garbage do not seem more prone to illness.

VIEW OF A DUST YARD.

(From a Sketch taken on the spot.)

Fig. 9: "View of a Dust Yard."

and he snapped his fingers contemptuously in the air, and, thrusting both hands into his breeches pockets, strutted about, apparently satisfied that he had the best of the argument. He was, in fact, a stout, jolly, red-faced man. Indeed, the dustmen, as a class, appear to be healthy, strong men, and extraordinary instances of longevity are common among them. I heard of one dustman who lived to be 115 years; another, named Wood, died at 100; and the well-known Richard Tyrrell died only a short time back at the advanced age of 97.[1] The misfortune is, that we have no large series of facts on this subject, so that the longevity and health of the dustmen might be compared with those of other classes.

In almost all their habits the Dustmen are similar to the Costermongers, with the exception that they seem to want their cunning and natural quickness, and that they have little or no predilection for gaming. Costermongers, however, are essentially traders, and all trade is a species of gambling—the risking of a certain sum of money to obtain more; hence spring, perhaps, the gambling propensities of low traders, such as costers, and Jew clothes-men; and hence, too, that natural sharpness which characterizes the same classes. The dustmen, on the contrary, have regular employment and something like regular wages, and therefore rest content with what they can earn in their usual way of business.

[...]

Chimney Sweepers.
Of the London Chimney-Sweepers.[2]

[...]

To understand the *necessity* for chimney-sweepers, and the extent of the work for them to do, that is to say, the quantity of soot deposited in our chimneys during the combustion of the three and a half millions of tons of coals that are now annually consumed in London, we must first comprehend the conditions upon which the evolution of soot depends, soot being simply the fine carbonaceous particles condensed from the smoke of coal fuel, and deposited against the sides of the chimneys during its ascent between the walls to the tops of our houses. These conditions appear to have been determined somewhat accurately during the investigations of the Smoke Prevention Committee.[3]

---

1 According to "Health of Nightmen, Scavengers, and Dustmen," in the *Journal of the Royal Statistical Society* (v. 11), Richard Tyrrell lived to be 97, after working in the trade for his whole life.

2 First published in the weekly serial version of *London Labour*, spanning what was likely No. 45, 18 October 1851, and No. 46, 25 October 1851.

3 The Select Committee on Smoke Prevention, 1843, was "appointed to inquire into the Means and the Expediency of preventing the Nuisance of Smoke arising from Fires or Furnaces."

There are two kinds of smoke from the ordinary materials of combustion—(A) *Opaque*, or black smoke; (B) *Transparent*, or invisible smoke.

A. The *Opaque* smoke, though the most offensive and annoying from its dirtying properties, is, like the muddiest water, the least injurious to animal or vegetable health. It consists of the particles of unconsumed carbon which have not been deposited in the form of soot in the flue or chimney. This is the black smoke which will be further described.

B. *Transparent* smoke is composed of gases which are for the most part invisible, such as carbonic acid and carbonic oxide; also of sulphurous acid, but smokes with that component are both visible and invisible. The sulphurous acid is said by Professor Brande[1] to destroy vegetation, for it has long been a cause of wonder why vegetation in towns did not flourish, since carbonic acid (which is so largely produced from the action of our fires) is the vital air of trees, shrubs, and plants.[2]

I may here observe, that several of the scientific men who gave the results of years of observation and study in their evidence to the Committee of the House of Commons, remarked on the popular misunderstanding of what smoke was, it being generally regarded as something *visible*. But in the composition of smoke, it appears, one product may be visible, and another invisible, and both offensive; while "occasionally you may have from the same materials varieties of products, all invisible, according to the manner to which they are supplied with air."

---

1 Likely chemist William Thomas Brande (1788–1866).

2 [Mayhew's note:] It has been notorious for many years, that flowers will not bloom in any natural luxuriance and that fruit will not properly ripen, in the heart of the city. Whilst this is an unquestionable fact, it is also a fact, that greatly as suburban dwellings have increased, and truly as London may be said to have "gone into the country," the greater quantity of the large, excellent, unfailing, and cheap supply of the fruits and vegetables in the London "green" markets are grown within a circle of from ten to twelve miles from St. Paul's. In the course of my inquiries (in the series of letters on Labour and the Poor in the *Morning Chronicle*) into the supply, &c., to the "green markets" of the metropolis, I was told by an experienced market-gardener, who had friends and connections in several of the suburbs, that he fancied, and others in the trade were of the same opinion, that no gardening could be anything but a failure if attempted within "where the fogs went." My informant explained to me that the fogs, so peculiar to London, did not usually extend beyond three or four miles from the heart of the city. He was satisfied, he said, that within half a mile or so of this reach of fog the gardener's labours might be crowned with success. He knew nothing of any scientific reason for his opinion, but as far as a purely London fog extended (without regard to any mist pervading the whole country as well as the neighbourhood of the capital), he thought it was the boundary within which there could be no proper growth of fruit or flowers. That the London fog has its *limits* as regards the manifestation of its greatest density, there can be no doubt. My informant was frequently asked, when on his way home, by omnibus drivers and others whom he knew, and met on their way to town a few miles from it: "How's the fog, sir? *How far?*" [...]

[...]

What may be called the *peculiarities* of a smoky and sooty atmosphere are of course more strongly developed in London than elsewhere, as the following curious statements show:—

Dr. Reid,[1] in describing metropolitan smoke, spoke of "those black portions of soot that every one is familiar with, which annoy us, for instance, at the Houses of Parliament to such an extent that I have been under the necessity of putting up a veil, about 40 feet long and 12 feet deep, on which, on a single evening, taking the worst kind of weather for the production of soot, we can count occasionally 200,000 visible portions of soot excluded at a single sitting. We count with the naked eye the number of pieces entangled upon a square inch. I have examined the amount deposited on different occasions in different parts of London at the tops of some houses; and on one occasion at the Horse Guards[2] the amount of soot deposited was so great, that it formed a complete and continuous film, so that when I walked upon it I saw the impression of my foot left as distinctly on that occasion as when snow lies upon the ground. The film was exceedingly thin, but I could discover no want of continuity. On other occasions I have noticed in London that the quantity that escapes into individual houses is so great that in a single night I have observed a mixture of soot and of hoar frost collecting at the edge of the door, and forming a stripe three-quarters of an inch in breadth, and bearing an exact resemblance to a pepper and salt gray cloth. Those that I refer to are extreme occasions."

Mr. Booth[3] mentioned, that one of the gardeners of the Botanic Garden in the Regent's-park, could tell the number of days sheep had been in the park from the blackness of their wool, its oleaginous power retaining the black.

Dr. Ure[4] informed the Committee that a column of smoke might be seen extending in different directions round London, according to the way of the wind, for a distance of from 20 to 30 miles; and that Sir William Herschel[5] had told him that when the wind blew from London he could not use his great telescope at Slough.

It was stated, moreover, that when a respirator[6] is washed, the water is rendered dirty by the particles of soot adhering to the wire gauze, and which, but for this, would have entered the mouth.

---

1 David Boswell Reid, Esq. MD (1805–63) provided testimony to the Select Committee on Smoke Prevention in 1843. A physician and chemist, Reid was well known for his work in sanitation and ventilation.

2 Located in Westminster, the Horse Guards building provided barracks and stables for the Household Cavalry of the British Army.

3 Abraham Booth was a professor and teacher of chemistry.

4 Andrew Ure, Esq. MD, FRS (1778–1857) was a prominent Scottish physician and professor of chemistry.

5 Herschel (1738–1822) was a British astronomer and composer.

6 Invented by Julius Jeffreys (1800–77) in 1835, the respirator warmed air as it was inhaled, by passing it through metal mesh.

Professor Brande said, on the subject of the public health being affected by smoke, "I cannot say that my opinion is that smoke produces any unhealthiness in London; it is a great nuisance certainly; but I do not think we have any good evidence that it produces disease of any kind."

"This Committee," said Mr. Beckett,[1] "have been told that, by the mechanical effects of smoke upon the chest and lungs, disease takes place; that is, by swallowing a certain quantity of smoke the respiratory organs are injured; can you give any opinion upon that?"—"One would conceive," replied the Professor, "that that is the case; but when we compare the health of London with that of any other town or place where they are comparatively free or quite free from smoke, we do not find that difference which we should expect in regard to health."

Mr. E. Solly, lecturer on chemistry at the Royal Institution,[2] expressed his opinion of the effect of smoke upon the health of towns:—

"My impression is," he said, "that it produces decided evil in two or three ways: first, mechanically; the solid black carbonaceous matter produces a great deal of disease; it occasions dirt amongst the lower orders, and, if they will not take pains to remove it, it engenders disease. If we could do away the smoke nuisance, I believe a great deal of that disease would be put an end to. But there is another point, and that is, the bad effects produced by the gases, sulphurous acid and other compounds of that nature, which are given out. If we do away with smoke, we shall still have those gases; and I have no doubt that those gases produce a great part of the disease that is produced by smoke."

On the other hand Dr. Reid thought that smoke was more injurious from the dirt it created than from causing impurity in the atmosphere, although "it was obvious enough that the inspiration of a sooty atmosphere must be injurious to persons of a delicate constitution." Dr. Ure pronounced smoke, in the common sense of visible black smoke, unwholesome, but "not so eminently as the French imagine."

Many witnesses stated their conviction that where poor people resided amongst smoke, they felt it impossible to preserve cleanliness in their persons or their dwellings, and that made them careless of their homes and indifferent to a decency of appearance, so that the public-house, and places where cleanliness and propriety were in no great estimation, became places of frequent resort, on the plain principle that if a man's home were uncomfortable, he was not likely to stay in it.

"I think," said Mr. Booth, "one great effect of the evil of smoke is upon the dwellings of the poor; it renders them less attentive to their personal appearance, and, in consequence, to their social condition."

---

1 William Beckett, Esq. MP (1784–1863) was a Member for Leeds and testified on behalf of his constituents.

2 Edward Solly, Esq. FRS (1819–86). The Royal Institution of Great Britain was founded by prominent British scientists in 1799 to promote scientific research and education.

It was also stated that there were "certain districts inhabited by the poor, where they will not hang out their clothes to be cleansed; they say it is of no use to do it, they will become dirty as before, and consequently they do not have their clothes washed." The districts specified as presenting this characteristic are St. George's-in-the-East and the neighbourhood of Old-street, St. Luke's.

It must not be lost sight of, that whatever evils, moral or physical, without regarding merely pecuniary losses, are inflicted by the excess of smoke, they fall upon the poor, and almost solely on the poor. It is the poor who must reside, as was said, and with a literality not often applicable to popular phrases, "in the thick of it," and consequently there must either be increased washing or increased dirt.

[...]

Of the General Characteristics of the Working Chimney-Sweepers.[1]

THERE are many reasons why the chimney-sweepers have ever been a distinct and peculiar class. They have long been looked down upon as the lowest order of workers, and treated with contumely by those who were but little better than themselves. The peculiar nature of their work giving them not only a filthy appearance, but an offensive smell, of itself, in a manner, prohibited them from associating with other working men; and the natural effect of such proscription has been to compel them to herd together apart from others, and to acquire habits and peculiarities of their own widely differing from the characteristics of the rest of the labouring classes.

Sweepers, however, have not from this cause generally been an hereditary race—that is, they have not become sweepers from father to son for many generations. Their numbers were, in the days of the climbing boys, in most intances increased by parish apprentices, the parishes usually adopting that mode as the cheapest and easiest of freeing themselves from a part of the burden of juvenile pauperism. The climbing boys, but more especially the unfortunate parish apprentices, were almost always cruelly used, starved, beaten, and over-worked by their masters, and treated as outcasts by all with whom they came in contact: there can be no wonder, then, that, driven in this manner from all other society, they gladly availed themselves of the companionship of their fellow-sufferers; quickly imbibed all their habits and peculiarities; and, perhaps, ended by becoming themselves the most tyrannical masters to those who might happen to be placed under their charge.

Notwithstanding the disrepute in which sweepers have ever been held, there are many classes of workers beneath them in intelligence. All the

1 First published in the weekly serial version of *London Labour*, likely in No. 47, 1 November 1851.

tribe of finders and collectors (with the exception of the dredgermen, who are an observant race, and the sewer-hunters, who, from the danger of their employment, are compelled to exercise their intellects) are far inferior to them in this respect; and they are clever fellows compared to many of the dustmen and scavagers.[1] The great mass of the agricultural labourers are known to be almost as ignorant as the beasts they drive; but the sweepers, from whatever cause it may arise, are known, in many instances, to be shrewd, intelligent, and active.

But there is much room for improvement among the operative chimney-sweepers. Speaking of the men generally, I am assured that there is scarcely one out of ten who can either read or write. One man in Chelsea informed me that some ladies, in connection with the Rev. Mr. Cadman's church,[2] made an attempt to instruct the sweepers of the neighbourhood in reading and writing; but the master sweepers grew jealous, and became afraid lest their men should get too knowing for them. When the time came, therefore, for the men to prepare for the school, the masters always managed to find out some job which prevented them from attending at the appointed time, and the consequence was that the benevolent designs of the ladies were frustrated.

The sweepers, as a class, in almost all their habits, bear a strong resemblance to the costermongers. The habit of going about in search of their employment has, of itself, implanted in many of them the wandering propensity peculiar to street people. Many of the better-class costermongers have risen into coal-shed men and greengrocers, and become settled in life; in like manner the better-class sweepers have risen to be masters, and, becoming settled in a locality, have gradually obtained the trade of the neighbourhood; then, as their circumstances improved, they have been able to get horses and carts, and become nightmen;[3] and there are many of them at this moment men of wealth, comparatively speaking. The great body of them, however, retain in all their force their original characteristics; the masters themselves, although shrewd and sensible men, often betray their want of education, and are in no way particular as to their expressions, their language being made up, in a great measure, of the terms peculiar to the costermongers, especially the denominations of the various sorts of money. I met with some sweepers, however, whose language was that in ordinary use, and their manners not vulgar. I might specify one, who, although a workhouse orphan and apprentice, a harshly-

1 Mayhew alternates between scavengers and scavagers, the latter being an older variant of the word that referred to someone whose official duty was to clean the streets.

2 Likely a reference to William Cadman, pastor of St. George the Martyr in the Borough district of South London. Cadman founded several ragged schools in the area around St. George. See p. 185, note 1.

3 Workers who collected and carried human waste from cesspools. Such work was legislated to be performed only after midnight. See "Of the London Dustmen, Nightmen, Sweeps, and Scavengers," p. 186.

treated climbing-boy, is now prospering as a sweeper and nightman, is a regular attendant at all meetings to promote the good of the poor, and a zealous ragged-school[1] teacher, and teetotaller.

When such men are met with, perhaps the class cannot be looked upon as utterly cast away, although the need of reformation in the habits of the working sweepers is extreme, and especially in respect of drinking, gambling, and dirt. The journeymen (who have often a good deal of leisure) and the single-handed men are—in the great majority of cases at least—addicted to drinking, beer being their favourite beverage, either because it is the cheapest or that they fancy it the most suitable for washing away the sooty particles which find their way to their throats. These men gamble also, but with this proviso—they seldom play for money; but when they meet in their usual houses of resort—two famous ones are in Back C—— lane and S—— street, Whitechapel—they spend their time and what money they may have in tossing for beer, till they are either drunk or penniless. Such men present the appearance of having just come out of a chimney. There seems never to have been any attempt made by them to wash the soot off their faces. I am informed that there is scarcely one of them who has a second shirt or any change of clothes, and that they wear their garments night and day till they literally rot, and drop in fragments from their backs. Those who are not employed as journeymen by the masters are frequently whole days without food, especially in summer, when the work is slack; and it usually happens that those who are what is called "knocking about on their own account" seldom or never have a farthing in their pockets in the morning, and may, perhaps, have to travel till evening before they get a threepenny or sixpenny chimney to sweep. When night comes, and they meet their companions, the tossing and drinking again commences; they again get drunk; roll home to wherever it may be, to go through the same routine on the morrow; and this is the usual tenour of their lives, whether earning 5*s.* or 20*s.* a week.

[...]

I had occasion to visit the house of one of the persons from whom I obtained much information. He is a master in a small way, a sensible man, and was one of the few who are teetotallers. His habitation, though small—being a low house only one story high—was substantially furnished with massive mahogany chairs, table, chests of drawers, &c., while on each side of the fire-place, which was distinctly visible from the street over a hall door, were two buffets, with glass doors, well filled with glass and china vessels. It was a wet night, and a fire burned brightly in the stove, by the light of which might be seen the master of the establishment sitting on one side, while his wife and daughter occupied the other; a neighbour sat before the fire with his back to the door, and altogether it

1 See p. 185, note 1.

struck me as a comfortable-looking evening party. They were resting and chatting quietly together after the labour of the day, and everything betokened the comfortable circumstances in which the man, by sobriety and industry, had been able to place himself. Yet this man had been a climbing-boy, and one of the unfortunates who had lost his parents when a child, and was apprenticed by the parish to this business. From him I learned that his was not a solitary instance of teetotalism (I have before spoken of another); that, in fact, there were some more, and one in particular, named Brown, who was a good speaker, and devoted himself during his leisure hours at night in advocating the principles which by experience he had found to effect such great good to himself; but he also informed me that the majority of the others were a drunken and dissipated crew, sunk to the lowest degree of misery, yet recklessly spending every farthing they could earn in the public-house.

Different in every respect was another house which I visited in the course of my inquiries, in the neighbourhood of H—street, Bethnal-green. The house was rented by a sweeper, a master on his own account, and every room in the place was let to sweepers and their wives or women, which, with these men, often signify one and the same thing. The inside of the house looked as dark as a coal-pit; there was an insufferable smell of soot, always offensive to those unaccustomed to it; and every person and every thing which met the eye, even to the caps and gowns of the women, seemed as if they had just been steeped in Indian ink. In one room was a sweep and his woman quarrelling. As I opened the door I caught the words, "I'm d——d if I has it any longer. I'd see you b——y well d——d first, and you knows it." The savage was intoxicated, for his red eyes flashed through his sooty mask with drunken excitement, and his matted hair, which looked as if it had never known a comb, stood out from his head like the whalebone ribs of his own machine.[1] "B——y Bet," as he called her, did not seem a whit more sober than her man; and the shrill treble of her voice was distinctly audible till I turned the corner of the street, whither I was accompanied by the master of the house, to whom I had been recommended by one of the fraternity as an intelligent man, and one who knew "a thing or two." "You see," he said, as we turned the corner, "there isn't no use a talkin' to them ere fellows—they're all tosticated now, and they doesn't care nothink for nobody; but they'll be quiet enough to-morrow, 'cept they yarns somethink, and if they do then they'll be just as bad to-morrow night. They're a awful lot, and nobody ill niver do anythink with them." This man was not by any means in such easy circumstances as the master first mentioned. He was merely a man working for himself, and unable to employ any one else in the business; as is customary with some of these people, he had taken the

1 The 1830s saw the production of chimney-sweeping machines, which reduced the need for climbing boys to enter chimneys. Like earlier tools, their brushes were made from whale bones.

house he had shown me to let to lodgers of his own class, making something by so doing; though, if his own account be correct, I'm at a loss to imagine how he contrived even to get his rent. From him I obtained the following statement:—

"Yes, I was a climbing-boy, and sarved a rigler printiceship for seven years. I was out on my printiceship when I was fourteen. Father was a silk-weaver, and did all he knew to keep me from being a sweep, but I would be a sweep, and nothink else." [This is not so very uncommon a predilection, strange as it may seem.] "So father, when he saw it was no use, got me bound printice. Father's alive now, and near 90 years of age. I don't know why I wished to be a sweep, 'cept it was this—there was sweeps always lived about here, and I used to see the boys with lots of money a tossin' and gamblin', and wished to have money too. You see they got money where they swept the chimneys; they used to get 2*d.* or 3*d.* for theirselves in a day, and sometimes 6*d.* from the people of the house, and that's the way they always had plenty of money. I niver thought anythink of the climbing; it wasn't so bad at all as some people would make you believe. There are two or three ways of climbing. In wide flues you climb with your elbows and your legs spread out, your feet pressing against the sides of the flue; but in narrow flues, such as nine-inch ones, you must slant it; you must have your sides in the angles, it's wider there, and go up just that way." [Here he threw himself into position—placing one arm close to his side, with the palm of the hand turned outwards, as if pressing the side of the flue, and extending the other arm high above his head, the hand apparently pressing in the same manner.] "There," he continued, "that's slantin'. You just put yourself in that way, and see how small you make yourself. I niver got to say stuck myself, but a many of them did; yes, and were taken out dead. They were smothered for want of air, and the fright, and a stayin' so long in the flue; you see the waistband of their trowsers sometimes got turned down in the climbing, and in narrow flues, when not able to get it up, then they stuck. I had a boy once—we were called to sweep a chimney down at Poplar. When we went in he looked up the flues, 'Well, what is it like?' I said. 'Very narrow,' says he, 'don't think I can get up there'; so after some time we gets on top of the house, and takes off the chimney-pot, and has a look down—it was wider a' top, and I thought as how he could go down. 'You had better buff it, Jim,' says I. I suppose you know what that means; but Jim wouldn't do it, and kept his trowsers on. So down he goes, and gets on very well till he comes to the shoulder of the flue, and then he couldn't stir. He shouts down, 'I'm stuck.' I shouts up and tells him what to do. 'Can't move,' says he, 'I'm stuck hard and fast.' Well, the people of the house got fretted like, but I says to them, 'Now my boy's stuck, but for Heaven's sake don't make a word of noise; don't say a word, good or bad, and I'll see what I can do.' So I locks the door, and buffs it, and forces myself up till I could reach him with my hand, and as soon as he got his foot on my hand he begins to prize himself up, and gets loosened, and comes out at the top again. I was stuck myself, but I was stronger nor he, and I manages to get out again. Now I'll

THE SWEEPS' HOME.

(*From a sketch taken on the spot.*)

Fig. 10: "The Sweeps' Home."

be bound to say if there was another master there as would kick up a row and a-worrited, that ere boy 'ud a niver come out o' that ere flue alive. There was a many o' them lost their lives in that way. Most all the printices used to come from the 'House' (workhouse). There was nobody to care for them, and some masters used them very bad. I was out of my time at fourteen, and began to get too stout to go up the flues; so after knockin' about for a year or so, as I could do nothink else, I goes to sea on board a man-o'-war, and was away four year. Many of the boys, when they got too big and useless, used to go to sea in them days—they couldn't do nothink else. Yes, many of them went for sodgers;[1] and I know some who went for Gipsies, and others who went for play-actors, and a many who got on to be swell-mobsmen,[2] and thieves, and housebreakers, and the like o' that ere. There ain't nothink o' that sort a-goin' on now since the Ack of Parliament."[3] [...]

[...]

Of the Subterranean Character of the Sewers.[4]

In my inquiries among that curious body of men, the "Sewer Hunters," I found them make light of any danger, their principal fear being from the attacks of rats in case they became isolated from the gang with whom they searched in common, while they represented the odour as a mere nothing in the way of unpleasantness. But these men pursued only known and (by them) beaten tracks at low water, avoiding any deviation, and so becoming but partially acquainted with the character and direction of the sewers. And had it been otherwise, they are not a class competent to describe what they saw, however keen-eyed after silver spoons.

The following account is derived chiefly from official sources. I may premise that where the deposit is found the greatest, the sewer is in the worst state. This deposit, I find it repeatedly stated, is of a most miscellaneous character. Some of the sewers, indeed, are represented as the dust-bins and dung-hills of the immediate neighbourhood. The deposit has been found to comprise all the ingredients from the breweries, the gas-works, and the several chemical and mineral manufactories; dead dogs, cats, kittens, and rats; offal from slaughter-houses, sometimes even including the entrails of the animals; street-pavement dirt of every variety; vegetable refuse; stable-dung; the refuse of pig-styes; night-soil; ashes; tin

1 Soldiers.

2 Swell mobs were gangs of thieves who dressed in fashionable clothing to avoid suspicion and detection.

3 Several parliamentary acts passed in the nineteenth century attempted to regulate the chimney-sweeping trade and mitigate its worst effects on children. The speaker is likely referring to acts passed in either 1834 or 1840, which prohibited the employment of child sweeps under a certain age. The enforcement of these acts was rare and uneven.

4 First published in the weekly serial version of *London Labour*, No. 48, 8 November 1851.

kettles and pans (pansherds); broken stoneware, as jars, pitchers, flower-pots, &c.; bricks; pieces of wood; rotten mortar and rubbish of different kinds; and even rags. Our criminal annals of the previous century show that often enough the bodies of murdered men were thrown into the Fleet[1] and other ditches, then the open sewers of the metropolis, and if found washed into the Thames, they were so stained and disfigured by the foulness of the contents of these ditches, that recognition was often impossible, so that there could be but one verdict returned—"Found drowned." Clothes stripped from a murdered person have been, it was authenticated on several occasions in Old Bailey[2] evidence, thrown into the open sewer ditches, when torn and defaced, so that they might not supply evidence of identity. So close is the connection between physical filthiness in public matters and moral wickedness.

The following particulars show the characteristics of the underground London of the sewers. The subterranean surveys were made after the commissions were consolidated.[3]

"An old sewer, running between Great Smith-street and St. Ann-street (Westminster), is a curiosity among sewers, although it is probably only one instance out of many similar constructions that will be discovered in the course of the subterranean survey. The bottom is formed of planks laid upon transverse timbers, 6 inches by 6 inches, about 3 feet apart. The size of the sewer varies in width from 2 to 6 feet, and from 4 to 5 feet in height. The inclination of the bottom is very irregular: there are jumps up at two or three places, and it contains a deposit of filth averaging 9 inches in depth, the sickening smell from which escapes into the houses and yards that drain into it. In many places the side walls have given way for lengths of 10 and 15 feet. Across this sewer timbers have been laid, upon which the external wall of a workshop has been built; the timbers are in a decaying state, and should they give way, the wall will fall into the sewer."

From the further accounts of this survey, I find that a sewer from the Westminster Workhouse, which was of all shapes and sizes, was in so wretched a condition that the leveller could scarcely work for the thick scum that covered the glasses of the spirit-level in a few minutes after being wiped. "At the outfall into the Dean-street sewer, it is 3 feet 6 inches by 2 feet 8 inches for a short length. From the end of this, a wide sewer branches in each direction at right angles, 5 feet 8 inches by 5 feet 5 inches. Proceeding to the eastward about 30 feet, a chamber is reached about 30 feet in length, from the roof of which hangings of putrid matter *like stalactites* descend *three feet in length*. At the end of this chamber, the sewer passes under the public privies, the ceilings of which can be seen from it. Beyond this it is not possible to go."

[...]

---

1 See p. 179, note 2.

2 The central criminal court of England and Wales, located next to Newgate prison.

3 See p. 149, note 1.

THE RAT-CATCHERS OF THE SEWERS.

[*From a Daguerreotype by* BEARD.]

Fig. 11: "The Rat-Catchers of the Sewers."

Crossing-Sweepers.

Crossing-Sweepers.[1]

THAT portion of the London street-folk who earn a scanty living by sweeping crossings constitute a large class of the Metropolitan poor. We can scarcely walk along a street of any extent, or pass through a square of the least pretensions to "gentility," without meeting one or more of these private scavengers. Crossing-sweeping seems to be one of those occupations which are resorted to as an excuse for begging; and, indeed, as many expressed it to me, "it was the last chance left of obtaining an honest crust."

The advantages of crossing-sweeping as a means of livelihood seem to be:

1st, the smallness of the capital required in order to commence the business;

2ndly, the excuse the apparent occupation it affords for soliciting gratuities without being considered in the light of a street-beggar;

And 3rdly, the benefits arising from being constantly seen in the same place, and thus exciting the sympathy of the neighbouring householders, till small weekly allowances or "pensions" are obtained.

The first curious point in connexion with this subject is what constitutes the "*property*," so to speak, in a crossing, or the *right* to sweep a pathway across a certain thoroughfare. A nobleman, who has been one of her Majesty's Ministers, whilst conversing with me on the subject of crossing-sweepers, expressed to me the curiosity he felt on the subject, saying that he had noticed some of the sweepers in the same place for years. "What were the rights of property," he asked, "in such cases, and what constituted the title that such a man had to a particular crossing? Why did not the stronger sweeper supplant the weaker? Could a man bequeath a crossing to a son, or present it to a friend? How did he first obtain the spot?"

The answer is, that crossing-sweepers are, in a measure, under the protection of the police. If the accommodation afforded by a well-swept pathway is evident, the policeman on that district will protect the original sweeper of the crossing from the intrusion of a rival. I have, indeed, met with instances of men who, before taking to a crossing, have asked for and obtained permission of the police; and one sweeper, who gave me his statement, had even solicited the authority of the inhabitants before he applied to the inspector at the station-house.

---

1 Date of first publication uncertain, but likely November or December of 1851. This section on crossing sweepers was likely written by Henry Mayhew's brother Augustus Mayhew (1826–75). In Augustus's 1858 novel *Paved with Gold*, he claims that his investigations on crossing sweepers "were originally undertaken by me at the request of my brother, Mr. Henry Mayhew, and will, I believe, form part of his invaluable work on 'London Labour and the Poor.'"

If a crossing have been vacant for some time, another sweeper may take to it; but should the original proprietor again make his appearance, the officer on duty will generally re-establish him. One man to whom I spoke, had fixed himself on a crossing which for years another sweeper had kept clean on the Sunday morning only. A dispute ensued; the one claimant pleading his long Sabbath possession, and the other his continuous every-day service. The quarrel was referred to the police, who decided that he who was oftener on the ground was the rightful owner; and the option was given to the former possessor, that if he would sweep there every day the crossing should be his.

[...]

The irregular sweepers mostly consist of boys and girls who have formed themselves into a kind of company, and come to an agreement to work together on the same crossings. The principal resort of these is about Trafalgar-square, where they have seized upon some three or four crossings, which they visit from time to time in the course of the day.

One of these gangs I found had appointed its king and captain, though the titles were more honorary than privileged. They had framed their own laws respecting each one's right to the money he took, and the obedience to these laws was enforced by the strength of the little fraternity.

One or two girls whom I questioned, told me that they mixed up ballad-singing or lace-selling with crossing-sweeping, taking to the broom only when the streets were wet and muddy. These children are usually sent out by their parents, and have to carry home at night their earnings. A few of them are orphans with a lodging-house for a home.

Taken as a class, crossing-sweepers are among the most honest of the London poor. They all tell you that, without a good character and "the respect of the neighbourhood," there is not a living to be got out of the broom. Indeed, those whom I found best-to-do in the world were those who had been longest at their posts.

Among them are many who have been servants until sickness or accident deprived them of their situations, and nearly all of them have had their minds so subdued by affliction, that they have been tamed so as to be incapable of mischief.

[...]

Gander—The "Captain" of the Boy Crossing-Sweepers.[1]

GANDER, the captain of the gang of boy crossing-sweepers, was a big lad of sixteen, with a face devoid of all expression, until he laughed, when the cheeks, mouth, and forehead instantly became crumpled up with a won-

1 Date of first publication uncertain, but likely November or December of 1851.

derful quantity of lines and dimples. His hair was cut short, and stood up in all directions, like the bristles of a hearth-broom, and was a light dust tint, matching with the hue of his complexion, which also, from an absence of washing, had turned to a decided drab, or what house-painters term a stone-colour.

He spoke with a lisp, occasioned by the loss of two of his large front teeth, which allowed the tongue as he talked to appear through the opening in a round nob like a raspberry.

The boy's clothing was in a shocking condition. He had no coat, and his blue-striped shirt was as dirty as a French-polisher's rags, and so tattered, that the shoulder was completely bare, while the sleeve hung down over the hand like a big bag.

From the fish-scales on the sleeves of his coat, it had evidently once belonged to some coster in the herring line. The nap was all worn off, so that the lines of the web were showing like a coarse carpet; and instead of buttons, string had been passed through holes pierced at the side.

Of course he had no shoes on, and his black trousers, which, with the grease on them, were gradually assuming a tarpaulin look, were fastened over one shoulder by means of a brace and bits of string.

During his statement, he illustrated his account of the tumbling backwards—the "caten-wheeling"—with different specimens of the art, throwing himself about on the floor with an ease and almost grace, and taking up so small a space of the ground for the performance, that his limbs seemed to bend as though his bones were flexible like cane.

"To tell you the blessed truth, I can't say the last shilling I handled."

"Don't you go a-believing on him," whispered another lad in my ear, whilst Gander's head was turned: "he took thirteenpence last night, he did."

It was perfectly impossible to obtain from this lad any account of his average earnings. The other boys in the gang told me that he made more than any of them. But Gander, who is a thorough street-beggar, and speaks with a peculiar whine, and who, directly you look at him, puts on an expression of deep distress, seemed to have made up his mind, that if he made himself out to be in great want I should most likely relieve him—so he would not budge an inch from his twopence a-day, declaring it to be the maximum of his daily earnings.

"Ah," he continued, with a persecuted tone of voice, "if I had only got a little money, I'd be a bright youth! The first chance as I get of earning a few halfpence, I'll buy myself a coat, and be off to the country, and I'll lay something I'd soon be a gentleman then, and come home with a couple of pounds in my pocket, instead of never having ne'er a farthing, as now."

One of the other lads here exclaimed, "Don't go on like that there, Goose; you're making us out all liars to the gentleman."

The old woman also interfered. She lost all patience with Gander, and reproached him for making a false return of his income. She tried to shame him into truthfulness, by saying,—

"Look at my Johnny—my grandson, sir, he's not a quarther the Goose's size, and yet he'll bring me home his shilling, or perhaps eighteenpence or two shillings—for shame on you, Gander! Now, did you make six shillings last week?—now, speak God's truth!"

"What! six shillings?" cried the Goose—"six shillings!" and he began to look up at the ceiling, and shake his hands. "Why, I never heard of sich a sum. I did *once* see a half-crown; but I don't know as I ever touched e'er a one."

"Thin," added the old woman, indignantly, "it's because you're idle, Gander, and you don't study when you're on the crossing; but lets the gintlefolk go by without ever a word. That's what it is, sir."

The Goose seemed to feel the truth of this reproach, for he said with a sigh, "I knows I am fickle-minded."

He then continued his statement,—

"I can't tell how many brooms I use; for as fast as I gets one, it is took from me. God help me! They watch me put it away, and then up they comes and takes it. What kinds of brooms is the best? Why, as far as I am concerned, I would sooner have a stump on a dry day—it's lighter and handier to carry; but on a wet day, give me a new un.

"I'm sixteen, your honour, and my name's George Gandea, and the boys calls me 'the Goose' in consequence; for it's a nickname they gives me, though my name ain't spelt with a *har* at the end, but with a *h'ay*, so that I ain't Gand*er* after all, but Gand*ea*, which is a sell for 'em.

"God knows what I am—whether I'm h'Irish or h'*I*talian, or what; but I was christened here in London, and that's all about it.

"Father was a bookbinder. I'm sixteen now, and father turned me away when I was nine year old, for mother had been dead before that. I was told my right name by my brother-in-law, who had my register. He's a sweep, sir, by trade, and I wanted to know about my real name when I was going down to the *Waterloo*—that's a ship as I wanted to get aboard as a cabin-boy.

"I remember the fust night I slept out after father got rid of me. I slept on a gentleman's door-step, in the winter, on the 15th January. I packed my shirt and coat, which was a pretty good one, right over my ears, and then scruntched myself into a doorway, and the policeman passed by four or five times without seeing on me.

"I had a mother-in-law at the time; but father used to drink, or else I should never have been as I am; and he came home one night, and says he, 'Go out and get me a few ha'pence for breakfast,' and I said I had never been in the streets in my life, and couldn't; and, says he, 'Go out, and never let me see you no more,' and I took him to his word, and have never been near him since.

"Father lived in Barbican at that time, and after leaving him, I used to go to the Royal Exchange,[1] and there I met a boy of the name of Michael,

1 London's centre of commerce.

and he first learnt me to beg, and made me run after people, saying, 'Poor boy, sir—please give us a ha'penny to get a mossel of bread.' But as fast as I got anythink, he used to take it away, and knock me about shameful; so I left him, and then I picked up with a chap as taught me tumbling. I soon larnt how to do it, and then I used to go tumbling after busses. That was my notion all along, and I hadn't picked up the way of doing it half an hour before I was after that game.

"I took to crossings about eight year ago, and the very fust person as I asked, I had a fourpenny-piece give to me. I said to him, 'Poor little Jack, yer honour,' and, fust of all, says he, 'I haven't got no coppers,' and then he turns back and give me a fourpenny-bit. I thought I was made for life when I got that.

"I wasn't working in a gang then, but all by myself, and I used to do well, making about a shilling or ninepence a-day. I lodged in Church-lane at that time.

"It was at the time of the Shibition year (1851)[1] as these gangs come up. There was lots of boys that came out sweeping, and that's how they picked up the tumbling off me, seeing me do it up in the Park, going along to the Shibition.

"The crossing at St. Martin's Church was mine fust of all; and when the other lads come to it I didn't take no heed of 'em—only for that I'd have been a bright boy by now, but they carnied[2] me over like; for when I tried to turn 'em off they'd say, in a carnying way, 'Oh, let us stay on,' so I never took no heed of 'em.

"There was about thirteen of 'em in my gang at that time.

"They made me cap'an over the lot—I suppose because they thought I was the best tumbler of 'em. They obeyed me a little. If I told 'em not to go to any gentleman, they wouldn't, and leave him to me. There was only one feller as used to give me a share of his money, and that was for larning him to tumble—he'd give a penny or twopence, just as he yearnt a little or a lot. I taught 'em all to tumble, and we used to do it near the crossing, and at night along the streets.

"We used to be sometimes together of a day, some a-running after one gentleman, and some after another; but we seldom kept together more than three or four at a time.

"I was the fust to introduce tumbling backards, and I'm proud of it—yes, sir, I'm proud of it. There's another little chap as I'm larning to do it; but he ain't got strength enough in his arms like. ('Ah!' exclaimed a lad in the room, 'he is a one to tumble, is Johnny—go along the streets like anythink.')

"He is the King of the Tumblers," continued Gander—"King, and I'm Cap'an."

The old grandmother here joined in. "He was taught by a furreign gintleman, sir, whose wife rode at a circus. He used to come here twice a-

1 1851; the year of the Great Exhibition (see p. 116, note 1).

2 Persuaded; cajoled.

day and give him lessons in this here very room, sir. That's how he got it, sir."

"Ah," added another lad, in an admiring tone, "see him and the Goose have a race! Away they goes, but Jacky will leave him a mile behind."

The history then continued:—"People liked the tumbling backards and forards, and it got a good bit of money at fust, but they is getting tired with it, and I'm growing too hold, I fancy. It hurt me awful at fust. I tried it fust under a railway arch of the Blackwall Railway; and when I goes backards, I thought it'd cut my head open. It hurts me if I've got a thin cap on.

"The man as taught me tumbling has gone on the stage. Fust he went about with swords, fencing, in public-houses, and then he got engaged. Me and him once tumbled all round the circus at the Rotunda[1] one night wot was a benefit, and got one-and-eightpence a-piece, and all for only five hours and a half—from six to half-past eleven, and we acting and tumbling, and all that. We had plenty of beer, too. We was wery much applauded when we did it.

"I was the fust boy as ever did ornamental work in the mud of my crossings. I used to be at the crossing at the corner of Regent-suckus; and that's the wery place where I fust did it. The wery fust thing as I did was a hanker (anchor)—a regular one, with turn-up sides and a rope down the centre, and all. I sweeped it away clean in the mud in the shape of the drawing I'd seen. It paid well, for I took one-and-ninepence on it. The next thing I tried was writing 'God save the Queen'; and that, too, paid capital, for I think I got two bob. After that I tried We Har (V. R.)[2] and a star, and that was a sweep too. I never did no flowers, but I've done imitations of laurels, and put them all round the crossing, and very pretty it looked, too, at night. I'd buy a farthing candle and stick it over it, and make it nice and comfortable, so that the people could look at it easy. Whenever I see a carriage coming I used to douse the glim and run away with it, but the wheels would regularly spile the drawings, and then we'd have all the trouble to put it to rights again, and that we used to do with our hands.

"I fust learnt drawing in the mud from a man in Adelaide-street, Strand; he kept a crossing, but he only used to draw 'em close to the kerbstone. He used to keep some soft mud there, and when a carriage come up to the Lowther Arcade, after he'd opened the door and let the lady out, he would set to work, and by the time she come back he'd have some flowers, or a We Har, or whatever he liked, done in the mud, and underneath he'd write, 'Please to remember honnest hindustry.'

"I used to stand by and see him do it, until I'd learnt, and when I knowed, I went off and did it at my crossing.

"I was the fust to light up at night though, and now I wish I'd never done it, for it was that which got me turned off my crossing, and a capital

1 A circular building at Blackfriars Road, Southwark, used, variously, as a museum, lecture theatre, and music hall before it was converted to a pub in 1855.

2 The queen's initials: Victoria Regina.

one it was. I thought the gentlemen coming from the play would like it, for it looked very pretty. The policeman said I was destructing (obstructing) the thoroughfare, and making too much row there, for the people used to stop in the crossing to look, it were so pretty. He took me in charge three times on one night, cause I wouldn't go away; but he let me go again, till at last I thought he would lock me up for the night, so I hooked it.

"It was after this as I went to St. Martin's Church, and I haven't done half as well there. Last night I took three-ha'pence; but I was larking, or I might have had more."

As a proof of the very small expense which is required for the toilette of a crossing-sweeper, I may mention, that within a few minutes after Master Gander had finished his statement, he was in possession of a coat, for which he had paid the sum of fivepence.

When he brought it into the room, all the boys and the women crowded round to see the purchase.

"It's a very good un," said the Goose. "It only wants just taking up here and there; and this cuff putting to rights." And as he spoke he pointed to tears large enough for a head to be thrust through. "I've seen that coat before, sum'ares," said one of the women; "where did you get it?"

"At the chandly-shop," answered the Goose.

VOLUME 3.

The Destroyers of Vermin. A Night at Rat-Killing.[1]

CONSIDERING the immense number of rats which form an article of commerce with many of the lower orders, whose business it is to keep them for the purpose of rat matches, I thought it necessary, for the full elucidation of my subject, to visit the well-known public-house in London,[2] where, on a certain night in the week, a pit is built up, and regular rat-killing matches take place, and where those who have sporting dogs, and are anxious to test their qualities, can, after such matches are finished, purchase half a dozen or a dozen rats for them to practise upon, and judge for themselves of their dogs' "performances."

To quote the words printed on the proprietor's card, "he is always at his old house at home, as usual, to discuss the FANCY[3] generally."

I arrived at about eight o'clock at the tavern where the performances were to take place. I was too early, but there was plenty to occupy my leisure in looking at the curious scene around me, and taking notes of the habits and conversation of the customers who were flocking in.

The front of the long bar was crowded with men of every grade of society, all smoking, drinking, and talking about dogs. Many of them had brought with them their "fancy" animals, so that a kind of "canine exhibition" was going on; some carried under their arm small bull-dogs, whose flat pink noses rubbed against my arm as I passed; others had Skye-terriers, curled up like balls of hair, and sleeping like children, as they were nursed by their owners. The only animals that seemed awake, and under continual excitement, were the little brown English terriers, who, despite the neat black leathern collars by which they were held, struggled to get loose, as if they smelt the rats in the room above, and were impatient to begin the fray.

There is a business-like look about this tavern which at once lets you into the character of the person who owns it. The drinking seems to have been a secondary notion in its formation, for it is a low-roofed room without any of those adornments which are now generally considered so necessary to render a public-house attractive. The tubs where the spirits are kept are blistered with the heat of the gas, and so dirty that the once brilliant gilt hoops are now quite black.

Sleeping on an old hall-chair lay an enormous white bulldog, "a great beauty," as I was informed, with a head as round and smooth as a

---

1 A version of this text was first published in Augustus Mayhew's novel *Paved with Gold* (1858) before its appearance in Vol. 3 of *London Labour.*

2 Most likely either the Blue Anchor Tavern, Bunhill Row, or the Queen's Head Tavern, Haymarket, both owned by Jemmy Shaw, a prominent organizer of tavern dog shows and ratting events. See p. 220, note 1 for more on Shaw.

3 Dog fancying is the activity of showing and breeding dogs. In the mid-nineteenth century, dogs bred for ratting sports were shown in public houses.

clenched boxing-glove, and seemingly too large for the body. Its forehead appeared to protrude in a manner significant of water on the brain, and almost overhung the short nose, through which the animal breathed heavily. When this dog, which was the admiration of all beholders, rose up, its legs were as bowed as a tailor's, leaving a peculiar pear-shaped opening between them, which, I was informed, was one of its points of beauty. It was a white dog, with a sore look, from its being peculiarly pink round the eyes, nose, and indeed at all the edges of its body.

On the other side of the fire-place was a white bull-terrier dog, with a black patch over the eye, which gave him rather a disreputable look. This animal was watching the movements of the customers in front, and occasionally, when the entrance-door was swung back, would give a growl of inquiry as to what the fresh-comer wanted. The proprietor was kind enough to inform me, as he patted this animal's ribs, which showed like the hoops on a butter-firkin,[1] that he considered there had been a "little of the greyhound in some of his back generations."

About the walls were hung clusters of black leather collars, adorned with brass rings and clasps, and pre-eminent was a silver dog-collar, which, from the conversation of those about me, I learnt was to be the prize in a rat-match to be "killed for" in a fortnight's time.

As the visitors poured in, they, at the request of the proprietor "not to block up the bar," took their seats in the parlour, and, accompanied by a waiter, who kept shouting, "Give your orders, gentlemen," I entered the room.

I found that, like the bar, no pains had been taken to render the room attractive to the customers, for, with the exception of the sporting pictures hung against the dingy paper, it was devoid of all adornment. Over the fireplace were square glazed boxes, in which were the stuffed forms of dogs famous in their day. Pre-eminent among the prints was that representing the "Wonder" Tiny, "five pounds and a half in weight," as he appeared killing 200 rats. This engraving had a singular look, from its having been printed upon a silk handkerchief. Tiny had been a great favourite with the proprietor, and used to wear a lady's bracelet as a collar.

Among the stuffed heads was one of a white bull-dog, with tremendous glass eyes sticking out, as if it had died of strangulation. The proprietor's son was kind enough to explain to me the qualities that had once belonged to this favourite. "They've spoilt her in stuffing, sir," he said; "made her so short in the head; but she was the wonder of her day. There wasn't a dog in England as would come nigh her. There's her daughter," he added, pointing to another head, something like that of a seal, "but she wasn't reckoned half as handsome as her mother, though she was very much admired in her time.

"That there *is* a dog," he continued, pointing to one represented with a rat in its mouth, "it was as good as any in England, though it's so small.

1 A hooped wooden cask for storing butter.

I've seen her kill a dozen rats almost as big as herself, though they killed *her* at last; for sewer-rats are dreadful for giving dogs canker in the mouth, and she wore herself out with continually killing them, though we always rinsed her mouth out well with peppermint and water while she were at work. When rats bite they are pisonous, and an ulcer is formed, which we are obleeged to lance; that's what killed her."

The company assembled in "the parlour" consisted of sporting men, or those who, from curiosity, had come to witness what a rat-match was like. Seated at the same table, talking together, were those dressed in the costermonger's suit of corduroy, soldiers with their uniforms carelessly unbuttoned, coachmen in their livery, and tradesmen who had slipped on their evening frock-coats, and run out from the shop to see the sport.

The dogs belonging to the company were standing on the different tables, or tied to the legs of the forms, or sleeping in their owners' arms, and were in turn minutely criticised—their limbs being stretched out as if they were being felt for fractures, and their mouths looked into, as if a dentist were examining their teeth. Nearly all the little animals were marked with scars from bites. "Pity to bring him up to rat-killing," said one, who had been admiring a fierce-looking bull-terrier, although he did not mention at the same time what line in life the little animal ought to pursue.

At another table one man was declaring that his pet animal was the exact image of the celebrated rat-killing dog "Billy,"[1] at the same time pointing to the picture against the wall of that famous animal, "as he performed his wonderful feat of killing 500 rats in five minutes and a half."

There were amongst the visitors some French gentlemen, who had evidently witnessed nothing of the kind before; and whilst they endeavoured to drink their hot gin and water, they made their interpreter translate to them the contents of a large placard hung upon a hatpeg, and headed—

> "Every Man has his Fancy.
> RATTING SPORTS IN REALITY."

About nine o'clock the proprietor took the chair in the parlour, at the same time giving the order to "shut up the shutters in the room above, and light up the pit." This announcement seemed to rouse the spirits of the impatient assembly, and even the dogs tied to the legs of the tables ran out to the length of their leathern thongs, and their tails curled like eels, as if they understood the meaning of the words.

"Why, that's the little champion," said the proprietor, patting a dog with thighs like a grasshopper, and whose mouth opened back to its ears.

1 Billy's feat of killing five hundred rats in five and a half minutes noted here is either an exaggeration or an error, as the celebrated ratting dog's still impressive record was only one hundred rats killed in that time frame. There is little consensus in Victorian sources about what Billy's exact record was, but comparisons to Billy were widely used as a measure of rat-killing success long after his death in 1829. See p. 149, note 2.

"Well, it *is* a beauty! I wish I could gammon you to take a 'fiver' for it." Then looking round the room, he added, "Well, gents, I'm glad to see you look so comfortable."

The performances of the evening were somewhat hurried on by the entering of a young gentleman, whom the waiters called "Cap'an."

"Now, Jem,[1] when is this match coming off?" the Captain asked impatiently; and despite the assurance that they were getting ready, he threatened to leave the place if kept waiting much longer. This young officer seemed to be a great "fancier" of dogs, for he made the round of the room, handling each animal in its turn, feeling and squeezing its feet, and scrutinising its eyes and limbs with such minuteness, that the French gentlemen were forced to inquire who he was.

There was no announcement that the room above was ready, though everybody seemed to understand it; for all rose at once, and mounting the broad wooden staircase, which led to what was once the "drawing-room," dropped their shillings into the hand of the proprietor, and entered the rat-killing apartment.

"The pit," as it is called, consists of a small circus, some six feet in diameter. It is about as large as a centre flower-bed, and is fitted with a high wooden rim that reaches to elbow height. Over it the branches of a gas lamp are arranged, which light up the white painted floor, and every part of the little arena. On one side of the room is a recess, which the proprietor calls his "private box," and this apartment the Captain and his friend soon took possession of, whilst the audience generally clambered upon the tables and forms, or hung over the sides of the pit itself.

All the little dogs which the visitors had brought up with them were now squalling and barking, and struggling in their masters' arms, as if they were thoroughly acquainted with the uses of the pit; and when a rusty wire cage of rats, filled with the dark moving mass, was brought forward, the noise of the dogs was so great that the proprietor was obliged to shout out—"Now, you that have dogs *do* make 'em shut up."

The Captain was the first to jump into the pit. A man wanted to sell him a bull-terrier, spotted like a fancy rabbit, and a dozen of rats was the consequent order.

The Captain preferred pulling the rats out of the cage himself, laying hold of them by their tails and jerking them into the arena. He was cautioned by one of the men not to let them bite him, for "believe me," were the words, "you'll never forget, Cap'an; these 'ere are none of the cleanest."

Whilst the rats were being counted out, some of those that had been taken from the cage ran about the painted floor and climbed up the young officer's legs, making him shake them off and exclaim, "Get out, you

---

1 Owner of the Blue Anchor Pub and later the Queen's Head Tavern, Jemmy (Jimmy) Shaw (1815–86) was a well-known promoter of the sport of rat-baiting. See p. 217, note 2.

varmint!" whilst others of the ugly little animals sat upon their hind legs, cleaning their faces with their paws.

When the dog in question was brought forth and shown the dozen rats, he grew excited, and stretched himself in his owner's arms, whilst all the other animals joined in a full chorus of whining.

"Chuck him in," said the Captain, and over went the dog; and in a second the rats were running round the circus, or trying to hide themselves between the small openings in the boards round the pit.

Although the proprietor of the dog endeavoured to speak up for it, by declaring "it was a good 'un, and a very pretty performer," still it was evidently not worth much in a rat-killing sense; and if it had not been for his "second," who beat the sides of the pit with his hand, and shouted "Hi! hi! at 'em!" in a most bewildering manner, we doubt if the terrier would not have preferred leaving the rats to themselves, to enjoy their lives. Some of the rats, when the dog advanced towards them, sprang up in his face, making him draw back with astonishment. Others, as he bit them, curled round in his mouth and fastened on his nose, so that he had to carry them as a cat does its kittens. It also required many shouts of "Drop it—dead 'un," before he would leave those he had killed.

We cannot say whether the dog was eventually bought; but from its owner's exclaiming, in a kind of apologetic tone, "Why, he never saw a rat before in all his life," we fancy no dealings took place.

The Captain seemed anxious to see as much sport as he could, for he frequently asked those who carried dogs in their arms whether "his little 'un would kill," and appeared sorry when such answers were given as—"My dog's mouth's a little out of order, Cap'an," or "I've only tried him at very small 'uns."

One little dog was put in the pit to amuse himself with the dead bodies. He seized hold of one almost as big as himself, shook it furiously till the head thumped the floor like a drumstick, making those around shout with laughter, and causing one man to exclaim, "He's a good 'un at shaking heads and tails, ain't he?"

Preparations now began for the grand match of the evening, in which fifty rats were to be killed. The "dead 'uns" were gathered up by their tails and flung into the corner. The floor was swept, and a big flat basket produced, like those in which chickens are brought to market, and under whose iron wire top could be seen small mounds of closely packed rats.

This match seemed to be between the proprietor and his son, and the stake to be gained was only a bottle of lemonade, of which the father stipulated he should have first drink.

It was strange to observe the daring manner in which the lad introduced his hand into the rat cage, sometimes keeping it there for more than a minute at a time, as he fumbled about and stirred up with his fingers the living mass, picking out, as he had been requested, "only the big 'uns."

When the fifty animals had been flung into the pit, they gathered themselves together into a mound which reached one-third up the sides, and which reminded one of the heap of hair-sweepings in a barber's shop after a heavy day's cutting. These were all sewer and water-ditch rats, and the smell that rose from them was like that from a hot drain.

The Captain amused himself by flicking at them with his pocket handkerchief, and offering them the lighted end of his cigar, which the little creatures tamely snuffed at, and drew back from, as they singed their noses.

It was also a favourite amusement to blow on the mound of rats, for they seemed to dislike the cold wind, which sent them fluttering about like so many feathers; indeed, whilst the match was going on, whenever the little animals collected together, and formed a barricade as it were to the dog, the cry of "Blow on 'em! blow on 'em!" was given by the spectators, and the dog's second puffed at them as if extinguishing a fire, when they would dart off like so many sparks.

The company was kept waiting so long for the match to begin that the impatient Captain again threatened to leave the house, and was only quieted by the proprietor's reply of "My dear friend, be easy, the boy's on the stairs with the dog"; and true enough we shortly heard a wheezing and a screaming in the passage without, as if some strong-winded animal were being strangled, and presently a boy entered, carrying in his arms a bull-terrier in a perfect fit of excitement, foaming at the mouth and stretching its neck forward, so that the collar which held it back seemed to be cutting its throat in two.

The animal was nearly mad with rage—scratching and struggling to get loose. "Lay hold a little closer up to the head or he'll turn round and nip yer," said the proprietor to his son.

Whilst the gasping dog was fastened up in a corner to writhe its impatience away, the landlord made inquiries for a stop-watch, and also for an umpire to decide, as he added, "whether the rats were dead or alive when they're 'killed,' as Paddy says."

When all the arrangements had been made the "second" and the dog jumped into the pit, and after "letting him see 'em a bit," the terrier was let loose.

The moment the dog was "free," he became quiet in a most business-like manner, and rushed at the rats, burying his nose in the mound till he brought out one in his mouth. In a short time a dozen rats with wetted necks were lying bleeding on the floor, and the white paint of the pit became grained with blood.

In a little time the terrier had a rat hanging to his nose, which, despite his tossing, still held on. He dashed up against the sides, leaving a patch of blood as if a strawberry had been smashed there.

"He doesn't squeal, that's one good thing," said one of the lookers-on.

As the rats fell on their sides after a bite they were collected together in the centre, where they lay quivering in their death-gasps!

"Hi, Butcher! hi, Butcher!" shouted the second, "good dog! bur-r-r-r-h!" and he beat the sides of the pit like a drum till the dog flew about with new life.

"Dead 'un! drop it!" he cried, when the terrier "nosed" a rat kicking on its side, as it slowly expired of its broken neck.

"Time!" said the proprietor, when four of the eight minutes had expired, and the dog was caught up and held panting, his neck stretched out like a serpent's, staring intently at the rats which still kept crawling about.

The poor little wretches in this brief interval, as if forgetting their danger, again commenced cleaning themselves, some nibbling the ends of their tails, others hopping about, going now to the legs of the lad in the pit, and sniffing at his trousers, or, strange to say, advancing, smelling, to within a few paces of their enemy the dog.

The dog lost the match, and the proprietor, we presume, honourably paid the bottle of lemonade to his son. But he was evidently displeased with the dog's behaviour, for he said, "He won't do for me—he's not one of my sort! Here, Jim, tell Mr. G. he may have him if he likes; I won't give him house room."

A plentiful shower of halfpence was thrown into the pit as a reward for the second who had backed the dog.

A slight pause now took place in the proceedings, during which the landlord requested that the gentlemen "would give their minds up to drinking; you know the love I have for you," he added jocularly, "and that I don't care for any of you"; whilst the waiter accompanied the invitation with a cry of "Give your orders, gentlemen," and the lad with the rats asked if "any other gentleman would like any rats."

Several other dogs were tried, and amongst them one who, from the size of his stomach, had evidently been accustomed to large dinners, and looked upon rat-killing as a sport and not as a business. The appearance of this fat animal was greeted with remarks such as "Why don't you feed your dog?" and "You shouldn't give him more than five meals a-day."

Another impatient bull-terrier was thrown into the midst of a dozen rats. He did his duty so well, that the admiration of the spectators was focussed upon him.

"Ah," said one, "*he'd* do better at a hundred than twelve"; whilst another observed, "Rat-killing's *his* game, I can see"; while the landlord himself said, "He's a very pretty creetur', and I'd back him to kill against anybody's dog at eight and a half or nine."

The Captain was so startled with this terrier's "cleverness," that he vowed that if she could kill fifteen in a minute "he'd give a hundred guineas for her."

It was nearly twelve o'clock before the evening's performance concluded. Several of the spectators tried their dogs upon two or three rats, either the biggest or the smallest that could be found: and many offers as to what "he wanted for the dog," and many inquiries as to "who was its father," were made before the company broke up.

At last the landlord, finding that no "gentleman would like a few rats," and that his exhortations to "give their minds up to drinking" produced

RATTING—"THE GRAHAM ARMS," GRAHAM STREET.

[*From a Photograph.*]

Fig. 12: Ratting—"The Graham Arms," Graham Street.

no further effect upon the company, spoke the epilogue of the rat tragedies in these words;—

"Gentlemen, I give a very handsome solid silver collar to be killed for next Tuesday. Open to all the world, only they must be novice dogs, or at least such as is not considered *phee*nomenons. We shall have plenty of sport, gentlemen, and there will be loads of rat-killing. I hope to see all my kind friends, not forgetting your dogs, likewise; and may they be like the Irishman all over, who had good trouble to catch and kill 'em, and took good care they didn't come to life again. Gentlemen, there is a good parlour down-stairs, where we meets for harmony and entertainment."

Her Majesty's Bug-Destroyer.

THE vending of bug-poison in the London streets is seldom followed as a regular source of living. We have met with persons who remember to have seen men selling penny packets of vermin poison, but to find out the vendors themselves was next to an impossibility. The men seem merely to take to the business as a living when all other sources have failed. All, however, agree in acknowledging that there is such a street trade, but that the living it affords is so precarious that few men stop at it longer than two or three weeks.

Perhaps the most eminent firm of the bug-destroyers in London is that of Messrs. Tiffin and Son; but they have pursued their calling in the streets, and rejoice in the title of "Bug-Destroyers to Her Majesty and the Royal Family."

Mr. Tiffin, the senior partner in this house, most kindly obliged me with the following statement. It may be as well to say that Mr. Tiffin appears to have paid much attention to the subject of bugs, and has studied with much earnestness the natural history of this vermin.

"We can trace our business back," he said, "as far as 1695, when one of our ancestors first turned his attention to the destruction of bugs. He was a lady's stay-maker—men used to make them in those days, though, as far as that is concerned, it was a man that made my mother's dresses. This ancestor found some bugs in his house—a young colony of them, that had introduced themselves without his permission, and he didn't like their company, so he tried to turn them out of doors again, I have heard it said, in various ways. It is in history, and it has been handed down in my own family as well, that bugs were first introduced into England after the fire of London,[1] in the timber that was brought for rebuilding the city, thirty years after the fire, and it was about that time that my ancestor first discovered the colony of bugs in his house. I can't say whether he studied the subject of bug-destroying, or whether he found out his stuff by accident, but he certainly *did* invent a compound which completely destroyed the bugs, and, having been so successful in his own house, he named it to

1 See p. 167, note 2.

some of his customers who were similarly plagued, and that was the commencement of the present connexion, which has continued up to this time.

"At the time of the illumination for the Peace, I thought I must have something over my shop, that would be both suitable for the event and to my business; so I had a transparency done, and stretched on a big frame, and lit up by gas, on which was written—

MAY THE
DESTROYERS OF PEACE
BE DESTROYED BY US.
TIFFIN & SON,
BUG-DESTROYERS TO HER MAJESTY.

"Our business was formerly carried on in the Strand, where both my father and myself were born; in fact, I may say I was born to the bug business.

"I remember my father as well as possible; indeed, I worked with him for ten or eleven years. He used, when I was a boy, to go out to his work killing bugs at his customers' houses with a sword by his side and a cocked-hat and bag-wig on his head—in fact, dressed up like a regular dandy. I remember my grandmother, too, when she was in the business, going to the different houses, and seating herself in a chair, and telling the men what they were to do, to clean the furniture and wash the woodwork.

"I have customers in our books for whom our house has worked these 150 years; that is, my father and self have worked for them and their fathers. We do the work by contract, examining the house every year. It's a precaution to keep the place comfortable. You see, servants are apt to bring bugs in their boxes; and, though there may be only two or three bugs perhaps hidden in the woodwork and the clothes, yet they soon breed if left alone.

"We generally go in the spring, before the bugs lay their eggs; or, if that time passes, it ought to be done before June, before their eggs are hatched, though it's never too late to get rid of a nuisance.

"I mostly find the bugs in the bedsteads. But, if they are left unmolested, they get numerous and climb to the tops of the rooms, and about the corners of the ceilings. They colonize anywhere they can, though they're very high-minded and prefer lofty places. Where iron bedsteads are used the bugs are more in the *rooms*, and that's why such things are bad. They don't keep a bug away from the person sleeping. Bugs'll come, if they're thirty yards off.

"I knew a case of a bug who used to come every night about thirty or forty feet—it was an immense large room—from a corner of the room to visit an old lady. There was only one bug, and he'd been there for a long time. I was sent for to find him out. It took me a long time to catch him. In that instance I had to examine every part of the room, and when I got him I gave him an extra nip to serve him out. The reason why I was so bothered was, the bug had hidden itself near the window, the last place I should have thought of looking for him, for a bug never by choice faces the light; but when I came to inquire about it, I found that this old lady never rose till three o'clock in the day, and the window-curtains were always drawn, so that there was no light like.

"Lord! yes, I am often sent for to catch a single bug. I've had to go many, many miles—even 100 or 200—into the country, and perhaps catch only half-a-dozen bugs after all; but then that's all that are there, so it answers our employer's purpose as well as if they were swarming.

"I work for the upper classes only; that is, for carriage company and such-like approaching it, you know. I have noblemen's names, the first in England, on my books.

"My work is more method; and I may call it a scientific treating of the bugs rather than wholesale murder. We don't care about the thousands, it's the last bug we look for, whilst your carpenters and upholsterers leave as many behind them, perhaps, as they manage to catch."

[...]

OUR STREET FOLK.
I. Street Exhibitors.
Exhibitor of the Microscope.

"I EXHIBIT with a microscope that I wouldn't take fifty guineas for, because it suits my purpose, and it is of the finest quality. I earn my living with it. If I were to sell it, it wouldn't fetch more than 15*l*. It was presented to me by my dear sister, who went to America and died there. I'll show you that it is a valuable instrument. I'll tell you that one of the best lens-makers in the trade looked through it, and so he said, 'I think I can improve it for you'; and he made me a present of a lens, of extreme high power, and the largest aperture of magnifying power that has ever been exhibited. I didn't know him at the time. He did it by kindness. He said, after looking through, 'It's very good for what it professes, but I'll make you a present of a lens made out of the best Swiss metal.' And he did so from the interest he felt in seeing such kinds of exhibitions in the streets. With the glass he gave me I can see cheese-mites as distinctly as possible, with their eight legs and transparent bodies, and heads shaped like a hedgehog's. I see their jaw moving as they eat their food, and can see them lay their eggs, which are as perfect as any fowl's, but of a bright blue colour; and I can also see them perform the duties of nature. I can also see them carry their young on their backs, showing that they have affection for their offspring. They lay their eggs through their ribs, and you can tell when they are going to lay for there is a bulging out just by the hips. They don't sit on their eggs, but they roll them about in action till they bring forth their object. A million of these mites can walk across a flea's back, for by Lardner's micrometer[1] the surface of a flea's back measures 24 inches from the proboscis to the posterior. The micrometer is an instrument used for determining microscopic power, and it is all graduated to a scale. By Lardner's micrometer the mite looks about the size of a large black-beetle, and then it is magnified 100,000 times. This will give you some idea of the power and value of my instrument. Three hundred gentlemen have viewed through it in one week, and each one delighted; so much so, that many have given double the money I have asked (which was a penny), such was the satisfaction my instrument gave.

[...]

"I was apprenticed when I was 13 years of age to a shoemaker, who was a profound philosopher, and very fond of making experiments and of lecturing on various branches of science. I could produce bills—I have them at home—such as that at the Friar's-mount Sunday-school,[2] some six or seven years ago, where it states that William Knock,[3] minister and lecturer, will lecture on zoology and natural history. He's about 70 now. Electricity is his favourite science. Whilst I was his apprentice, he had an observatory built at the top of his house in Underwood-street, Spitalfields, for the purpose of taking astronomical observations. My being in his house, and seeing him so busy with his instruments, gave me a great taste for science. I was his assistant when he went lecturing. I was apprenticed with him for five years. He was a kind and good master, and very affectionate. He encouraged me in my scientific studies, and gave me access to his library, which was immense, and consisted of 3000 volumes. Amongst other employment I used to copy out sermons for him, and he gave me a penny each, which by saving up enabled me to buy a watch of him for 5*l.* 5*s.* He was a shoemaker and manufacturer of ladies and children's boots and shoes, so that he might have made from his 2*l.* to 3*l.* a-week, for he was not a journeyman, but an employer. [...]

"I began my street-life with exhibiting a telescope, and here is the origin of my doing so. I had a sister living at the west-end of the town who was a professed cook, and I used to visit her three times a-week. One night I saw a man in the Regent-circus exhibiting a telescope. I went up to him, and I said, 'Sir, what is the object to-night?' And he told me it was Jupiter. I was very much interested with looking at Jupiter, and I stopped with that man for two hours, conversing with him, and I saw exactly how much he took. Then I thought, 'Why shouldn't I do this?' So I wrote to my brother-in-law, and I told him this man was taking at the rate of 1*d.* per minute,

1 Presumably named after Dionysius Lardner (1793–1859), author and lecturer who popularized scientific and mathematical ideas.

2 Located on Church Street in Bethnal Green, and one of thousands of Sunday schools that instructed London's children in both religious and academic subjects. The schools also hosted annual meetings and lectures.

3 Unknown.

and I offered, if he would provide me with a telescope, that I should be very happy and contented to take half of the receipts as my share, and give him the other for the use of his instrument. He did so, and bought a telescope which cost him 14*l*. I took up my stand on London-bridge, and did very well, taking on the average 6*s*. a-night. I gave up the telescope for this reason,—my brother-in-law was going to America, and was anxious to call in all his money. The telescope was sold, and my sister, the professed cook, fearing that I should be left without a means of living, bought for me a microscope out of her own earnings, which cost her 5*l*. She said to me, 'The microscope is better than the telescope, for the nights are so uncertain.' She was quite right, for when the telescopes have been idle for three months at a time, I can exhibit my microscope day and night. She gave it to me as a mark of her respect. She died in America, just after she arrived. That instrument has enabled me to support an afflicted and aged mother, and to bury her comfortably when she died.

"My microscope contains six objects, which are placed on a wheel at the back, which I turn round in succession. The objects are in cell-boxes of glass. The objects are all of them familiar to the public, and are as follows:—1. The flea. 2. The human hair, or the hair of the head. 3. A section of the old oak tree. 4. The animalculæ[1] in water. 5. Cheese-mites. And 6. The transverse section of cane used by schoolmasters for the correction of boys.

"I always take up my stand in the day-time in Whitechapel, facing the London Hospital, being a large open space, and favourable for the solar rays—for I light up the instrument by the direct rays of the sun. At night-time I am mostly to be found on Westminster-bridge, and then I light up with the best sperm oil there is. I am never interfered with by the police; on the contrary, they come and have a look, and admire and recommend, such is the interest excited.

"The first I exhibit is the flea, and I commence a short lecture as follows:—'Gentlemen,' I says, 'the first object I have to present to your notice is that of a flea. I wish to direct your attention especially to the head of this object. Here you may distinctly perceive its proboscis or dart. It is that which perforates the cuticle or human skin, after which the blood ascends by suction from our body into that of the flea. Thousands of persons in London have seen a flea, have felt a flea, but have never yet been able by the human eye to discover that instrument which made them sensible of the flea about their person, although they could not catch the old gentleman. This flea, gentlemen, by Dr. Lardner's micrometer, measures accurate 24 inches in length, and 11 across the back. My instrument, mark you, being of high magnifying power, will not show you the whole of the object at once. Mark you, gentlemen, this is not the flea of the dog or the cat, but the human flea, for each differ in their formation, as clearly

1 Common nineteenth-century term for microscopic organisms, from the Latin meaning "little animal."

proved by this powerful instrument. For they all differ in their form and shape, and will only feed upon the animal on which they are bred. Having shown you the head and shoulders, with its dart, I shall now proceed to show you the posterior view of this object, in which you may clearly discover every artery, vein, muscle and nerve, exact like a lobster in shape, and quite as large as one at 2*s*. 6*d*.' That pleases them, you know; and sometimes I add, to amuse them, 'An object of that size would make an excellent supper for half-a-dozen persons.' That pleases them.

"One Irishwoman, after seeing the flea, threw up her arms and screamed out, 'O J——! and I've had hundreds of them in my bed at once.' She got me a great many customers from her exclamations. You see, my lecture entices those listening to have a look. Many listeners say, 'Ain't that true, and philosophical, and correct?' I've had many give me 6*d*. and say, 'Never mind the change, your lecture is alone worth the money.'

"I'll now proceed to No. 2. 'The next object I have to present to your notice, gentlemen, is that of the hair of the human head. You perceive that it is nearly as large as yonder scaffolding poles of the House of Lords.' I say this when I am on Westminster-bridge, because it refers to the locality, and is a striking figure, and excites the listeners. 'But mark you, it is not, like them, solid matter, through which no ray of light can pass.' That's where I please the gentlemen, you know, for they say, 'How philosophical!' 'You can readily perceive, mark you, that they are all tubes, like tubes of glass; a proof of which fact you have before you, from the light of the lamp shining direct through the body of the object, and that light direct portrayed in the lens of your eye, called the retina, on which all external objects are painted.' 'Beautiful!' says a gentleman. 'Now, if the hair of the head be a hollow tube, as you perceive it is, then what caution you ought to exercise when you place your head in the hands of the hair-dresser, by keeping your hat on, or else you may be susceptible to catch cold; for that which we breathe, the atmosphere, passing down these tubes, suddenly shuts to the doors, if I may be allowed such an expression, or, in other words, closes the pores of the skin and thereby checks the insensible perspiration, and colds are the result. Powdering the head is quite out of date now, but if a little was used on those occasions referred to, cold in the head would not be so frequent.' What do you think of that? I never had an individual complain of my lecture yet.

"Now comes No. 3. 'This, gentlemen, is the brave old oak, a section of it not larger than the head of a pin. Looking at it through this powerful instrument, you may accurately perceive millions of perforations, or pores, through which the moisture of the earth rises, in order to aid its growth. Of all the trees of the forest, none is so splendid as the brave old oak. This is the tree that braves the battle and the breeze, and is said to be in its perfection at 100 years. Who that looks at it would not exclaim, in the language of the song, "Woodman, spare that tree, and cut it not down?" Such is the analogy existing between vegetable and animal physiology, that a small portion of the cuticle or human skin would present the same appearance, for there are millions of pores in the human skin which a grain of sand is said to cover; and here are millions of perforations through which the moisture of the earth is said to rise to aid the growth of the tree. See the similitude between the vegetable and animal physiology. Here is the exhibition of nature—see how it surpasses that of art. See the ladies at the Great Exhibition[1] admiring the shawls that came from India: yet they, though truly deserving, could not compare with this bit of bark from the brave old oak. Here is a pattern richer and more deserving than any on any shawl, however wonderful. Where is the linendraper in this locality that can produce anything so beautiful as that on this bit of bark? Such are the works of art as compared with those of nature.'

"No. 4 is the animalculæ in water. 'Gentlemen, the object now before you is a drop of water, that may be suspended on a needle's point, teeming with millions of living objects. This one drop of water contains more inhabitants than the globe on which I stand. See the velocity of their motion, the action of their stomachs! the vertebræ is elegantly marked, like the boa-constrictor in the Zoological Gardens.[2] They are all moving with perfect ease in this one drop, like the mighty monsters of the vast deep.'

"On one occasion a gentleman from St. Thomas's Hospital disputed my statement about its being only one drop of water, so I said to the gent: 'If you will accompany me to some coffee-house the drop of water shall be removed, and perhaps what you see you may believe,' which he did, and he paid me 1*s*. for my experiment. He told me he was a doctor, and I told him I was surprised that he was not better acquainted with the instrument; for, said I, 'how can you tell the effects of inoculation on the cuticle, or the disease called the itch, unless you are acquainted with such an instrument?' He was quite ashamed as he paid me for my trouble. I tell this anecdote on the bridge, and I always conclude with, 'Now, gentlemen, whilst I was paid 1*s*. by the faculty for showing one object alone, I am only charging you 1*d*. for the whole six.' Then I address myself to the person looking into the microscope, and say, 'What do you think of this one drop of water, sir?' and he says, 'Splendid!' Then I add, 'Few persons would pass and re-pass this instrument without having a glance into it, if they knew the wonders I exhibit'; and the one looking says, 'That's true, very true.'

"The next object is the cheese-mite—No. 5. I always begin in this way,—'Those who are unacquainted with the study of entomology declare that these mites are beetles, and not mites; but could I procure a beetle with eight legs, I should present it to the British Museum as a curiosity.' This is the way I clench up the mouths of those sceptics who would try to ridicule me, by showing that I am philosophic. 'Just look at them. Notice, for instance, their head, how it represents the form of an

1 See p. 116, note 1.

2 Founded by the Zoological Society of London in 1828, providing its members with a collection of animals and research materials for their own use. The Zoological Gardens opened to the public in 1847 and later became the London Zoo.

hedgehog. The body presents that of the beetle shape. They have eight legs and eight joints. They have four legs forward and four legs back; and they can move with the same velocity forwards as they can back, such is their construction. They are said to be moving with the velocity of five hundred steps in one minute. Read Blair's "Preceptor,"[1] where you may see a drawing of the mite accurately given, as well as read the description just given.' A cheesemonger in Whitechapel brought me a few of these objects for me to place in my microscope. He invited his friends, which were taking supper with him, to come out and have a glance at the same objects. He gave me sixpence for exhibiting them to him, and was highly gratified at the sight of them. I asked him how he could have the impudence to sell them for a lady's supper at 10*d.* a-pound. The answer he gave me was,—'What the eye cannot see the heart never grieves.' Then I go on,—'Whilst this lady is extending her hand to the poor, and doing all the relief in her power, she is slaying more living creatures with her jaw-bone than ever Samson did with his.' If it's a boy looking through, I say, 'Now, Jack, when you are eating bread and cheese don't let it be said that you slay the mites with the jaw-bone of an ass. Cultivate the intellectual and moral powers superior to the passions, and then you will rise superior to that animal in intellect.' 'Good,' says a gentleman, 'good; here's sixpence for you'; and another says, 'Here's twopence for you, and I'm blessed if I want to see anything after hearing your lecture.' Then I continue to point out the affection of the mite for its young. 'You see fathers looking after their daughters, and mothers after their sons, when they are taking their walks; and such is their love for their young, that when the young ones are fatigued with their journey the parents take them up on their backs. Do you not see it?' And then some will say, 'I'll give a penny to see that'; and I've had four pennies put in my hand at once to see it. Excitement is everything in this world, sir.

"Next comes the cane—No. 6. 'The object before you, gentlemen, is a transverse section of cane,—common cane,—such, mark you, as is used by schoolmasters for the correction of boys who neglect their tasks, or play the wag.' I make it comic, you know. 'This I call the tree of knowledge, for it has done more for to learn us the rules of arithmetic than all the vegetable kingdom combined. To it we may attribute the rule of three, from its influence on the mind,'—that always causes a smile,—'just look at it for one moment. Notice, in the first place, its perforations. Where the human hand has failed to construct a micrometer for microscopic or telescopic purposes, the spider has lent its web in one case, and the cane in the other. Through the instrumentality of its perforations, we may accurately infer the magnifying power of other objects, showing the law of

---

1 *The Universal Preceptor: Being a General Grammar of Arts, Sciences, and Useful Knowledge* by Rev. David Blair, a pseudonym of Sir Richard Phillips (1767–1840), was first published in 1811 and later reprinted in many editions throughout England and the United States.

STREET TELESCOPE EXHIBITOR.

[*From a Photograph.*]

Fig. 13: "Street Telescope Exhibitor."

analogy. The perforations of this cane, apart from this instrument, would hardly admit a needle's point, but seem now large enough for your arm to enter. This cane somewhat represents a telescopic view of the moon at the full, when in conjunction with the sun, for instance. Here I could represent inverted rocks and mountains. You may perceive them yourself, just as they would be represented in the moon's disc through a powerful telescope of 250 times, such as I have exhibited to a thousand persons in St. Paul's Churchyard.[1] On the right of this piece of cane, if you are acquainted with the science of astronomy, you may depicture very accurately Mount Tycho, for instance, representing a beautiful burning mountain, like Mount Vesuvius or Etany, near the fields of Naples.[2] You might discover accurately all the diverging streaks of light emanating from the crater. Further on to the right you may perceive Mount St. Catherine, like the blaze of a candle rushing through the atmosphere. On the left you may discover Mount Ptolemy.[3] Such is a similar appearance of the moon's mountainous aspect. I ask you, if the school-boy had but an opportunity of glancing at so splendid an object as the cane, should he ever be seen to shed a tear at its weight?'

"This shows that I am scientific, and know astronomy. The last part makes them laugh.

"This is the mode in which I exhibit my instrument, and such is the interest been excited in the public mind, that though a penny is the small charge which I make, that amount has been doubled and trebled by gentlemen who have viewed the instrument; and on one occasion a clergyman in the Commercial-road presented me with half-a-sovereign, for the interest he felt at my description, as well as the objects presented to his view. It has given universal satisfaction."

[...]

The Snake, Sword, and Knife-Swallower.

HE was quite a young man, and, judging from his countenance, there was nothing that could account for his having taken up so strange a method of gaining his livelihood as that of swallowing snakes.

He was very simple in his talk and manner. He readily confessed that the idea did not originate with him, and prided himself only on being the second to take it up. There is no doubt that it was from his being startled by the strangeness and daringness of the act that he was induced to make

1 St. Paul's Cathedral was London's most prominent church.

2 The Tycho moon crater was named after Danish astronomer Tycho Brahe (1546–1601) in the seventeenth century. Mayhew compares it to Mount Vesuvius and, presumably, Mount Etna, both active volcanoes near Naples, Italy.

3 Mount St. Catherine and Mount Ptolemy presumably refer to the Catharina and Ptolemaeus lunar craters.

the essay. He said he saw nothing disgusting in it; that people liked it; that it served him well in his "professional" engagements; and spoke of the snake in general as a reptile capable of affection, not unpleasant to the eye, and very cleanly in its habits.

"I swallow snakes, swords, and knives; but, of course, when I'm engaged at a penny theatre I'm expected to do more than this, for it would only take a quarter of an hour, and that isn't long enough for them. They call me in the perfession a 'Sallementro,' and that is what I term myself; though p'raps it's easier to say I'm a 'swallower.'

"It was a mate of mine that I was with that first put me up to sword-and-snake swallowing. I copied off him, and it took me about three months to learn it. I began with a sword first—of course not a sharp sword, but one blunt-pointed—and I didn't exactly know how to do it, for there's a trick in it. I see him, and I said, 'Oh, I shall set up master for myself, and practise until I can do it.'

"At first it turned me, putting it down my throat past my swallow, right down—about eighteen inches. It made my swallow sore—very sore, and I used lemon and sugar to cure it. It was tight at first, and I kept pushing it down further and further. There's one thing, you mustn't cough, and until you're used to it you want to very bad, and then you must pull it up again. My sword was about three-quarters of an inch wide.

"At first I didn't know the trick of doing it, but I found it out this way. You see the trick is, you must oil the sword—the best sweet oil, worth fourteen pence a pint—and you put it on with a sponge. Then, you understand, if the sword scratches the swallow it don't make it sore, 'cos the oil heals it up again. When first I put the sword down, before I oiled it, it used to come up quite slimy, but after the oil it slips down quite easy, is as clean when it comes up as before it went down.[1]

"As I told you, we are called at concert-rooms where I perform the 'Sallementro.' I think it's French, but I don't know what it is exactly; but that's what I'm called amongst us.

"The knives are easier to do than the sword because they are shorter. We puts them right down till the handle rests on the mouth. The sword is about eighteen inches long, and the knives about eight inches in the blade. People run away with the idea that you slip the blades down your breast, but I always hold mine right up with the neck bare, and they see it go into the mouth atween the teeth. They also fancy it hurts you; but it don't, or what a fool I should be to do it. I don't mean to say it don't hurt you at first, 'cos it do, for my swallow was very bad, and I couldn't eat anything but liquids for two months whilst I was learning. I cured my swallow whilst I was stretching it with lemon and sugar.

---

1 Sword-swallowers relax the throat and stomach muscles to disable the gag reflex and manoeuvre the foreign object past vital internal organs. Likely injuries include intestinal bleeding, lacerated pharynx, slashed esophagus, and hemorrhaging.

"I was the second one that ever swallowed a snake. I was about seventeen or eighteen years old when I learnt it. The first was Clarke as did it. He done very well with it, but he wasn't out no more than two years before me, so he wasn't known much. In the country there is some places where, when you do it, they swear you are the devil, and won't have it nohow.

"The snakes I use are about eighteen inches long, and you must first cut the stingers out, 'cos it might hurt you. I always keep two or three by me for my performances. I keep them warm, but the winter kills 'em. I give them nothing to eat but worms or gentles.[1] I generally keep them in flannel, or hay, in a box. I've three at home now.

"When first I began swallowing snakes they tasted queer like. They draw'd the roof of the mouth a bit. It's a roughish taste. The scales rough you a bit when you draw them up. You see, a snake will go into ever such a little hole, and they are smooth one way.

"The head of the snake goes about an inch and a half down the throat, and the rest of it continues in the mouth, curled round like. I hold him by the tail, and when I pinch it he goes right in. You must cut the stinger out or he'll injure you. The tail is slippery, but you nip it with the nails like pinchers. If you was to let him go, he'd go right down; but most snakes will stop at two inches down the swallow, and then they bind like a ball in the mouth.

"I in generally get my snakes by giving little boys ha'pence to go and catch 'em in the woods. I get them when I'm pitching in the country. I'll get as many as I can get, and bring 'em up to London for my engagements.

"When first caught the snake is slimy, and I have to clean him by scraping him off with the finger-nail as clean as I can, and then wiping him with a cloth, and then with another, until he's nice and clean. I have put 'em down slimy, on purpose to taste what it was like. It had a nasty taste with it—very nasty.

"I give a man a shilling always to cut the stinger out—one that knows all about it, for the stinger is under the tongue. It was this Clark I first see swallow a snake. He swallowed it as it was when he caught it, slimy. He said it was nasty. Then he scraped it with his nail and let it crawl atween his hands, cleaning itself. When once they are cleaned of the slime they have no taste. Upon my word they are clean things, a'most like metal. They only lives on worms, and that ain't so nasty; besides, they never makes no mess in the box, only frothing in the mouth at morning and evening: but I don't know what comes from 'em, for I ain't a doctor.

"When I exhibit, I first holds the snake up in the air and pinches the tail, to make it curl about and twist round my arm, to show that he is alive. Then I holds it above my mouth, and as soon as he sees the hole in he goes. He goes wavy-like, as a ship goes,—that's the comparison. You

---

1 Maggots.

see, a snake will go in at any hole. I always hold my breath whilst his head is in my swallow. When he moves in the swallow, it tickles a little, but it don't make you want to retch. In my opinion he is more glad to come up than to go down, for it seems to be too hot for him. I keep him down about two minutes. If I breathe or cough, he draws out and curls back again. I think there's artfulness in some of them big snakes, for they seem to know which is the master. I was at Wombwell's menagerie of wild beasts[1] for three months, and I had the care of a big snake, as thick round as my arm. I wouldn't attempt to put that one down my throat, I can tell you, for I think I might easier have gone down his'n. I had to show it to the people in front of the carriages to draw 'em in, at fair time.[2] I used to hold it up in both hands, with my arms in the air. Many a time it curled itself three or four times round my neck and about my body, and it never even so much as squeeged me the least bit. I had the feeding on it, and I used to give it the largest worms I could find. Mr. Wombwell has often said to me, 'It's a dangerous game you're after, and if you don't give the snake plenty of worms and make it like you, it'll nip you some of these times.' I'm sure the snake know'd me. I was very partial to it, too. It was a furren snake, over spots, called a boa-constructor. It never injured me, though I'm told it is uncommon powerful, and can squeege a man up like a sheet of paper, and crack his bones as easy as a lark's. I'm tremendous courageous, nothing frightens me; indeed, I don't know what it is to be afraid.

"The one I was speaking of I have often held up in the air in both hands, and it was more than four yards long, and let it curl round my neck in five or six twirls. It was a boa-constructor, and I believe it know'd me, and that's why it didn't hurt me, for I feed him. He had nothing but long great worms, and he grew to know me.

"My performance with the snake is always very successful. The women is frightened at first, but they always stop to see, and only hide their eyes. There's no danger as long as you keep hold.

"I generally perform at concert-rooms, and penny theatres, and cheap circuses, and all round the country, such as in the street, or at farm-houses, or in tap-rooms. I have done it in the streets of London too, and then I'm dressed-up in fleshing tights, skin dress, and trunks. I carry the snake in a box. When I swallow it some holloa out, 'O my God, don't do that!' but when I'm finished, they say, 'It's hardly wonderful to be believed,' and give money.

"I generally mix up the sword-and-snake performances with my other ones; and it's the same in the streets.

---

1 Wombwell's Traveling Menagerie, founded in 1810, was owned and operated by George Wombwell (1777–1850). The menagerie owned several exotic animals and was widely celebrated.

2 A travelling exhibit, Wombwell's was a frequent attraction at the yearly Bartholomew Fair in London.

"Sometimes I go out to tap-rooms in my every-day dress, with the snake in my pocket, and a sword. Then I go and offer to show my performance. First I'll do some tumbling, and throw a somerset over a table. Then I takes out the snake and say, 'Gentlemen, I shall now swallow a live snake, anybody is at liberty to feel it.' I have—according to the company, you know—made such a thing as five shillings, or one shilling and sixpence, or whatever it may be, by snake-swallowing alone.

"I'm the only one in London who can swallow a snake. There's nobody else besides me. It requires great courage. I've great courage. One night I was sleeping in a barn at a public-house, called the Globe, at Lewes, seven miles from Brighton. A woman who had cut her throat used to haunt the place. Well, I saw her walking about in a long white shroud, the doors opening and shutting before her. A man who was in the room with us jumped up in his bed and cried, 'Tumblers!'

"I must tell you one thing before you finish, just to prove what tremendous courage I've got. I was out showing the sword-and-snake swallowing in the country, and I travelled down to near Lewes, which is seven miles from Brighton, and there I put up at a house called the Falcon. We slept in a barn, and at night, when all was asleep except myself, I see a figure all in white come into the room with her throat cut, and her face as white as chalk. I knowed she was a apperition, 'cos I'd been told the house was haunted by such. Well, in she come, and she stopped and looked at me, seeing that I was awake. The perspiration poured out of me like a shower; but I warn't afeard, I've that courage. I says, 'God help me!' for I knew I'd done no harm as I could call to mind; so I hadn't no fear of ghosts and such-like spirits. No, I'm certain it wern't no fancy of mine, 'cos others see it as well as me. There was a mate in the same room, and he woke up and sees the ghosts, and up he jumps in bed and cries out: 'Tumblers! Tumblers! here's a woman haunting us!' I told him to lie down and go to sleep, and hold his noise. Then I got out of bed, and it wanished past me, close as could be,—as near as I am to this table. The door opened itself to let her out, and then closed again. I didn't feel the air cold like, nor nothing, nor was there any smell or anythink. I'm sure I wasn't dreaming, 'cos I knows pretty well when I'm awake. Besides the doors kept bouncing open, and then slamming-to again for more than an hour, and woke everybody in the room. This kept on till one o'clock. Yet, you see, though the sweat run down me to that degree I was wetted through, yet I had that courage I could get out of bed to see what the spirit was like. I said, 'God help me! for I've done no harm as I knows of,' and that give me courage."

Whilst the "Salamentro" told me this ghost story, he spoke it in a half voice, like that of a nervous believer in such things. When he had finished he seemed to have something on his mind, for after a moment's silence he said, in a confidential tone, "Between ourselves, sir, I'm a Jew." I then asked him if he thought the ghost was aware of it, and had visited him on that account, and the following was his reply: "Well, it ain't unlikely; for, you see, some of our scholars know what to say to the poor things, and they know what to do to rest 'em. Now, pr'aps she thought I knew these secrets,—but, I'm no scholard—for, you see, we Jews always carry prayers about with us to keep off evil spirits. That's one reason why I was so bold as to go up to her."

Street Clown.[1]

HE was a melancholy-looking man, with the sunken eyes and other characteristics of semi-starvation, whilst his face was scored with lines and wrinkles, telling of paint and premature age.

I saw him performing in the streets with a school of acrobats soon after I had been questioning him, and the readiness and business-like way with which he resumed his professional buffoonery was not a little remarkable. His story was more pathetic than comic, and proved that the life of a street clown is, perhaps, the most wretched of all existence. Jest as he may in the street, his life is literally no joke at home.

"I have been a clown for sixteen years," he said, "having lived totally by it for that time. I was left motherless at two years of age, and my father died when I was nine. He was a carman, and his master took me as a stable-boy, and I stayed with him until he failed in business. I was then left destitute again, and got employed as a supernumerary at Astley's,[2] at one shilling a-night. I was a 'super' some time, and got an insight into theatrical life. I got acquainted, too, with singing people, and could sing a good song, and came out at last on my own account in the streets, in the Jim Crow line.[3] My necessities forced me into a public line, which I am far from liking. I'd pull trucks at one shilling a-day, rather than get twelve shillings a-week at my business. I've tried to get out of the line. I've got a friend to advertise for me for any situation as groom. I've tried to get into the police, and I've tried other things, but somehow there seems an impossibility to get quit of the street business. Many times I have to play the clown, and indulge in all kinds of buffoonery, with a terrible heavy heart. I have travelled very much, too, but I never did overwell in the profession. At races I may have made ten shillings for two or three days, but that was only occasional; and what is ten shillings to keep a wife and family on, for a month maybe? I have three children, one now only eight weeks old. You can't imagine, sir, what a curse the street business often becomes, with its insults and starvations. The day before my

---

1 First published as part of Letter LIV of "Labour and the Poor" in the *Morning Chronicle*, 30 May 1850.

2 Astley's Royal Amphitheatre, founded by Philip Astley (1742–1814) in the late eighteenth century. It was originally home to an equestrian show, but Astley's popular performances grew to include pantomimes, acrobatic acts, and trained animal performances.

3 A caricature of a slave made popular in 1828 by Thomas D. Rice (1806–60), an American actor who performed a song-and-dance routine entitled "Jump Jim Crow" in blackface.

wife was confined, I jumped and labour'd doing Jim Crow for twelve hours—in the wet, too—and earned one shilling and threepence; with this I returned to a home without a bit of coal, and with only half-a-quartern loaf in it. I know it was one shilling and threepence; for I keep a sort of log of my earnings and my expenses; you'll see on it what I've earn'd as clown, or the funnyman, with a party of acrobats, since the beginning of this year."

He showed me this log, as he called it, which was kept in small figures, on paper folded up as economically as possible. His latest weekly earnings were, 12*s.* 6*d.*, 1*s.* 10*d.*, 7*s.* 7*d.*, 2*s.* 5*d.*, 3*s.* 11½*d.*, 7*s.* 7½*d.*, 7*s.* 9¼*d.*, 6*s.* 4½*d.*, 10*s.* 10½*d.*, 9*s.* 7*d.*, 6*s.* 1½*d.*, 15*s.* 6¼*d.*, 6*s.* 5*d.*, 4*s.* 2*d.*, 12*s.* 10¼*d.*, 15*s.* 5½*d.*, 14*s.* 4*d.* Against this was set off what the poor man had to expend for his dinner, &c., when out playing the clown, as he was away from home and could not dine with his family. The ciphers intimate the weeks when there was no such expense, or in other words, those which had been passed without dinner. 0, 0, 0, 0, 2*s.* 2½*d.*, 3*s.* 9¼*d.*, 4*s.* 2*d.*, 4*s.* 5*d.*, 5*s.* 8¼*d.*, 5*s.* 11¼*d.*, 4*s.* 10½*d.*, 2*s.* 8¾*d.*, 3*s.* 7¾*d.*, 3*s.* 4¼*d.*, 6*s.* 5¼*d.*, 4*s.* 6¾*d.*, 4*s.* 3*d.* This account shows an average of 8*s.* 6½*d.* a-week as the gross gain, whilst, if the expenses be deducted, not quite six shillings remain as the average weekly sum to be taken home to wife and family.

"I dare say," continued the man, "that no persons think more of their dignity than such as are in my way of life. I would rather starve than ask for parochial relief. Many a time I have gone to my labour without breaking my fast, and played clown until I could raise dinner. I have to make jokes as clown, and could fill a volume with all I knows."

He told me several of his jests; they were all of the most venerable kind, as for instance:—"A horse has ten legs: he has two fore legs and two hind ones. Two fores are eight, and two others are ten." The other jokes were equally puerile, as, "Why is the City of Rome," (he would have it Rome), "like a candle wick? Because it's in the midst of Greece." "Old and young are both of one age: your son at twenty is young, and your horse at twenty is old: and so old and young are the same." "The dress," he continued, "that I wear in the streets consists of red striped cotton stockings, with full trunks, dotted red and black. The body, which is dotted like the trunks, fits tight like a woman's gown, and has full sleeves and frills. The wig or scalp is made of horse-hair, which is sown on to a white cap, and is in the shape of a cock's comb. My face is painted with dry white lead. I grease my skin first and then dab the white paint on (flake-white is too dear for us street clowns); after that I colour my cheeks and mouth with vermilion. I never dress at home; we all dress at public-houses. In the street where I lodge, only a very few know what I do for a living. I and my wife both strive to keep the business a secret from our neighbours. My wife does a little washing when able, and often works eight hours for sixpence. I go out at eight in the morning and return at dark. My children hardly know what I do. They see my dresses lying about, but that is all. My eldest is a girl of thirteen. She has seen me dressed at Stepney fair,[1] where she brought me my tea (I live near there); she laughs when she sees me in my clown's dress, and wants to stay with me: but I would rather see her lay dead before me (and I had two dead in my place at one time, last Whitsun Monday was a twelvemonth) than she should ever belong to my profession."

I could see the tears start from the man's eyes as he said this.

"Frequently when I am playing the fool in the streets, I feel very sad at heart. I can't help thinking of the bare cupboards at home; but what's that to the world? I've often and often been at home all day when it has been wet, with no food at all, either to give my children or take myself, and have gone out at night to the public-houses to sing a comic song or play the funnyman for a meal—you may imagine with what feelings for the part—and when I've come home I've call'd my children up from their beds to share the loaf I had brought back with me. [...] When I go out as a street clown, the first thing I do is a comic medley dance; and then after that I crack a few jokes, and that is the whole of my entertainment. The first part of the medley dance is called 'the good St. Anthony'[2] (I was the first that ever danced the polka in the streets); then I do a waltz, and wind up with a hornpipe. After that I go through a little burlesque business. I fan myself, and one of the school asks me whether I am out of breath? I answer, 'No, the breath is out of me.' The leading questions for the jokes are all regularly prepared beforehand. The old jokes always go best with our audiences. The older they are, the better for the streets. I know, indeed, of nothing new in the joking way; but even if there was, and it was in any way deep, it would not do for the public thoroughfares. I have read a great deal of 'Punch,'[3] but the jokes are nearly all too high there; indeed, I can't say I think very much of them myself. The principal way in which I've got up my jokes is through associating with other clowns. We don't make our jokes ourselves; in fact, I never knew one clown who did. I must own that the street clowns like a little drop of spirits, and occasionally a good deal. They are in a measure obligated to it. I can't fancy a clown being funny on small beer; and I never in all my life knew one who was a teetotaller. I think such a person would be a curious character, indeed. Most of the street clowns die in the workhouses. In their old age they are generally very wretched and poverty-stricken. I can't say what I think will be the end of me. I daren't think of it, sir."

1 After its revival in 1843, Stepney Fair was a source of income for entertainers and dealers in wares of all kinds; London costermongers made money by transporting visitors from various locations to the fairground in Stepney Green.

2 The clown's dance possibly references Saint Anthony of Padua (1195–1231), the subject of a comic song called "The Temptations of Good Saint Anthony," in which the saint successfully avoids temptation before finally succumbing to a devil in the form of a beautiful woman.

3 A sophisticated humour and satire magazine founded by Mayhew and Ebenezer Landells in 1841 and running, with one break between 1992 and 1996, until 2002. It was an early pioneer of the political cartoon.

A few minutes afterwards I saw this man dressed as Jim Crow, with his face blackened, dancing and singing in the streets as if he was the lightest-hearted fellow in all London.

Street Reciter.

STREET reciters are somewhat scarce now-a-days, and I was a long time before meeting with one; for though I could always trace them through their wanderings about the streets, and learn where they had been seen the night before, still I could never find one myself. I believe there are not more than ten lads in London,—for they seem to be all lads,—who are earning a livelihood by street-reciting.

At length I heard that some street actors, as they call themselves, lived in a court in the City.[1] There were two of them—one a lad, who was dressed in a man's ragged coat and burst boots, and tucked-up trowsers, and seemingly in a state of great want; and the other decently enough attired in a black paletot with a flash white-and-red handkerchief, or "fogle," as the costermongers call it, jauntily arranged so as to bulge over the closely-buttoned collar of his coat. There was a priggish look about the latter lad, while his manner was "cute," and smacked of Petticoat-lane; and though the other one seemed to slink back, *he* pushed himself saucily forward, and at once informed me that he belonged "to the profession" of street declaimer. "I and this other boy goes out together," he said, as he took a short pipe from his mouth; and in proof of his assertion, he volunteered that they should on the spot give me a specimen of their histrionic powers.

I preferred listening to the modest boy. He was an extremely good-looking lad, and spoke in a soft voice, almost like a girl's. He had a bright, cheerful face, and a skin so transparent and healthy, and altogether appeared so different from the generality of street lads, that I felt convinced that he had not long led a wandering life, and that there was some mystery connected with his present pursuits. He blushed when spoken to, and his answers were nervously civil.

When I had the better-natured boy alone with me, I found that he had been well educated; and his statement will show that he was born of respectable parents, and the reason why he took to his present course of life. At first he seemed to be nervous, and little inclined to talk; but as we became better acquainted, he chatted on even faster than my pen could follow. He had picked up several of the set phrases of theatrical parlance, such as, "But my dream has vanished in air"; or, "I felt that a blight was on my happiness"; and delivered his words in a romantic tone, as though he fancied he was acting on a stage. He volunteered to show me his declamatory powers, and selected "Othello's Apology."[2] He went to the

1 See p. 127, note 2.

2 Likely referring to Othello's last speech in Shakespeare's *Othello* 5.2.

back of the room, and after throwing his arms about him for a few seconds, and looking at the ceiling as if to inspire himself, he started off.

Whilst he had been chatting to us his voice was—as I said before—like a girl's; but no sooner did he deliver his, "Most potent, grave, and reverend Signiors,"[1] than I was surprised to hear him assume a deep stomachic voice—a style evidently founded upon the melo-dramatic models at minor theatres. His good-looking face, however, became flushed and excited during the delivery of the speech, his eyes rolled about, and he passed his hands through his hair, combing it with his fingers till it fell wildly about his neck like a mane.

When he had finished the speech he again relapsed into his quiet ways, and resuming his former tone of voice, seemed to think that an apology was requisite for the wildness of his acting, for he said, "When I act Shakspeare I cannot restrain myself,—it seems to master my very soul."

He had some little talent as an actor, but was possessed of more memory than knowledge of the use of words. Like other performers, he endeavoured to make his "points" by dropping his voice to almost a whisper when he came to the passage, "I' faith 'twas strange, 'twas passing strange."[2]

In answer to my questions he gave me the following statement:—

"I am a street reciter, that is, I go about the streets and play Shakspeare's tragedies, and selections from poets. The boys in the streets call me Shakspeare. The first time they called me so I smiled at them, and was honoured by the name, though it's only passing! it's only fleet!

"I was born in Dublin, and my father was in the army, and my mother was a lady's nurse and midwife, and used to go out on urgent business, but only to ladies of the higher classes. My mother died in Dublin, and my father left the army and became a turnkey in Dublin prison. Father left Dublin when I was about ten years of age, and went to Manchester. Then I went into an office—a herring-store, which had agents at Yarmouth and other fishing-ports; and there I had to do writing. Summer-time was our busiest time, for we used to have to sit up at night waiting for the trains to come in with the fish. I used to get 3*d.* an hour for every hour we worked over, and 6*d.* in the morning for coffee, and 8*s.* 6*d.* standing wages, whether I worked or played. I know all about herrings and herring-packing, for I was two years there, and the master was like a father to me, and would give me money many times, Christmas-boxes, and new-years' gifts, and such-like. I might have been there now, and foreman by this time, in the Isle of Man, where we had a house, only I was too foolish—going to theatres and such-like.

"You see, I used, before I went out as clerk, to go to a school in Manchester, where the master taught recitation. We used to speak pieces from

1 *Othello* 1.3.79.

2 *Othello* 1.3.163.

Uwin's 'Elocution,'[1] and we had to get a piece off to elocution, and attitude, and position; indeed, elocution may be said to be position and attitude. We used to do 'The Downfall of Poland,' and 'Lord Ullen's Daughter,' and 'My name is Norval,' and several others—'Rolla,' and all them. Then we used to speak them one at a time, and occasionally we would take different parts, such as the 'Quarrel of Brutus,' and 'Cassius,' and 'Rolla,' and the 'American Patriot,' and such-like. I will not boast of myself, but I was one of the best in the class, though since I have gone out in the streets it has spoiled my voice and my inclinations, for the people likes shouting. I have had as many as 500 persons round me in the Walworth-road at one time, and we got 4*s*. between us; and then we lost several halfpence, for it was night, and we could not see the money that was thrown into the ring. We did the 'Gipsy's Revenge,' and 'Othello's Apology.'

"Whilst I was at the herring-stores I used to be very fond of the theatre, and I'd go there every night if I could, and I did nearly manage to be there every evening. I'd save up my money, and if I'd none I'd go to my master and ask him to let me have a few halfpence; and I've even wanted to go to the play so much that, when I couldn't get any money, I'd sell my clothes to go. Master used to caution me, and say that the theatre would ruin me, and I'm sure it has. When my master would tell me to stop and do the books, I'd only just run them over at night and cast them up as quickly as I could, and then I'd run out and go to the twopenny theatre on the Victoria-bridge, Manchester. Sometimes I used to perform there for Mr. Row, who was the proprietor. It was what is called a travelling 'slang,' a booth erected temporarily. I did William Tell's son,[2] and I've also done the 'Bloody Child'[3] in Macbeth, and go on with the witches. It was a very little stage, but with very nice scenery, and shift-scenes and all, the same as any other theatre. On a Saturday night he used to have as many as six houses; start off at three o'clock, after the factory hands had been paid off. I never had any money for acting, for though he offered me half-a-sovereign a-week to come and take a part, yet I wouldn't accept of it, for I only did it for my own amusement like. They used to call me King Dick.[4]

[...]

1 Most likely Thomas Ewing's *Principles of Elocution* (1814), a widely reprinted collection of excerpts from famous literary works used to teach the art of public speaking.

2 A scene from Friedrich Schiller's *Wilhelm Tell* (1804). In this scene (3.3), Tell, a legendary Swiss hero and marksman, is forced by the governor to shoot an arrow through an apple placed on his son's head.

3 A reference to Shakespeare's *Macbeth* 4.1.77–86, in which the apparition of a "Bloody Child" appears before Macbeth.

4 Several slang dictionaries define this term as Cockney rhyming slang for brick or bricklayer. In this context, it is possible that the term refers to Shakespeare's *King Richard* plays. Some slang dictionaries also define "Dick" as dictionary, implying that the Street Reciter has a vast vocabulary.

"When I go out to recite, I generally go with another boy, and we take parts. The pieces that draw best with the public are, 'The Gipsy's Revenge,' 'The Gold Digger's Revenge,' 'The Miser,' 'The Robber,' 'The Felon,' and 'The Highwayman.'[1] We take parts in these, and he always performs the villain, and I take the noble characters. He always dies, because he can do a splendid back-fall, and he looks so wicked when he's got the moustaches on. I generally draws the company by giving two or three recitations, and then we perform a piece; and whilst he goes round with the hat, I recite again. My favourite recitations are, 'Othello's Apology,' beginning with 'Most potent, grave, and reverend Signiors,' and those from Hamlet, Richard III., and Macbeth. Of the recitations I think the people prefer that from Othello, for the ladies have often asked me to give them that from Othello (they like to hear about Desdemona), but the gentlemen ask for that from Hamlet, 'To be, or not to be?'

"My principal place for giving performances is the Commercial-road, near Limehouse, but the most theatrically inclined neighbourhood is the Walworth-road. The most money I ever took at one time in the streets was 4*s*. in the Walworth-road.

"The best receipts I ever had was got in a public-house near Brick-lane, for I took 12*s*., and I was alone. There was a 'lead' up there for a friend, and I knew of it, and I had my hair curled and got myself decently habited, I was there for about three or four hours, and in the intervals between the dances I used to recite. There were girls there, and they took my part, though they made me drink so much I was nearly tipsy.

"The only theatrical costume I put on is moustachios, and I take a stick to use as a sword. I put myself into attitudes, and look as fierce as I can. When first the people came to hear me they laughed, and then they became quiet; and sometimes you could hear a pin drop.

"When I am at work regularly—that's when I am in voice and will—I make about 10*s*. a-week, if there's not much rain. If it's wet, people don't go to the public-houses, and they are my best paying audiences. The least I have ever taken in a week is about 6*s*.

"There isn't many going about London reciting. It is a very rare class to be found; I only know about four who live that way, and I have heard of the others from hearsay—not that I have seen them myself.

"I'm very fond of music, and know most of the opera. That organ's playing something by Verdi; I heard it at the theatre at Dublin. I amuse them sometimes in the kitchen at my lodgings by playing on a penny tin whistle. I can do 'Still, so gently,' from 'La Sonnambula,'[2] and hornpipes, and jigs, and Scotch airs, as well as 'Cheer boys, cheer,' and 'To the

1 Scenes from popular stage plays from the eighteenth and nineteenth centuries.

2 An aria from Act 2 of Vincenzo Bellini's 1831 opera *La Sonnambula* (The Sleep-walker).

West,'[1] and many others. They get me to play when they want to dance, and they pay me for them. They call me Shakspeare by name."

II. Street Musicians.
"Old Sarah."[2]

ONE of the most deserving and peculiar of the street musicians was an old lady who played upon a hurdy-gurdy.[3] She had been about the streets of London for upwards of forty years, and being blind, had had during that period four guides, and worn out three instruments. Her cheerfulness, considering her privation and precarious mode of life, was extraordinary. Her love of truth, and the extreme simplicity of her nature, were almost childlike. Like the generality of blind people, she had a deep sense of religion, and her charity for a woman in her station of life was something marvellous; for, though living on alms, she herself had, I was told, two or three little pensioners. When questioned on this subject, she laughed the matter off as a jest, though I was assured of the truth of the fact. Her attention to her guide was most marked. If a cup of tea was given to her after her day's rounds, she would be sure to turn to the poor creature who led her about, and ask, "You comfortable, Liza?" or "Is your tea to your liking, Liza?"

When conveyed to Mr. Beard's[4] establishment to have her daguerreotype[5] taken, she for the first time in her life rode in a cab; and then her fear at being pulled "back'ards" as she termed it (for she sat with her back to the horse), was almost painful. She felt about for something to lay hold of, and did not appear comfortable until she had a firm grasp of the pocket. After

---

1 Two songs written and adapted to traditional English melodies by poet and songwriter Charles MacKay (1812–89). Both songs promote emigration to North America and were part of a series of MacKay's poems and songs published in the *Illustrated London News* between 1851 and 1855.

2 Mayhew refers to the unnamed Sarah in Letter LV of the "Labour and the Poor" series for the *Morning Chronicle*, 6 June 1850. The article features a condensed version of her narrative.

3 A lecture by Mayhew called "The curiosities of life among the labourers and poor of London" describes Sarah as "the best, the kindest, and noblest creature he ever knew." In the lecture, Mayhew claimed that he and Sarah had a personal relationship: that she had drunk tea at his house regularly, and that he visited her often in the hospital following her accident ("Polytechnic Institution—Lecture by Mr. Mayhew," *The Daily News*, 17 June 1856).

4 See Introduction, p. 16, note 1.

5 The daguerrotype process was one of the first practical methods of creating permanent photographs. It was named after Louis Jacques Mande Daguerre (1787–1851), a French artist, and had been developed in collaboration with Joseph Nicéphore Niépce (1765–1833), a French scientist. The process involved capturing an image with a camera on a sensitized plate of silver-coated copper. The image was then "brought out" by exposing the plate to heated mercury and was finally fixed in a bath of hyposulphate of soda.

"OLD SARAH," THE WELL-KNOWN HURDY-GURDY PLAYER.

[*From a Daguerreotype by* BEARD.]

Fig. 14: "'Old Sarah,' the Well-Known Hurdy-Gurdy Player."

her alarm had in a measure subsided, she turned to her guide and said, "We must put up with those trials, Liza." In a short time, however, she began to find the ride pleasant enough. "Very nice, ain't it Liza?" she said; "but I shouldn't like to ride on them steamboats, they say they're shocking dangerous; and as for them railways, I've heard tell they're dreadful; but these cabs, Liza, is very nice." On the road she was continually asking "Liza" where they were, and wondering at the rapidity at which they travelled. "Ah!" she said, laughing, "if I had one of these here cabs, my 'rounds' would soon be over." Whilst ascending the high flight of stairs that led to the portrait-rooms, she laughed at every proposal made to her to rest. "There's twice as many stairs as these to our church, ain't there, Liza?" she replied when pressed. When the portrait was finished she expressed a wish to feel it.

The following is the history of her life, as she herself related it, answering to the variety of questions put to her on the subject:—

"I was born the 4th April, 1786 (it was Good Friday that year), at a small chandler's shop, facing the White Horse, Stuart's-rents, Drury-lane. Father was a hatter, and mother an artificial-flower maker and feather finisher. When I was but a day old, the nurse took me out of the warm bed and carried me to the window, to show some people how like I was to father. The cold flew to my eyes and I caught inflammation in them. Owing to mother being forced to be from home all day at her work, I was put out to dry-nurse when I was three weeks old. My eyes were then very bad, by all accounts, and some neighbours told the woman I was with, that Turner's cerate[1] would do them good. She got some and put it on my eyes, and when poor mother came to suckle me at her dinner-hour, my eyes was all 'a gore of blood.' From that time I never see afterwards. She did it, poor woman, for the best; it was no fault of her'n, and I'm sure I bears her no malice for it. I stayed at home with mother until I was thirteen, when I was put to the Blind-school,[2] but I only kept there nine months; they turned me out because I was not clever with my hands, and I could not learn to spin or make sash-lines; my hands was ocker'd like. I had not been used at home to do anything for myself—not even to dress myself. Mother was always out at her work, so she could not learn me, and no one else would, so that's how it was I was turned out. I then went back to my mother, and kept with her till her death. I well remember that; I heard her last. When she died I was just sixteen year old. I was sent to the Union—'Pancridge' Union[3] it was—and father with me (for he was ill at the time). He died too, and left me, in seven weeks after mother. When

1 An ointment containing calamine powder, yellow wax, and olive oil melted together. Commonly used to treat burns, wounds, and ulcers.

2 The School for the Indigent Blind, established 1799 in St. George's Fields in Southwark. The school's pupils, aged 12 to 30, resided at the school and were trained in trades such as making wicker baskets and brushes for the men, and sewing and spinning for the women.

3 "Pancridge" was a common pronunciation for the area of St. Pancras; here Sarah refers to the St. Pancras workhouse.

they was both gone, I felt I had lost my only friends, and that I was all alone in the world and blind. But, take it altogether, the world has been very good to me, and I have much to thank God for and the good woman I am with. I missed mother the most, she was so kind to me; there was no one like her; no, not even father. I was kept in the Union until I was twenty; the parish paid for my learning the 'cymbal': God bless them for it, I say. A poor woman in the workhouse first asked me to learn music; she said it would always be a bit of bread for me; I did as she told me, and I thank her to this day for it. It took me just five months to learn the—cymbal, if you please—the hurdy-gurdy ain't it's right name. The first tune I ever played was 'God save the King,' the Queen as is now; then 'Harlequin Hamlet,' that took me a long time to get off; it was three weeks before they put me on a new one. I then learnt 'Moll Brook'; then I did the 'Turnpike-gate' and 'Patrick's day in the morning': all of them I learnt in the Union. I got a poor man to teach me the 'New-rigged ship.' I soon learnt it, because it was an easy tune. Two-and-forty years ago I played 'The Gal *I* left behind me.' A woman learnt it me; she played my cymbal and I listened, and so got it. 'Oh, Susannah!' I learnt myself by hearing it on the horgan. I always try and listen to a new tune when I am in the street, and get it off if I can: it's my bread. I waited to hear one to-day, quite a new one, but I didn't like it, so I went on. 'Hasten to the Wedding' is my favourite; I played it years ago, and play it still. I like 'Where have you been all the night?'[1] it's a Scotch tune. The woman as persuaded me to learn the cymbal took me out of the Union with her; I lived with her, and she led me about the streets. When she died I took her daughter for my guide. She walked with me for more than five-and-twenty year, and she might have been with me to this day, but she took to drinking and killed herself with it. She behaved very bad to me at last, for as soon as we got a few halfpence she used to go into the public and spend it all; and many a time I'm sure she's been too tipsy to take me home. One night I remember she rolled into the road at Kensington, and as near pulled me with her. We was both locked up in the station-house, for she couldn't stand for liquor, and I was obligated to wait till she could lead me home. It was very cruel of her to treat me so, but, poor creature, she's gone, and I forgive her I'm sure. I'd many guides arter her, but none of them was honest like Liza is: I don't think she'd rob me of a farden. Would you, Liza? Yes, I've my reg'lar rounds, and I've kept to 'em for near upon fifty year. All the children like to hear me coming along, for I always plays my cymbal as I goes. At Kentish-town they calls me Mrs. Tuesday, and at Kensington I'm Mrs. Friday, and so on. At some places they likes polkas, but at one house I plays at in Kensington they always ask me for 'Haste to the Wedding.' No, the

1 Sarah's list of songs includes well-known ditties and jigs. Some songs are of eighteenth-century Gaelic origins and might have been considered old-fashioned by her contemporary listeners in the London streets; in contrast, the popular American minstrel song "Oh, Susannah!" by Stephen Foster (1826–64) was first published in 1848.

cymbal isn't very hard to play; the only thing is, you must be very particular that the works is covered up, or the halfpence is apt to drop in. King David, they say, played on one of those here instruments. We're very tired by night-time; ain't we, Liza? but when I gets home the good woman I lodges with has always a bit of something for me to eat with my cup of tea. She's a good soul, and keeps me tidy and clean. I helps her all I can; when I come in, I carries her a pail of water up-stairs, and such-like. Many ladies as has known me since they was children allows me a trifle. One maiden lady near Brunswick-square has given me sixpence a week for many a year, and another allows me eighteenpence a fortnight; so that, one way and another, I am very comfortable, and I've much to be thankful for."

It was during one of old Sarah's journeys that an accident occurred, which ultimately deprived London of the well-known old hurdy-gurdy woman. In crossing Seymour-street, she and her guide Liza were knocked down by a cab, as it suddenly turned a corner. They were picked up and placed in the vehicle (the poor guide dead, and Sarah with her limbs broken), and carried to the University Hospital.[1] Old Sarah's description of that ride is more terrible and tragic than I can hope to make out to you. The poor blind creature was ignorant of the fate of her guide, she afterwards told us, and kept begging and praying to Liza to speak to her as the vehicle conveyed them to the asylum. She shook her, she said, and intreated her to say if she was hurt, but not a word was spoken in answer, and then she felt how terrible a privation was her blindness; and it was not until they reached the hospital, and they were lifted from the cab, that she knew, as she heard the people whisper to one another, that her faithful attendant was dead. In telling us this, the good old soul forgot her own sufferings for the time, as she lay with both her legs broken beneath the hooped bed-clothes of the hospital bed; and when, after many long weeks, she left the medical asylum, she was unable to continue her playing on the hurdy-gurdy, her hand being now needed for the crutch that was requisite to bear her on her rounds.

The shock, however, had been too much for the poor old creature's feeble nature to rally against, and though she continued to hobble round to the houses of the kind people who had for years allowed her a few pence per week, and went limping along musicless through the streets for some months after she left the hospital, yet her little remaining strength at length failed her, and she took to her bed in a room in Bell-court, Gray's-inn-lane,[2] never to rise from it again.[3]

---

1 In the 1850s, the University Hospital was located at Gower Street in Bloomsbury. It was a teaching hospital, founded in 1828, and served the poor of the neighbourhood.

2 In "Of the Low Lodging-houses of London," Mayhew identifies Bell-court in Gray's-inn Lane as the location of one of several low-lodging houses in High Holborn, within two kilometres of the University Hospital.

3 The *London Evening Standard* on 28 April 1852 confirms Mayhew's account that a cab struck two women on Molton-street, Euston-square, causing the death of Eliza Ann Croney, and "seriously injured another woman of advanced age,

Tom-Tom Players.

WITHIN the last few years East Indians playing on the tom-tom have occasionally made their appearance in the London streets. The Indian or Lascar[1] crossing-sweepers, who earned their living by alternately plying the broom and sitting as models to artists—the Indian converted to Christianity, who, in his calico clothes, with his brown bosom showing, was seen, particularly on cold days, crouching on the pavement and selling tracts, have lately disappeared from our highways, and in their stead the tom-tom players have made their appearance.

I saw two of these performers in one of the West-end streets, creeping slowly down the centre of the road, and beating their drums with their hands, whilst they drawled out a kind of mournful song. Their mode of parading the streets is to walk one following the other, beating their oyster-barrel-shaped drums with their hands, which they make flap about from the wrist like flounders out of water, whilst they continue their droning song, and halt at every twenty paces to look round.

One of these performers was a handsome lad, with a face such as I have seen in the drawings of the princes in the "Arabian Nights Entertainments."[2] He had a copper skin and long black hair, which he brushed behind his ears. On his head was a white turban, made to cock over one ear, like a hat worn on one side, and its rim stood out like the stopper to a scent-bottle.

The costume of the man greatly resembled that of a gentleman wearing his waistcoat outside his shirt, only the waistcoat was of green merino, and adorned with silk embroidery, his waist being bound in with a scarf. Linen trowsers and red knitted cuffs, to keep his wrists warm, completed his costume.

This man was as tall, slim, and straight, and as gracefully proportioned, as a bronze image. His face had a serious, melancholy look, which seemed to work strongly on the feelings of the nurses and the servant-girls who stopped to look at him. His companion, although dressed in the same costume, (the only difference being that the colour of his waistcoat was red instead of green,) formed a comical contrast to his sentimental Othello-looking[3]

---

named Sarah Chandler," who was a well-known hurdy-gurdy player. The article consults witnesses to the accident and states that the magistrate believed that the incident was accidental.

1 See p. 92, note 1.

2 Though various editions of tales designated as belonging to the *The Arabian Nights* had circulated in the eighteenth century, Mayhew is here likely referring to the edition produced by Edward William Lane (1801–76), which was first published serially and then in three bound volumes in 1838–41. Lane's volumes, which included over one hundred illustrations, featured copious annotations on Egyptian life and approached the tales as ethnographic and historical texts.

3 The name of the hero of Shakespeare's tragedy was commonly used as a racial slur against black men.

partner, for he was what a Yankee would call "a rank nigger."[1] His face, indeed, was as black and elastic-looking as a printer's dabber.

The name of the negro boy was Peter. Beyond "Yes" and "No," he appeared to be perfectly unacquainted with the English language. His Othello friend was 17 years of age, and spoke English perfectly. I could not help taking great interest in this lad, both from the peculiarity of his conversation, which turned chiefly upon the obedience due from children to their parents, and was almost fanatical in its theory of perfect submission, and also from his singularly handsome countenance; for his eyes were almond-shaped, and as black as elder-berries, whilst, as he spoke, the nostrils of his aquiline nose beat like a pulse.

When I attempted to repeat after them one of their Indian songs, they both burst out into uproarious merriment. Peter rolling about in his chair like a serenader playing "the bones,"[2] and the young Othello laughing as if he was being tickled.

In speaking of the duties which they owed to their parents, the rules of conduct which they laid down as those to be followed by a good son were wonderful for the completeness of the obedience which they held should be paid to a father's commands. They did not seem to consider that the injunctions of a mother should be looked upon as sacredly as those of the male parent. They told me that the soul of the child was damned if even he disputed to obey the father's command, although he knew it to be wrong, and contrary to God's laws. "Allah," they said, would visit any wickedness that was committed through such obedience upon the father, but he would bless the child for his submission. Their story was as follows:—

"Most of the tom-tom players are Indians, but we are both of us Arabs. The Arabs are just equally as good as the Indians at playing the tom-tom, but they haven't got exactly to the learning of the manufacture of them yet. I come from Mocha, and so does Peter, my companion; only his father belongs to what we call the Abshee tribe,[3] and that's what makes him so much darker than what I am. The Abshee tribe are now outside of Arabia, up by the Gulf of Persia. They are much the same as the Mucdad people,—it's all the same tribe like.

"My name is Usef Asman, and my father has been over here twelve years now. He came here in the English army, I've heard him say, for he was in the 77th Bengal Native Infantry;[4] but he wasn't an Indian, but

1 While terms such as this were used in Mayhew's time, they are now considered offensive due to their racist nature.

2 Folk percussion instrument typically consisting of two short animal bones, or sticks. The reference here evokes the minstrel show tradition, in which the bones were commonly played.

3 The name "Abshee" likely refers to people from Abyssinia, the northern half of present-day Ethiopia.

4 The infantry of the Bengal Army, whose troops were recruited from India and neighbouring areas. The Army was established in 1757 and belonged to the East India Company until 1858.

enlisted in the service and fought through the Sikh war,[1] and was wounded. He hasn't got a pension, for he sent his luggage through Paris to England, and he lost his writings. The East India Company[2] only told him that he must wait until they heard from India, and that's been going on for now six years.

"Mother came home with father and me, and two brothers and a sister. I'm the second eldest. My brother is thirty-six, and he was in the Crimea,[3] as steward on board the Royal Hydaspes, a steam screw[4] she is. He was 17 and I was 6 years old when I came over. My brother is a fine strapping fellow, over six feet high, and the muscles in his arms are as big round as my thigh.

"I don't remember my native country, but Peter does, for he's only been here for two years and five months. He likes his own country better than England. His father left Arabia to go to Bombay, and there he keeps large coffee-shops. He's worth a little money. His shops are in the low quarter of the town, just the same as Drury Lane may be, though it's the centre of the town. They call the place the Nacopoora taleemoulla.

"Before father went into the army he was an interpreter in Arabia. His father was a horse-dealer. My father can speak eight or nine different languages fluently, besides a little of others. He was the interpreter who got Dr. Woolfe out of Bokhara prison,[5] when he was put in because they thought he was a spy. Father was sent for by the chief to explain what this man's business was. It is the Mogul language[6] they speak there. My father was told to get him out of the country in twenty-four hours, and my father killed his own horse and camel walking so hard to get him away.

"We was obliged to put ourselves up to going about the streets. Duty and necessity first compelled me to do it. Father couldn't get his pension, and, of course, we couldn't sit at home and starve; so father was obliged to go out and play the drum. He got his tom-toms from an Arab vessel which came over, and they made them a present to him.

---

1 Refers to either the First Anglo-Sikh War of 1845–46 or the Second Anglo-Sikh War of 1848–49 between the Sikh Empire and the British East India Company.

2 British trading company established by royal charter in 1600 to secure a foothold in the East Indian spice trade. It became a powerful agent of British colonial rule in India until it was dissolved following the events of the "Indian Mutiny" of 1857 (see p. 339, note 1).

3 A region in eastern Europe. In support of its allies, England declared war on Russia in 1854 to prevent Russian expansion and keep trade routes open. A peace treaty that ended the Crimean War was signed in March of 1856.

4 A steamship. The Hydaspes was used to transport soldiers to Crimea in 1855 and 1856.

5 Joseph Wolff (1795–1862), a Jewish Christian missionary, made a journey to Bukhara—a city in Uzbekistan and a centre of Islamic culture and learning—in 1843 to search for two missing British military officers, who had already been executed by the time Wolff arrived.

6 An older spelling of Mughal, referring to Persian, or Farsi.

"We used before now, father and myself, to go to artists or modelers, to have our likenesses taken. We went to Mr. Armitage,[1] when he was painting a battle in India. If you recollect, I'm leaning down by the rocks, whilst the others are escaping. I've also been to Mr. Dobson,[2] who used to live in Newman-street. I've sat to him in my costume for several pictures. In one of them I was like a chief's son, or something of that, smoking a hubble-bubble.[3] Father used to have a deal of work at Mr. Gale's,[4] in Fitzroy-square. I don't know the subjects he painted, for I wasn't there whilst father used to sit. It used to tire me when I had to sit for two or three hours in one position. Sometimes I had to strip to the waist. I had to do that at Mr. Dobson's in the winter time, and, though there was a good fire in the room, it was very wide, and it didn't throw much heat out, and I used to be very cold. He used to paint religious subjects. I had a shilling an hour, and if a person could get after-work at it, I could make a better living at it than in the streets; in fact, I'd rather do it any time, though it's harder work, for there is a name for that, but there is no name for going about playing the tom-tom; yet it's better to do that than sit down and see other people starving.

"Father is still sitting to artists. He doesn't go about the streets—he couldn't face it out.

"It's about eight years ago since father got the tom-toms. They are very good ones, and one of them is reckoned the best in England. They are made out of mango tree. It grows just the same as the bamboo tree; and they take a joint of it, and take out the pith—for it's pithy inside, just like elderberry wood, with the outside hard. Father had these tom-toms for a month before we went out with them.

"The first day father went out with me, and kept on until he got employ; and then I went out by myself. I was about for four years by myself, along with sister; and then I went with Peter; and now we go out together. My sister was only about seven years old when she first went out, and she used to sing. She was dressed in a costume with a short jacket, with a tight waistcoat, and white trowsers. She had a turban and a sash.

"When we first went out we done very well. We took 6, 7, or 8*s.* a-day. We was the first to appear with it; indeed there's only me and my cousin and another man that does it now. Peter is my cousin. His real name is Busha, but we call him Peter, because it's more a proper name like, because several people can call him that when they can't Busha. We are all turned Christians; we go to school every Sunday, in Great Queen-street, Lincoln's Inn, and always to chapel. They are joined together.

---

1 Edward Armitage (1817–96), a painter best known for historical subjects. The painting described in the passage likely refers to his oil painting *The Battle of Meanee* (1847).

2 William C.T. Dobson (1817–98), an artist known for biblical subjects.

3 A water pipe; a rudimentary version of a hookah.

4 William Gale (1823–1909), a painter whose diverse output included historical and biblical subjects. He has been loosely associated with the Pre-Raphaelite school and Orientalist art.

"I and Peter take now, on a fine day in summer-time, generally 5 or 6*s*., but coming on winter as it does now it's as much as we can do to take 2*s*. or 3*s*. Sometimes in winter we don't take more than 1*s*. 6*d*., and sometimes 1*s*. Take the year round it would come, I should think, to 3*s*. a-day. On wet days we can't do nothing.

"We were forced to become Christians when we came here. Of course a true Mussulman[1] won't take anything to eat that has been touched by other people's hands. We were forced to break caste. The beasts were slaughtered by other people,[2] and we wanted meat to eat. The bread, too, was made by Christians. The school-teachers used to come to father. We remained as Mussulmen as long as we could, but when winter came on, and we had no money, we was obliged to eat food from other people's hands.

"Persons wouldn't believe it, but little family as we are it takes 4*s*. a-day to keep us. Yet mother speaks English well. I'm sure father doesn't go out and drink not half-a pint a beer of a night, but always waits till we come home, and then our 3*s*. or 4*s*. go to get bread and rice and that, and we have a pot of beer between us.

"Peter's father married my father's sister, that's how we are cousins. He came over by ship to see us. He sent a message before to say that he was coming to see his uncle, and he expected to go back by the same ship, but he was used so cruelly on board that he preferred staying with us until we can all return together. Because he couldn't understand English and his duty, and coming into a cold country and all, he couldn't do his work, and they flogged him. Besides, they had to summon the captain to get their rights. He very much wants to get back to India to his father, and our family wants to get back to Mocha. I've forgot my Arabic, and only talk Hindostanee. I did speak French very fluently, but I've forgot it all except such things as Venez ici, or Voulez-vous danser? or such-like.

"When we are at home we mostly eat rice. It's very cheap, and we like it better than anything else, because it fills our bellies better. It wouldn't be no use putting a couple of half-quartern loaves before us two if we were hungry, for, thank God, we are very hearty-eating, both of us. Rice satisfies us better than bread. We mix curry-powder and a little meat or fish with it. If there's any fish in season, such as fresh herrings or mackerel, we wash it and do it with onions, and mix it with the curry-powder, and then eat it with rice. Plaice is the only fish we don't use, for it makes the curry very watery. We wash the rice two or three times after looking over it to take out any dirt or stones, and then we boil it and let it boil about five minutes. Rice-water is very strengthening, and the Arabs drink a deal of

---

1 Archaic term for Muslim.

2 A reference to halal food that is prepared according to Islamic dietary law. Halal animal slaughter is regulated by specific practices and is carried out by trained Islamic butchers.

it, because whenever it lays in the stomach it becomes solid. It turns, when cold, as thick as starch, and with some salt it's not a bad thing.

"Our best places for playing the tom-tom is the West-end in summer-time, but in winter we goes round by Islington and Shoreditch, and such-like, for there's no quality at home, and we have to depend on the trades-people. Sometimes we very often happen to meet with a gentleman —when the quality's in town—who has been out in India, and can speak the language, and he will begin chatting with us and give us a shilling, or sometimes more. I've got two or three ladies who have taken a fancy to us, and they give me 6*d*. or 1*s*. whenever I go round. There's one old lady and two or three young ones, at several houses in different places, who have such kindness for us. I was in place once with Captain Hines, and he was very kind to me. He had been out in India, and spoke the language very fluently. I didn't leave him, he left me to go to the Crimea; and he told me he was very sorry, but he had a servant allowed him by the Government, and couldn't take me.

"Some of the servant-girls are very kind to us, and give us a 1*d*. or 2*d*. We in general tries to amuse the people as much as we can. All the people are very fond of Peter, he makes them laugh; and the same people generally gives us money when we goes round again.

"When we are out we walk along side by side beating the tom-toms. We keep on singing different songs,—foreign ones to English tunes. The most favourite tune is what we calls in Hindostanee,—

'Tasa bi tasa, no be no
Mutra bakooch, no arber go;
Tasa bi tasa, no be no
Attipa ho gora purgeen
Mara gora gora chelopageen.
Tasa bi tasa, no be no.
O senna key taho baroo
Dilla chungay gurrey kumahayroo.
Tasa bi tasa, no be no
Lutfellee karu basha bud
Shibbe de lum sesta bud
Tasa bi tasa, no be no.'

"This means:—

"'I want something fresh (such as fish) in the value of nine. And after he went and bought these fresh goods he looked at them, and found them so good, that he was very pleased with them ('mutra bakooch' is pleased), that he says to his servant that he will give him leave to go about his business, because he's made such a good bargain.'

"That's all the meaning of that, sir, and we sing it to its original Indian tune. We sometimes sing Arab songs—one or two. They are very different, but we can't explain them so well as we can the Hindostanee. They're more melancholy, and towards the parents sentimental-like. There's one song they sing in Arabia, that it puts them in that way they don't know what they are doing of. They begin the song, and then they bend the body about and beat their knees, and keep on so until they tumble off their chairs. They nearly strangle themselves sometimes. It's about love to their parents, and as if they left them and went far away. It's a sort of a cutting song, and very sentimental. There's always a man standing in one corner, looking after those singing, and when he sees them get into a way, he reads a book and comes and rouses them. He's a kind of magician-like. Father sings it, and I know a verse or two of it. I've seen father and another man singing it, and they kept on see-sawing about, and at last they both fell off the chair. We got a little water and sprinkled their faces, and hit them on the back very hard, and said, 'Sallee a nabbee,' which is just the same as 'Rise, in the name of the Lord,' and they came to instantly, and after they got up was very calm—ah, very tame afterwards!

"The tom-tom hasn't got much music in it beyond beating like a drum. There are first-rate players in India, and they can make the tom-tom speak in the same way as if you was to ask a gentleman, 'How do you do?' and they'll answer you, 'Very well, thank you.' They only go to the feasts, which are called 'madggeless,' and then the noblemen, after hearing them, will give them great sums of money as a handsome present. The girls, too, dance to the tom-tom in India. Peter is a very good player, and he can make the tom-tom to answer. One side of the drum asks the question, that is the treble side, and the bass one answers it, for in a tom-tom each end gives a different note.

"Father makes all our clothes for us. We wear flannel under our shirts, which a lady made me a present of, or else we never used to wear them before. All through that sharp winter we never used to wear anything but our dress. All the Arab boys are brought up to respect their parents. If they don't they will be punished. For myself, I always obey mine. My father has often called shame on the laws of this country, to hear the children abusing their parents. In our country, if a son disobeys his father's command, he may, even though the child be as tall as a giant, take up his sword and kill him. My brother, who is on board ship, even though he has learnt the laws of this country, always obeys my father. One night he wouldn't mind what was said, so my father goes up and hit him a side slap on the chops, and my brother turned the other cheek to him, and said in Arabic, 'Father, hit this cheek, too; I have done wrong.' He was about 30 then. Father said he hoped he'd never disobey his orders again.

"The Arabs are very clean. In our country we bathe three times a-day; but over here we only go to the bath in Endell-street[1] (a public one) twice a-week. We always put on clean things three times a-week.

"There's a knack in twisting the turban. A regular Arab always makes the rim bind over the right ear, like Peter's. It don't take more than five

---

1 A public bathhouse in High Holborn near St. Giles.

minutes to put the turban on. We do it up in a roll, and have nothing inside it to stiffen it. Some turbans have 30 yards in them, all silk, but mine is only 3½ yards, and is calico. The Arab waistcoat always has a pocket on each side of the breast, with a lengthways opening, and a bit of braid round the edge of the stuff, ending where the waist is, so that the flaps are not bound.

"The police are very kind to us, and never interfere with us unless there is somebody ill, and we are not aware of it. The tom-tom makes a very humming sound, and is heard to a great distance."

IV. Street Artists.
Street Photography.

WITHIN the last few years photographic portraits have gradually been diminishing in price, until at the present time they have become a regular article of street commerce. Those living at the west-end of London have but little idea of the number of persons who gain a livelihood by street photography.

There may be one or two "galleries" in the New-road, or in Tottenham-court-road, but these supply mostly shilling portraits. In the eastern and southern districts of London, however, such as in Bermondsey, the New-cut,[1] and the Whitechapel-road, one cannot walk fifty yards without passing some photographic establishment, where for sixpence persons can have their portrait taken, and framed and glazed as well.

It was in Bermondsey that I met with the first instance of what may be called pure street photography. Here a Mr. F——l was taking sixpenny portraits in a booth built up out of old canvas, and erected on a piece of spare ground in a furniture-broker's yard.

Mr. F——l had been a travelling showman, but finding that photography was attracting more attention than giants and dwarfs, he relinquished the wonders of Nature for those of Science.

Into this yard he had driven his yellow caravan, where it stood like an enormous Noah's ark, and in front of the caravan (by means of clothes-horses and posts, over which were spread out the large sail-like paintings (show-cloths), which were used at fairs to decorate the fronts of booths), he had erected his operating-room, which is about as long and as broad as a knife-house, and only just tall enough to allow a not particularly tall customer to stand up with his hat off: whilst by means of two window-sashes a glazed roof had been arranged for letting light into this little tent.

On the day of my visit Mr. F——l was, despite the cloudy state of the atmosphere, doing a large business. A crowd in front of his tent was admiring the photographic specimens, which, of all sizes and in all kinds of frames, were stuck up against the canvas-wall, as irregularly as if a bill-sticker had placed them there. Others were gazing up at the chalky-

1 See p. 53, note 2.

looking paintings over the door-way, and on which a lady was represented photographing an officer, in the full costume of the 11th Hussars.[1]

Inside the operating room we found a crowd of women and children was assembled, all of them waiting their turn to be taken. Mr. F——l remarked, as I entered, that 'It was wonderful the sight of children that had been took'; and he added, 'when *one* girl comes for her portrait, there's a *dozen* comes along with her to see it took.'

The portraits I discovered were taken by Mrs. F——l, who, with the sleeves of her dress tucked up to the elbows, was engaged at the moment of my visit in pointing the camera at a lady and her little boy, who, from his wild nervous expression, seemed to have an idea that the operatress was taking her aim previous to shooting him. Mr. F——l explained to me the reason why his wife officiated. "You see," said he, "people prefers more to be took by a woman than by a man. Many's a time a lady tells us to send that man away, and let the missis come. It's quite natural," he continued; "for a lady don't mind taking her bonnet off and tucking up her hair, or sticking a pin in here and there before one of her own sect, which before a man proves objectionable."

After the portrait had been taken I found that the little square piece of glass on which it was impressed was scarcely larger than a visiting card,[2] and this being handed over to a youth, was carried into the caravan at the back, where the process was completed. I was invited to follow the lad to the dwelling on wheels.

The outside of the caravan was very remarkable, and of that peculiar class of architecture which is a mixture of coach-and-ship building. In the centre of the front of the show were little folding-doors with miniature brass knockers, and glass let into the upper panels. On each side of the door were long windows, almost big enough for a shop-front, whilst the white curtains, festooned at their sides, gave them a pleasant appearance. The entire erection was coloured yellow, and the numerous little wooden joists and tie-beams, which framed and strengthened the vehicle, conferred upon it a singular plaid-like appearance.

I mounted the broad step-ladder and entered. The room reminded me of a ship's cabin, for it was panelled and had cross-beams to the arched roof, whilst the bolts and fastenings were of bright brass. If the windows had not been so large, or the roof so high, it would have resembled the fore-cabin of a Gravesend steamer.[3] There were tables and chairs, as in an ordinary cottage room. At one end was the family bed, concealed during the day by chintz curtains, which hung down like a drop-scene before a

---

1 A cavalry regiment of the British Army that wore extravagant and expensive uniforms.

2 A small card printed with a person's name and sometimes with other practical details (e.g., social position or address). In the Victorian era, visiting cards were exchanged by the upper and upper-middle classes as proper etiquette for social visits.

3 Thames passenger steamboats that travelled downriver via Gravesend, a town east of London.

miniature theatre; and between the openings of these curtains I could catch sight of some gaudily attired wax figures stowed away there for want of room, but standing there like a group of actors behind the scenes.

Along one of the beams a blunderbuss and a pistol rested on hooks, and the showman's speaking trumpet (as large as the funnel to a grocer's coffee-mill) hung against the wall, whilst in one corner was a kind of cabin stove of polished brass, before which a boy was drying some of the portraits that had been recently taken.

"So you've took him at last," said the proprietor, who accompanied us as he snatched the portrait from the boy's hand. "Well, the eyes ain't no great things, but as it's the third attempt it must do."

On inspecting the portrait I found it to be one of those drab-looking portraits with a light back-ground, where the figure rises from the bottom of the plate as straight as a post, and is in the cramped, nervous attitude of a patient in a dentist's chair.

After a time I left Mr. F——l's, and went to another establishment close by, which had originally formed part of a shop in the penny-ice-and-bull's-eye line[1]—for the name-board over "Photographic Depôt" was still the property of the confectioner—so that the portraits displayed in the window were surmounted by an announcement of "Ginger beer 1*d.* and 2*d.*"

A touter at the door was crying out "Hi! hi!—walk inside! walk inside! and have your c'rect likeness took, frame and glass complete, and only 6*d.*!—time of sitting only four seconds!"

A rough-looking, red-faced tanner, who had been staring at some coloured French lithographs[2] which decorated the upper panes, and who, no doubt, imagined that they had been taken by the photographic process, entered, saying, "Let me have my likeness took."

The touter instantly called out, "Here, a shilling likeness for this here gent."

The tanner observed that he wanted only a sixpenny.

"Ah, very good, sir!" and raising his voice, the touter shouted louder than before—"A sixpenny one first, and a shilling one afterwards."

"I tell yer I don't want only sixpennorth," angrily returned the customer, as he entered.

At this establishment the portraits were taken in a little alley adjoining the premises, where the light was so insufficient, that even the blanket hung up at the end of it looked black from the deep shadows cast by the walls.

1 A shop that sells candies: penny ices were frozen syrups and bull's-eye candies were a type of boiled sweet.

2 Invented in Bavaria in 1796, lithography was an inexpensive method of printing using stone or metal plates and was capable of reproducing thousands of images rapidly. France became the centre of production of lithographs, which were the preferred medium for images of daily life before the invention of photography.

When the tanner's portrait was completed it was nearly black; and, indeed, the only thing visible was a slight light on one side of the face, and which, doubtlessly, accounted for the short speech which the operator thought fit to make as he presented the likeness to his customer.

"There," he said, "there is your likeness, if you like! look at it yourself; and only eightpence"—"Only sixpence," observed the man.—"Ah!" continued the proprietor, "but you've got a patent American preserver, and that's twopence more."[1]

Then followed a discussion, in which the artist insisted that he lost by every sixpenny portrait he took, and the tanner as strongly protesting that he couldn't believe that, for they must get *some* profit any how. "You don't tumble to the rig,"[2] said the artist; "it's the half-guinea ones, you see, that pays us."

The touter, finding that this discussion was likely to continue, entered and joined the argument. "Why, it's cheap as dirt," he exclaimed indignantly; "the fact is, our governor's a friend of the people, and don't mind losing a little money. He's determined that everybody shall have a portrait, from the highest to the lowest. Indeed, next Sunday, he *do* talk of taking them for threepence-ha'penny, and if that ain't philandery,[3] what is?"

After the touter's oration the tanner seemed somewhat contented, and paying his eightpence left the shop, looking at his picture in all lights, and repeatedly polishing it up with the cuff of his coat-sleeve, as if he were trying to brighten it into something like distinctness.

Whilst I was in this establishment a customer was induced to pay twopence for having the theory of photography explained to him. The lecture was to the effect, that the brass tube of the "camerer" was filled with clockwork, which carried the image from the lens to the ground glass at the back. To give what the lecturer called "hockeylar proof"[4] of this, the camera was carried to the shopdoor, and a boy who was passing by ordered to stand still for a minute.

"Now, then," continued the lecturer to the knowledge-seeker, "look behind here; there's the himage, you see"; and then addressing the boy, he added, "Just open your mouth, youngster"; and when the lad did so, the student was asked, "Are you looking down the young un's throat?" and on his nodding assent, he was informed, "Well, that's the way portraits is took."

---

1 This is a sales tactic indicating that American patents were more highly regarded than British and European patents. The preserver is a sheet of paper that could be used to regulate exposure in some printing processes.

2 "You don't fall for that kind of con."

3 Philanthropy.

4 Ocular (visible) proof. The most famous use of this expression is from Shakespeare's *Othello*, where the protagonist demands "ocular proof" of his wife's infidelity (3.3.362).

V. Exhibitors of Trained Animals.
The Happy Family Exhibitor.[1]

"HAPPY Families," or assemblages of animals of diverse habits and propensities living amicably, or at least quietly, in one cage, are so well known as to need no further description here. Concerning them I received the following account:—

"I have been three years connected with happy families, living by such connexion. These exhibitions were first started at Coventry, sixteen years ago, by a man who was my teacher. He was a stocking-weaver, and a fancier of animals and birds, having a good many in his place—hawks, owls, pigeons, starlings, cats, dogs, rats, mice, guinea-pigs, jackdaws, fowls, ravens, and monkeys. He used to keep them separate and for his own amusement, or would train them for sale, teaching the dogs tricks, and such-like. He found his animals agree so well together, that he had a notion—and a snake-charmer, an old Indian, used to advise him on the subject—that he could show in public animals and birds, supposed to be one another's enemies and victims, living in quiet together. He did show them in public, beginning with cats, rats, and pigeons in one cage; and then kept adding by degrees all the other creatures I have mentioned. He did very well at Coventry, but I don't know what he took. His way of training the animals is a secret, which he has taught to me. It's principally done, however, I may tell you, by continued kindness and petting, and studying the nature of the creatures. Hundreds have tried their hands at happy families, and have failed. The cat has killed the mice, the hawks have killed the birds, the dogs the rats, and even the cats, the rats, the birds, and even one another; indeed, it was anything but a happy family. By our system we never have a mishap; and have had animals eight or nine years in the cage—until they've died of age, indeed. In our present cage we have 54 birds and animals, and of 17 different kinds; 3 cats, 2 dogs (a terrier and a spaniel), 2 monkeys, 2 magpies, 2 jackdaws, 2 jays, 10 starlings (some of them talk), 6 pigeons, 2 hawks, 2 barn fowls, 1 screech owl, 5 common-sewer rats, 5 white rats (a novelty), 8 guinea-pigs, 2 rabbits (1 wild and 1 tame), 1 hedgehog, and 1 tortoise. Of all these, the rat is the most difficult to make a member of a happy family: among birds, the hawk. The easiest trained animal is a monkey, and the easiest trained bird a pigeon. They live together in their cages all night, and sleep in a stable, unattended by any one. They were once thirty-six hours, as a trial, without food—that was in Cambridge; and no creature was injured; but they were very peckish, especially the birds of prey. I wouldn't allow it to be tried (it was for a scientific gentleman) any longer, and I fed them well to begin upon. There are now in London five happy families, all belonging to two families of men. Mine, that is the one I have the care of, is the strongest—

1 First published as part of Letter LVI of the "Labour and the Poor" series for the *Morning Chronicle*, 13 June 1850.

fifty-four creatures: the others will average forty each, or 214 birds and beasts in happy families. Our only regular places now are Waterloo-bridge and the National Gallery. The expense of keeping my fifty-four is 12*s*. a-week; and in a good week—indeed, the best week—we take 30*s*.; and in a bad week sometimes not 8*s*. It's only a poor trade, though there are more good weeks than bad: but the weather has so much to do with it. The middle class of society are our best supporters. When the happy family—only one—was first in London, fourteen years ago, the proprietor took 1*l*. a-day on Waterloo-bridge; and only showed in the summer. The second happy family was started eight years ago, and did as well for a short time as the first. Now there are too many happy families. There are none in the country."

SKILLED AND UNSKILLED LABOUR.

The Coal-Heavers.

The Coal-Heavers.[1]

THE transition from the artisan to the labourer is curious in many respects. In passing[2] from the skilled operative of the west-end to the unskilled workman of the eastern quarter of London, the moral and intellectual change is so great, that it seems as if we were in a new land, and among another race. The artisans are almost to a man red-hot politicians. They are sufficiently educated and thoughtful to have a sense of their importance in the State. It is true they may entertain exaggerated notions of their natural rank and position in the social scale, but at least they have read, and reflected, and argued upon the subject, and their opinions are entitled to consideration. The political character and sentiments of the working classes appear to me to be a distinctive feature of the age, and they are a necessary consequence of the dawning intelligence of the mass. As their minds expand, they are naturally led to take a more enlarged view of their calling, and to contemplate their labours in relation to the whole framework of society. They begin to view their class, not as a mere isolated body of workmen, but as an integral portion of the nation, contributing their quota to the general welfare. If property has its duties as well as its rights; labour, on the other hand, they say, has its rights as well as its duties. The artisans of London seem to be generally well-informed upon these subjects. That they express their opinions violently, and often savagely, it is my duty to acknowledge; but that they are the unenlightened and unthinking body of people that they are generally considered by those who never go among them, and who see them only as "the dangerous

---

1 First published as part of Letter XIX of the "Labour and the Poor" series for the *Morning Chronicle*, 21 December 1849.

2 In a section omitted from this edition, Mayhew has just discussed skilled tradespeople like cabinet-makers and doll's-eye makers.

classes," it is my duty also to deny. So far as my experience has gone, I am bound to confess, that I have found the skilled labourers of the metropolis the very reverse, both morally and intellectually, of what the popular prejudice imagines them.

The unskilled labourers are a different class of people. As yet they are as unpolitical as footmen, and instead of entertaining violent democratic opinions, they appear to have no political opinions whatever; or, if they do possess any, they rather lead towards the maintenance of "things as they are," than towards the ascendancy of the working people. I have lately been investigating the state of the coalwhippers,[1] and these reflections are forced upon me by the marked difference in the character and sentiments of these people from those of the operative tailors. Among the latter class there appeared to be a general bias towards the six points of the Charter;[2] but the former were extremely proud of their having turned out to a man on the 10th of April, 1848, and become special constables for the maintenance of law and order on the day of the great Chartist demonstration.[3] As to which of these classes are the better members of the state, it is not for me to offer an opinion; I merely assert a social fact. The artisans of the metropolis are intelligent, and dissatisfied with their political position: the labourers of London appear to be the reverse; and in passing from one class to the other, the change is so curious and striking, that the phenomenon deserves at least to be recorded in this place.

[...]

The following statistics, carefully collected from official returns, will furnish our readers with some idea of the amazing increase in the importation of coal:—

"About 300 years ago (say about 1550) one or two ships were sufficient for the demand and supply of London. In 1615, about 200 were equal to its demand; in 1705, about 600 ships were engaged in the London coal-trade; in 1805, 4856 cargoes, containing about 1,350,000 tons; in 1820, 5884 cargoes, containing 1,692,992 tons; in 1830, 7108 cargoes, containing 2,079,275 tons; in 1840, 9132 cargoes, containing 2,566,899 tons; in 1845, 2695 ships were employed in carrying 11,987 cargoes, containing 3,403,320 tons; and during the year 1848, 2717 ships, making 12,267 voyages, and containing 3,418,340 tons. The increase in the importation from the year 1838 to 1848, when the respective importa-

---

1 See p. 184, note 1.

2 The six points of the Charter laid out the primary demands of the Chartists. See p. 56, note 1, and Introduction, p. 19.

3 More than 100,000 private citizens were sworn in as special constables to help the police control a mass meeting and march organized by the Chartist movement for 10 April 1848. The meeting ostensibly shut down the city, as hundreds of thousands of people both rallied at, and policed, the event.

tions were 2,518,085 tons and 3,418,340 tons, is upwards of 90 per cent. Now, by taking 2700 vessels as the actual number now employed, and by calculating such vessels to average 300 tons burden per ship, and giving to a vessel of that size a crew of eight men, it will appear that at the present time 21,600 seamen are employed in the carrying department of the London coal-trade."

[...]

The coalwhippers, previous to the passing of the Act of Parliament in 1843, were employed and paid by the publicans in the neighbourhood of the river, from Tower-hill to Limehouse. Under this system, none but the most dissolute and intemperate obtained employment; in fact, the more intemperate they were the more readily they found work. The publicans were the relatives of the northern shipowners; they mostly had come to London penniless, and being placed in a tavern by their relatives, soon became shipowners themselves. There were at that time seventy taverns on the north side of the Thames, below bridge, employing coalwhippers, and all of the landlords making fortunes out of the earnings of the people. When a ship came to be "made up," that is, for the hands to be hired, the men assembled round the bar in crowds and began calling for drink, and outbidding each other in the extent of their orders, so as to induce the landlord to give them employment. If one called for beer, the next would be sure to give an order for rum; for he who spent most at the public-house had the greatest chance of employment. After being "taken on," their first care was to put up a score at the public-house, so as to please their employer, the publican. In the morning before going to their work, they would invariably call at the house for a quartern of gin or rum; and they were obliged to take off with them to the ship "a bottle," holding nine pots of beer, and that of the worst description, for it was the invariable practice among the publicans to supply the coalwhippers with the very worst articles at the highest prices. When the men returned from their work they went back to the public-house, and there remained drinking the greater part of the night. He must have been a very steady man indeed, I am told, who could manage to return home sober to his wife and family. The consequence of this was, the men used to pass their days, and chief part of their nights, drinking in the public-house; and I am credibly informed that frequently, on the publican settling with them after leaving the ship, instead of having anything to receive they were brought in several shillings in debt; this remained as a score for the next ship: in fact, it was only those who were in debt to the publican who were sure of employment on the next occasion. One publican had as many as fifteen ships; another had even more; and there was scarcely one of them without his two or three colliers.[1] The children of the coalwhippers were almost reared in the

1 Coal ships.

tap-room, and a person who has had great experience in the trade, tells me he knew as many as 500 youths who were transported, and as many more who met with an untimely death. At one house there were forty young robust men employed, about seventeen years ago, and of these there are only two living at present. My informant tells me that he has frequently seen as many as 100 men at one time fighting pell-mell at King James's-stairs,[1] and the publican standing by to see fair play. The average money spent in drink by each man was about 12*s.* to each ship. There were about 10,000 ships entered the Pool each year, and nine men were required to clear each ship. This made the annual expenditure of the coalwhippers in drink, 54,000*l.*, or 27*l.* a-year per man. This is considered an extremely low average. The wives and families of the men at this time were in the greatest destitution, the daughters invariably became prostitutes, and the mothers ultimately went to swell the number of paupers at the union. This state of things continued till 1843, when, by the efforts of three of the coalwhippers, the Legislature was induced to pass an Act forbidding the system, and appointing Commissioners for the registration and regulation of coalwhippers in the port of London, and so establishing an office where the men were in future employed and paid. Under this Act, every man then following the calling of a coalwhipper was to be registered. For this registration 4*d.* was to be paid; and every man desirous of entering upon the same business had to pay the same sum, and to have his name registered. The employment is open to any labouring man; but every new hand, after registering himself, must work for twenty-one days on half-pay before he is considered to be "broken in," and entitled to take rank and receive pay as a regular coalwhipper.

[...]

The coalwhippers all present the same aspect—they are all black. In summer, when the men strip more to their work, perspiration causes the coal-dust to adhere to the skin, and blackness is more than ever the rule. All about the ship partakes of the grimness of the prevailing hue. The sails are black; the gilding on the figurehead of the vessel becomes blackened, and the very visitor feels his complexion soon grow sable. The dress of the whippers is of every description; some have fustian jackets,[2] some have sailors' jackets, some loose great coats, some Guernsey frocks.[3] Many of them work in strong shirts, which once were white with a blue stripe: loose cotton neckerchiefs are generally worn by the whippers. All have black hair and black whiskers—no matter what the original hue; to the more stubbly beards and moustachios the coal-dust adheres freely between the bristles, and may even be seen, now and then, to glitter in the light amidst

---

1 See p. 183, note 1.

2 See p. 54, note 1.

3 See p. 160, note 2.

the hair. The barber, one of these men told me, charged nothing extra for shaving him, although the coal-dust must be a formidable thing to the best-tempered razor. In approaching a coal-ship in the river, the side has to be gained over barges lying alongside—the coal crackling under the visitor's feet. He must cross them to reach a ladder of very primitive construction, up which the deck is to be reached. It is a jest among the Yorkshire seamen that every thing is black in a collier, especially the soup. When the men are at work in whipping or filling, the only spot of white discernible on their hands is a portion of the nails.

[...]

I was now desirous of obtaining some information from the men collectively. Accordingly I entered the basket-men's waiting-room,[1] where a large number of them were "biding their turn"; and no sooner had I made my appearance in the hall, and my object became known to the men, than a rush was made from without, and the door was obliged to be bolted to prevent the overcrowding of the room. As it was, the place was crammed so full, that the light was completely blocked by the men piled up on the seats and lockers, and standing before the windows. The room was thus rendered so dark that I was obliged to have the gas lighted, in order to see to take my notes; I myself was obliged to mount the opposite locker to take the statistics of the meeting.

There were eighty-six present. To show how many had no employment whatever last week, forty-five hands were held up. One had had no employment for a fortnight; twenty-four no work for eight days. Of those who had worked during the previous week, eight had received 20*s.*; sixteen between 15*s.* and seventeen between 10*s.* and 15*s.*; ten between 5*s.* and 10*s.*; one had received under 5*s.*; twelve had received nothing. The average of employment as to time is this:—None are employed for thirty weeks during the year; all for twenty-five weeks or upwards, realizing 12*s.* perhaps, yearly, per week—so many of the men said; but the office returns show 1*s.* 1½*d.* per day as the average for the last nine months. "Waterage" costs the whipper an average of 6*d.* a-week the year through. "Waterage" means the conveyance from the vessels to the shore. Fourteen of the men had wives or daughters who work at slop needlework,[2] the husbands being unable to maintain the family by their own labour. A coalwhipper stated that there were more of the wives of the coalwhippers idle, because they couldn't get work, than were at work. All the wives and daughters would have worked if they could have got it. "Why, your honour," one man said, "we are better off in this office than under the old system. We were then

1 In Mayhew's Letter XIX to the *Morning Chronicle* (21 December 1849), he explains that the basket-men, or foremen, wrote the names of their whippers in the office's rotation book and then waited in the basket-men's room for their turn to clear a ship.

2 See p. 77, note 1.

compulsory drunkards, and often in debt to a publican after clearing the ship." The men employed generally spent 12*s.* to 15*s.* a-week. Those unemployed had abundant credit at the publican's. One man said, "I worked for a publican who was also a butcher; one week I had to pay 9*s.* for drink, and 11*s.* for meat, and he said I hadn't spent sufficient. I was one of his constant men." At the time a ship was cleared, the whipper had often nothing to take home. "Nothing but sorrow," said one. The publican swept all; and some publicans would advance 2*s.* 6*d.* towards the next job, to allow a man to live. Many of the whippers now do not drink at all. The average of the drinking among the men, when at hard work, does not exceed three half-pints a-day. The grievances that once afflicted the coal-whipper, are still felt by the ballast-men.[1] The men all stated the fact as to the 9*d.* allowed, and the 8*d.* per ton paid for whipping. They all represented that a lighterman, engaged by the gas companies, was doing them great injury, by employing a number of "bonafides,"[2] and taking the best ships away from the regular office, and giving them to the "bonafides" who "whip" the vessel at a lower rate of wages—about 6*d.* a-ton. He is connected with a beer-shop, and the men are expected to buy his beer. If this man gets on with his system (all this the men concurred in stating), the bad state of things prevailing under the publican's management might be brought back. Sixteen years ago each whipper received 11¼*d.* per ton, prices steady, and the men in union. "If it wasn't for this office," one man said, "not one man who worked sixteen years ago would be alive now." The Union was broken up about twelve years ago, and prices fell and fluctuated down as low as 6*d.*, and even 5½*d.*, sometimes rising and falling 1¼*d.* a-week. The prices continued fluctuating until the present office was established, in 1844. The shipowners and merchants agreed, at the commencement of the office, to give the whippers 9*d.* a-ton, and in three months reduced it to 8*d.* The publicans, it was stated, formed themselves into a compact body for the purpose of breaking down the present system, and they introduced hundreds of fresh hands to undersell the regular workers. In 1847 wages rose again to 9*d.*; the whippers appealing to the trade, urging the high price of provisions, and their appeal being allowed. This 9*d.* a-ton continued until the 1st of June last. At that time the "bonafides" were generally introduced, and greatly increased, and getting three times the work the regular men did, they (the regular men) consented again to lower the prices. The "bonafides" are no better off than

1 As described by Mayhew in Letter XXII to the *Morning Chronicle*, once the ships had offloaded their coal, they needed to be weighed down with ballast—typically gravel or sand dredged up from the bed of the Thames—in order to sail back to the north of England safely. Mayhew describes three types of ballast labourers, the third of whom suffers the most abuse: the ballast-getters who collect the ballast, the ballast-lighters who then transport it to the ships, and the ballast-heavers who load it onto the ships.

2 Subcontractors charging their own, cheaper, rates rather than being employed directly by the office.

the regular hands; for though they have much more work they have less per ton, and have to spend more in drink. The coalwhippers represented themselves as benefited by the cheapness of provisions. With dear provisions they couldn't, at their present earnings, live at all. The removal of the backing system had greatly benefited the whippers. On being asked how many had things in pawn, there was a general laugh, and a cry of "All of us." [...]

[...]

I then proceeded to take the statement of some of the different classes of the men. The first was a coalwhipper, whom the men had selected as one knowing more about their calling than the generality. He told me as follows:—

"I am about forty, and am a married man with a family of six children. I worked under the old system, and that to my sorrow. If I had been paid in money, according to the work I then did, I could have averaged 30*s.* a-week. Instead of receiving that amount in money, I was compelled to spend in drink 15*s.* to 18*s.* per week, when work was good; and the publican even then gave me the residue very grudgingly, and often kept me from eleven to twelve on Saturday night, before he would pay me. The consequences of this system were, that I had a miserable home to go to: I would often have faced Newgate as soon. My health didn't suffer, because I didn't drink the liquor I was forced to pay for. I gave most of it away. The liquors were beer, rum, and gin, all prepared the night before, adulterated shamefully for our consumption, as we dursn't refuse it,—dursn't even grumble. The condition of my poor wife and children was then most wretched. Now the thing is materially altered, thank God; my wife and children can go to chapel at certain times, when work is pretty good, and our things are not in pawn. By the strictest economy, I can do middling well—very well when compared with what things were. When the new system first came into operation, I felt almost in a new world. I felt myself a free man; I wasn't compelled to drink; my home assumed a better aspect, and keeps it still. Last Monday night I received 19*s.* 7*d.* for my work (five days) in the previous week. I shall now (Thursday) have to wait until Monday next before I can get to work at my business. Sometimes I get a job in idle times at the docks, or otherwise, and wish I could get more. I may make, one week with another, by odd jobs, 1*s.* a-week. Perhaps for months I can't get a job. All that time I have no choice but to be idle. One week with another, the year through (at 8*d.* per ton), I may earn 14*s.* The great evil is the uncertainty of the work. We have all to take our rotation. This uncertainty has this effect upon many of the men—they are compelled to live on credit." [...]

I visited this man's cottage, and found it neat and tidy. His children looked healthy. The walls of the lower room were covered with some cheap prints; a few old books, well worn, as if well used, were to be seen;

and everything evinced a man who was struggling bravely to rear a large family well on small means. I took the family at a disadvantage, moreover, as washing was going on.

Hearing that accidents were frequent among the class, I was anxious to see a person who had suffered by the danger of the calling. A man was brought to me with his hand bound up in a handkerchief. The sleeve of his coat was ripped open and dangled down beside his injured arm. He walked lame; and on my inquiring whether his leg was hurt, he began pulling up his trousers and unlacing his boot, to show me that it had not been properly set. He had evidently once been a strong, muscular man, but little now remained as evidence of his physical power but the size of his bones. He furnished me with the following statement:—

"I was a coalwhipper. I had a wife and two children. Four months ago, coming off my day's work, my foot slipped, and I fell and broke my leg. I was taken to the hospital, and remained there ten weeks. At the time of my accident I had no money at all by me, but was in debt to the amount of 10*s*. to my landlord. I had a little furniture, and a few clothes of myself and wife. While I was in the hospital, I did not receive anything from our benefit society,[1] because I had not been able to keep up my subscription. My wife and children lived while I was in the hospital by pawning my things, and going from door to door to every one she knowed to give her a bit. The men who worked in the same gang as myself, made up 4*s*. 6*d*. for me, and that, with two loaves of bread that they had from the relieving officer, was all they got. While I was in the hospital the landlord seized for rent the few things that my wife had not pawned, and turned her and my two little children into the street. One was a boy three years old, and the other a baby just turned ten months. My wife went to her mother, and she kept her and my little ones for three weeks, till she could do so no longer. My mother, poor old woman, was most as bad off as we were. My mother only works on the ground, out in the country, at gardening. She makes about 7*s*. a-week in the summer, and in the winter she has only 9*d*. a-day to live upon; but she had at least a shelter for her child, and she willingly shared that with her daughter and her daughter's children. She pawned all the clothes she had, to keep them from starving; but at last everything was gone from the poor old woman, and then I got my brother to take my family in. My brother worked at garden-work, the same as my mother-in-law did. He made about 15*s*. a-week in the summer, and about half that in the winter time. He had a wife and two children of his own, and found it hard enough to keep them, as times go. But still he took us all in, and shared what he had with us, rather than let us go to the workhouse. When I was told to leave the hospital—which I was forced to do upon my crutches, for my leg

1 An article on coal-whippers in *The Working Man's Friend and Family Instructor* (March 1852) explains that a few years earlier, the coal-whippers formed a benefit society, which kept a common pool of money to aid those needing financial assistance, especially in instances of illness and death.

was very bad still—my brother took me in too. He had only one room, but he got in a bundle of straw for me, and we lived and slept there for seven weeks. He got credit for more than a pound's worth of bread, and tea, and sugar for us; and now he can't pay, and the man threatens to summon him for it. After I left my brother's, I came to live in the neighbourhood of Wapping, for I thought I might manage to do a day's work at coalwhipping, and I couldn't bear to live upon his little earnings any longer—he could scarcely keep himself then. At last I got a ship to deliver; but I was too weak to do the work, and in pulling at the ropes my hands got sore, and festered for want of nourishment." [He took the handkerchief off and showed that it was covered with plaster. It was almost white from deficient circulation.] "After this I was obliged to lay up again, and that's the only job of work I've been able to do for these last four months. My wife can't do anything; she is a delicate, sickly little woman as well, and has the two little children to mind, and to look after me likewise. I had one pennyworth of bread this morning. We altogether had half-a-quartern loaf among the four of us, but no tea nor coffee. Yesterday we had some bread, and tea, and butter; but wherever my wife got it from I don't know. I was three days but a short time back without a taste of food." [Here he burst out crying.] "I had nothing but water that passed my lips. I had merely a little at home, and that my wife and children had. I would rather starve myself than let them do so: indeed, I've done it over and over again. I never begged: I'll die in the streets first. I never told nobody of my life. The foreman of my gang was the only one besides God that knew of my misery; and his wife came to me and brought me money and brought me food, and himself, too, many a time." ["I had a wife and five children of my own to maintain, and it grieved me to my heart," said the man who sat by, "to see them want, and I unable to do more for them."] "If any accident occurs to any of us who are not upon the society, they must be as bad off as I am. If I only had a little nourishment to strengthen me, I could do my work again; but, poor as I am, I can't get strength to do it, and not being totally incapacitated from ever resuming my labour, I cannot get any assistance from the superannuation fund of our men."

I told the man I wished to see him at his own home, and he and the foreman who had brought him to me, and who gave him a most excellent character, led me into a small house in a court near the Shadwell entrance to the London Docks. When I reached the place I found the room almost bare of furniture. A baby lay sprawling on its back on a few rags beside the handful of fire. A little shoeless boy, with only a light washed-out frock to cover him, ran shyly into a corner of the room as we entered. There was only one chair in the room, and that had been borrowed down stairs. Over the chimney hung to dry a few ragged infant's chemises that had been newly washed. In front of the fire, on a stool, sat the thinly-clad wife; and in the corner of the apartment stood a few old tubs. On a line above these were two tattered men's shirts, hanging to dry, and a bed was thrown on some boxes. On a shelf stood a physic-bottle that the man had got from the parish doctor,

BALLAST-HEAVERS AT WORK IN THE POOL.

[From a Sketch.

Fig. 15: "Ballast-Heavers at Work in the Pool."

and in the empty cupboard was a slice of bread—all the food, they said, they had in the world, and they knew not where on earth to look for more.

[...]

The Dock-Labourers.
The London Dock.[1]

[...]

As you enter the dock[2] the sight of the forest of masts in the distance, and the tall chimneys vomiting clouds of black smoke, and the many coloured flags flying in the air, has a most peculiar effect; while the sheds with the monster wheels arching through the roofs look like the paddle-boxes of huge steamers. Along the quay you see, now men with their faces blue with indigo, and now gaugers,[3] with their long brass-tipped rule dripping with spirit from the cask they have been probing. Then will come a group of flaxen-haired sailors chattering German; and next a black sailor, with a cotton handkerchief twisted turban-like round his head. Presently a blue-smocked butcher, with fresh meat and a bunch of cabbages in the tray on his shoulder; and shortly afterwards a mate, with green paroquets in a wooden cage. Here you will see sitting on a bench a sorrowful-looking woman, with new bright cooking tins at her feet, telling you she is an emigrant preparing for her voyage. As you pass along this quay the air is pungent with tobacco; on that it overpowers you with the fumes of rum; then you are nearly sickened with the stench of hides, and huge bins of horns; and shortly afterwards the atmosphere is fragrant with coffee and spice. Nearly everywhere you meet stacks of cork, or else yellow bins of sulphur, or lead-coloured copper-ore. As you enter this warehouse, the flooring is sticky, as if it had been newly tarred, with the sugar that has leaked through the casks; and as you descend into the dark vaults, you see long lines of lights hanging from the black arches, and lamps flitting about midway. Here you sniff the fumes of the wine, and there the peculiar fungus-smell of dry rot; then the jumble of sounds as you pass along the dock blends in anything but sweet concord. The sailors are singing boisterous nigger songs[4] from the Yankee ship just entering; the cooper is hammering at the casks on the quay; the chains of the cranes, loosed of their weight, rattle as they fly up up again; the ropes splash

1 First published as part of Letter III of the "Labour and the Poor" series for the *Morning Chronicle*, 26 October 1849.

2 London Dock was one of many dock systems built along the Thames in east and southeast London during the dock-building boom of the nineteenth century. It was situated in Wapping and completed between 1802 and 1805. It was known for its massive tobacco and wine warehouses.

3 Tax officers who inspected imported bulk goods, such as wine and beer, to ensure duty payment and prevent smuggling.

4 On this terminology, see p. 252, note 1.

in the water; some captain shouts his orders through his hands; a goat bleats from some ship in the basin; and empty casks roll along the stones with a heavy drum-like sound. Here the heavily-laden ships are down far below the quay, and you descend to them by ladders; whilst in another basin they are high up out of the water, so that their green copper sheathing is almost level with the eye of the passenger; while above his head a long line of bowsprits stretches far over the quay; and from them hang spars and planks as a gangway to each ship.

[...]

It will be easy to judge what may be the condition and morals of a class who to-day, as a body, may earn near upon 400*l.*, and tomorrow only 150*l.* I had hoped to have been able to have shown the fluctuations in the total amount of wages paid to the dock-labourers for each week throughout the whole year; and so, by contrasting the comparative affluence and comfort of one week with the distress and misery of the other, to have afforded the reader some more vivid idea of the body of men who are performing, perhaps, the heaviest labour, and getting the most fickle provision of all. But still I will endeavour to impress him with some faint idea of the struggle there is to gain the uncertain daily bread. Until I saw with my own eyes this scene of greedy despair, I could not have believed that there was so mad an eagerness to work, and so biting a want of it, among so vast a body of men. A day or two before I had sat at midnight in the room of the starving weaver;[1] and as I heard him tell his bitter story, there was a patience in his misery that gave it more an air of heroism than desperation. But in the scenes I have lately witnessed the want has been positively tragic, and the struggle for life partaking of the sublime. The reader must first remember what kind of men the casual labourers generally are. They are men, it should be borne in mind, who are shut out from the usual means of life by the want of character. Hence, you are not astonished to hear from those who are best acquainted with the men, that there are hundreds among the body who are known thieves, and who go to the docks to seek a living; so that, if taken for any past offence, their late industry may plead for some little lenity in their punishment.

He who wishes to behold one of the most extraordinary and least-known scenes of this metropolis, should wend his way to the London Dock gates at half-past seven in the morning. There he will see congregated within the principal entrance masses of men of all grades, looks, and kinds. Some in half-fashioned surtouts burst at the elbows, with the dirty shirts showing through. Others in greasy sporting jackets, with red

1 London's silk weavers were gradually thrown out of work as factory mechanization and power looms replaced hand-loom weaving carried out in homes and small-scale workshops in London's East End neighbourhoods, especially Spitalfields. Here, Mayhew refers to a previous letter in *The Morning Chronicle* that focused on these weavers.

pimpled faces. Others in the rags of their half-slang gentility, with the velvet collars of their paletots worn through to the canvas. Some in rusty black, with their waistcoats fastened tight up to the throat. Others, again, with the knowing thieves' curl on each side of the jaunty cap; whilst here and there you may see a big-whiskered Pole, with his hands in the pockets of his plaited French trousers. Some loll outside the gates, smoking the pipe which is forbidden within; but these are mostly Irish.

Presently you know, by the stream pouring through the gates and the rush towards particular spots, that the "calling foremen" have made their appearance. Then begins the scuffling and scrambling forth of countless hands high in the air, to catch the eye of him whose voice may give them work. As the foreman calls from a book the names, some men jump up on the backs of the others, so as to lift themselves high above the rest, and attract the notice of him who hires them. All are shouting. Some cry aloud his surname, some his christian name, others call out their own names, to remind him that they are there. Now the appeal is made in Irish blarney—now in broken English. Indeed, it is a sight to sadden the most callous, to see thousands of men struggling for only one day's hire; the scuffle being made the fiercer by the knowledge that hundreds out of the number there assembled must be left to idle the day out in want. To look in the faces of that hungry crowd is to see a sight that must be ever remembered. Some are smiling to the foreman to coax him into remembrance of them; others, with their protruding eyes, eager to snatch at the hoped-for pass. For weeks many have gone there, and gone through the same struggle—the same cries; and have gone away, after all, without the work they had screamed for.

From this it might be imagined that the work was of a peculiarly light and pleasant kind, and so, when I first saw the scene, I could not help imagining myself. But, in reality, the labour is of that heavy and continuous character that you would fancy only the best fed could stand it. The work may be divided into three classes. 1. Wheel-work, or that which is moved by the muscles of the legs and weight of the body; 2. jigger, or winch-work, or that which is moved by the muscles of the arm. In each of these the labourer is stationary; but in the truck work, which forms the third class, the labourer has to travel over a space of ground greater or less in proportion to the distance which the goods have to be removed.

[...]

This labour, though requiring to be seen to be properly understood, must still appear so arduous that one would imagine it was not of that tempting nature, that 3000 men could be found every day in London desperate enough to fight and battle for the privilege of getting 2*s*. 6*d*. by it; and even if they fail in "getting taken on" at the commencement of the day, that they should then retire to the appointed yard, there to remain hour after hour in the hope that the wind might blow them some stray ship, so that other gangs might be wanted, and the calling foreman seek them there. It is a curious sight to see the men waiting in these yards to be hired at 4*d.* per hour, for such are the terms given in the after part of the day. There, seated on long benches ranged against the wall, they remain, some telling their miseries and some their crimes to one another, whilst others doze away their time. Rain or sunshine, there can always be found plenty ready to catch the stray 1*s.* or 8*d.* worth of work. By the size of the shed you can tell how many men sometimes remain there in the pouring rain, rather than run the chance of losing the stray hours' work. Some loiter on the bridges close by, and presently, as their practised eye or ear tells them that the calling foreman is in want of another gang, they rush forward in a stream towards the gate, though only six or eight at most can be hired out of the hundred or more that are waiting there. Again the same mad fight takes place as in the morning. There is the same jumping on benches, the same raising of hands, the same entreaties, and the same failure as before. It is strange to mark the change that takes place in the manner of the men when the foreman has left. Those that have been engaged go smiling to their labour. Indeed, I myself met on the quay just such a chuckling gang passing to their work. Those who are left behind give vent to their disappointment in abuse of him whom they had been supplicating and smiling at a few minutes before. Upon talking with some of the unsuccessful ones, they assured me that the men who had supplanted them had only gained their ends by bribing the foreman who had engaged them. This I made a point of inquiring into, and the deputy-warehousekeeper, of whom I sought the information, soon assured me, by the production of his book, that he himself was the person who chose the men, the foreman merely executing his orders: and this, indeed, I found to be the custom throughout the dock.

[...]

[T]o arrive at a fair estimate as to the character and the earnings of labourers generally, I directed my guide, after the closing of the docks, to take me to one of the largest lodging-houses in the neighbourhood. The young man who was with me happened to know one of the labourers who was lodging there, and having called him out, I told him the object of my visit, and requested to be allowed to obtain information from the labourers assembled within. The man assented, and directing me to follow him, he led me through a narrow passage into a small room on the ground floor, in which sat, I should think, at least twenty or thirty of the most wretched objects I ever beheld. Some were shoeless—some coatless—others shirtless; and from all these came so rank and foul a stench, that I was sickened with a moment's inhalation of the fetid atmosphere. Some of the men were seated in front of a table, eating soup out of yellow basins. As they saw me enter, they gathered round me; and I was proceeding to tell them what information I wished to gather from them, when in swaggered a drunken man, in a white canvas suit, who announced himself as the landlord of the place, asking whether there had been a robbery in the house, that people should come in without saying "with your leave" or "by your leave." I explained to him that I had mistaken the person who had introduced me for the proprietor of the house, when he grew very abusive, and declared I should not remain there. Some of the men, however, swore as lustily that I should; and after a time succeeded in pacifying him. He then bade me let him hear what I wanted, and I again briefly stated the object of my visit. I told him I wished to publish the state of the dock-labourers in the newspapers, on which the man burst into an ironical laugh, and vowed with an oath that *he* knowed me, and that the men were a set of b——y flats[1] to be done in that way. "I know who you are well enough," he shouted. I requested to be informed for whom he took me. "Take you for!" he cried; "why, for a b——y spy! You come here from the Secretary of State, you know you do, to see how many men I've got in the house, and what kind they are." This caused a great stir among the company, and I could see that I was mistaken for one of the detective police. I was located in so wretched a court, and so far removed from the street, with a dead wall opposite, that I knew any atrocity might be committed there almost unheard: indeed, the young man who had brought me to the house had warned me of its dangerous character before I went; but, from the kind reception I had met with from other labourers, I had no fear. At last the landlord flung the door wide open, and shouted from his clenched teeth, "By G—! if you ain't soon mizzled, I'll crack your b——y skull open for you!" And so saying, he prepared to make a rush towards me, but was held back by the youth who had brought me to the place. I felt that it would be dangerous to remain; and rising, informed the man that I would not trouble him to proceed to extremities.

[...]

The scenes witnessed at the London Dock were of so painful a description, the struggle for one day's work—the scramble for twenty-four hours' extra-subsistence and extra-life were of so tragic a character, that I was anxious to ascertain if possible the exact number of individuals in and around the metropolis who live by dock labour. I have said that at one of the docks alone I found that 1823 stomachs would be deprived of food by the mere chopping of the breeze. "It's an ill wind," says the proverb, "that blows nobody good"; and until I came to investigate the condition of the dock-labourer I could not have believed it possible that near upon 2000 souls in one place alone lived, chameleon-like, upon the air, or that an easterly wind, despite the wise saw, could deprive so many of bread. It is indeed "a nipping and an eager air." That the sustenance of thousands of families should be as fickle as the very breeze itself; that the weathercock should be the index of daily want or daily ease to such a vast number of men, women, and children, was a climax of misery and wretchedness that I could not have imagined to exist; and since that I have witnessed such scenes of squalor, and crime, and suffering, as oppress the mind even to a feeling of awe.

---

1 Bloody flats; a flat is a naïve or gullible person.

The docks of London are to a superficial observer the very focus of metropolitan wealth. The cranes creak with the mass of riches. In the warehouses are stored goods that are as it were ingots of untold gold. Above and below ground you see piles upon piles of treasure that the eye cannot compass. The wealth appears as boundless as the very sea it has traversed. The brain aches in an attempt to comprehend the amount of riches before, above, and beneath it. There are acres upon acres of treasure, more than enough, one would fancy, to stay the cravings of the whole world, and yet you have but to visit the hovels grouped round about all this amazing excess of riches to witness the same amazing excess of poverty. If the incomprehensibility of the wealth rises to sublimity, assuredly the want that co-exists with it is equally incomprehensible and equally sublime. Pass from the quay and warehouses to the courts and alleys that surround them, and the mind is as bewildered with the destitution of the one place as it is with the superabundance of the other. Many come to see the riches, but few the poverty, abounding in absolute masses round the far-famed port of London.

According to the official returns, there belonged to this port on the 31st of December, 1842, very nearly 3000 ships, of the aggregate burden of 600,000 tons. Besides that there were 239 steamers, of 50,000 tons burden; and the crews of the entire number of ships and steamers amounted to 35,000 men and boys. The number of British and foreign ships that entered the port of London during the same year was 6400 and odd, whose capacity was upwards of a million and a quarter of tons, and the gross amount of customs duly collected upon their cargoes was very nearly 12,000*l.* of money. So vast an amount of shipping and commerce, it has been truly said, was never concentrated in any other single port.

[...]

It may then be safely asserted, that though the wages of the casual labourer at the docks average 5*s.* per week, still the weekly earnings are of so precarious and variable a nature, that when the time of the men is fully employed, the money which is gained over and above the amount absolutely required for subsistence is almost sure to be spent in intemperance, and that when there is little or no demand for their work, and their gains are consequently insufficient for the satisfaction of their appetites, they and those who depend upon their labour for their food must at least want, if not starve. The improvidence of the casual dock-labourer is due, therefore, not to any particular malformation of his moral constitution, but to the precarious character of his calling. His vices are the vices of ordinary human nature. Ninety-nine in every hundred similarly circumstanced would commit similar enormities. If the very winds could whistle away the food and firing of wife and children, I doubt much whether, after a week's or a month's privation, we should many of us be able to prevent ourselves from falling into the very same excesses.

It is consoling to moralise in our easy chairs, after a good dinner, and to assure ourselves that we should do differently. Self-denial is not very difficult when our stomachs are full and our backs are warm; but let us live a month of hunger and cold, and assuredly we should be as self-indulgent as they.

[...]

LONDON VAGRANTS.

London Vagrants' Asylums for the Houseless.[1]

To give the reader an idea of the motley assemblage to be found in these places, I subjoin the following table (taken from the Report),[2] by which it will be seen that almost every quarter of the globe contributes its quota of wretchedness:—

PLACES TO WHICH THE INDIVIDUALS SHELTERED BY THE HOUSELESS POOR SOCIETY[3] DURING THE WINTER 1848–49 APPEARED TO BELONG.

Africa	12	Hampshire	414	Rutlandshire	24
America	78	Herefordshire	45	Scotland	230
Bedfordshire	55	Hertfordshire	181	Shropshire	42
Berkshire	267	Huntingdonshire	25	Somersetshire	246
Buckinghamshire	88	Ireland	8068	Spain	10
Cambridgeshire	88	Italy	7	St. Helena	8
Cheshire	40	Jersey	15	Staffordshire	129
Cornwall	32	Kent	523	Suffolk	133
Cumberland	12	Lancashire	811	Surrey	204
Denmark	6	Leicestershire	75	Sussex	147
Derbyshire	48	Lincolnshire	85	Wales	122
Devonshire	209	London	343	Warwickshire	160
Dorsetshire	46	Middlesex	214	West Indies	25
Durham	54	Norfolk	163	Westmoreland	6
East Indies	19	Northamptonshire	67	Wiltshire	87
Essex	392	Northumberland	72	Worcestershire	36
France	14	Nottinghamshire	68	Yorkshire	126
Germany	53	Oxfordshire	100	Unknown	29
Gibraltar	3	Poland	4	Born at sea	5
Gloucestershire	163	Portugal	5		
Guernsey	32	Russia	7		

1 First published as part of Letter XXV of the "Labour and the Poor" series for the *Morning Chronicle*, 11 January 1850.

2 Presumably refers to the "Medical Report for 1848–49" mentioned in the second table below.

3 Alternative name for the Society for the Relief of the Houseless Poor, founded in the 1820s, which provided shelter during the winter months.

These places of shelter for the houseless are only open at certain periods of the year; and at this season a large proportion of the country labourers who are out of employ flock to London, either to seek for work in the wintertime, or to avail themselves of the food and lodging afforded by these charitable institutions. Others, again, who are professional vagrants, tramping through the country, and sleeping at the different unions on their road, come to town as regularly as noblemen every winter, and make their appearance annually in these quarters. Moreover, it is at this season of the year that the sufferings and privations of the really poor and destitute are rendered tenfold more severe than at any other period; and it is at the houses of refuge that the great mass of London, or rather English and Irish, poverty and misery, is to be met with.

The congregation at the Refuges for the Destitute[1] is, indeed, a sort of ragged congress of nations—a convocation of squalor and misery—a synopsis of destitution, degradation, and suffering, to be seen, perhaps, nowhere else.

Nor are the returns of the bodily ailments of the wretched inmates of these abodes less instructive as to their miserable modes of life, their continual exposure to the weather, and their want of proper nutriment. The subjoined medical report of the diseases and bodily afflictions to which these poor creatures are liable, tells a tale of suffering which, to persons with even the smallest amount of pathological knowledge, must need no comment. The catarrh and influenza, the rheumatism, bronchitis, ague, asthma, lumbago—all speak of many long night's exposure to the wet and cold; whereas the abscesses, ulcers, the diarrhœa, and the excessive debility from starvation, tell, in a manner that precludes all doubt, of the want of proper sustenance and extreme privation of these, the very poorest of all the poor.

Medical Report for 1848–49. Of the persons who applied at the general asylum, there were afflicted with—

Catarrh and influenza	149
Incipient fever	52
Rheumatism	50
Atrophy	3
Dropsy	3
Incised wounds	3
Diarrhœa	60
Cholera	2
Bronchitis	13
Abscess	15

1 The Female Refuge for the Destitute opened in 1805 at Cupars Bridge, Lambeth, and moved to Hackney Road in 1811. The Male Refuge (at Hoxton) opened shortly thereafter.

Ulcers	11
Affections of the head	12
Ague	13
Excessive debility from starvation	17
Inflammation of lungs	2
Asthma	10
Epilepsy	4
Diseased joints	4
Erysipelas	3
Rupture	3
Cramps and pains in bowels	2
Spitting of blood	4
Lumbago	1
Rheumatic ophthalmia	2
Strumous disease	2
Sprains	1
Fractures	4
Pregnant	30

[...]

I will now proceed to a description of the Refuge itself.

The only refuge for the houseless now open which is really a home for the homeless, is that in Playhouse-yard, Cripplegate. The doors open into a narrow by-street, and the neighbourhood needs no other announcement that the establishment is open for the reception of the houseless, than the assembly of a crowd of ragged shivering people, certain to be seen on the night of opening, as if they knew by instinct where they might be housed under a warm and comfortable roof. The crowd gathers in Playhouse-yard, and many among them look sad and weary enough. Many of the women carry infants at the breast, and have children by their sides holding by their gowns. The cries of these, and the wrangling of the hungry crowds for their places, is indeed disheartening to hear. The only sounds of merriment come from the errand-boys, as they call themselves, whom even starvation cannot make sorrowful for two hours together. The little struggle that there usually is among the applicants is not for a rush when the doors are opened, but for what they call the "front rank." They are made to stand clear of the footpath; and when five o'clock—the hour of admission—comes, an officer of the Refuge steps out, and quietly, by a motion of his hand, or a touch on the shoulder, sends in about 150 men and boys, and about 50 women and girls. He knows the great majority of those who have tickets which entitle them to one or two nights' further lodging (the tickets are generally for three nights), and these are commonly in the foremost rank. The number thus admitted show themselves more or less at home. Some are quiet and abashed; but some proceed briskly, and in a business-like way, to the first process, to wash themselves. This is done in two large vessels, in what may be called the hall or vestibule of the building. A man keeps pumping fresh water into the vessels as fast as that used is drained off, and soap and clean towels are supplied when thought necessary; the clean towels, which are long, and attached to rollers, soon becoming, in truth, exceedingly dirty. I noticed some little contention—whether to show an anxiety to conform to the rules of the Refuge, or to hurry through a disagreeable but inevitable task, or really for the comfort of ablution, I will not pretend to determine—but there was some little contention for the first turn among the young men at the washing. To look down upon them from the main staircase, as I did, was to survey a very motley scene. There they were—the shirtless, the shoeless, the coatless, the unshaven, the uncouth, ay, and the decent and respectable. There were men from every part of the United Kingdom, with a coloured man or two, a few seamen, navigators, agricultural labourers, and artizans. There were no foreigners on the nights that I was there; and in the returns of those admitted there will not be found one Jew. It is possible that Jews may be entered under the heads of "Germans" or "Poles"—I mean, foreign Jews; but on my visits I did not see so much as any near approach to the Hebrew physiognomy. To attempt to give an account of anything like a prevailing garb among these men is impossible, unless I described it as rags. As they were washing, or waiting for a wash, there was some stir, and a loud buzz of talk, in which "the brogue" strongly predominated. There was some little fun, too, as there must be where a crowd of many youths is assembled. One in a ragged, coarse, striped shirt, exclaimed as he shoved along, "By your leave, gentlemen!" with a significant emphasis of his "gentlemen." Another man said to his neighbour, "The bread's fine, Joe; but the sleep, isn't that plummy?" Some few, I say, seemed merry enough, but that is easily accounted for. Their present object was attained, and your real professional vagabond is always happy by that—for a forgetfulness of the past, or an indifference to it, and a recklessness as to the future, are the primary elements of a vagrant's enjoyment. Those who had tickets were of course subjected to no further examination, unless by the surgeon subsequently; but all the new candidates for admission—and the officers kept admitting fresh batches as they were instructed—were not passed before a rigid examination, when a ticket for three nights was given to each fresh applicant. On the right hand, as you enter the building, is the office. The assistant-superintendant sits before a large ledger, in which he enters every name and description. His questions to every fresh candidate are:—"Your name?" "How old are you?" "What trade?" "How do you live (if no trade)?" "Where did you sleep last night?" "To what parish do you belong?" In order to answer these questions, each fresh applicant for admission stands before the door of the office, a portion of the upper division of the door being thrown open. Whilst I was present, there was among a portion of the male applicants but little hesitation in answering the inquiries glibly and promptly. Others answered reluctantly. The answers of some of the boys, especially the Irish boys, were curious.

"Where did you sleep last night?" "Well, then, sir, I sleep walking about the streets all night, and very cowld it was, sir." Another lad was asked, after he had stated his name and age, how he lived? "I beg, or do anything," he answered. "What's your parish?" "Ireland." (Several pronounced their parish to be the "county Corruk.") "Have you a father here?" "He died before we left Ireland." "How did you get here, then?" "I came with my mother." "Well, and where's she?" "She died after we came to England." So the child had the streets for a stepmother.

[...]

Every part of the building was scrupulously clean. On the first night of the opening, the matron selects from the women who have sought an asylum there, three, who are engaged for the season to do the household work. This is done during the day when the inmates are absent. All must leave by eight in the morning, the doors being open for their departure at five, in case any wish to quit early—as some do for the chance of a job at Covent-garden, Farringdon, or any of the early markets. The three women-helpers receive 7*s.* a-week each, the half of that sum being paid them in money every Saturday, and the other half being retained and given to each of them, in a round sum, at the closing of the Refuge. The premises in which this accommodation to the houseless is now supplied were formerly a hat manufactory on a large scale; but the lath and plaster of the ceilings, and the partitions, have been removed, so that what was a suite of apartments on one floor is now a long ward. The rafters of the ceilings are minutely whitewashed, as are the upright beams used in the construction of the several rooms before the place was applied to its present charitable end. Those now are in the nature of pillars, and add to the catacomb-like aspect that I have spoken of. In different parts of each ward are very large grates, in which bright fires are kept glowing and crackling; and as these are lighted some time before the hour of opening, the place has a warmth and cosiness which must be very grateful to those who have encountered the cold air all the day, and perhaps all the night before.

In order to arrive at a correct estimate as to the number of the really poor and houseless who availed themselves of the establishment (to afford nightly shelter to whom the refuge was originally instituted by the benevolent founder, Mr. Hick,[1] the City mace-bearer) I consulted with the superintendent as to the class of persons he found most generally seeking refuge there. These were—among the men—mostly labourers out of work—agricultural, railway, and dock; discharged artisans, chiefly carpenters and painters; sailors, either cast away or without their registry tickets;

1 Charles William Hick, Esq., the city's mace-bearer, chaired the Special Committee appointed to respond to petitions to restore the London Workhouse to serve the "houseless poor" in 1824.

broken-down tradesmen, clerks, shopmen, and errand-boys, who either through illness or misfortune had been deprived of their situations; and, above all, Irish immigrants, who had been starved out of their own country. These he considered the really deserving portion of the inmates for whom the institution was designed. Among the females, the better and largest class of poor were needlewomen, servants, charwomen, garden-women, sellers of laces in the street, and occasionally a beggar-woman. Under his guidance I selected such as appeared the most meritorious among the classes he had enumerated, and now subjoin the statements of a portion of the number.

The first of the houseless that I saw was a railway navigator. He was a fine, stoutly-built fellow, with a fresh-coloured open countenance, and flaxen hair—indeed, altogether a splendid specimen of the Saxon labourer. He was habited in a short blue smockfrock, yellow in parts with clay, and he wore the heavy high lace-up boots, so characteristic of the tribe. These were burst, and almost soleless with long wear.

The poor fellow told the old story of the labourer compelled to squander the earnings at the public-house of his master:—

"I have been a navvy for about eighteen years. The first work that I done was on the Manchester and Liverpool.[1] I was a lad then. I used to grease the railway waggons, and got about 1*s.* 6*d.* a-day. There we had a tommy-shop,[2] and we had to go there to get our bit of victuals, and they used to charge us an extra price. The next place I had after that was on the London and Brummagem.[3] There I went as horse-driver, and had 2*s.* 6*d.* a-day. Things was dear then, and at the tommy-shop they was much dearer; for there was tommy-shops on every line then; and indeed every contractor and sub-contractor had his shop that he forced his men to deal at, or else he wouldn't have them in his employ. [...] Then I went on to the London and Cambridge, and there it was the same story over and over again. Just about this time, railway work began to get slack, and then farmers' work was slack too; and you see that made things worse for the navvies, for all came to look for employment on the railroads. This is about seven years ago. After that some more fresh lines started throughout Lancashire and Yorkshire, and trade being bad in them parts, all the weavers applied for work on the railways, and the regular navvies had a hard time of it then. But we managed to get on somehow—kept lingering on—till about three years agone, when trade got a little bit better. That was about the time when things was very dear, and our wages was rose to 3*s.* 6*d.* a-day.: they'd been only 2*s.* 6*d.* and 3*s.* before that; and we did much better when our pay was increased, because we had the ready-money then, and there was no tommy-shops that summer, for the

1 Early railway line in England.

2 A system in which wages are paid in goods and workers are often obliged to purchase these goods from shops owned by their employer. Also known as truck wages.

3 The London and Birmingham was an early railway line.

company wouldn't have them on that line. At the end of that year the work was all stopped, on account of the Chartist rising,[1] and then there was hundreds of men walking about begging their bread from door to door, with nothing to do. [...] I come to London, and I've looked all about for a job, and I can't find nothing to do. I went to a lodging-house in the Borough, and I sold all my things—shovel and grafting-tool and all, to have a meal of food. When all my things was gone, I didn't know where to go. One of my mates told me of this Refuge, and I have been here two nights. All that I have had to eat since then is the bread night and morning they gives us here. This will be the last night I shall have to stop here, and after that I don't know what I shall do. There's no railway work—that is, there's none to speak of, seeing the thousands of men that's walking about with nothing to do, and not knowing where to lay their heads. If I could get any interest, I should like to go away as an emigrant. I shouldn't like to be sent out of my native country as a rogue and a vagabone; but I'm tired of stopping here, and if I can't get away, why I must go home and go to the parish, and it's hard for a young man that's willing and able like me to work, and be forced to want because he can't get it. I know there is thousands—thousands, sir, like I am—I know there is, in the very same condition as I am at this moment: yes, I know there is." [This he said with very great feeling and emphasis.] "We are all starving. We are all willing to work, but it ain't to be had. This country is getting very bad for labour; it's so overrun with Irish that the Englishman hasn't a chance in his own land to live. Ever since I was nine years old I've got my own living, but now I'm dead beat, though I'm only twenty-eight next August."

[...]

To complete the picture of this Irish destitution, I add the following.[2]

One wretched creature had come to the Refuge with her four children. She herself was habited in a large blue cloth cloak, her toes were through the end of her shoes, and her gown clung tight to her limbs, telling that she was utterly destitute of under clothing. In her arms she carried an infant, round which were wound some old woollen rags. As the little thing sucked at its mother's breast, it breathed so hard that it needed no words to tell of its long exposure to the cold. Though the mother was half-clad, still there was the little bit of clean net inside the old rusty straw bonnet. The children were respectively eleven, six, and three years old. The eldest (a good-looking grey-eyed girl, who stood with her forefinger in her mouth, half simple) was covered with a tattered plaid shawl. This, at her mother's bidding, she drew from her shoulder with an ostentation of poverty, to show that what had before appeared a gown beneath was

---

1 See p. 51, note 1.

2 This section includes nine portraits of London vagrants. The portrait that follows is the fifth in the series.

nothing more than a bombazine petticoat. On her feet were a pair of women's old fashionable shoes, tied on with string. These had been given in charity to her by a servant a week back. The next child—a boy—laughed as I looked at him, and seemed, though only six years old, to have been made prematurely "knowing" by his early street education. He put out his foot as he saw my eye glance downward to his shoes, to show me that he had one boot and one shoe on. He was clad in all kinds of rags, and held in his hand a faded velvet cap. The youngest boy was almost a dwarf. He was three years old, but so stunted that he seemed scarce half that age.

"I come from the county of Corruk, the worst and the poorest part of it—yes, indeed, sir, it is," said the woman; "and the gintlemen know that I do. When I had it to do, I manufactured at flax and wool. I knit and sewed, to be sure I did; but God Almighty was plazed to deprive me of it. It was there I was married. My husband was a miner. Distress and want, and hunger and poverty—nothing else—druv us to this counthry. It was the will of God—glory be to his holy and blessed name!—to fail the 'taties. To be sure, I couldn't dig one out of the ground not fit to ate. We lived on 'taties, and milk, and fish, and eggs. We used to have hins then. And the mining failed, too; and the captains came over here. Yes, to be sure; for here they lived, sir. Yes, sir, indeed; and I could tell you that I used to be eight days—yes, that I did—before I could get one ha'porth to ate—barring the wather I boiled and drank to keep the life in myself and children. It was Doctor O'Donovan[1] that paid for our passage. When he see all the hunger, and distress, and want—yes, indeed, sir—that I went through, he gave a letther to the stame-packet office, and then they brought me and my three childer over. It was here that this baby was borrun. My husband was here before me, he was, about seven or eight months. He hadn't sent me any money, for he couldn't a penny. He wrote home to see if I lived, for he didn't think I lived; and then I showed the letther to Dr. O'Donovan. My husband niver got a day's work since he came over; indeed, he couldn't give the childer their breakfast the next morning after they came. I came to London-bridge, and met my husband there. Well, indeed, that is nearly three years agone. Oh, thin, I had nothing to do since but what little we done at the harvest. It was tin weeks before Christmas that I came over, and I don't know what month it was, for I don't read or write, you know. Oh, thin, indeed, we had to live by begging from that up to harvest time. I had to beg for him sooner than let him die with the hunger. He didn't do any work, but he'd be glad of a sixpence he'd earn. He'd rather have it that way than if he'd begged tin pound—it would be more plisure. Never a day's work could he get; and many beside him. Oh, Lord, there is many, sir. He never does anything but at the harvest-time, and then he works at raping the corrun. I know nothing else that he does; and I bind the shaves afther him. Why, indeed,

1 Unknown.

we get work then for about a fortnight or three weeks—it don't howld a month. Oh no, sir, no; how could my children do anything, but as fast as we'd earn it to ate it? I declare I don't know how much we'd make a-week then. They got only eight shillings an acre last year for it. I declare I don't know what we made; but whatever we had, we hadn't two shillings laving it. Ah, indeed, I had to beg all the rest of my time. My husband doesn't beg—I'll tell you the thruth. The thruth is the best. When he has e'er a penny, he tries to sell a handful of oranges; and, indeed, he had to lave off silling, for he couldn't buy half a hundred of 'em to sill back. He done pritty well when the onions were in season, he did, sir; but there's so many silling oranges, he can't sill one of 'em. Now he does nothing, for he has nothing to reach half a hundred of limons with, and that isn't much. When I gets a pinny to pay for the lodgings, then we lodges and sleeps together; but when I can't, I must go about this way with my children. When I go out begging, he remains at home in the lodging-house; he has nothing else to do, sir. I always go out with my childer; sure I couldn't look at 'em die with hunger. Where's the use of laving them with the husband; what has he to give them? Indeed, if I had left them last night with him, he couldn't have give them as much as they'd put in their mouths onced. Indeed, I take them out in the cowld to big with me to get a bit of victuals for 'em. Sure God knows I can't hilp it—he knows I can't—glory be to his holy name! Indeed, I have a part of the brid I got here last night to carry to my poor husband, for I know he wanted it. Oh, if I'm to go to the gallows, I'm telling you the thruth. Oh, to be sure, yes, sir; there's many a one would give a bit to the childer when they wouldn't to me—sure the world knows that; and maybe the childer will get ha'pence, and that will pay my lodging or buy a loaf of brid for 'em. Oh, sir, to be sure, you know I'd get more with all my little childer out than I would with one, and that's the rason indeed. Yes, indeed, that's why I take them out! Oh, then, that's what you want to know! Why, there's some people wouldn't believe I'd have so many. Maybe, some days I wouldn't get a pinny, and maybe I'd git a shilling. I met a gintleman the other day that gave me a shilling together. I'd all my childer out with me then. The sister carries the little fellow on her back, no more would he stop afther me nayther. Only twice I've left him at home. Oh thin, indeed, he do cry with the cowld, and often again with the hunger; and some of the people says to me it's myself that makes him cry; but thin, indeed, it ain't. Maybe I've no home to give my husband, maybe it's at some union he slept last night. My husband niver goes bigging, he didn't, sir—I won't tell a lie—he didn't, indeed; but he sinds me out in the cowld, and in the wit, and in the hate, too: but thin he can't help it. He's the best man that iver put a hat on his hid, and the kindest."

She persisted in asseverating this, being apparently totally incapable of perceiving the inhumanity of her husband's conduct.

"He don't force me—he don't, indeed—but he sits idle at home while I go out. Ah, if you knew what I suffers! Oh, yes, he'd rather work, if I'd got a guinea in gowld for him to-night; and yesterday morning he prayed to God Almighty to put something in his way to give him a day's work. I was in prison onced for bigging. My children was taken away from me, and sint to some union. I don't know the name of it. That was the time my husband was silling the limons. He niver came to spake for me when I was going to prison, and he doesn't know whether I'm in prisin to-night. Ah, I beg your honour's pardon, he would care, but he can't help me. I thought I'd ind my life in the prisin, for I wouldn't be allowed to spake a word. The poor man, my husband, can't help it. He was niver counted lazy in his counthry; but God Almighty plazed to deprive him of his work, and what can he do?"

[...]

A pretty, pleasant-spoken young woman, very tidy in her poor attire, which was an old cloak wrapped close round her, to cover her scanty dress, gave me the following statement very modestly:—

"I am twenty-two; my mother died six years ago; my father I never knew, for I'm an unlawful child. My mother had a small income from my father, and kept me at school. I can't even guess who my father was. I am an only child. I was taken from school to wait upon my mother; very kind indeed she was to me, but she died in three weeks after I came from school. She'd been in a consumption for six years; she fretted sadly about me. She never told me I was an unlawful child. My aunt, my mother's sister, told me one day afterwards. My mother always said my father lived in the country. I loved my mother, so I seldom spoke of my father, for she would say, 'I don't wish to hear about him.' There was nothing for me at my mother's death, so I put myself to learn fancy-box-making for grocers and pastrycooks, for their sweetmeats, and for scents. My aunt assisted me. She is now poor, and a widow. I could never earn more than 3*s*. or 4*s*. a-week at box-making, the pay is so bad. I lived this way for four or five years, lodging with my aunt, and giving her all I earned, and she kept me for it. I then went to learn the Macintosh coat-making. I went into lodgings, my aunt being unable to help me any longer, as at my uncle's death she could only keep a room for herself and children. She makes pill-boxes. I could earn at the Macintoshes only 4*s*. a-week and my tea, when in full work, and when work was bad, I earned only 2*s*. 6*d*. It was 8*d*. a-day and my tea. I parted with a good box of clothes to keep myself; first one bit of dress went, and another. I was exposed to many a temptation, but I have kept my character, I am happy to say. On Monday night I was in the streets all night—I hardly knew in what part, I was so miserable—having no place to put my head in, and frightened to death almost. I couldn't pay my lodgings, and so lost them—I was locked out. I went to the station-house, and asked to sit there for a shelter, but the policeman said it was no place for me, as I was not guilty of any offence; they could do nothing for me: they were all very civil. I walked the streets all that cold night; I feel the cold of that night in my limbs still. I thought it never would be over. I wasn't exposed to any insults. I had to walk about all Tuesday, without a bite either Monday or Tuesday. On Tuesday evening I got admitted into this place, and was very thankful. Next day I tried for work, but got none. I had a cup of tea from my aunt to live on that day."

This girl wished to get into the parish, in order to be sent out as an emigrant, or anything of that kind; but her illegitimacy was a bar, as no settlement could be proved.[1]

[...]

From the opening of the Refuges for the Houseless in 1820, until 1852, as many as 189,223 homeless individuals received "nightly shelter" there, being an average of upwards of 6000 a-year. Some of these have remained three or four nights in the same establishment; so that, altogether, no less than 1,141,558 nights' lodgings were afforded to the very poor, and 2,778,153 lbs., or nearly 25,000 cwt. of bread distributed among them.

1 Under the Poor Law, the poor could emigrate from Britain if the cost was covered by their home parish.

Appendix A: Full Table of Contents of London Labour and the London Poor

[The table of contents of the four "complete" volumes of *London Labour and the London Poor*, including subheadings, reflects Mayhew's complex system of classification and the range of his investigations. The further he explored, the more subcategories and subdivisions he required, until his taxonomy of street folk and their work became, in the words of one critic, an "active disorganizing principle" (K. Williams 241). Mayhew himself acknowledged the difficulties of his project: "It is no easy matter ... to classify the different kinds of labour scientifically. To arrange the several varieties of work into 'orders,' and to group the manifold species of arts under a few comprehensive genera—so that the mind may grasp the whole at one effort—is a task of a most perplexing character" (*London Labour* vol. 4, p. 4). Titles marked with an asterisk are included in this edition.]

VOLUME 1

Of the Orange and Nut Market.
Of Orange and Lemon Selling in the Streets.
Of Nut Selling in the Streets.
Of Roasted Chestnuts and Apples.
Of "Dry" Fruit Selling in the Streets.
Of the Street-Sale of Vegetables.
Of the "Aristocratic" Vegetable-Sale.
Of Onion Selling in the Streets.
Of Pot-Herbs and Celery.
Gross Value of the Fruit and Vegetables Sold annually in the London Streets.

Of the Stationary Street-Sellers of Fish, Fruit, and Vegetables.

Of the Number of Street Stalls.
Of the Character of the Street-Stalls.
Of Fruit-Stall Keepers.
Of a Public Meeting of Street-Sellers.

****Of the Street-Irish.***

Of the Causes Which Have Made the Irish Turn Costermongers.
How the Street-Irish Displanted the Street-Jews in the Orange Trade.
Of the Religion of the Street-Irish.
*Of the Education, Literature, Amusements, and Politics of the Street-Irish.
*The Homes of the Street-Irish.
Irish Lodging-Houses for Immigrants.
Of the Diet, Drink, and Expense of Living of the Street-Irish.
Of the Resources of the Street-Irish as Regards "Stock-Money," Sickness, Burials, &c.
Of the History of Some Irish Street-Sellers.
Of the Irish "Refuse"-Sellers.

Of the Street-Sellers of Game, Poultry (Live and Dead), Rabbits, Butter, Cheese, and Eggs.

Of the Quantity of Game, Rabbits, and Poultry, Sold in the Streets.
Of the Street-Purchasers of Game and Poultry.
Of the Experience of a Game Hawker.
Statement of Two Poultry Hawkers.
Of the Street Sale of Live Poultry.
Of Rabbit Selling in the Streets.
Of the Street Sale of Butter, Cheese, and Eggs.

Of the Sellers of Trees, Shrubs, Flowers (Cut and In Pots), Roots, Seeds, and Branches.

Of the Quantity of Shrubs, "Roots," Flowers, Etc., Sold in the Streets, and of the Buyers.
Of the Street Sale of Trees and Shrubs.
The London Flower Girls.
Of Two Orphan Flower Girls.
Of the Life of a Flower Girl.
Of the Street Sale of Lavender.
Cut Flowers.
Of the Street Sale of Flowers in Pots, Roots, Etc.

*Of the London Chimney-Sweepers.
Of the Sweepers of Old, and the Climbing Boys.
Of the Chimney-Sweepers of the Present Day.
*Of the General Characteristics of the Working Chimney-Sweepers.
Sweeping of the Chimneys of Steam-Vessels.
Of the "Ramoneur" Company.
Of the Brisk and Slack Seasons, and the Casual Trade among the Chimney-Sweepers.
Of the "Leeks" Among the Chimney-Sweepers.
Of the Inferior Chimney-Sweepers—the "Knullers" and "Queriers."
Of the Fires of London.
Of the Sewermen and Nightmen of London.
Of the Wet House-Refuse of London.
Of the Means of Removing the Wet House-Refuse.
Of the Quantity of Metropolitan Sewage.
Of Ancient Sewers.
Of the Kinds and Characteristics of Sewers.
*Of the Subterranean Character of the Sewers.
Of the House-Drainage of the Metropolis as Connected with the Sewers.
Of the London Street-Drains.
Of the Length of the London Sewers and Drains.
Of the Cost of Constructing the Sewers and Drains of the Metropolis.
Of the Uses of Sewers as a Means of Subsoil Drainage.
Of the City Sewerage.
Of the Outlets, Ramifications, Etc., of the Sewers.
Of the Qualities, Etc., of the Sewage.
Of the New Plan of Sewerage.
Of the Management of the Sewers and the Late Commissions.
Of the Powers and Authority of the Present Commissions of Sewers.
Of the Sewers Rate.
Of the Cleansing of the Sewers—Ventilation.
Of "Flushing" and "Plonging," and Other Modes of Washing the Sewers.
Of the Working Flushermen.
Of the Rats in the Sewers.
Of the Cesspoolage and Nightmen of the Metropolis.
Of the Cesspool System of London.
Of the Cesspool and Sewer System of Paris.
Of the Emptying of the London Cesspools by Pump and Hose.
Statement of a Cesspool-Sewerman.
Of the Present Disposal of the Night-Soil.
Of the Working Nightmen and the Mode of Work.

Crossing-Sweepers.

I. Of the Adult Crossing-Sweepers.
A. The Able-Bodied Sweepers.
1. The Able-Bodied Male Crossing-Sweepers.
The "Aristocratic" Crossing-Sweeper.
The Bearded Crossing-Sweeper at the Exchange.

VOLUME 3
THE DESTROYERS OF VERMIN.

*Her Majesty's Bug-Destroyer.
Black-Beetles.
Beetle Destroyers.
Crickets.

OUR STREET FOLK.

I.—Street Exhibitors.

Punch.
The Fantoccini Man.
Guy Fawkeses.
Guy Fawkes (Man).
Guy Fawkes (Boy).
An Old Street Showman.
The Chinese Shades.
Exhibitor of Mechanical Figures.
The Telescope Exhibitor.
*Exhibitor of the Microscope.
Peep-Shows.
Acrobat, or Street-Posturer.
The Street Risley.
The Strong Man.
The Street Juggler.
The Street Conjurer.
Statement of Another Street Conjurer.
The Street Fire-King, or Salamander.
*The Snake, Sword, and Knife-Swallower.
*Street Clown.
The Penny-Gaff Clown.
The Canvas Clown.
The Penny-Circus Jester.
Silly Billy.
Billy Barlow.
Strolling Actors.
Ballet Performers.
The Tight-Rope Dancers and Stilt-Vaulters.
*Street Reciter.
Blind Reader.
Gun-Exercise Exhibitor—One-Legged Italian.

II.—Street Musicians.

*"Old Sarah."
"Farm-Yard" Player.
Blind Performer on the Bells.
Blind Female Violin Player.
Blind Scotch Violoncello Player.
Blind Irish Piper.
The English Street Bands.
The German Street Bands.
Of the Bagpipe Players.

VOLUME 4

Of Prostitution in Turkey.
Of Prostitution in Circassia.
Of Prostitution among the Tartar Races.

Of the Mixed Northern Nations.

Introductory.
Of Prostitution in Russia.
Of Prostitution in Siberia.
Iceland and Greenland.
Of Prostitution in Lapland and Sweden.
Of Prostitution in Norway.
Of Prostitution in Denmark.

Of Prostitution in Civilized States.

Introduction.
Of Prostitution in Spain.
Amsterdam.
Belgium.
Hamburg.
Prussia—Germany.
Berlin.
Austria.
Modern Rome.
Turin.
Berne.
The City of Paris.

Prostitution in London. By Bracebridge Hemyng.

Seclusives, or those that live in Private Houses and Apartments.
Board Lodgers.
Those who live in Low Lodging Houses.
Sailors' Women.
Soldiers' Women.
Thieves' Women.
Park Women, or those who frequent the Parks at night and other retired places.
The Dependants of Prostitutes.
Bawds.
Followers of Dress-Lodgers.
Keepers of Accommodation Houses.
Procuresses, Pimps, and Panders.
Fancy-men.
Bullies.
Clandestine Prostitutes.
**Female Operatives.*
Maid-Servants.
Ladies of Intrigue and Houses of Assignation.
Cohabitant Prostitutes.
Narrative of a Gay Woman at the West End of the Metropolis.
Criminal Returns.
Traffic in Foreign Women.

THIEVES AND SWINDLERS. By John Binny.

Smuggling.
Felonies by Lightermen.
The River Pirates.
Narrative of a Mudlark.

Receivers of Stolen Property.

Dolly Shops.
Pawnbrokers, &c.
Narrative of a Returned Convict.

Coining.

Forgers.

Cheats.

Embezzlers.
Magsmen, or Sharpers.
Swindlers.

BEGGARS AND CHEATS. By Andrew Halliday.

The Origin and History of the Poor Laws.
Statistics of the Poor Laws.
Report of the Poor Law Board (1860).
Street Beggars in 1816.
Mendicant Pensioners.
Begging Letter Writers in 1816.
Begging-Letter Writers.
Advertising Begging-Letter Writers.
Ashamed Beggars.
The Swell Beggar.
Clean Family Beggars.

Naval and Military Beggars.

Turnpike Sailor.
Street Campaigners.

Foreign Beggars.

The French Beggar.
Destitute Poles.
*Hindoo Beggars.
*Negro Beggars.

Disaster Beggars.

A Shipwrecked Mariner.
Blown-up Miners.
Burnt-out Tradesmen.
Lucifer Droppers.
Bodily Affected Beggars.
Seventy Years a Beggar.
Having Swollen Legs.
Cripples.
A Blind Beggar.
Beggars Subject to Fits.
Being in a Decline.
"Shallow Coves."

Appendix B: Contemporary Reviews

[Both the *Morning Chronicle* series "Labour and the Poor" and *London Labour and the London Poor* attracted attention in the press. Influential journals such as the *Quarterly Review*, *British Quarterly Review*, *Fraser's Magazine*, and *Edinburgh Review* all commented on Mayhew's work. The reviews included here from the *Eclectic Review* and the *Athenaeum*—journals aimed at middle-class readers—are generally positive. Letters to the editor printed in *Reynolds's Newspaper*, a weekly paper read by working-class audiences, are much more critical of the way in which Mayhew represented street sellers in *London Labour*.]

1. From *Eclectic Review*[1] (October 1851): 424–36

THE revelations of this work should give a new tone and colour to the contemporary history of these times. A picture of England in the middle of the nineteenth century is usually drawn in vivid tints to flatter the vanity of our civilization. Political supremacy in Europe; the enjoyment of true liberty; the glories of extended empire; a commerce which visits the remotest shores, and colonies which make a chain round the globe—these, with inferior sources of congratulation, form the invariable substance of our complacent hymns in praise of our own achievements. We forget, or we have hitherto neglected to notice, the existence of a large class, in our metropolis, more degraded than the savages of New Zealand, than the blacks of the Great Karroo,[2] or the insular communities of the Pacific. It is not a petty tribe, composed of outcasts and vagrants, incident to every social system; but a nation, numbered by thousands, which daily wanders through our streets, and carries on perpetual warfare against society. Such a fact should be remembered by us when we indulge in grandiloquent panegyrics upon the refined and polished state of manners, the general happiness, the public riches, and the universal freedom, under the discipline of just laws, which render England the Corinthian capital—the moral Acropolis—of Europe. We despise other times and other systems; we look on this as the illuminated age, whose lustre radiates from our own central city; but Athens had no such class, nor had Rome. North America has no such class, nor have the Swiss cantons.

Henry Mayhew has dug up the foundations of society, and exposed them to light. He has travelled through the unknown regions of our metropolis, and returned with full reports concerning the strange tribes of men which he may be said to have discovered. For, until his researches had taken place, who knew of the nomade race which daily carries on its predatory operations in our streets, and nightly disappears in quarters wholly unvisited as well by the portly

1 A monthly magazine published between 1805 and 1868. The author of this review is Cyrus Read Edmonds.

2 The Karoo is a semi-desert region in South Africa.

citizens of the East as by perfumed whiskerandoes of the West End? An important and valuable addition has thus been made to our knowledge. In a volume replete with curious facts, authenticated by absolute proof, as well as by the high character of the author, we have a description of a class of the population perfectly marvellous to contemplate. We shall lay before our readers the leading facts which our author has brought to light, but refer them to the book itself for the wonderful details, for the innumerable anecdotes, for the episodes of romance, for the philosophic reflections, and the infinite variety of pictures, which render it the most remarkable work of the age.

[...]

[...] There is a sleeping volcano in the bosom of the State.

Formidable as they are in a political point of view, the members of this class should be dreaded for the moral disease which they perpetuate and spread. The social law with them is little binding. Not more than one-tenth of the couples living together are married; but in Clerkenwell, where the incumbent performs the ceremony without a fee, a fifth of the whole are lawfully wedded—a fact for the consideration of the ministers of religion. [...]

[...]

[...] Yet there is a literature among these barbarians, and there are those who can read it to the others. Tales of vice, with pretended revelations and real accounts of courts, with other loathsome subjects, they greedily devour. Cruickshank's "Bottle"[1] was highly admired, but men who pronounced it "prime," became drunk three hours afterwards. Altogether, the kind of writing relished among them is of a low order, and the most contemptible scrawlers, for the most part, fill the high places in their literary Pantheon.

Among men so removed in sentiment and practice from all that appears virtuous or pure, it seems remarkable to find honesty a characteristic. [...]

[...]

[...] We have, we believe, justified our assertion that there is a nation of men, women, and children in London, overwhelmed by ignorance, vice, and poverty—a dangerous leaven in our society, a slumbering fire which may one day break out and devastate the higher regions of the commonwealth. As long as they continue as they actually are, our civilization will be but a partial scheme, excluding the poor from its advantages. We have made laws for hundreds of years; we have achieved great social triumphs; we have become the first nation; we have piled up, in various stores, the accumulated trophies of our art, our industry, and our versatile skill; we have acquired naval and military fame; and the benignant influences of order, peace, and happiness, have

1 See p. 61, note 5.

sprung from our bosom to bless whole millions in distant parts of the world. In India we have substituted a wise and beneficent government for a desolating tyranny; in Australia we are reclaiming the desert; in New Zealand we are redeeming the savage; but in our own metropolis vast tribes of barbarians remain unvisited by religion, unrefined in manners, unenlightened by education. Are these debased, immoral, irreligious, fraudulent, and reckless classes civilized? If they are, then we have no right to call the Fingoes[1] barbarians; but if they are not, we have no right to boast of our social institutions. We should rather blush that fifty thousand human beings are thus abandoned in the capital of our empire to the most degrading and dangerous influences. It is not for charity to help them. It is not for private enterprise to elevate them—it is for the Legislature, and until a new spirit is infused into the Legislature, reform among the poor is hopeless. Can the reader imagine what men and women must grow from children who never knew what play was; never enjoyed a gambol in the fields; never breathed one breeze of country air; children that pass at one step from the helplessness of infancy to the self-dependence of maturity, and are taught to labour almost as soon as they leave the mother's breast! [...]

[...]

We entreat public attention to Mr. Mayhew's revelations of London. If ignorance could, up to this time, be pleaded in defence of our neglect, there is no longer any such retreat for the consciences of indolent politicians. It is idle to reiterate the hollow remark that legislation cannot deal with such classes, that law cannot elevate them, purify their morals, or refine their manners. Parliament can and must effect a change, or we may be awakened from an indifference by a catastrophe not the less portentous because it should have been foreseen. This is by no means mere speculation. It is impossible to deny that a large class of men, such as we have shown the street-wanderers to be, must form a dangerous element in society. That element is continually increasing its power, because it is perpetually multiplied. The process will not go on for ever. Combustible materials will not for ever accumulate, without an explosion one day taking place. It is, consequently, imperative on the Legislature to direct an inquiry into the means of reforming these people. We cannot here suggest a plan, but Henry Mayhew has, doubtless, matured one, and his opinion will be very valuable. He now proposes to deal with the immoral classes of London, and to extend a comparative view of the same subject over all the world—a most interesting investigation.

Meanwhile we recommend our readers to examine Mr. Mayhew's noble work for themselves. They will find it more entertaining than any fiction. It is a history of the poor in the nineteenth century, and is illustrated by numerous woodcuts from daguerreotypes by Beard. The interest of the volume is enhanced by an admirable portrait of the author. We should mention, also, that

---

1 See p. 51, note 2.

it is dedicated to one of the most kindly and brilliant writers of his age—Douglas Jerrold.[1]

2. From *Athenaeum*[2] (15 November 1851): 1199–1201

An inquiry into the actual condition of the London poor has long been desired by the statist and philanthropist. Committees of the House of Commons, Special Commissioners, and "own Correspondents" have examined witnesses and made reports on mines, factories, coal-pits, and many other subjects; and if they cannot be said to have made the general public familiar with the state of the population engaged in these great branches of English industry, they have at least collected a body of authentic information, and laid it up in an accessible shape for the use of statesmen and public writers. But the idea of a free inquiry into the actual state of the million poor of London—embracing an intelligible account of their occupations, modes of living, earnings, education, amusements, morals, and, in fact, a distinct portraiture of the entire aspect of their moral and material life—seems not to have occurred to any one in office. Yet, there is scarcely any species of knowledge so valuable to the politician. London covers so large a surface—our habits of local government render its several parts so independent of ministerial action—the swell and subsidence of the mere tide of physical life are so vast—the power to check any abnormal movement is so slight compared with the surface to be acted on,—that an intimate knowledge of every part of the great city, of the conditions under which the population subsists, of the temptations which assail it, and indeed of all the elements of social disorder which exist and operate in this mighty metropolis, would seem to be indispensable to any prudent and sagacious minister. No effort, however, was ever made by the State to obtain this knowledge. Census returns have told us that nearly two millions and a half of human beings are gathered round the common centre of St. Paul's. We have been proud to tell foreigners of the square miles comprised within the limits of our great city,—of the parks, squares, docks, workshops, which adorn and occupy "the vast province covered with houses." But of the more human interests we have been content as a people to remain in great ignorance.

A private inquirer at length undertook to do for us that which the State had so long neglected. In connexion with the *Morning Chronicle*, Mr. Henry Mayhew—up to that time known chiefly as a writer of comic stories and editor of the "Comic Almanac"[3]—began a series of letters, which he entitled "Labour and the Poor," on the subject. The courage with which the task was under-

---

1 A popular dramatist and journalist, Jerrold (1803–57) was an influential figure in Victorian literary culture. Like Mayhew, Jerrold was a contributor to *Punch* magazine (see p. 241, note 3). His daughter, Jane Matilda, married Mayhew in 1844. Mayhew dedicated *London Labour and the London Poor* to Jerrold in Volume 1.

2 Influential weekly literary magazine published in London between 1828 and 1921.

3 An annual collection of humorous stories, poems, jokes, and illustrations published from 1835–53. George Cruikshank (1792–1878) was the main illustrator and compiler, with contributions by Horace Mayhew (1816–72), Henry Mayhew, William Makepeace Thackeray (1811–63), and others. Henry Mayhew was editor in 1850–51.

taken—the ability and energy with which it was put in course of execution—were admirable. The work was good work in most respects:—and had it been effected in a severe spirit of truth, fairness, and neutrality, its record would have commanded a place in every library, and gained for its enterprising conductor an abiding place in the social history of England. But, unfortunately, the papers no sooner began to appear than a suspicion arose that the accounts were exaggerated. The nature of the author's previous writings lent a certain air of probability to this suspicion. Many of his sketches were highly effective,—and some of them looked as if they had been drawn for the mere sake of effect. Then came out in one of their series an attack on the Ragged Schools,[1] based, as our readers know, on statements which could not afterwards be sustained; and the proved exaggeration in one case helped to throw a degree of doubt over the whole series of the writer's London "revelations."

But while we admitted, and admit, that these doubts were to some extent justifiable, we would guard against being thought to condemn Mr. Mayhew's labours. On the contrary, while we cannot but regret that his literary habits should have led him to adopt a style of treatment less simple than his subject required, we consider his book to be one of very considerable importance. The manner is much toned down in this reprint,—the classification is improved,—and the information is rendered more copious and precise.

[...]

3. From *Reynolds's Newspaper*[2] (18 May 1851): 14

A numerous meeting of the London street-sellers was held in Westminster, on Wednesday evening last, for the purpose of refuting the statements put forth by Mr. Mayhew, in his work entitled, "London Labour and the London Poor." Delegates from the different street trades attended.

Mr. Taylor,[3] the chairman, said he thought Mr. Mayhew's conduct was ungentlemanly and unjust. He had been invited to attend there that evening, but he had not thought fit to appear. He (Mr. Taylor) wished he had, for two reasons. First, that he might hear the truth—an article, he was sorry to say, Mr. Mayhew did not deal largely in as respects his publication; and, secondly, to hear the refutations of those he had calumniated. Mr. Mayhew had endeavoured to wage war against one of the poorest, the lowest, and the most illiterate classes of the community. Mr. Mayhew had tried to injure a class of society that never injured him; he had endeavoured to show that the street-sellers were devoid of honesty, decency, and of every virtue. He had got up his book to suit the tastes and views of the upper and middle classes, and he had selected a

1 In the spring of 1850, Mayhew criticized the premise of the ragged school movement in the *Morning Chronicle* by arguing that ragged schools fostered juvenile crime instead of preventing it. Mayhew's criticism led to a series of rebuttals from ragged school supporters, who questioned the accuracy of his reporting and his journalistic integrity. For more on ragged schools, see p. 185, note 1.

2 *Reynolds's Newspaper* was founded in 1850 by George W.M. Reynolds (see p. 61, note 1).

3 Unknown.

helpless class to be the victim of his slanders—the butt and target to be fired at by public scorn and ridicule. Mr. Mayhew took care never to state anything on his own authority, but always on hearsay—a ready and safe mode of circulating falsehood and calumny. (Cheers.) His object had been to paint blemishes, not to show virtues. He had held up one particular class of the poor to scorn and opprobrium, and that class feeling aggrieved, with reason complained. Mr. Mayhew had been remonstrated with on the falsity of his statements; he replied that he would be happy to set right any errors that might have appeared. But would a small note in the column of correspondence prove an antidote to the poisonous calumnies he had spread over pages? Mr. Mayhew's offer was declined, and the poor street-vendors of the metropolis would appeal to the public for redress. (Loud cheering.)

[...]

4. From *Reynolds's Newspaper* (15 June 1851): 14

We willingly insert the following letter, and consider it a duty to open our columns for the purpose of correcting misrepresentation or exposing exaggeration. We cannot, however, on our own authority, charge Mr. Mayhew with having deliberately outstepped the bounds of truth, although we must say that he appears to have drawn somewhat extensively on the credulity of his readers.

TO THE EDITOR OF "REYNOLDS'S NEWSPAPER."

Sir,—

[...]

When Mr. Mayhew was special correspondent for the *Morning Chronicle*, he convened a meeting of street people, at the National Hall, Holborn.[1] No person who obtained a living in the streets was debarred admission; on the contrary, large tickets were plentifully distributed throughout the public thoroughfares, earnestly inviting all of the above class to attend. The result was a crowded hall. Mr. Mayhew addressed those assembled, professing a very great affection for them. But he met with some opposition; for several present charged Mr. Mayhew with having an ulterior pecuniary object in eliciting information from those in the hall. They believed that his design was to publish a work upon the classes. Finding that he could not gull the whole of the meeting with his smooth words, Mr. Mayhew adjourned the meeting; but in the next assembly he restricted admission to costermongers only.

Since then, the statements of his opponents at that meeting have been verified. *He has published a work about them.* And the infamous accusations against street

1 The building was owned by the National Association for Promoting the Political and Social Improvement of the People from its opening in 1842 until 1849, when the association folded and the building came under ownership of a group of trustees.

folk are so great and so many in that work, that the class injured have formed themselves into a society chiefly to repel the unprincipled attacks made against them by this gentleman. Two public meetings have been held on the subject, both of which were reported in this paper; and notwithstanding Mr. Mayhew's having been invited, he declined attending the first; for he "could not see the good that would result from so doing." This is from a letter which his agent, Mr. Knight,[1] delivered at the meeting. The second invitation was unheeded. And although since then the first volume of the work has been completed, no notice, either directly or indirectly, has been taken. But a preface has been attached to the work, which, in my opinion, is indeed amazing, when we consider that Mr. Mayhew has recently met with strong opposition from the class of which he has been writing.

In this preface Mr. Mayhew speaks thus: "It is believed that the book is curious for many reasons.

"It surely may be considered curious, as being the first attempt to publish the history of a people from the lips of the people themselves—giving a literal description of their labour, their earnings, their trials, and their sufferings, in their own 'unvarnished' language; and to pourtray the condition of their homes and their families, by personal observation of the places, and direct communion with the individuals."

Concerning this, I declare, in behalf of the body of street people, that Mr. Mayhew has not generally obtained the information from "the people" themselves. Nor has he given a literal description of our labour, our earnings, our trials, or our sufferings. The "unvarnished language" to which he alludes, is neither ours, nor of those belonging to us. But that Mr. Mayhew has charged us with vices he cannot prove—that he has misrepresented our labour and our earnings—that he or his agents have used petty and disgraceful tricks to elicit statements from poor men addicted to intoxication—that he has exaggerated the information received, and that he has caricatured, and sneered, and vilified, and exposed the worst and hidden the best of our nature,—all these, I dare affirm, and can prove against Mr. Mayhew.

Also, that he, notwithstanding the injury that he has done to us, has been treated in a gentlemanly and respectful manner—far more than his conduct merited; that he was respectfully invited to attend our public meetings to substantiate his statements; and that every thing open, candid, and reasonable, has been pursued by us as a body in investigating those unfair and illiberal charges; all these I declare to have been done by the *degraded* "Street People."

[...]

I regret, Mr. Editor, that the necessity under which I struggle, impelling me to procure a scanty living in the public thoroughfares, prevents me from entering more fully into this subject this week. Should you continue to insert the articles forwarded, Mr. Mayhew's publication shall be methodically examined, and the fallacies, inaccuracies, and absurdities therein contained shall be exposed to the public.

1 Likely the same as Richard Knight (see p. 48, note 1).

At the same time, in conclusion, permit me, on the part of the body of street folk, to offer our very respectful thanks for the humane and gentlemanly manner in which you have offered a space in your valuable paper to a class who has been too much judged as beyond commiseration or sympathy. There is many a man now in the streets forced to many painful tasks to procure an honest living, who, if in the station fitted for his abilities, would be a bright and useful ornament.

I beg to remain, Sir, your obedient servant,

GEORGE MARTIN, Secretary to the Street Traders' Protection Association.[1]

5. From *Reynolds's Newspaper* (20 July 1851): 3

TO THE EDITOR OF REYNOLDS'S NEWSPAPER.

Sir,—

[...]

The highly amusing assertion of Mr. Mayhew's, that mechanics when tramping, street-sellers, when either wandering or settled, as well as sailors and pickpockets, are all more or less distinguished for high cheek-bones and protruding jaws is, I verily believe, too far from truth for any rational individual to coincide with it. Were this a fact, the street people would be a distinct tribe, bearing certain peculiar physical qualities to be found in them and a few others only. But that this is *not* the fact Mr. Mayhew must soon know if he were to attend one of our public meetings. I would challenge him to select from the individuals assembled those of the "*wandering tribes*," and I am assured that his theory would prove to be grievously at fault. Indeed, Mr. Mayhew's features would give the lie to it; for, judging from my personal experience of several hundreds of "*nomads*," I am certain that they cannot claim such a vast amount of cheekbone or protuberance of jaw as Henry Mayhew, Esq.

Moreover, if these changes occur "through the mere act of wandering," as Mr. Mayhew surmises,—if every individual changes his physical qualities so strikingly as Mr. Mayhew represents, surely his generalizing of the classes influenced by this natural law must be very imperfect. For in addition to cabmen, street-sellers, pickpockets, and prostitutes, he must add, if he dare carry his theory to its boundaries, three-fourths of the aristocracy, the gentry, and a host of authors, lecturers, actors, and philosophers. If the "mere act of wandering" promotes protuberance of jaw, what may we expect from many of the higher classes who are constantly "wandering"? Nothing but a very striking protuberance indeed can result—that is, if H. Mayhew be correct.

I truly believe this is too absurd to require any further observation. I regret that a gentleman, an author of established reputation, should thus far permit

1 The group was created to challenge Mayhew and his depictions of the street traders. Additional information about Martin is unknown.

his imagination to overrule his judgment; that he should plume himself upon having discovered that which a Buffon, a Bluminbark, or a Lavater's[1] deep research never detected; and that he, in order to thrust what he doubtless considers proofs of great sagacity upon a credulous mass of readers, that he should tamper with, and wound the best feelings of human nature, because that human nature is enveloped in a coarse garb,—all this is deeply to be regretted.

Let Mr. Mayhew learn from this time, that there is no individual, however lowly, but has some claim of sympathy from his fellow-creatures; and that it is not the province of any man removed above the average, as Mr. Mayhew probably is, to play with or insult the self-dignity of manhood. Let him not for the future endeavour to debase the poor street-seller by painting him in odious colours; but let him, if he is the sincere friend he proposes to be,—let him aim at raising the degraded and the fallen, stretching out his right hand in charitable good-will to all, however lowly, and, in humble imitation of a mighty teacher, bid them "Go and sin no more."

Yours, obediently,
GEORGE MARTIN.
Secretary to the Street Traders' Protection Association.

1 Georges-Louis Leclerc, Comte de Buffon (1707–99) and Johann Kaspar Lavater (1741–1801) both contributed to the field of physiognomy, which linked one's appearance to personality and moral character. Bluminbark is unknown.

Appendix C: Selection of Entries from the Morning Chronicle[1] *and Volume 4 of* London Labour and the London Poor

[Mayhew's surveys of London workers began with two articles on the "cholera districts" for the *Morning Chronicle* newspaper. Volume 4 of *London Labour and the London Poor*, published in 1862, contained almost no material by Mayhew himself. One exception was his "Classification of the Workers and Non-Workers of Great Britain," part of which is included here. The other entries in Volume 4 were probably all contributed by other writers; Mayhew had no direct involvement in the production of Volume 4 of *London Labour*.]

1. From the *Morning Chronicle*

a. "A Visit to the Cholera Districts of Bermondsey [by Henry Mayhew]" (24 September 1849): 4

There is an Eastern fable which tells us that a certain city was infested by poisonous serpents that killed all they fastened upon; and the citizens, thinking them sent from Heaven as a scourge for their sins, kept praying that the visitation might be removed from them, until scarcely a house remained unsmitten. At length, however, concludes the parable, the eyes of the people were opened; for, after all their prayers and fastings, they found that the eggs of the poisonous serpents were hatched in the muck-heaps that surrounded their own dwellings.

The history of the late epidemic,[2] which now seems to have almost spent its fatal fury upon us, has taught us that the masses of filth and corruption round the metropolis are, as it were, the nauseous nests of plague and pestilence. Indeed, so well known are the localities of fever and disease, that London would almost admit of being mapped out pathologically, and divided into its morbid districts and deadly cantons. We might lay our fingers on the Ordnance map,[3] and say here is the typhoid parish, and there the ward of cholera; for as truly as the West-end rejoices in the title of Belgravia,[4] might the southern shores of the Thames be christened Pestilentia. As season follows season, so does disease follow disease in the quarters that may be more literally than metaphorically styled the plague-spots of London. If the seasons are favourable, and typhus does not bring death to almost every door, then influenza and scarlatina fill the workhouses with the families of the sick. So

1 For more on the *Morning Chronicle* newspaper and Mayhew's involvement with it, see Introduction, p. 15.

2 The cholera epidemic reached London in 1832, where it killed more than 6,500 people. The epidemic returned to London in 1849, claiming more than 14,000 lives.

3 A detailed map created by the British Ordnance Survey.

4 An upper-class neighbourhood of London developed in the early nineteenth century.

certain and regular are the diseases in their returns, that each epidemic, as it comes back summer after summer, breaks out in the self-same streets as it appeared on its former visit, with but this slight difference, that if at its last visitation it began at the top of the street, and killed its way down, this time it begins at the bottom, and kills its way as surely up the lines of houses.

Out of the 12,800 deaths which, within the last three months, have arisen from cholera, 6,500 have occurred on the southern shores of the Thames; and to this awful number no localities have contributed so largely as Lambeth, Southwark, and Bermondsey, each, at the height of the disease, adding its hundred victims a week to the fearful catalogue of mortality. Any one who has ventured a visit to the last-named of these places in particular, will not wonder at the ravages of the pestilence in this malarious quarter, for it is bounded on the north and east by filth and fever, and on the south and west by want, squalor, rags, and pestilence. Here stands, as it were, the very capital of cholera, the Jessore[1] of London—JACOB'S ISLAND,[2] a patch of ground insulated by the common sewer. Spared by the fire of London,[3] the houses and comforts of the people in this loathsome place have scarcely known any improvement since that time. The place is a century behind even the low and squalid districts that surround it.

In the days of Henry II., the foul stagnant ditch that now makes an island of this pestilential spot, was a running stream, supplied with the waters which poured down from the hills about Sydenham and Nunhead, and was used for the working of the mills that then stood on its banks. These had been granted by charter to the monks of St. Mary and St. John,[4] to grind their flour, and were dependencies upon the Priory of Bermondsey. Tradition tells us that what is now a straw yard skirting the river, was once the City Ranelagh, called "Cupid's Gardens," and that the trees, which are now black with mud, were the bowers under which the citizens loved, on the sultry summer evenings, to sit beside the stream drinking their sack and ale. But now the running brook is changed into a tidal sewer, in whose putrid filth staves are laid to season; and where the ancient summer-houses stood, nothing but hovels, sties, and muck-heaps are now to be seen.

Not far from the Tunnel there is a creek opening into the Thames. The entrance to this is screened by the tiers of colliers[5] which lie before it. This creek bears the name of the Dock Head. Sometimes it is called St. Saviour's, or, in jocular allusion to the odour for which it is celebrated, Savory Dock. The walls of the warehouses on each side of this muddy stream are green and slimy, and barges lie beside them, above which sacks of corn are continually dangling from the cranes aloft. This creek was once supplied by the streams from the

---

1 It was believed that the cholera outbreak originated in Jessore, a district of then–British Bengal (modern-day Bangladesh), in 1817, before making its way to Europe.

2 Slum on the south bank of the Thames in Bermondsey, London, created during conditions of nineteenth-century industrialization. Jacob's Island suffered notoriously from poverty and crime and was depicted in Dickens's *Oliver Twist*.

3 See p. 167, note 2.

4 Saint John's Abbey (1096–1539), in Colchester, and Saint Mary's Abbey (1088–1539), in York, were both part of the Benedictine order.

5 See p. 265, note 1.

Surrey hills, but now nothing but the drains and refuse of the houses that have grown up round about it thicken and swell its waters.

On entering the precincts of the pest island, the air has literally the smell of a graveyard, and a feeling of nausea and heaviness comes over any one unaccustomed to imbibe the musty atmosphere. It is not only the nose, but the stomach, that tells how heavily the air is loaded with sulphuretted hydrogen; and as soon as you cross one of the crazy and rotting bridges over the reeking ditch, you know, as surely as if you had chemically tested it, by the black colour of what was once the white-lead paint upon the door-posts and window-sills, that the air is thickly charged with this deadly gas. The heavy bubbles which now and then rise up in the water show you whence at least a portion of the mephitic compound comes, while the open doorless privies that hang over the water side on one of the banks, and the dark streaks of filth down the walls where the drains from each house discharge themselves into the ditch on the opposite side, tell you how the pollution of the ditch is supplied.

The water is covered with a scum almost like a cobweb, and prismatic with grease. In it float large masses of green rotting weed, and against the posts of the bridges are swollen carcasses of dead animals, almost bursting with the gases of putrefaction. Along its shores are heaps of indescribable filth, the phosphoretted smell from which tells you of the rotting fish there, while the oyster shells are like pieces of slate from their coating of mud and filth. In some parts the fluid is almost as red as blood from the colouring matter that pours into it from the reeking leather-dressers' close by.

The striking peculiarity of Jacob's Island consists in the wooden galleries and sleeping-rooms at the back of the houses which overhang the dark flood, and are built upon piles, so that the place has positively the air of a Flemish street, flanking a sewer instead of a canal; while the little ricketty bridges that span the ditches and connect court with court, give it the appearance of the Venice of drains, where channels before and behind the houses do duty for the ocean. Across some parts of the stream whole rooms have been built, so that house adjoins house; and here, with the very stench of death rising through the boards, human beings sleep night after night, until the last sleep of all comes upon them years before its time. Scarce a house but yellow linen is hanging to dry over the balustrade of staves, or else run out on a long oar where the sulphur-coloured clothes hang over the waters, and you are almost wonder-struck to see their form and colour unreflected in the putrid ditch beneath.

At the back of nearly every house that boasts a square foot or two of outlet—and the majority have none at all—are pig-sties. In front waddle ducks, while cocks and hens scratch at the cinder-heaps. Indeed, the creatures that fatten on offal are the only living things that seem to flourish here.

The inhabitants themselves show in their faces the poisonous influence of the mephitic air they breathe. Either their skins are white, like parchment, telling of the impaired digestion, the languid circulation, and the coldness of the skin peculiar to persons suffering from chronic poisoning, or else their cheeks are flushed hectically, and their eyes are glassy, showing the wasting fever and general decline of the bodily functions. The brown, earth-like complexion of some, and their sunk eyes, with the dark areolæ round them, tell you that the sulphuretted hydrogen of the atmosphere in which they live has been absorbed into the blood; while others are remarkable for the watery eye exhibiting the increased secretion of tears so peculiar to those who are exposed to the exhalations of hydro-sulphate of ammonia.

Scarcely a girl that has not suffusion and soreness of the eyes, so that you would almost fancy she had been swallowing small doses of arsenic;[1] while it is evident, from the irritation and discharge from the mucous membranes of the nose and eyes for which all the children are distinguished, that the poor emaciated things are suffering from the continual inhalation of the vapour of carbonate of ammonia and other deleterious gases.

Nor was this to be wondered at, when the whole air reeked with the stench of rotting animal and vegetable matter: for the experiment of Professor Donovan[2] has shown that a rabbit, with only its body enclosed in a bladder filled with sulphuretted hydrogen, and allowed to breathe freely, will die in ten minutes. Thénard[3] also has proved that one eight hundredth part of this gas in the atmosphere is sufficient to destroy a dog, and one two hundred and fiftieth will kill a horse; while Mr. Taylor,[4] in his book on poisons, assures us that the men who were engaged in excavating the Thames Tunnel suffered severely during the work from the presence of this gas in the atmosphere in which they were obliged to labour. "The air, as well as the water which trickled through the roof," he tells us, "was found to contain sulphuretted hydrogen. This was probably derived from the action of the iron pyrites[5] in the clay. By respiring this atmosphere the strongest and most robust men were, in the course of a few months, reduced to a state of extreme exhaustion and died. They became emaciated, and fell into a state of low fever, accompanied with delirium. In one case which I saw," he adds, "the face of the man was pale, the lips of a violet hue, the eyes sunk and dark all round, and the whole muscular system flabby and emaciated." To give the reader some idea as to the extent with which the air in Jacob's Island is charged with this most deadly compound, it will be sufficient to say that a silver spoon of which we caught sight in one of the least wretched dwellings was positively chocolate-coloured by the action of the sulphur on the metal.

On approaching the tidal ditch from the Neckinger-road, the shutters of the house at the corner were shut from top to bottom. Our intelligent and oblig-

---

1 The poisonous chemical was used in many products in nineteenth-century Britain. It could also be found in the drinking water, leading to gradual arsenic poisoning, whose symptoms could present as those of common ailments.

2 Michael Donovan (1790–1876), professor of chemistry to the Company of Apothecaries in Ireland. The chemist's findings on sulphuretted hydrogen are published in his *Treatise on Chemistry* (1839) and repeated in various more popular works, such as the *Rural Cyclopedia*, vol. 4, and *The Magazine of Domestic Economy and Family Review*, vol. 1.

3 Louis-Jacques Thénard (1777–1857). In 1832, the French chemist submitted a plan to the Academy of Sciences to use sulphuretted hydrogen to kill mice and other unwanted creatures.

4 Alfred Swaine Taylor (1806–80). The British toxicologist, a pioneer in forensic medicine, published *On Poisons in Relation to Medical Jurisprudence and Medicine* in 1848.

5 Also known as fool's gold, pyrite is composed of iron sulfide and is a common impurity in clay.

ing guide, Dr. Martin,[1] informed us that a girl was then lying dead there from cholera, and that but very recently another victim had fallen in the house adjoining it. This was the beginning of the tale of death, for the tidal ditch was filled up to this very point. Here, however, its putrefying waters were left to mingle their poison with the 267 cubic feet of air that each man daily takes into his lungs, and this was the point whence the pestilence commenced its ravages. As we walked down George-row, our informant told us that at the corner of London-street he could see, a short time back, as many as nine houses in which there were one or two persons lying dead of the cholera at the same time; and yet there could not have been more than a dozen tenements visible from the spot.

We crossed the bridge, and spoke to one of the inmates. In answer to our questions, she told us she was never well. Indeed, the signs of the deadly influence of the place were painted in the earthy complexion of the poor woman. "Neither I nor my children know what health is," said she. "But what is one to do? We must live where our bread is. I've tried to let the house, and put a bill up, but cannot get any one to take it." From this spot we were led to narrow close courts, where the sun never shone, and the air seemed almost as stagnant and putrid as the ditch we had left. The blanched cheeks of the people that now came out to stare at us, were white as vegetables grown in the dark, and as we stopped to look down the alley, our informant told us that the place teemed with children, and that if a horn was blown they would swarm like bees at the sound of a gong. The houses were mostly inhabited by "corn-runners," coal-porters, and "longshore-men," getting a precarious living—earning some times as much as 12*s.* a day, and then for weeks doing nothing. Fevers prevailed in these courts we were told more than at the side of the ditch.

By this way we reached a dismal stack of hovels called, by a strange incongruity, Pleasant-row. Inquiring of one of the inmates, we were informed that they were quite comfortable now! The stench had been all removed, said the woman, and we were invited to pass to the back-yard as evidence of the fact. We did so; the boards bent under our feet, and the air in the cellar-like yard was fœtid to positive nausea. As we left the house a child sat nursing a dying half-comatose baby on a door step. The skin of its little arms, instead of being plumped out with health, was loose and shrivelled, like an old crone's, and had a flabby monkey-like appearance more than the character of human cuticle. The almost jaundiced colour of the child's skin, its half paralyzed limbs, and state of stupor, told it was suffering from some slow poison; indeed the symptoms might readily have been mistaken for those of chronic poisoning from acetate of lead. At the end of this row our friend informed us that the last house on either side was *never* free from fever.

Continuing our course we reached "The Folly," another street so narrow that the names and trades of the shopmen were painted on boards that stretched, across the street, from the roof of their own house to that of their neighbour's. We were here stopped by our companion in front of a house "to let." The building was as narrow and as unlike a human habitation as the wooden houses in a child's

1 Unknown.

box of toys. "In this house," said our friend, "when the scarlet fever was raging in the neighbourhood, the barber who was living here suffered fearfully from it; and no sooner did the man get well of this than he was seized with typhus, and scarcely had he recovered from the first attack than he was struck down a second time with the same terrible disease. Since then he has lost his child with cholera, and at this moment his wife is in the workhouse suffering from the same affliction. The only wonder is that they are not all dead, for as the man sat at his meals in his small shop, if he put his hand against the wall behind him, it would be covered with the soil of his neighbour's privy, sopping through the wall. At the back of the house was an open sewer, and the privies were full to the seat."

One fact, says an eminent writer in toxicology, is worthy of the attention of medical jurists, namely, that the respiration of an atmosphere only slightly impregnated with the gases emanating from drains and sewers, may, if long continued, seriously affect an individual and cause death. M. D'Arcet[1] had to examine a lodging in Paris, in which three young and vigorous men had died successively in the course of a few years, under similar symptoms. The lodging consisted of a bed-room with a chimney, and an ill-ventilated ante-room. The pipe of a privy passed down one side of the room, by the head of the bed, and the wall in this part was damp from infiltration. At the time of the examination there was no perceptible smell in the room, though it was small and low. M. D'Arcet attributed the mortality in the lodging to the slow and long-continued action of the emanations from the pipe (Ann. d'Hyg., Juillet, 1836).

We then journeyed on to London-street, down which the tidal ditch continues its course. In No. 1 of this street the cholera first appeared seventeen years ago, and spread up it with fearful virulence; but this year it appeared at the opposite end, and ran down it with like severity. As we passed along the reeking banks of the sewer the sun shone upon a narrow slip of the water. In the bright light it appeared the colour of strong green tea, and positively looked as solid as black marble in the shadow—indeed it was more like watery mud than muddy water; and yet we were assured this was the only water the wretched inhabitants had to drink. As we gazed in horror at it, we saw drains and sewers emptying their filthy contents into it; we saw a whole tier of doorless privies in the open road, common to men and women, built over it; we heard bucket after bucket of filth splash into it, and the limbs of the vagrant boys bathing in it seemed, by pure force of contrast, white as Parian marble. And yet, as we stood doubting the fearful statement, we saw a little child, from one of the galleries opposite, lower a tin can with a rope to fill a large bucket that stood beside her. In each of the balconies that hung over the stream the self-same tub was to be seen in which the inhabitants put the mucky liquid to stand, so that they may, after it has rested for a day or two, skim the fluid from the solid particles of filth, pollution, and disease. As the little thing dangled her tin cup as gently as possible into the stream, a bucket of night-soil was poured down from the next gallery.

---

1 Jean-Pierre-Joseph d'Arcet (1777–1844). The French chemist and industrialist published "Observations d'asphyxie lente due à l'insalubrité des habitations, et à des émanations métalliques" with Henri Braconnot (1780–1855) in *Annales d'hygiène publique et de médecine légale*, July 1836.

In this wretched place we were taken to a house where an infant lay dead of the cholera. We asked if they *really did* drink the water? The answer was, "They were obliged to drink the ditch, without they could beg a pailfull or thieve a pailfull of water." But have you spoken to your landlord about having it laid on for you? "Yes, sir; and he says he'll do it, and do it, but we know him better than to believe him." "Why, sir," cried another woman, who had shot out from an adjoining room, "he won't even give us a little whitewash, though we tell him we'll willingly do the work ourselves: and look here, sir," she added, "all the tiles have fallen off, and the rain pours in wholesale."

We had scarcely left the house when a bill caught our eye, announcing that "this valuable estate" was to be sold!

From this spot we crossed the little shaky bridge into Providence-buildings—a narrow neck of land set in sewers. Here, in front of the houses, were small gardens that a table-cloth would have covered. Still the one dahlia that here raised its round red head made it a happier and brighter place. Never was colour so grateful to the eye. All we had looked at had been so black and dingy, and had smelt so much of churchyard clay, that this little patch of beauty was brighter and greener than ever was oasis in the desert. Here a herd of children came out, and stared at us like sheep. One child our guide singled out from the rest. She had the complexion of tawed leather, and her bright, glassy eyes were sunk so far back in her head, that they looked more like lights shining through the hollow sockets of a skull than a living head, and her bones seemed ready to start through the thin layer of skin. We were told she had had the cholera twice. Her father was dead of it. "But she, sir," said a woman addressing us, "won't die. Ah! if she'd had plenty of victuals and been brought up less hardy she would have been dead and buried long ago, like many more. And here's another," she added, pushing forward a long thin woman in rusty black. "Why, I've know'd her eat as much as a quartern loaf at a meal, and you can't fatten her no how." Upon this there was a laugh, but in the woman's bloodless cheeks and blue lips we saw that she like the rest was wasting away from the influence of the charnel-like atmosphere around her.

The last place we went to was in Joiner's-court, with four wooden houses in it, in which there had lately been as many as five cases of cholera. In front, the poor souls, as if knowing by an instinct that plants were given to purify the atmosphere, had pulled up the paving-stones before their dwellings, and planted a few stocks here and there in the rich black mould beneath. The first house we went to, a wild ragged-headed boy shot out in answer to our knock, and putting his hands across the doorway, stood there to prevent our entrance. Our friend asked whether he could enter, and see the state of the drainage? "No; t'ain't convenient," was the answer, given so quickly and sharply, that the lad forced some ugly and uncharitable suspicion upon us. In the next house, the poor inmate was too glad to meet with any one ready to sympathise with her sufferings. We were taken up into a room, where we were told she had positively lived for nine years. The window was within four feet of a high wall, at the foot of which, until very recently, ran the open common sewer. The room was so dark that it was several minutes before we could see anything within it, and there was a smell of must and dry rot that told of damp and imperfect ventilation, and the unnatural size of the pupils of the wretched woman's eyes convinced us how much too long she had dwelt in this gloomy place.

Here, as usual, we heard stories that made one's blood curdle, of the cruelty of those from whom they rented the sties called dwellings. They had begged for pure water to be laid on, and the rain to be shut out; and the answer for eighteen years had been, that the lease was just out. "They knows it's handy for a man's work," said one and all, "and that's the reason why they impose on a body." This, indeed, seems to us to be the great evil. Out of these wretches' health, comfort, and even lives, small capitalists reap a petty independence; and until the poor are rescued from the fangs of these mercenary men, there is but little hope either for their physical or moral welfare.

The extreme lassitude and deficient energy of both body and mind induced by the mephitic vapours they continually inhale leads them—we may say, *forces* them to seek an unnatural stimulus in the gin-shop; indeed, the publicans of Jacob's Island drive even a more profitable trade than the landlords themselves. What wonder, then, since debility is one of the predisposing conditions of cholera, that—even if these stenches of the foul tidal ditch be not the *direct* cause of the disease—that the impaired digestive functions, the languid circulation, the depression of mind produced by the continued inhalation of the noxious gases of the tidal ditch, together with the intemperance that it induces—the cold, damp houses—and, above all, the quenching of the thirst and cooking of the food with water saturated with the very excrements of their fellow-creatures, should make Jacob's Island notorious as the Jessore of England.

b. From "Labour and the Poor: The Metropolitan Districts. From our Special Correspondent. Letter I [by Henry Mayhew]" (19 October 1849): 5

The plan of publishing in this journal a series of communications descriptive of the condition of the poor was fully explained in *The Morning Chronicle* of yesterday. To me has been confided the office of examining into the condition of the poor of London; and I shall now proceed to state the view I purpose taking of the subject.

Under the term poor I shall include all those persons whose incomings are insufficient for the satisfaction of their wants—a want being, according to my idea, contra-distinguished from a mere desire by a positive physical pain, instead of a mental uneasiness, accompanying it. The large and comparatively unknown body of people included in this definition I shall contemplate in two distinct classes, viz., the *honest* and *dishonest* poor; and the first of these I purpose subdividing into the *striving* and the *disabled*—or, in other words, I shall consider the whole of the metropolitan poor under three separate phases, according as they *will* work, they *can't* work, and they *won't* work. Of those that will work, and yet are unable to obtain sufficient for their bodily necessities, I shall devote my attention first to such as receive no relief from the parish; and under this head will be included the poorly-paid—the unfortunate—and the improvident. While treating of the poorly-paid, I shall endeavour to lay before the reader a catalogue of such occupations in London as yield a bare subsistence to the parties engaged in them. At the same time I purpose, when possible, giving the weekly amount of income derived from each, together with the cause—if discoverable—of the inadequate return. After this, it is my intention to visit the dwellings of the unrelieved poor—to ascertain, by positive inspection, the condition of their homes—to learn, by close communion with them, the real or fancied wrongs of their lot—to discover, not only on how little they subsist, but how large a rate of profit they have to pay for the little upon which they do subsist—to ascertain what weekly rent they are charged for their waterless, drainless, floorless, and almost roofless tenements; and to calculate the interest that the petty capitalist reaps from their necessities. Nor shall I fail to point out how, when the poor are driven to raise a meal on their clothes or their bedding, he who makes the advance is licensed by law to receive as much as 20 per cent. for the petty loan upon the shirt or the blanket, though more than five per cent. is forbidden to be charged for the loan upon the land. But, however alive I may be to the wrongs of the poor, I shall not be misled by a morbid sympathy to see them only as suffering from the selfishness of others. Their want of prudence, want of temperance, want of energy, want of cleanliness, want of knowledge, and want of morality, will each be honestly set forth. This done, I shall proceed to treat of the poor receiving parish relief, outside and inside the union; after which, the habits, haunts, and tricks of the beggars of London will be duly set forth; and, finally, those of the thieves and prostitutes.

In the present article I shall endeavour to give the reader a general idea of the wealth and poverty, the power and weakness, the knowledge and ignorance, the luxury and want, the crime and charity, which all lie huddled together in London, in such vast and striking confusion. But before doing so, let me briefly draw attention to the extraordinary change of feeling which has taken place of late years, and which makes the poor of the present day of such moment to us that, from high to low, from one corner of the land to the other—in the mansion, the counting-house, and the tap-room—the sufferings and privations of the labouring classes should be listened to with so lively an interest that the columns of a morning newspaper are judged a fit place for the exposition of them. Indeed, the chief distinction of the present age from the past, consists, not in the substitution of steam for human labour—in the use of cranks and levers for thews and sinews—nor does it lie in the iron bands which now link town to town, and brace county to county, nor in the nerve-like wires that carry our wishes from one corner of the land to the other with the same marvellous instantaneousness as our muscles act in obedience to our will. These, it is true, are salient points of difference between us and our forefathers. Still the broad line of demarcation separating our own times from all others is to be found in the fuller and more general development of the human sympathies.

[...]

The city of London, within the walls, occupies a space of only 370 acres, and is but the hundred and fortieth part of the extent covered by the whole metropolis. Nevertheless, it is the parent of a mass of united and far spreading tenements, stretching from Hammersmith to Blackwall, from Holloway to

Camberwell. A century ago, according to Maitland,[1] the metropolis had drawn into its vortex one city, one borough, and forty-three villages. Despite its vast extent, still its increase continues to be so rapid, that every year further house room has to be provided for twenty thousand persons—so that London increases annually by the addition of a town of considerable size. At all times there are 4,000 extra houses in the course of erection. By the last return the metropolis covered an extent of nearly 45,000 acres, and contained upwards of two hundred and sixty thousand houses, occupied by one million eight hundred and twenty thousand souls, constituting not only the densest, but the busiest hive, the most wondrous workshop, and the richest bank in the world. The mere name of London awakens a thousand trains of varied reflections. Perhaps the first thought that it excites in the mind, paints it as the focus of modern civilization, of the hottest, the most restless activity of thc social elements. Some, turning to the west, see it as a city of palaces, adorned with parks, ennobled with triumphal arches, grand statues, and stately monuments; others, looking at the east, see only narrow lanes and musty counting-houses, with tall chimneys vomiting black clouds, and huge masses of warehouses with doors and cranes ranged one above another. Yet all think of it as a vast bricken multitude, a strange incongruous chaos of wealth and want—of ambition and despair—of the brightest charity and the darkest crime, where there are more houses and more houseless, where there is more feasting and more starvation, than on any other spot on earth—and all grouped round the one giant centre, the huge black dome,[2] with its ball of gold looming through the smoke (apt emblem of the source of its riches!) and marking out the capital, no matter from what quarter the traveller may come.

Those who have only seen London in the daytime, with its flood of life pouring through its arteries to its restless heart, know it not in its grandest aspect. It is not in the noise and roar of the cataract of commerce pouring through its streets, nor in its forest of ships, nor in its vast docks and warehouses, that its true solemnity is to be seen. To behold it in its greatest sublimity, it must be contemplated by night, afar off, from an eminence. The noblest prospect in the world, it has been well said, is London viewed from the suburbs on a clear winter's evening. The stars are shining in the heavens, but there is another firmament spread out below, with its millions of bright lights glittering at our feet. Line after line sparkles, like the trails left by meteors, cutting and crossing one another till they are lost in the haze of the distance. Over the whole there hangs a lurid cloud, bright as if the monster city were in flames, and looking afar off like the sea by night, made phosphorescent by the million creatures dwelling within it. At night it is that the strange anomalies of London are best seen. Then, as the hum of life ceases and the shops darken, and the gaudy gin palaces thrust out their ragged and squalid crowds, to pace the streets, London puts on its most solemn look of all. On the benches of the parks, in the

1 William Maitland (c. 1693–1757), historian and author of *The History of London, from Its Foundation by the Romans to the Present Time*, first published in 1739 with later editions issued throughout the eighteenth century.

2 St. Paul's Cathedral, with its dome at the time blackened from air pollution, is positioned on Ludgate Hill, the highest point of the City of London.

nitches of the bridges, and in the litter of the markets, are huddled together the homeless and the destitute. The only living things that haunt the streets are the poor wretches who stand shivering in their finery, waiting to catch the drunkard as he goes shouting homewards. Here on a door-step crouches some shoeless child, whose day's begging has not brought it enough to purchase it even the twopenny bed that its young companions in beggary have gone to. There, where the stones are taken up and piled high in the road, and the gas streams from a tall pipe in the centre of the street in a flag of flame—there, round the red glowing coke fire, are grouped a ragged crowd smoking or dozing through the night beside it. Then, as the streets grow blue with the coming light, and the church spires and chimney tops stand out against the sky with a sharpness of outline that is seen only in London before its million fires cover the town with their pall of smoke—then come sauntering forth the unwashed poor, some with greasy wallets on their back, to hunt over each dirt heap, and eke out life by seeking refuse bones or stray rags and pieces of old iron. Others, on their way to their work, gathered at the corner of the street round the breakfast stall, and blowing saucers of steaming coffee drawn from tall tin cans, with the fire shining crimson through the holes beneath; whilst already the little slattern girl, with her basket slung before her, screams watercresses through the sleeping streets.

Yet who, to see the squalor and wretchedness of London by night, would believe that twenty-nine only of the London bankers have cleared through their clearing-house as much as *nine hundred and fifty-four million pounds sterling in one year*, the average being more than three millions of money daily—or that the loans of merely one house in the City throughout the year exceed thirty millions? Who could have visited the Rookery of St. Giles's as it existed but a few months back,[1] and have seen the unutterable abominations of this retreat of wretchedness, this nest of disease, at once the nursery and sanctuary of vice—where in one house alone, Mr. Smirke[2] tells us, were huddled together eleven men, thirteen women, and thirty children—where as many as sixty of the foulest of the London lazzaroni often sleep in the same abode—who could witness this want and wretchedness, and yet believe that this country is "the bank for the whole world," as the late Mr. Rothschild[3] called it in 1832; or that

---

1 Most likely a reference to a controversy following from a letter sent to the *Times* in July 1849 from the inhabitants of a cellar in St. Giles. It prompted extensive print commentary in the weeks and months to follow. One of London's worst slums, St. Giles's rookery saw an influx of Irish immigrants arriving in 1845 and 1849, many of whom died in the cholera epidemic of 1848–49.

2 Sydney Smirke (1797–1877). British architect and author of "Suggestions for the Architectural Improvement of the Western Part of London" (1834), in which he details the living conditions in St. Giles, including this particular house on Monmouth Street, which was subject to a fire.

3 Nathan Rothschild (1777–1836), member of the Rothschild banking family and one of the richest men in the world. Rothschild testified to the Committee of Secrecy on the Bank of England Charter (1832) that the Bank of England could "never guide the Exchanges for long.... This country in general is the Bank for the whole world; I mean, that all transactions in India, in China, in Germany, in Russia, and in the whole world, are all guided here and settled through this country."

"all transactions in India, in China, in Russia, and indeed every other empire, are guided and settled in this country"?

[...]

2. From *London Labour and the London Poor,* Volume 4 (1862)

a. "Classification of the Workers and Non-Workers of Great Britain," p. 12

CLASSIFICATION

OF

THE WORKERS AND NON-WORKERS

OF GREAT BRITAIN.

THOSE WHO WILL WORK.

I. Enrichers, as the Collectors, Extractors, or Producers of Exchangeable Commodities.

II. Auxiliaries, as the Promoters of Production, or the Distributors of the Produce.

III. Benefactors, or those who confer some permanent benefit, as Educators and Curators engaged in promoting the physical, intellectual, or spiritual well-being of the people.

IV. Servitors, or those who render some temporary service, or pleasure, as Amusers, Protectors, and Servants.

THOSE WHO CANNOT WORK.

V. Those who are provided for by some public Institution, as the Inmates of workhouses, prisons, hospitals, asylums, almshouses, dormitories, and refuges.

VI. Those who are unprovided for, and incapacitated for labour, either from want of power, from want of means, or from want of employment.

THOSE WHO WILL NOT WORK.

VII. Vagrants.

VIII. Professional Beggars.

IX. Cheats.

X. Thieves.

XI. Prostitutes.

THOSE WHO NEED NOT WORK.

XII. Those who derive their income from rent.

XIII. Those who derive their income from dividends.

XIV. Those who derive their income from yearly stipends.

XV. Those who derive their income from obsolete or nominal offices.

XVI. Those who derive their income from trades in which they do not appear.

XVII. Those who derive their income by favour from others.

XVIII. Those who derive their support from the head of the family.

b. From "Female Operatives,"[1] pp. 255–57

When alluding casually to this subject before, I enumerated some of the trades that supplied women to swell the ranks of prostitution, amongst which are milliners, dress-makers, straw bonnet-makers, furriers, hat-binders, silk-winders, tambour-workers,[2] shoe-binders, slop-women, or those who work for cheap tailors, those in pastry-cook, fancy and cigar-shops, bazaars, and ballet-girls.

I have heard it asserted in more than one quarter, although of course such assertions cannot be authenticated, or made reliable, for want of data, that one out of three of all the female operatives in London are unchaste, and in the habit of prostituting themselves when occasion offers, either for money, or more frequently for their own gratification.

I met a woman in Fleet Street,[3] who told me that she came into the streets now and then to get money not to subsist upon, but to supply her with funds to meet the debts her extravagance caused her to contract. But I will put her narrative into a consecutive form.

"Ever since I was twelve," she said, "I have worked in a printing office where a celebrated London morning journal is put in type and goes to press. I get enough money to live upon comfortably; but then I am extravagant, and spend a great deal of money in eating and drinking, more than you would imagine. My appetite is very delicate, and my constitution not at all strong. I long for certain things like a woman in the family way, and I must have them by hook or by crook. The fact is the close confinement and the night air upset me and disorder my digestion. I have the most expensive things sometimes, and when I can, I live in a sumptuous manner, comparatively speaking. I am attached to a man in our office, to whom I shall be married some day. He does not suspect me, but on the contrary believes me to be true to him, and you do not suppose that I ever take the trouble to undeceive him. I am nineteen now, and have carried on with my 'typo'[4] for nearly three years now. I sometimes go to the Haymarket,[5] either early in the evening, or early in the morning, when I can get away from the printing; and sometimes I do a little in the day-time. This is not a frequent practice of mine; I only do it when I want money to pay any-thing. I am out now with the avowed intention of picking up a man, or making

---

1 Written by Bracebridge Hemyng (1841–1901), who contributed the interviews with London prostitutes to the fourth volume of *London Labour and the London Poor*. Trained as a lawyer, Hemyng was the author of popular penny dreadfuls and adventure stories for boys in the 1860s and 1870s.

2 A tambour is a circular frame used to stretch fabric so that it can be embroidered.

3 Major London thoroughfare named after the Fleet River (see p. 179, note 2) and long associated with printers, publishers, booksellers, literary coffeehouses and pubs, and the newspaper business. The original office for *London Labour* was located on Fleet Street before moving to Wellington Street.

4 A person who works as a typographer, or printer.

5 A central London street where a market for hay and straw was established in the seventeenth century. By the nineteenth century the area had become a theatre district and was associated with the sex trade.

an appointment with some one for to-morrow or some time during the week. I always dress well, at least you mayn't think so, but I am always neat, and respectable, and clean, if the things I have on ain't worth the sight of money that some women's things cost them. I have good feet too, and as I find they attract attention, I always parade them. And I've hooked many a man by showing my ankle on a wet day. I shan't think anything of all this when I'm married. I believe my young man would marry me just as soon if he found out I went with others as he would now. I carry on with him now, and he likes me very much. I ain't of any particular family; to tell the truth, I was put in the workhouse when I was young, and they apprenticed me. I never knew my father or my mother, although 'my father was, as I've heard say, a well-known swell of capers gay, who cut his last fling with great applause';[1] or, if you must know, I heard that he was hung for killing a man who opposed him when committing a burglary. In other words, he was 'a macing-cove what robs,'[2] and I'm his daughter, worse luck. I used to think at first, but what was the good of being wretched about it? I couldn't get over for some time, because I was envious, like a little fool, of other people, but I reasoned, and at last I did recover myself, and was rather glad that my position freed me from certain restrictions. I had no mother whose heart I shou'd break by my conduct, or no father who could threaten me with bringing his grey hairs with sorrow to the grave. I had a pretty good example to follow set before me, and I didn't scruple to argue that I was not to be blamed for what I did. Birth is the result of accident. It is the merest chance in the world whether you're born a countess or a washerwoman. I'm neither one nor t'other; I'm only a mot who does a little typographing by way of variety. Those who have had good nursing, and all that, and the advantages of a sound education, who have a position to lose, prospects to blight, and relations to dishonour, may be blamed for going on the loose, but I'll be hanged if I think that priest or moralist is to come down on me with the sledge-hammer of their denunciation. You look rather surprised at my talking so well. I know I talk well, but you must remember what a lot has passed through my hands for the last seven years, and what a lot of copy I've set up. There is very little I don't know, I can tell you. It's what old Robert Owen[3] would call the spread of education."

I had to talk some time to this girl before she was so communicative; but it must be allowed my assiduity was amply repaid. The common sense she displayed was extraordinary for one in her position; but, as she said, she certainly had had superior opportunities, of which she had made the most. And her arguments, though based upon fallacy, were exceedingly clever and well put. So much for the spread of education amongst the masses. Who knows to what it will lead?

---

1 A reference to "Jerry Juniper's Chant" in William Harrison Ainsworth's 1834 Newgate novel *Rookwood*.

2 A swindler.

3 Owen (1771–1858) was best known for the model society he developed in New Lanark, Scotland, based on principles of cooperation and collective living. He inspired the Owenite movement (a precursor to socialism) and advocated reforms to factory working conditions, trade unionism, and free education for all.

[...]

Many causes may be enumerated to account for the lax morality of our female operatives. Among the chief of which we must class—

1. Low wages inadequate to their sustenance.
2. Natural levity and the example around them.
3. Love of dress and display, coupled with the desire for a sweetheart.
4. Sedentary employment, and want of proper exercise.
5. Low and cheap literature of an immoral tendency.
6. Absence of parental care and the inculcation of proper precepts. In short, bad bringing up.

c. From "Pickpockets and Shoplifters,"[1] pp. 303–06

IN tracing the pickpocket from the beginning of his career, in most cases we must turn our attention to the little ragged boys living by a felon's hearth, or herding with other young criminals in a low lodging-house, or dwelling in the cold and comfortless home of drunken and improvident parents. The great majority of the pickpockets of the metropolis, with few exceptions, have sprung from the dregs of society—from the hearths and homes of London thieves—so that they have no reason to be proud of their lineage. Fifteen or twenty years ago many of those accomplished pickpockets, dressed in the highest style of fashion, and glittering in gold chains, studs, and rings, who walk around the Bank of England and along Cheapside, and our busy thoroughfares, were poor ragged boys walking barefooted among the dark and dirty slums and alleys of Westminster and the Seven Dials, or loitering among the thieves' dens of the Borough and Whitechapel.

Step by step they have emerged from their rags and squalor to a higher position of physical comfort, and have risen to higher dexterity and accomplishment in their base and ignoble profession.

We say there are a few exceptions to the general rule, that the most of our habitual thieves have sprung from the loins of felon parents. We blush to say that some have joined the ranks of our London thieves, and are living callous in open crime, who were trained in the homes of honest and industrious parents, and were surrounded in early life with all those influences which are fitted to elevate and improve the mind. But here our space forbids us to enlarge.

The chief sources whence our pickpockets spring are from the low lodging-houses—from those dwellings in low neighbourhoods, where their parents are thieves, and where improvident and drunken people neglect their children, such as Whitechapel, Shoreditch, Spitalfields, New Cut, Lambeth, the Borough, Clerkenwell, Drury Lane, and other localities. Many of them are the children of Irish parents, costermongers, bricklayers' labourers, and others.

1 Written by John Binny. Little is known about Binny compared to the other contributors to Volume 4. He was a contributor to Mayhew's *The Criminal Prisons of London* (1862).

They often begin to steal at six or seven years of age, sometimes as early as five years, and commit petty sneaking thefts, as well as pick handkerchiefs from gentlemen's pockets. Many of these ragged urchins are taught to steal by their companions, others are taught by trainers of thieves, young men and women, and some middle-aged convicted thieves. They are learned to be expert in this way. A coat is suspended on the wall with a bell attached to it, and the boy attempts to take the handkerchief from the pocket without the bell ringing. Until he is able to do this with proficiency he is not considered well trained. Another way in which they are trained is this: The trainer—if a man—walks up and down the room with a handkerchief in the tail of his coat, and the ragged boys amuse themselves abstracting it until they learn to do it in an adroit manner. We could point our finger to three of these execrable wretches, who are well known to train schools of juvenile thieves—one of them, a young man at Whitechapel; another, a young woman at Clerkenwell; and a third, a middle-aged man residing about Lambeth Walk. These base wretches buy the stolen handkerchiefs from the boys at a paltry sum. We have also heard of some being taught to pick pockets by means of an effigy; but this is not so well authenticated.

Great numbers of these ragged pickpockets may be seen loitering about our principal streets, ready to steal from a stall or shop-door when they find an opportunity. During the day they generally pick pockets two or three in a little band, but at dusk a single one can sometimes do it with success. They not only steal handkerchiefs of various kinds, but also pocket-books from the tails of gentlemen's coats. We may see them occasionally engaged at this work on Blackfriars Bridge and London Bridge, also along Bishopsgate, Shoreditch, Whitechapel, Drury Lane, and similar localities. They may be seen at any hour of the day, but chiefly from 10 to 2 o'clock. They are generally actively on the look-out on Saturday evening in the shopping streets where the labouring people get their provisions in for the Sunday. At this early stage the boys occasionally pick pockets, and go about cadging and sneaking (begging and committing petty felonies).

The next stage commences—we shall say—about fourteen years of age, when the stripling lays aside his rags, and dresses in a more decent way, though rather shabby. Perhaps in a dark or gray frock-coat, dark or dirty tweed trousers, and a cap with peak, and shoes. At this time many of them go to low neighbourhoods, or to those quieter localities where the labouring people reside, and pick the pockets of the wives and daughters of this class of persons; others steal from gentlemen passing along thoroughfares, while a few adroit lads are employed by men to steal from ladies' pockets in the fashionable streets of the metropolis.

[...]

Walking along Cheapside one day, toward the afternoon, we observed a well-dressed, good-looking man of about thirty years of age, having the appearance of a smart man of business, standing by the side of an elderly looking, respectably dressed lady at a jeweller's window. The lady appeared to belong to the country, from her dress and manner, and was absorbed looking into the window at the gold watches, gold chains, lockets, pins, and other trinkets glittering within. Meantime the gentleman also appeared to be engrossed looking at these articles beside her, while crowds of people were passing to and fro in the street, and the carts, cabs, omnibuses, and other vehicles were rumbling by, deadening the footsteps of the passers by. Our eye accidentally caught sight of his left hand drooping by his side in the direction of the lady's pocket. We observed it glide softly in the direction of her pocket beneath the edge of her shawl with all the fascination of a serpent's movement. While the hand lay drooping, the fingers sought their way to the pocket. From the movement we observed that the fingers had found the pocket, and were seeking their way farther into the interior. The person was about to plunge his hand to abstract the contents, when we instinctively hooked his wrist with the curve of our walking-stick and prevented the robbery. With great address and tact he withdrew his hand from the lady's pocket, and his wrist from our grasp, and walked quietly away. Meantime a group of people had gathered round about us, and a gentleman asked if we had observed a pocket picked. We said nothing, but whispered to the lady, who stood at the window unaware of the attempted felony, that we had prevented her pocket being picked, and had just scared a thief with his hand in her pocket, then walked over to the other side of the street and passed on.

[...]

d. "Hindoo Beggars,"[1] pp. 423–25

[Hindoo beggars] are those spare, snake-eyed Asiatics who walk the streets, coolly dressed in Manchester cottons,[2] or chintz of a pattern commonly used for bed-furniture, to which the resemblance is carried out by the dark, polished colour of the thin limbs which it envelopes. They very often affect to be converts to the Christian religion, and give away tracts; with the intention of entrapping the sympathy of elderly ladies. They assert that they have been high-caste Brahmins, but as untruth, even when not acting professionally, is habitual to them, there is not the slightest dependence to be placed on what they say. Sometimes, in the winter, they "do shallow," that is, stand on the kerbstone of the pavement, in their thin, ragged clothes, and shiver as with cold and hunger, or crouch against a wall and whine like a whipped animal; at others they turn out with a small, barrel-shaped drum, on which they make a monotonous noise with their fingers, to which music they sing and dance. Or they will "stand pad with a fakement," *i.e.* wear a placard upon their breasts, that describes them as natives of Madagascar, in distress, converts to Christianity,

1 Andrew Halliday (1830–77) is the author of "Hindoo Beggars" and "Negro Beggars." Halliday was born in Scotland and started writing for the *Morning Chronicle* in 1849 before going on to write for magazines edited by Dickens and Thackeray.

2 Nineteenth-century Manchester was the global centre of cotton textile production, displacing India as the leading exporter of well-made, inexpensive cotton.

anxious to get to a seaport where they can work their passage back. This is a favourite artifice with Lascars[1]—or they will sell lucifers, or sweep a crossing, or do anything where their picturesque appearance, of which they are proud and conscious, can be effectively displayed. They are as cunning as they look, and can detect a sympathetic face among a crowd. They never beg of soldiers, or sailors, to whom they always give a wide berth as they pass them in the streets.

From the extraordinary mendacity of this race of beggars—a mendacity that never falters, hesitates, or stumbles, but flows on in an unbroken stream of falsehood,—it is difficult to obtain any reliable information respecting them. I have, however, many reasons for believing that the following statement, which was made to me by a very dirty and distressed Indian, is moderately true. The man spoke English like a cockney of the lowest order. I shall not attempt to describe the peculiar accent or construction which he occasionally gave to it.

"My name is Joaleeka. I do not know where I was born. I never knew my father. I remember my mother very well. From the first of my remembrance I was at Dumdum,[2] where I was servant to a European officer—a great man—a prince—who had more than a hundred servants beside me. When he went away to fight, I followed among others—I was with the baggage. I never fought myself, but I have heard the men (Sepoys)[3] say that the prince, or general, or colonel, liked nothing so well as fighting, except tiger-hunting. He was a wonderful man, and his soldiers liked him very much. I travelled over a great part of India with Europeans. I went up country as far as Secunderabad,[4] and learned to speak English very well—so well that, when I was quite a young man, I was often employed as interpreter, for I caught up different Indian languages quickly. At last I got to interpret so well that I was recommended to ——, a great native prince who was coming over to England. I was not his interpreter, but interpreter to his servants. We came to London. We stopped in an hotel in Vere-street, Oxford-street. We stayed here some time. Then my chief went over to Paris, but he did not take all his servants with him. I stopped at the hotel to interpret for those who remained. It was during this time that I formed a connexion with a white woman. She was a servant in the hotel. I broke my caste, and from that moment I knew that it would not do for me to go back to India. The girl fell in the family-way, and was sent out of the house. My fellow-servants knew of it, and as many of them hated me, I knew that they would tell my master on his return. I also knew that by the English laws in England I was a free man, and that my master could not take me back against my will. If I had gone back, I should have been put to death for breaking my caste. When my master returned from France, he sent for me. He told me that he had heard of my breaking my caste, and of the girl, but that he should take no notice of it; that I was to return to Calcutta with him, where he would get me employment with some European officer; that I need not fear, as he would order his servants to keep silent on the subject. I

1 See p. 92, note 1.

2 A suburb of Kolkata.

3 A low-ranking Indian soldier serving in the British or other European military.

4 A city in south-central India. The British established a military headquarters there in 1806.

salaamed and thanked him, and said I was his slave for ever; but at the same time I knew that he would break his word, and that when he had me in his power, he would put me to death. He was a very severe man about caste. I attended to all my duties as before, and all believed that I was going back to India—but the very morning that my master started for the coast, I ran away. I changed my clothes at the house of a girl I knew—not the same one as I had known at the hotel, but another. This one lived at Seven Dials. I stopped in-doors for many days, till this girl, who could read newspapers, told me that my master had sailed away. I felt very glad, for though I knew my master could not force me to go back with him, yet I was afraid for all that, for he knew the King and the Queen, and had been invited by the Lord Mayor to the City. I liked England better than India, and English women have been very kind to me. I think English women are the handsomest in the world. The girl in whose house I hid, showed me how to beg. She persuaded me to turn Christian, because she thought that it would do me good—so I turned Christian. I do not know what it means, but I am a Christian, and have been for many years. I married that girl for some time. I have been married several times. I do not mean to say that I have ever been to church as rich folks do; but I have been married without that. Sometimes I do well, and sometimes badly. I often get a pound or two by interpreting. I am not at all afraid of meeting any Indian who knew me, for if they said anything I did not like, I should call out 'Police!' I know the law better than I did. Every thing is free in England. You can do what you like, if you can pay, or are not found out. I do not like policemen. After the mutiny in 1857[1] I did very badly. No one would look at a poor Indian then—much less give to him. I knew that the English would put it down soon, because I know what those rascals over there are like. I am living now in Charles Street, Drury Lane. I have been married to my present wife six years. We have three children and one dead. My eldest is now in the hospital with a bad arm. I swept a crossing for two years; that was just before the mutiny. All that knew me used to chaff me about it, and call me Johnny Sepoy. My present wife is Irish, and fought two women about it. They were taken to Bow-street by a policeman, but the judge would not hear them. My wife is a very good wife to me, but she gets drunk too often. If it were not for that, I should like her better. I ran away from her once, but she came after me with all the children. Sometimes I make twelve shillings a week. I could make much more by interpreting, but I do not like to go among the nasty natives of my country. I believe I am more than fifty years of age."

e. "Negro Beggars," pp. 425–26

The negro beggar so nearly resembles the Hindoo that what I have said of one, I could almost say of the other. There are, however, these points of difference.

1 A resistance against the East India Company, a British trading company that controlled much of India. The resistance began with the company's sepoys in northern India and spread to more powerful elites. The "Mutiny of 1857," as it came to be known, was a turning point in British–Indian relations and led to the demise of the East India Company (see p. 253, note 2).

The negro mendicant, who is usually an American negro, never studies the picturesque in his attire. He relies on the abject misery and down-trodden despair of his appearance, and generally represents himself as a fugitive slave—with this exception, his methods of levying contributions are precisely the same as his lighter-skinned brother's.

Some years ago it was a common thing to see a negro with tracts in his hand, and a placard upon his breast, upon which was a wood-cut of a black man, kneeling, his wrists heavily chained, his arms held high in supplication, and round the picture, forming a sort of proscenium or frame, the words: "Am I not a man and a brother?"[1] At the time that the suppression of the slave trade created so much excitement, this was so excellent a "dodge" that many white beggars, fortunate enough to possess a flattish or turned-up nose, *dyed themselves black* and "stood pad" as real Africans. The imposture, however, was soon detected and punished.

There are but few negro beggars to be seen now. It is only common fairness to say that negroes seldom, if ever, shirk work. Their only trouble is to obtain it. Those who have seen the many negroes employed in Liverpool, will know that they are hard-working, patient, and, too often, underpaid. A negro will sweep a crossing, run errands, black boots, clean knives and forks, or dig, for a crust and a few pence. The few impostors among them are to be found among those who go about giving lectures on the horrors of slavery, and singing variations on the "escapes" in that famous book "Uncle Tom's Cabin."[2] Negro servants are seldom read of in police reports, and are generally found to give satisfaction to their employers. In the east end of London negro beggars are to be met with, but they are seldom beggars by profession. Whenever they are out of work they have no scruples, but go into the streets, take off their hats, and beg directly.

I was accosted by one in Whitechapel, from whom I obtained the following statement:—

"My father was a slave, so was my mother. I have heard my father say so. I have heard them tell how they got away, but I forget all about it. It was before I was born. I am the eldest son. I had only one brother. Three years after his birth my mother died. My father was a shoe-black in New York. He very often had not enough to eat. My brother got a place as a servant, but I went out in the streets to do what I could. About the same time that my father, who was an old man, died, my brother lost his place. We agreed to come to England together. My brother had been living with some Britishers, and he had heard them say that over here niggers were as good as whites; and that the whites did not look down on them and illtreat them, as they do in New York. We went

---

1 The woodcut image with the quotation referred to here would have been a copy of a famous medallion produced for the British anti-slavery movement by pottery manufacturer Josiah Wedgwood (1730–95) in 1787. Reproduced in mass quantities, the image and inscription appeared on Wedgwood products, including crockery and jewellery, and in print media.

2 Anti-slavery novel by American author Harriet Beecher Stowe (1811–96), published in 1852.

about and got odd jobs on the quay, and at last we hid ourselves in the hold of a vessel, bound for Liverpool. I do not know how long we were hid, but I remember we were terribly frightened lest we should be found out before the ship got under weigh. At last hunger forced us out, and we rapped at the hatches; at first we were not heard, but when we shouted out, they opened the hatches, and took us on deck. They flogged us very severely, and treated us shamefully all the voyage. When we got to Liverpool, we begged and got odd jobs. At last we got engaged in a travelling circus, where we were servants, and used to ride about with the band in beautiful dresses, but the grooms treated us so cruelly that we were forced to run away from that. I forget the name of the place that we were performing at, but it was not a day's walk from London. We begged about for some time. At last, my brother—his name is Aaron—got to clean the knives and forks at a slap-bang (an eating-house) in the city. He was very fortunate, and used to save some bits for me. He never takes any notice of me now. He is doing very well. He lives with a great gentleman in Harewood-square, and has a coat with silver buttons, and a gold-laced hat. He is very proud, and I do not think would speak to me if he saw me. I don't know how I live, or how much I get a week. I do porter's work mostly, but I do anything I can get. I beg more than half the year. I have no regular lodging. I sleep where I can. When I am in luck, I have a bed. It costs me threepence. At some places they don't care to take a man of colour in. I sometimes get work in Newgate-market, carrying meat, but not often. Ladies give me halfpence oftener than men. The butchers call me 'Othello,'[1] and ask me why I killed my wife. I have tried to get aboard a ship, but they won't have me. I don't know how old I am, but I know that when we got to London, it was the time the Great Exhibition[2] was about. I can lift almost any weight when I have had a bit of something to eat. I don't care for beer. I like rum best. I have often got drunk, but never when I paid for it myself."

1 See p. 251, note 3.

2 See p. 116, note 1.

Appendix D: Answers to Correspondents

[In response to readers' requests, the fifth number of *London Labour* introduced an "Answers to Correspondents" feature to *London Labour*. Mayhew explained that the new "outer pages" were "a wrapper, intended to be cut off in binding" (Taithe 87), on which readers' queries and his answers would be printed. They present a fascinating window into how Mayhew's interviewees responded to his representations, offering new information and ideas of their own that often involved exchanges across several issues. Mayhew was eager to extend his database as widely as possible and used the letters as a valuable source of material for the production of *London Labour*. Further, the letters offer crucial clues, unavailable elsewhere, to the demographic profile of his readership in relation to class, age, gender, and occupation. Mayhew's responses allowed him both to answer specific queries and to expand on larger issues of importance to his work as a whole. The selections included here include three letters by Charles Alloway, a disabled man who sold nutmeg-graters and other items in the street,[1] as well as passages in which Mayhew addresses the method and theory that inform his thinking.]

1 See "The Crippled Street-seller of Nutmeg-graters" p. 140.

ANSWERS TO CORRESPONDENTS.

per week, and, whenever he can, substitutes their labour in the place of men's. These lads he treats most shamefully, making them, poor fellows, work night after night as *over time*, and then docking them if their fagged and overwrought bodies cannot do quite so much labour the next day.

"I am, Sir,
"Your obedient Servant,
"* * * * *."

"Boy labour or thief labour," said an enterprising shoe-factor to Mr. Mayhew, "it 's all the same to me, so long as I can get my work done cheap." This boy and apprentice labour is the great curse of the printer's trade.

The two following letters are touching the meaning of the term "*Daylye Oratour*" mentioned in the Notices to Correspondents attached to No. 38:—

MORPETH, OCT. 4, 1851.

"SIR,

"I think I can throw some light on the 'Office' of 'Daylye Oratour.' I believe that 'Anthoyne Master of London, haberdasher,' by so entitling himself, merely intended to intimate that he daily offered prayers for his Majesty's welfare. *Orare* means not only to speak or deliver an oration, but to entreat, to plead, to pray to the gods. Thence, of course, 'Oratory,' a place where prayer is wont to be made. But the question is, I think, set at rest by an expression which I remarked some time since in a MS. letter, of date early in the 17th century, which I regret I must quote from memory, as I have not now access to the papers. The context was to this effect: 'If God protract your life and grant you,' &c., 'for which' the writer continued, 'I shall be to Him a —— *orator*.' I leave a blank, for I am not certain what adjective was used; it might be 'constant' or 'daily.' But this use of the word 'orator' fixes, I think, the meaning in your correspondent's quotation.

"I have had thought of addressing you about 'trampers' lodging-houses in the country towns, but doubt whether what I could say would be of any value to you.

"I am, Sir,
"Truly and gratefully yours,
"W. T. S."

"As it is only once a month that I obtain your interesting work on London Labour, doubtless some one else has, ere now, attempted (and probably with success) to explain the term 'Daylye Oratour' (No. 38, fly-leaf); however, at the risk of being thought troublesome, I venture to forward the following:—'Daylye Oratour' I imagine means nothing more than daily petitioner, and is equivalent to saying that he was one who *prayed* daily for the welfare of his sovereign; the present concluding clause in petitions 'and your petitioners, as in duty bound, will ever pray,' &c., seems connected with the above.

"I am, Sir,
"Yours truly,
"T. L. L."

"Ashby-de-la-Zouch."

RIMMEL'S TOILET VINEGAR will be found far preferable to any Eau de Cologne as a tonic and refreshing lotion for the Toilet or Bath, removing all freckles, pimples, and irritation. It forms also a delightful and reviving perfume, a pleasant dentifrice, and a powerful disinfectant in apartments or sick rooms. Its useful and sanitary properties render it an indispensable requisite in all families. Price *2s. 6d.* and *5s.* To be had of E. RIMMEL, Perfumer, 39, Gerard-street, Soho, London; of all Perfumers and Chemists; and at the Exposition, 58, Baker-street.

Just Published, Price Sixpence,

A BRIEF INQUIRY into the Evils attendant upon the Present Method of Erecting, Purchasing, and Renting DWELLINGS for the INDUSTRIAL CLASSES, with Suggestions for their Remedy; being an apology for the formation of the METROPOLITAN BUILDINGS PURCHASE COMPANY, by One of its Promoters. London: published by HOULSTON and STONEMAN, 65, Paternoster-row.

On Monday, July 28th, was published, Volume I. (price *5s. 6d.*) of

LONDON LABOUR AND THE LONDON POOR.

A Cyclopædia of the Condition and Earnings of

(1) THOSE THAT WILL WORK; (2) THOSE THAT CANNOT WORK; and (3) THOSE THAT WILL NOT WORK.

THE STREET-FOLK.

BOOK THE FIRST.—CONTAINING ACCOUNTS OF

The London Costermongers.
The Street-Sellers of Fish.
The Street-Sellers of Fruit and Vegetables.
The Street Irish.
The Street-Sellers of Game and Poultry.
The Street-Sellers of Trees, Shrubs, Flowers, and Roots.
The Street-Sellers of Eatables and Drinkables.
The Street-Sellers of Stationery, Literature, and the Fine Arts.
The Low Lodging-houses.
The Street-Sellers of Manufactured Articles.
The Female Street-Sellers.
The Children Street-Sellers.

Including altogether upwards of FORTY THOUSAND INDIVIDUALS, whose gross yearly takings in the London Streets amount to more than 2,500,000*l.*

BY HENRY MAYHEW.

Office, 16, Upper Wellington-street, Strand.

Fig. 16: Advertising Supplement.

1. From No. 19 (19 April 1851)

[...]

The following sums have been received for the Crippled Street-seller of Nutmeg-graters, and have been handed to Mr. Howden,[1] who will see the money profitably applied:—Mr. P. (Temple), half a sovereign; and the subjoined sums in Postage Stamps: B.W., 3s.; E.H., 1*s.* a Purchaser from the First, 2s. 6d.; E.J.S., 5*s.*; a sympathiser, 5s.

Thirty shillings from Mr. P. (Temple), to be offered by way of loan to the Street-showman[2] whose letter appeared in No. 17.

THE CRIPPED STREET-SELLER OF NUTMEG-GRATERS has forwarded the subjoined:-

"Sir,

"I feel grateful for your Exertions in my behalf. I have received the sum of £2 1s. 0d. from the publisher, 69, fleet street. I am gazed at in the street with astonishment; and observations made within my hearing with respect to the Exact likeness of the portrait. I have purchaised with the money so kindly forwarded to me a few articles of furniture and a little stock, and I have taken a room in the Boro' Road, there not being sufficient room at my present Lodging.

"I am, Sir, with respect,

"Your Humble Servant,

"C—A—"

It is a rule with Mr. Mayhew not to reveal the addresses of his informants. If W.E.C. wishes to make any communications to the person mentioned in his letter, a note sent to the office, 16, Upper Wellington street shall be forwarded to him. W.E.C. will see that to choose to do other than this would be a breach of faith on Mr. Mayhew's part. This answer will apply to all other applications for addresses.

Mr. Mayhew begs to state, once more that he cannot become the dispenser of alms to any person. He therefore, wishes it to be distinctly understood that all monies forwarded to him for the relief of any poor street-seller are consid-

1 Mayhew's publisher, who had been appointed the honorary secretary of a "Loan-Office for the Poor" established in the *London Labour and the London Poor* office at 16 Wellington Street.

2 Refers to a letter that appeared in No. 17 of the "Answers to Correspondents" published 5 April 1851, from a street-showman of "peep-shows" whose statement had first been published on 13 June 1850 in *The Morning Chronicle* and would later be republished as "Peep-Shows" in Volume 3 of *London Labour and the London Poor*. His letter is an appeal for a loan of £1 10s. to keep him from the workhouse.

ered by him as loans, to be repaid by trimestrial instalments, and which when returned may be again advanced to others equally deserving. For the assurance of ladies and gentlemen forwarding money, a letter will be sent to them, informing them of the amounts having been applied as requested, as well as communicating to them the rate at which it is promised to be returned. The letter will also state that the donor can always withdraw as many of the instalments as might be in hand. Mr. Howden will be glad to show his arrangements on the subject to any one calling at North Wellington-street. It is necessary that in money matters of so peculiar a nature, the transactions should be beyond the shadow of a suspicion.

[...]

2. From No. 24 (24 May 1851)

[...]

The annexed is from the CRIPPLED NUTMEG-GRATER SELLER. It requires no comment:—

"24 Bond-street,
"June 2, 1851.

"Mr. Mayhew.

"Sir,—I cannot express my gratitude to you in this letter, for while writing I am so different in my feelings to what I was before I saw you, that I am inwardly quite another being. Had I been like others, I should have had no difficulty in expressing perhaps what to them would have been but ordinary gratitude, but to you and those who, through you, have so altered my condition, I can but give you my blessings and my thanks; and at the same time let you know what I have done with the money sent for my benefit. I have bought a good suit of new clothes, furniture for my home, a donkey and cart, and am getting in a stock of goods, to leave off going about the streets as I did before you saw me.

"I am having some bills printed, and shall go round London in the General Line. I have written to the Superintendent of the L division for leave to have a stand of goods in Lambeth-walk on each Saturday night, having obtained the permission of two shopkeepers (Mr. Hall and Mr. Page) to do so. Returning my most sincere thanks to you and those who have so kindly assisted me, and also to Mrs. Mayhew for her very great kindness to me,

"I am,
"Your very obedient humble
"& afflicted servant,
"CHARLES ALLOWAY."

3. From No. 33 (26 July 1851)

[...]

The Crippled Street-Seller of Nutmeg-Graters writes as follows:—

"24 Bond Street, Boro'-road.

"Sir,—Notwithstanding all my exertions to forward myself in the general line of dealing, I have been unfortunate. I purchased a donkey with the view of hawking hardware through the country, but had scarcely provided the necessaries when my donkey took ill, and broke out all over sores, and is now useless either for work or for sale: this circumstance, together with keeping a boy and doing no business within the last month, has entirely deprived me of money and considerably lessened my stock. A friend of mine having a little pony intended for sale, would be glad to give me the preference, and take my donkey in barter, could I but pay the difference; he thinks he can cure the donkey and make him answer his business. Unless I dispose of him in this manner, I have no chance of selling him, unless at an enormous sacrifice. To complete my trouble I gave an order for a little cart, for which I paid 30s. in advance; the man moved away and I have no clue to finding him or recovering my money. I have sufficient stock to go on with, but too heavy for a boy to wheel about with me as well. Sir, I have told you something respecting my father-in-law; he is since dead and willed all his property to his granddaughters. I expected he would repent in his last moments, and in pity leave me something, but such was not the case, and those who now hold the property are equally heartless. I would wish that these lines may meet their eyes; they may do from shame what they ought to do from generosity. Sir, what money I have received through the medium of your work I have laid out to what I believed the best advantage; but misfortune will sometimes happen to those more capable of conducting a business than me.

"Sir, my best respects to you and Mrs. Mayhew, and my hope to your welfare,

"C. ALLOWAY."

The Nutmeg-Grater Seller has already received upwards of £9, and it would be unjust to others to solicit any further aid on his behalf. The letter is printed in the hopes of shaming his relations into doing their duty to one whom Providence, for some inscrutable purpose, has almost deprived of the means of assisting himself.

4. Nos. 9 & 10 (8 and 15 February 1851)

The London coal-whippers have forwarded a Prospectus of a new journal which is about to be published by some members of their own body. These labouring men have long been celebrated for the many classical scholars included among their ranks; but curious as classical scholarship may be when found among such a class, still intelligence in a periodical will prove of much greater value. It is hoped therefore that the coal-whippers will not be so anxious to display their learning as their sense. If they will but avoid a perhaps pardonable demonstration of their scholastic acquirements, and determine to deal with the labour question judicially rather than emotionally, eschewing all that may savour of the platform—if they will but adhere to plain matters of fact, collecting and making known the statistics of labour, and so contributing their mite of truth to the general knowledge fund on this difficult question, they may be the means of doing incalculable good, not only to their own people, but to the great body of labouring men throughout the country. Let them rest assured that the labourer is to be benefitted solely by truth. No revolution in any country whatsoever can ever make two and two anything but four. If the working men are wronged, then let them demonstrate how the treatment they receive violates the laws of right, and depend upon it there are enough people wishing right to prevail, ultimately to put an end to the wrong. The process may seem a slow one, but there is no hastening it *by force*—conviction alone can work the change. Mr. MAYHEW himself believes that the working men of England are grossly wronged by capitalists. All production is according to the very first principles of political economy—a partnership between the man of money and the man of muscles, in which the monied man agrees to advance to the working man his share of the produce in the form of wages. Look at the labour question in whatever light we may, these are the very elements of it. It may offer some violence to the pride of the capitalist to be told that his labourers are partners in his business, but common sense and justice admit of no other view being taken of the transaction. That this fundamental contract is violated, and that the labourer does *not get his fair share of the produce at the present day, none can doubt*—the padlock, to quote a solitary instance, which is made for a halfpenny, is sold for a shilling. In place of the original compact a new law has been instituted, by which the *necessities* of the working man—instead of equity—are made to determine the value of his labour. This is what is called the law of supply and demand, which taking no heed of the result (that is to say, whether the value of the materials on which the workman has exercised his skill has been doubled or increased even a hundredfold by the operation), says, that the proportion of the wealth which is to come to the labourer is to be regulated by no other principle than what the capitalist can induce or force him (by starvation or chicanery) to accept. Now this to Mr. MAYHEW appears to be the very reverse of justice, and contrary to the fundamental principles of the very science of which it is said to be a part. Unfortunately, however, the law of supply and demand has got to be recognised by the rulers of the land, and to be considered almost as a part of the commercial creed of the country—the last "new commandment," as it were—against which it is political blasphemy to raise one's voice. Until the injustice of this principle is exposed and made generally known, there is no hope for the labouring man; for a necessary collorary (and certainly a most convenient one to all employers) of the law of supply and demand is the dogma of free labour, which asserts that in any way to restrict the liberty of the capitalist to buy his labour in the cheapest market and sell it (of course) in the dearest, is to interfere with the "rights of commerce." [...] Under these circumstances it behoves the great body of working men to protest loudly—but calmly and resolutely—against the iniquity of the law of supply and demand, and against the doctrine of free labour which seeks to make the remuneration of workmen depend on the greed of commercial men rather than the principles of justice. There are no men who can make this apparent better than the coal-whippers—no men who have had greater experience of the atrocities that can be perpetrated under the *free labour* principle, and none who if they will but tell all they know, and all they have seen, and tell it dispassionately—appealing, to the consciences rather than the passions of their fellow-creatures—can do more to bring about that state of right and truth which all good men desire. This is the sole object Mr. MAYHEW has in view—all he wishes is to make the public aware of the infamies that can be practised upon the labourer when the trader is allowed to use him as his own brutalizing love of gain may dictate; he hopes by showing these things to induce some change in our social state (though at present he hardly knows *what* change) by which the workman may ensure *his fair share of the produce.* There are many means proposed to obtain this end. Protection, Chartism, Co-operative Societies, Socialism, Communism, and many other social and political panacea; but with these Mr. MAYHEW has in his present vocation nothing to do, and he wishes it to be distinctly known and understood—without reservation or cavil—that he is in no way connected with any social or political party or sect whatever. MR. Mayhew is neither Chartist, Protectionist, Socialist, Communist, nor Co-operationist; but a mere collector of facts, endeavouring to discover the several phenomena of labour with a view of arriving ultimately at the laws and circumstance affecting, and controlling the operation and rewards the labourer, as well as of showing the importance of the poor and the working classes as members of the State.

5. From No. 16 (29 March 1851)

[...]

MR. MAYHEW, however, wishes it to be distinctly understood, that he in no way pledges himself to the principles here asserted from time to time. It should be remembered he is collecting facts, and merely avails himself of the *waste* pages of this periodical as a means of recording the opinions which are forced upon him in the course of his investigations (such opinions being at all times carefully excluded from the work itself). He reserves to himself therefore (as person unconnected with party), the right of changing or modifying his sentiments as often as a more enlarged series of facts, may present new views to his mind. It is in this light that he wishes his speculations to be received—for speculations they are, though, perhaps based upon a greater number of phenomena than any economist has as yet personally obtained. For the present he can only declare his determination to follow the facts, whithersoever they may lead (for he has no object but the truth), and if he be open to the charge of generalising, before he has made himself acquainted with all the particulars, he at least has a greater right to do so than any economist of the present day—seeing that he is perhaps the first who has sought to evolve the truths of the Labour Question by personal investigation. As yet political economy has been a purely armchair science—gentlemen who troubled their heads about the matter have done *no more than* trouble their heads; they have sat beside a snug sea-coal fire and tried to excogitate, or think out the several matters affecting the working classes—even as Adam Smith,[1] the great founder of the science retired for twelve years to an obscure village in Scotland to dream upon the laws concerning production and the producers. And yet it is upon the cobweb philosophy thus spun out that the whole of the legislation of the present day is made to depend!

MR. MAYHEW will at all times be glad to listen patiently to any *new* ideas, though he must object to disgorging of the old ones, in opposition to the sentiments he here propounds; he will also be pleased to receive any additional facts from working men, whose greater experience may cause them to detect omissions and errors in the enumeration of circumstances given here or hereafter. A desire for the public good precludes party bigotry.

[...]

6. From No. 21 (3 May 1851)

[...]

Mr. MAYHEW prints the following entire, because it shows how erroneous a view some persons may take as to the object of his labours.

"Sir,—I cannot deduce from your 'London Labour' what is the ultimate object intended by you—the good of the street seller or his injury.

"The exposé of the tricks of their trade in the several numbers already issued will surely injure far more than enhance the profits derived by the poor individuals seeking an existence by the sale of various articles in the streets of the metropolis.

"Since the appearance of the number of your work referring to the sale of oranges,[2] I have heard parties exclaim, when the orange-seller has offered his or her fruit for sale, 'Oh no! they've been biled'; and with various other articles doubtless the same thing occurs.

"The real cause of persons purchasing articles in the thoroughfares or environs of London is the hope of obtaining them much cheaper than by patronising the tradesmen, who certainly has his rent, together with many other expenses, to cover before making a profit; but if your publication benefits *him* (as I fear it may do), is it not to the injury of a very industrious hardworking class, who probably would be in the workhouse if not in the streets earning their 'half profits'?

1 Smith (1723–90) was a pioneering thinker in political economy.

2 The writer here refers to the article "The Tricks of Costermongers," which appeared in one of the early numbers of the serial. The article includes a statement from a costermonger, who chuckles as he describes selling boiled oranges, which makes the oranges appear to be of better quality, but actually spoils them.

"The deep distress and misery which many have to undergo, and which has been faithfully described by you may have done some good, as they have been relieved by contributions from the charitable and well-disposed; but this I fear would be found to be the exception, not the rule.

"Excuse me, therefore, when I say, that in my humble opinion your work tends to the injury rather than the welfare of the Street-Poor.

"Your obedient Servant,

"G.N."

Mr Mayhew's aim in the investigations that he is now making into the condition and earnings of the several classes of society is simply to *come at the truth* respecting them. It is impossible to benefit any class or any individual by falsity. If there are customs and practices among the street-sellers that are unjust, the mere fact of making them known will put the public on their guard against them, and so bring them to an end. It is the dishonest portion of the street-folk who injure the more honest members of that body. "How is it possible for us," said a costermonger, "to be just and fair in all our dealings, when, by using slangs, any of our people can sell twice as cheap as those who carry fair weights and measures, and get all their custom away from them." There are many of the street-sellers who mean well enough, but who are compelled to *compete* with the tricks of the unprincipled. Then again, the lurkers and sham street-sellers lead the public to look upon the street trade generally as a cloak for beggary, and an encouragement to idleness. The exposure of the lurkers' tricks will be sure to render them abortive, and *then*, and then only, they will be abandoned.

Moreover, Mr. Mayhew has no desire to depict the street-sellers other than as they really are. Were he to canonize the whole race of costermongers, and to paint the patterers as angels, what good could possibly come of such sickly sentimentalism? It is high time that the truth concerning all classes should be known, so that what is right among us may be cherished, and what is wrong put to an end to as soon as possible. This was and is the sole object of the beginning and continuing the inquiries concerning "Labour and the Poor."

[...]

7. From No. 23 (17 May 1851)

[...]

The POOR POET thus rhythmically acknowledges the receipt of the money sent for him:—

To H. MAYHEW, ESQ.

To the Labouring Classes
I know you are Kind,
And a Friend and Defender
In you They did find,—

For you've sought the Cot
Of the Wretched and Poor,
Where Merit sits shrouded
In silence obscure,
Oh would But the wealthy
Tread Those steps of thine,
What vice Might Be crushed—
And what Virtue Might Shine.
The sixteen Shillings you sent
Our Wants did decrease,
To pray for your Welfare
I shall never cease,
Your kind Benefaction
I did not abuse,
From your Bedridden Servant,
The Brazier,
JOHN HUGHES.
My Thanks are Sincere,
They are honest and true,
May Heaven Shower Blessings;
On Squire
MAYHEW.

Appendix E: Mayhew's Contemporaries and "Slum Journalism"

[Mayhew's work was a response to an increased interest in the living and labour conditions of the poor sparked by governmental reports, the fear of cholera, the influx of people to cities, and middle-class anxieties about social and political unrest. It, in turn, inspired many subsequent "eyewitness" accounts of the urban poor and their environs. The Reverend Thomas Beames's (d. 1864) *The Rookeries of London* (1850; second edition 1852) combines a history of the rookery (a term used in the period for highly-populated slum areas) dating back to the medieval period, documentary material on existing rookeries, and a call for legislative reform. George Godwin (1813–88), architectural journalist and long-time editor of *The Builder*, wrote extensively on the built environments of the poor and hoped, like Mayhew, to use print to catalyze social reform. *London Shadows* (1854) is the first of a series of three books Godwin wrote drawn from articles published in *The Builder*. Journalist and theatre manager John Hollingshead's (1827–1904) *Ragged London in 1861* (1861) is a compilation of articles originally written for the *Morning Post*. The distressing conditions he relates demonstrate how little traction had been made on social amelioration in the decade following Mayhew's *London Labour*.]

1. From Thomas Beames, *The Rookeries of London*, vol. 2 (London: Thomas Bosworth, 1852), 1–2, 20–22, 26–27, 75–76

Chapter 1

There is much in a name, one significant phrase which spares circumlocution, and the reader, without wading through two or three pages, sees what you mean. We had not otherwise been bold enough to call our book

"*The Rookeries of London.*"

There is a period in all languages, when words pass from the mint in which they are coined, their questionable origin is forgotten, and they are used among the current money of the realm of thought. We believe that such is the case with the word *Rookery*. The uninitiated may ask its meaning, and the philologist wish to know the stages by which it arrived at its present acceptation. It would be wrong to call the dwellings of the working classes generally *Rookeries*: in country villages they hardly lie close enough for that; they are not high enough—sufficiently crowded; there is not the same economy of space which *The legitimate Rookery* demands.

Doubtless there is some analogy between these pauper colonies and the nests of the birds from whom they take their name; the houses for the most part high and narrow, the largest possible number crowded together in a given space,—common necessity their bond of union: though the occupation of the different tenants varies, yet they belong to the same section of the social body, having all descended to the lowest scale which is compatible with human life. Other birds are broken up into separate families—occupy separate nests; rooks seem to know no such distinction. So it is with the class whose dwellings we are to describe. We must speak of the dwellings of the poor in crowded cities, where large masses of men are brought together; where, by the unwritten laws of competition, rents rise and room is economised in proportion; where, because there is no restraint to check the progress of avarice, no statute to make men do their duty, they turn to profit the necessities of their fellow-creatures, and riot on the unhallowed gains which injustice has amassed at the expense of the poor.

We must speak of human masses pent up, crowded, crammed into courts and allies; here, as by a fatal attraction, opposite houses grow together at the top, seem to nod one against one another, conspiring to shut out the little air which would pierce through for the relief of those beneath. We must speak of men and women sleeping in the same apartment, whom, in some cases, not even the tie of relationship unites; of a married couple with their offspring, who have already come to the age of maturity, with a common dormitory; and we ask, if a malignant spirit wished to demoralise the working classes of the country, could he find a plan more congenial to his wishes? We must speak of stories piled on stories in the older part of our towns; not each floor, but each room tenanted by a family; in some cases the dormitory of several occupants, thrown together without distinction of sex or age in the chance scramble for the night's lodging, each swelling the gains of some middleman, whose heart is seared by the recollection of his own poverty, and who learns to grind as he was once ground by others. We trust to the hands of the most ignorant and most injured, an instrument which even the best and the wisest can scarce wield as they should. We put an engine, fitted with momentous powers, into the hands of one trained to abuse it by a long course of oppression—of oppression which, under the name of custom and the sanction of law, eats into men's hearts; their natures are insensibly changed by it; against which they first rebel, then bear with, then submit to, then acquiesce in, then adopt, then exercise, then defend, to the injury of their brethren. But of this we will speak anon: the middleman and the broker are persons whom we must sketch at length, when we have proceeded further. Are not these colonies Rookeries, if the description given by the naturalist be correct? "A Rookery, a village in the air peopled with numerous inhabitants: it is the nature of birds to associate together, and they build in numbers in the same or adjoining trees." Rookeries they are, if rooks build high and lie thick together, young and old in one nest. Colonies are wedged up, not so much because of connection between families as by common wants and a common nature, and with the fierce discord and occasional combats of the inhabitants. The tenants of these Rookeries, like the birds from whom they take their names, have much in common—want, with its offspring, recklessness; they the pariahs, so to speak, of the body social, a distinct caste, yet not bound together otherwise than by common wants—with their jealousies, discords, and antipathies; as if it were not too true of them, as of others, that a man's foes may be they of his own household.

[...]

Chapter 3[1]

[...]

We have lately had an opportunity of visiting the worst district of St. Giles's[2]—George street and Church lane; through this part of the parish runs the New Oxford street, and they are thus the remains of the famous Rookery—the still standing plague-spots of that colony. You cannot gain an idea of what *The Rookery* was without visiting these streets. Rows of crumbling houses, flanked by courts and alleys, *culs de sac*, &c. in the very densest part of which the wretchedness of London takes shelter. You seem for a time to leave the day, and life, and habits of your fellow-creatures behind you—just to step out of the din and bustle of a crowded thoroughfare—to turn aside from streets whose shops teem with every luxury—where Art has brought together its most beautiful varieties,—and you have scarce gone a hundred yards when you are in *The Rookery*. The change is marvellous: squalid children, haggard men, with long uncombed hair, in rags, most of them smoking, many speaking Irish; women without shoes or stockings—a babe perhaps at the breast, with a single garment, confined to the waist by a bit of string; wolfish looking dogs; decayed vegetables strewing the pavement; low public houses; linen hanging across the street to dry; the population stagnant in the midst of activity; lounging about in remnants of shooting jackets, leaning on the window frames, blocking up the courts and alleys; with young boys gathered round them, looking exhausted as though they had not been to bed. Never was there so little connection between masses of living beings and their means of livelihood. And then these dens, the fronts of a small court—square you can scarce call it—more wretched, more utterly destitute of all that is needed for the purposes of life, than the lanes of which they are the background. These alleys were thickly populated, as though a close atmosphere had more attractions, and drew by a sympathetic cord more lodgers than the open thoroughfares; you could scarcely have an idea of the number of persons crowded together in a single room. At first, when the average proportion of sleepers is stated to you, you feel inclined to calculate the number of square feet contained in the area of the room, to see whether it is possible that so many human beings can lie down there. You begin to fancy that the process so familiar to the prisons of the middle ages must take place here; that persons do not sleep in a recumbent posture, but by leaning against the walls; or perhaps, at night, some purgatory like a steamer's cabin is erected, and men sleep in tiers, as in one of those marine Pandemoniums. Thus in one room, measuring six feet by five broad, we were assured that eight people, some of them, of course, children, slept. You will tell us this must be exaggeration; however, the tendency amongst the inhabitants, was to conceal, or qualify; for the landlords had made wholesale clearances in many houses, where they had

1 See "Of the Low Lodging-houses of London," p. 110.

2 See p. 331, note 1.

reason to believe that information on the subject of lodgings had been given by the tenants. The landlords were alarmed at the inquiries made of late, and determined to elude them. In one house 100 persons have been known to sleep on a given night. In a particular instance we ascertained that three rooms were thus occupied—first room, by eight persons, second by fifteen, third by twenty-four. We ourselves saw as many as twenty-four persons in the same room; they were assembled there even in the day-time, and yet you are assured that night alone affords a fair criterion. In these rooms are piled the wares by which *some* of the inhabitants gain their precarious living,—oranges, herrings, water-cresses, onions, seemed to be the most marketable articles; and there were sweepers, cadgers or beggars, stray luggage porters, &c. lounging about. In another house, the average number of persons who slept in a room was twelve; in others, of course larger, forty persons are known to have slept in a single night.

[...]

We do not aim in this sketch at describing minutely the condition of those who inhabit Rookeries, and have therefore contented ourselves with few details. We must otherwise, in the cause of truth, enter upon inquiries, whose results are too disgusting for our pages. Such descriptions very properly fill the reports of Sanatory Commissioners,[1] for, if they were left out, many an evil would be unchecked. *The Times*, *The Morning Chronicle*, and, above all, Mr. Mayhew, have told the naked tale. Thus, in the following pages, though much to the uninitiated may seem exaggeration, not one tithe of the nuisances which disgrace Rookeries, has been enumerated. [...]

[...]

Chapter 5

[...]

We do not say there is nothing to startle a stranger in the buildings of this place[2]—there is much; but, unhappily, twelve years of experience in crowded districts of London have shown us many such sights,—Chelsea, Whitechapel, St. Andrew's Holborn, have many such Rookeries. The floors of the houses being below the level of the foot-path must be flooded in wet weather; the rooms are mouldy and ill savoured; dark, small, and confined, they could not be peopled as the alleys of St. Giles's, because their size would not admit of it. There is the usual amount of decaying vegetable matter, the uneven footpath, the rotten doors, the broken windows patched with rags, ash heaps in front of the houses, dogs, &c. housed there, ragged children, and other features well

1 The detailed reports of living conditions in poor areas described in Edwin Chadwick's *Sanitary Report* (1842) and other works that followed in its wake.

2 Chapter 5 of Beames's book documents Jacob's Island (see p. 322, note 2).

known to those conversant with such neighbourhoods. But here the parallel ends:—there are peculiar nuisances in this spot which go far to justify the language used by the writer of the articles in *The Morning Chronicle*, and which he describes technically as perhaps a surgeon alone could do. These abominations we proceed to notice; not, of course, that we can go into many details;—the gentleman we have alluded to has done it much better than we could pretend to do,—done it too with a knowledge of the consequences involved in such neglect, and done it at a season when such supervision as he exercised involved the greatest results. He saw it while cholera was decimating its victims, making wholesale ravages; we now see it when frost and cold have purified the air; when what was a reeking flood of pestilence is now frozen over; so that you might walk on it. Some slight attempts have been made to supply the wants of the people,—public attention has been called to the nuisances which here, to the disgrace of our laws, still pollute this wretched district. The writer we have alluded to, says,—"The striking peculiarity of Jacob's Island consists in the wooden galleries and sleeping rooms at the back of the houses, which overhang the dark flood, and are built upon piles, so that the place has positively the air of a Flemish street flanking a sewer instead of a canal; while the little ricketty bridges that span the ditches and connect court with court, give it the appearance of the Venice of drains."[1] This is the source of all the disgust with which the visitor to these dens of wretchedness is inspired. This district, we have said before, is insulated by a quadrangular *ditch*; the very figure of the island tells you that such reservoirs must be stagnant; and stagnant they are until moved for a while by the tide, which does not at each rising pour fresh water into them, but which at intervals alone, twice or thrice a week, is sparingly introduced, and checked again when enough is supposed to have been done for the purposes of those who are concerned in traffic. Meanwhile this circumambient pond is *the common sewer of the neighbourhood, and the only source from which the wretched inhabitants can get the water which they drink—with which they wash—and with which they cook their victuals*: and because habit reconciles men to any anomaly, in the summer, boys are seeing bathing there, though the Thames is not far distant, and offers at least a cleaner bathing-place. Imagination will picture to itself much which we cannot describe, when we point to such a disgraceful condition of being as that entailed upon the denizens of Jacob's Island. We may well blush for the parish which can tolerate such a plague spot,—for our country, whose insulted laws do not at once sweep from the face of the earth such a record of its disgrace. Is it indeed come to pass, that men, women, and children habitually *drink* water whose ingredients decency forbids us to describe?—that with no affected squeamishness we shrink from picturing that on which our eyes have rested, which courts no secrecy, and which is naked and open to all who would inspect it? not carefully fenced off, lest the indignant spirit of Englishmen should doom it to destruction; not carefully guarded, lest perchance some wandering Christian should denounce it as the future city of God's wrath—the Babylon of his country? Is it indeed come to pass, that

1 A citation from Mayhew's *Morning Chronicle* article "A Visit to the Cholera Districts of Bermondsey," included in Appendix C1a.

heavy taxes are wrung from hard-pressed industry, and the poor man divides his loaf with the tax gatherer, and yet no shield is thrown between him and horrors like these? that fierce cabals agitate rival vestrymen, and some patriotic agitator, plethoric and bloated with good wishes for his country, wields his thunder, and yet no one is heard to decry these scenes, till at length a stranger comes and speaks, and men awake as from a dream, and go and see this new exhibition, and a few guineas drop in for the fund raised to relieve the poor sufferers, and then perhaps the wound will be scarred over, till when?—till it festers in some outbreak which shakes the nation.

[...]

Chapter 7[1]

[...]

[...] The houses are not so crowded as those in Church Lane or Saffron Hill, and there is not the same amount of squalid misery. It is said that instances are upon record of three families living together in the same room: in one room we saw three or four beds, but were told that they were all tenanted by members of the same family. The rooms are miserably small; mere closets, very dilapidated, quite unfit for human habitation, scarcely safe, below the level of the ground, with hardly any ventilation; until lately miserably, if at all, drained, their back parts very close in consequence of the cow-house we have described; so that the atmosphere is rendered still more fetid by the rank odour continually emitted from the animals confined. Some of the houses were occupied by chimney-sweepers, several by day labourers—some by men who get their living by selling baked potatoes. There are three costermongers living in one of these streets, from whom the potatoes are procured. Under the houses are large cellars, which are filled with these vegetables, and from which the tin cans of the vendors are replenished. There are also several rag shops in this part of the parish, the cellars being filled to overflowing with rags—which, at certain seasons, are carted away and sent to the paper makers. You are struck with the curious appearance of some of the lower windows in these houses,—old bonnets, veils, articles of dress, faded indeed, shorn of much of their original splendour, are exposed as if to tempt those who pass by; these are unlicensed pawn shops, where women deposit their wearing apparel, and with the money thus obtained gratify their passion for drinking at the next public house. Sometimes they redeem the goods, yet too often never return to claim them; after a time the goods are sold, though, whether a year elapses, as in the case of pawnbrokers, before the sale takes place, we could not learn. In the streets opening upon the quadrangle to which we have limited our inquiries, are two or three houses where thieves are

1 Ch. 7 documents the Berwick Street District of St. James, Westminster. In this particular passage, Beames is describing the houses along the square formed by Cock Court, New Street, Husband Street, and Hopkins Street, in the centre of which is a stable holding 30 cows.

harboured. Inquests are common in this locality—many persons die by violence. Not long since, three women of the town were residing here, two of them sisters; the youngest died of concussion of the brain arising from a blow she had received from one of her companions in a scuffle. There are several low lodging-houses in Husband Street, where the charge is 3*d.* a night, or 1*s.* 6*d.* a week, Sunday Evening being considered, according to the law adage, a *dies non*,[1] and therefore the lodgers pay only for six nights. The rooms are too small to admit of many sleeping together at the same time, accordingly, eight persons in a room seems as far as we could learn to be the maximum.

[...]

2. From George Godwin, *London Shadows: A Glance at the 'Homes' of the Thousands* (London: George Routledge & Co., 1854), vii–viii, 1–2, 7–8, 55

Prologue

The war of nations is a frightful evil (great the sin of those who render it necessary), but we must not shut our eyes to the direful operations of relentless foes at home, more costly and more deadly, though carried on with fewer trumpets. The miserable condition in which thousands of human beings are condemned to pass their lives in London and other large towns is a giant evil, a giant which should be slain if we would not have it slay us. And a war against this, fortunately, is a war which can be prosecuted without fear of loss, and with the certainty of success. There is no question about this,—no doubt. To whatever extent the endeavour is made, to that extent will advantages follow; as certainly as that two and two make four, and that we are all bound by the solemnest of injunctions to bear our part in the fight,—a fight against dirt, disease, disorder, degradation, and death;—a fight in a Holy War.

Only those who have examined into the evil for themselves can judge of its enormous extent and its frightful results. We are all interested in the removal of it, immediately and personally; and yet, blinded by ignorance or trusting to chance, we shut our eyes to the fact, and go on building gaols and forming penal settlements, to punish what might have been prevented; taxing our means to pay the cost of illness and death wickedly produced, and dying ourselves, it may be said without irreverence, long before there is any real necessity for doing so.

Part of the following statements with reference to the condition of London appeared originally in "THE BUILDER,"[2] and obtained the commendation of

---

1 Shortened from the Latin phrase *dies non juridicus*, translated as "day which is not juridical." Used for a day on which no legal business is carried out, or extended to mean a day that is not counted, or on which there is no activity.

2 A magazine founded in 1843 by Joseph Aloysius Hansom in order to provide guidance to those in the construction industry. Under George Godwin's editorship (1844–83), the *Builder* widened its scope to include views on architecture, sanitation, art, and history.

some whose good opinion is a reward. It has been urged that the further publication of them in a cheap form might be useful, and, believing it to be of the greatest importance that the extent of the disease should be widely known, in order to induce corresponding efforts for its cure, the suggestion has been adopted. In some few instances ameliorations may have been attempted since these remarks were written; but nothing has been done to any extent. I have visited places during the last fortnight not fit for dogs, and yet which hold in every room two or three families,—holes, ill-drained, ill-ventilated, and altogether unsuited for use. In the occupants of such places—men and women with bodies to suffer and souls to be lost—the feelings are blunted, the moral perceptions distorted; decency is out of the question, and degradation nearly certain. Goodness and virtue are sometimes to be found there, wonderful to say, but the majority have no hope; progress is impossible, the future a blank: in the dirt they are, and in the dirt they must remain. A remedy may be afforded at all events we may deal successfully with the next generation, and surely, surely this should be attempted. What is hereafter set forth has not been written to make a case, but to state plain facts. The examination has been painful and disheartening: still, to succeed to any extent in obtaining for the suffering thousands dwelling-places worthy the name of HOME, where the virtues and kindly feelings *might* be cultivated, and the household gods worthily set up, would be a reward so rich that the labour of the endeavour is not to be considered. Most earnestly then, and with deep feeling, I venture to implore the co-operation to this end of all who would advance society, lessen suffering, promote the happiness of their fellow creatures, and save the frightful amount of money, power, and life, now annually wasted in this kingdom. We may all do something, and moreover we are bound to do it.

> "This world is full of beauty as other worlds above,
> And if we did our duty, it might be full of love."[1]

Chapter 1

> "When every man is his own end, all things will come to a bad end."
> COLERIDGE.[2]

Deep are the "Mysteries of London,"[3] and so environed by difficulties, that few can penetrate them. The condition of large sections of its inhabitants is wholly unknown to the majority of those above them in the social pyramid, the wide base of which is made up of poverty, ignorance, degradation, crime, and misery. Much has been written on it within the last few years, and a large amount of good has

---

1 From "This World Is Full of Beauty," a poem by Chartist and amateur Egyptologist Gerald Massey (1828–1907), first published in *Cooper's Journal* on 6 April 1850.

2 The epigraph is from an aphorism in Samuel Taylor Coleridge's *Aids to Reflection, in the Formation of a Manly Character*, v. 1 (1825).

3 An allusion to the popular *The Mysteries of London* by George W.M. Reynolds (see p. 11, note 2).

been done. Still the great bulk of the people are ignorant and apathetic on the subject, blind to the extent to which they are themselves concerned in it: and, viewing the evil as a mighty one, and strongly impressed by the helpless—almost hopeless—condition of many thousands of fellow-creatures, who cannot make themselves heard unless the press speak for them, we propose entering into some particulars respecting the lodging-houses and other dwellings in London inhabited by the poorer classes, with the view of inducing efforts for their amelioration. It is quite possible to house the poorer classes comfortably and healthfully at as little cost to themselves as they now pay, and at infinitely less cost to the community at large; and what we desire is, to aid in bringing this about. As the writer has said elsewhere again and again, and the sentence has been echoed and reechoed far and wide,—homes are the manufactories of men,—*as* the home, *so* what it sends forth.

To investigate the condition of the houses of the very poor in this great metropolis is a task of no small danger and difficulty: it is necessary to brave the risks of fever and other injuries to health, and the contact of men and women often as lawless as the Arab or the Kaffir: in addition to these obstacles, there is amongst the very poor a strong feeling against intrusion: few persons venture into these haunts besides the regular inhabitants, the London missionaries, the parish surgeon, and the police, and thus the extent of this great evil is imperfectly understood. A few years ago it was a fashion to visit the "Rookery" of St. Giles's, and wonder at the peculiarities of that strange land (and it was, perhaps, partly owing to these visits that some improvements were carried into effect); yet few of those visitors, and not many others, are aware of the numerous places in London and the Borough which exist at the present day in as bad a condition as any part of St. Giles's in its worst time. These blots on London abound in Whitechapel, Westminster, Spitalfields, Camden-town, Somers-town, Clerkenwell, Islington, Bermondsey, various parts of the Borough, &c. &c. In many instances these hotbeds of fever and vice are so effectually hidden by goodly houses that the inhabitants of the latter are scarcely aware of the poverty and disease which exist within a stone's throw from their own doors. These densely-peopled clumps of houses, or "Rookeries" as they are called, are mostly inhabited by the poorest Irish lodging-house keepers, tramps, costermongers, thieves, and the lowest class of street-walkers. In addition to these there are small shopkeepers, receivers of stolen goods, brokers, and publicans.

Of the condition of the greater part of these people it is difficult to convey anything like a just idea. It is a certain and melancholy fact that this dangerous, and to the State, expensive class of persons is alarmingly increasing in London and other large towns; and this is easily to be accounted for. Many of the poor Irish who flock to these places are either unable to get employment, or are careless in looking for it. The women and children either beg, sweep crossings, or exist (for it is nothing better) on the profits of the sale of such trifling articles as they can procure. The parents are mostly ignorant, so are the children: few are sent to school: few are taught any trade; and the great majority, from an early age, gain a precarious living in the streets: many become thieves (little wonder), and in their turn teach others. Most of this class either marry young or form connections by which the numbers rapidly increase. There are other causes, which it is not our purpose in the present paper to inquire into.

It is, however, certain that one important and leading cause of this degradation is the condition of the dwellings in which thousands of these outcasts are born, and in which they live and die. Improving these would do much towards improving them. Let us then penetrate some of the London shadows, and show their distressing depth,—their degrading results. When the nature and extent of an evil are thoroughly known, efficient remedies become more probable. The Act for Improving the Condition of the Common Lodging Houses[1] seems to be working well; but in justice to the poor, it must be followed by other measures. [...]

3. From John Hollingshead, *Ragged London in 1861* (London: Smith, Elder and Co., 1861), 7–12, 55–62

[...]

A vast deal of life that skulks or struggles in London is only familiar to the hard-working clergy, certain medical practitioners, and a few parochial officers. It burrows in holes and corners, at the back of busy thoroughfares where few know of its existence, or care to follow it. The largest and most painstaking directories pass it by; writers upon London reject it as too mean, too repulsive, or too obscure; and novelists, when they condescend to touch it, for the sake of obtaining contrasts, often paint it in the colours of imagination, rather than in the hard outlines of fact. Its records, if truthfully given, have little romance, little beauty, and little variety. Poverty, ignorance, dirt, immorality, crime, are the five great divisions of its history. Immovability, love of place, a determination to huddle together, are some of its chief characteristics; and the growth of many courts and alleys, disgraceful to humanity, is the sure result. Whatever is demanded in London, whether in defiance of law or public decency, is promptly supplied; and ill-constructed, ill-ventilated lurking nests of dwellings exist in every quarter of the metropolis, in obedience to this rule of trade.

Those who wish to search London for gross examples of overcrowded dwellings may find them in the centre, or in any one of the four outskirts. Soho, St. James's, Westminster, and St. Martin's-in-the-Fields, can lay no claim to purity in this respect; and that part of Westminster known as Tothill Fields is notoriously one of the greatest offenders. In the west there is Knightsbridge, rendered filthy and immoral by the presence of its large military barracks, with Chelsea, and Brentford; in the south there are Lambeth, Walworth, embracing Lock's Fields, and the Borough, with its notorious Kent Street; in the north there is Agar Town,[2] built on a swamp, and running down to the canal in every

---

1 Legislation passed in 1851 and strengthened in 1853. It attempted to deal with overcrowding and sanitary concerns in lodging houses, which provided cheap short-term housing. The act empowered local authorities to regulate the number of permitted occupants, mandate reporting of disease, and ensure cleanliness and proper sanitation methods, such as adequate drainage.

2 A poor neighbourhood with low-grade housing near St. Pancras Station in Central London. The neighbourhood was demolished in the 1860s to make way for rail development.

stage of dirt and decay, with Somers' Town, Kentish Town, and Camden Town, each contributing its share to the general mass of misery; and in the east there are St. George's, Whitechapel, Bethnal Green, and overgrown Shoreditch. A melancholy list like this could be filled up for pages by any one familiar with the back streets of London. I have not touched upon the corners of Clerkenwell, of "merry Islington,"[1] and a dozen other districts; and I have purposely omitted St. Giles's and Saffron Hill, because they no longer represent the worst parts of London. I have merely taken a broad glance round the metropolis, to show that overcrowding amongst the poor, with all its attendant evils, is not peculiar to any particular parish or district.

The features of this huddling together vary slightly in different neighbourhoods, being governed, in some degree, by the character of the houses. In neighbourhoods that have "seen better days"—where family mansions that were once inhabited by city merchants, or the leading clerks and managers in banks or offices, have sunk gradually through all the different grades of lodging-houses, "classical and commercial" schools, down to workshops for cabinet-makers, turners, or ginger-beer brewers—the overcrowding takes the form of living in what are called "tenements." The old mansion, faded and dilapidated, with its garden cut off, it may be, for a skittle-ground[2] or a factory, is let out to a dozen or fifteen families, according to the number of its rooms. Its broad staircase, broken, shattered, and muddy, is always open to the street; and its long, narrow windows are patched with paper. Its broad closets and store-chambers are now filled with ragged children, who share their rough beds with coals, coke, wood, and a few cooking utensils. Its dark wainscotings, scratched and chipped, are hung with damp yellow clothes, that are always "in the wash"; its passages are often strewn with oyster-shells and broken tobacco-pipes; and its fore-court is filled with ashes, one or two rusty, broken saucepans, like old hats, and sometimes with a dead cat,—the playthings of the crowd of dirty children, who roll about on its hard, black earth. The iron railings that once closed it in from the thoroughfare have been long torn away, stolen, destroyed, sold; and all that remains of the low wall in which they were fixed may be a few rotten, jagged bricks standing on one side. I can find scores of such houses—containing forty, fifty, or even sixty human beings, surrounded by neighbourhoods crowded with gas factories, cooperages, and different workshops, or pierced by the dark arches of metropolitan railways—that stand within two miles of the Bank of England, and that once were looked upon as pleasant country retreats!

Dropping, however, this description of Ragged London, drawn from memory, let us go out into the ragged streets, and ragged houses, and see what the ragged people are doing in January, 1861. We will begin with Ragged London in the centre.

---

1 A village outside London, once known for its market gardens, coaching inns, pubs, theatres, and public amusements, hence the designation "merry." By the mid-nineteenth century it had been absorbed into greater London and had fallen on hard times.

2 Ground for lawn-bowling.

[...]

St. George's in the East

[...]

It is unnecessary for any writer to go over all the low streets of a particular district to give the public a faint picture of their chief characteristics, and he will do his duty if he carefully selects that representative thoroughfare which seems to him to present most of the features he wishes to depict. Such a representative hole and corner I believe I have found in Star Street, in the Christ Church division of St. George's in the East, a locality of forty-three acres, with a population of 13,300, untiringly watched over by the Rev. G.H. M'Gill.[1]

Star Street is a narrow avenue, leading out of the Commercial Road towards the river, the entrance to which is half blocked up with fruit-stalls, crossing-sweepers, and loiterers. Unlike most of its neighbours, it hangs out every sign of overcrowding for the most careless or hurried passer-by to look at, and it contains, perhaps, within an equal area, more hard-working, would-be-honest strugglers for dear life than any similar street in the same district. Its road is black and muddy, half filled with small pools of inky water, in which stand a number of trucks and barrows belonging to the poorest class of costermongers. The end is nearly blocked up with a public-house, which seems to thrive in the very citadel of want. At some of the low dirty doors wet baskets are standing half full of a common fish called "dabs"; in some of the wretched parlour windows, under sickly yellow curtains, a few rotten oranges are displayed on an old shutter for sale; another miserable front parlour seems to have been scooped out so as to form something like a shop, in which a few coals are thrown down in one corner as a sign of trade; another parlour has been turned into a cat's-meat store,[2] and there is one of those small chandler's-shops[3] where nearly everything is sold, and "weekly payments" are taken, which invariably flourish in such neighbourhoods.

I went down this thoroughfare with the chief clergyman of the district, and we were immediately surrounded by poor, thin women, in scanty dresses, representing every variety of dirt and poverty. They have nothing to pawn, nothing to take to the marine-store dealers. Their husbands can get no work for the present at the docks,[4] and they can get little or no needlework from the cheap clothiers in the neighbourhood. Their standard of living is so low that a few days of compulsory idleness brings them to the brink of starvation. One has a story to tell of fever and sickness, another of bread refused by the poor-law authorities on some technicality, another begs to be visited without delay, and

1 St. George's in the East was a poor, densely populated parish in east London that came under the auspices of the New Poor Law of 1834 (see Introduction, p. 20). Reverend George Henry M'Gill was known for establishing schools for poor children in his district and for his broad-minded attitude toward non-Anglican denominations.

2 A shop selling meat for cats, primarily from slaughtered horses.

3 See p. 167, note 1.

4 [Hollingshead's note:] January, 1861.

a dozen others present letters of recommendation for relief from the funds at the disposal of the clergyman. The same question seems always to bring the same melancholy answer:—

"How many children have you?"

"Eight, sir."

"What's your husband?"

"A dock labourer."

"How long has he been out of work?"

"Not done a stroke for thirteen weeks."

"Come to me, at the parsonage, at three."

We go into some of the houses to inspect the misery. The ground floor of one is occupied by a sweep. A short broom sticks out over the door. The front parlour contains two women, half covered with soot. A bed, as black as the women, stands in one corner, in which an infant is sleeping, with its little face looking pale, even under the dirt, and its head lying lower than its legs. Two other young children are playing on the black floor in front of the little glow-worm of a fire, eating what is literally bread and soot. Six other children, belonging to the same parents, are playing somewhere about in the inky puddles; and even this family only represents half the population of the small house. The rooms may be ten feet square—certainly not more[1]—and the rent averages about two shillings a room. The back parlour is also rented by the sweep, and it contains nothing but a mountain of soot—the store resulting from several weeks' work—an empty birdcage, and a fluttering green rag of a window-blind. Upstairs, in one room, is a street hawker, with a wife and five children, and in another room is a carpenter, also with a wife and five children. The latter has the same old painful story to tell of no work and no pay. He is a strong, healthy man, nearly fifty years of age, respectable in appearance, and civil in address. He is trying to still his evident hunger with a little weak tea, probably made from boiled tea-leaves, which his wife has begged from some family for whom she works. A few small lumps of precious bread are floating in the tea, and a hungry child is looking over the edge of the table at the remains of a small coarse loaf. Not a crumb is wasted of the scanty store; for the blank days of unproductive idleness may not be near their end, and the hateful workhouse must be kept at arm's length. The other children, if not in the ragged or national schools,[2] are rolling anywhere about the streets, like all other children of the very poor, in every back alley of the town. When they are gathered together at night—if they ever are so gathered—the roof of this stunted dwelling will cover twenty-five inmates. Other houses in the same poor street—not larger, not cleaner—shelter twenty-two and twenty-one inmates respectively; and thirteen lodgers for one house seems to be a very common number. Two of the rooms have eleven inmates, while one particular room has

---

1 [Hollingshead's note:] Average height—eight feet five inches; length, nine feet six inches; width, nine feet six inches.

2 Schools run by the Anglican Church for poor and working-class children. The schools stressed discipline and offered rudimentary training in literacy, numeracy, and the scriptures. For ragged schools, see p. 185, note 1.

nine, and another room has nine also. The general result seems to be—according to a local census taken by the Rev. Mr. M'Gill, on December 19, 1860—that in two hundred and thirty-five small rooms there is, self-crammed, a growing, breeding population of three hundred and forty-four adults and three hundred and fifty-seven children, making a total of seven hundred and one. A few of these unfortunates have been struck off the list since this melancholy account was taken; some by exhaustion, or long-settled disease, brought to an end by want. One labourer gave in, under a low fever, a few hours before we visited the street, and his dead body was stretched upon the only bed in the dark room, covered with a borrowed white sheet. Round the fire was a crowd of weeping women, and amongst them the widow, with two of the dead man's moaning children stricken with the same fever. Wretched as these people were, they would struggle to bury the dead body without assistance from the parish, for there is nothing the poor have such a horror of as a pauper's funeral.[1] No sooner have we left this abode of misery than we are almost dragged over to another, where a mere girl is suddenly left a widow with two helpless infants. Her husband was a dock labourer, twice as old as herself, and he died of asthma. He hung about the docks in the keen weather, day after day, waiting for ships that never came, and the afternoon before he came home wet, miserable, and hungry, took to his scanty bed, and never left it again. Death is bitter enough at all times, and in all places, but it is a hundred-fold more bitter where those who are left are haunted by the dreadful feeling that a few pence would have kept the body and soul together if they could only have been found.

[...]

1 Poor people whose families could not afford the expense of a private funeral were buried by the parish, often in common graves with no markers. Funeral customs for rich and poor alike were keenly observed in the Victorian period; poor and middle-income families would go to great lengths to ensure a respectable burial for their loved ones.

Works Cited and Select Bibliography

Agathocleous, Tanya. *Urban Realism and the Cosmopolitan Imagination in the Nineteenth Century: Visible City, Invisible World.* Cambridge UP, 2010.

Allen, Michelle. *Cleansing the City: Sanitary Geographies in Victorian London.* Ohio UP, 2008.

Altick, Richard D. *The English Common Reader: A Social History of the Mass Reading Public, 1800–1900.* 1957. 2nd ed. The Ohio State UP, 1998.

Anderson, Christopher Gangadin. *London Vagabond: The Life of Henry Mayhew.* Christopher Anderson, 2018.

Beier, A.L. "Identity, Language, and Resistance in the Making of the Victorian 'Criminal Class': Mayhew's Convict Revisited." *Journal of British Studies*, vol. 44, 2005, pp. 499–515.

Betensky, Carolyn. *Feeling for the Poor: Bourgeois Compassion, Social Action, and the Victorian Novel.* U of Virginia P, 2010.

Brantlinger, Patrick. *The Reading Lesson: The Threat of Mass Literacy in Nineteenth-Century Britain.* Indiana UP, 1998.

——. *The Spirit of Reform: British Literature and Politics, 1832–1867.* Harvard UP, 1977.

Chadwick, Edwin. *Report on the Sanitary Condition of the Labouring Population of Great Britain.* 1847. Edited by M.W. Flinn. Edinburgh UP, 1965.

Chase, Karen, and Michael Levenson. "Mayhew, the Prince, and the Poor: The Great Exhibition of Power and Dispossession." *Victorian Prism: Refractions of the Crystal Palace*, edited by James Buzard, Joseph W. Childers, and Eileen Gillooly. U of Virginia P, 2007, pp. 123–37.

Choi, Tina Young. *Anonymous Connections: The Body and Narratives of the Social in Victorian Britain.* U of Michigan P, 2016.

Clayton, Owen. "Hybrid Photographies in *London Labour and the London Poor.*" *Literature and Photography in Transition, 1850–1915.* Palgrave Macmillan, 2015, pp. 24–60.

Cuming, Emily. "'Home is home be it never so homely': Reading Mid-Victorian Slum Interiors." *Journal of Victorian Culture*, vol. 18, no. 3, 2013, pp. 368–86.

Feely, Catherine. "'What say you to free trade in literature?' *The Thief* and the Politics of Piracy in the 1830s." *Journal of Victorian Culture*, vol. 19, no. 4, 2014, pp. 497–506.

Gagnier, Regenia. *Subjectivities: A History of Self-Representation in Britain, 1832–1920.* Oxford UP, 1991.

Gallagher, Catherine. "The Body versus the Social Body in the Works of Thomas Malthus and Henry Mayhew." *Representations*, vol. 14, 1986, pp. 83–106.

Groth, Helen. "The Soundscapes of Henry Mayhew: Urban Ethnography and Technologies of Transcription." *Cultural Studies Review*, vol. 18, no. 3, 2012, pp. 109–30.

Guy, Josephine M. *The Victorian Social-Problem Novel: The Market, the Individual, and Communal Life*. Macmillan, 1996.

Hack, Daniel. "Sympathy for the Begging-Letter Writer." *The Material Interests of the Victorian Novel*. U of Virginia P, 2005, pp. 101–46.

Hamlin, Christopher. *Public Health and Social Justice in the Age of Chadwick: Britain, 1800–1854*. Cambridge UP, 1998.

Herbert, Christopher. "Mayhew's Cockney Polynesia." *Culture and Anomie: Ethnographic Imagination in the Nineteenth Century*. U of Chicago P, 1991, pp. 204–52.

——. "Rat Worship and Taboo in Mayhew's London." *Representations*, vol. 23, 1988, pp. 1–24.

Himmelfarb, Gertrude. *The Idea of Poverty: England in the Early Industrial Age*. Knopf, 1983.

Humpherys, Anne. *Henry Mayhew*. Twayne, 1984.

——. *Travels into the Poor Man's Country: The Work of Henry Mayhew*. U of Georgia P, 1977.

Jaffe, Audrey. "Detecting the Beggar: Arthur Conan Doyle, Henry Mayhew, and 'The Man with the Twisted Lip.'" *Representations*, vol. 31, 1990, pp. 96–117.

Jankiewicz, Stephen. "A Dangerous Class: The Street Sellers of Nineteenth-Century London." *Journal of Social History*, vol. 46, no. 2, 2012, pp. 391–415.

Jones, Gareth Stedman. *Outcast London: A Study in the Relationship between Classes in Victorian Society*. Oxford UP, 1971.

Joshi, Priti. "The Other Great Exhibition: Mayhew's Catalog of the Industrious." *Literature Compass*, vol. 9, no. 1, 2012, pp. 95–105.

Koven, Seth. *Slumming: Sexual and Social Politics in Victorian London*. Princeton UP, 2004.

Landon, Philip. "Great Exhibitions: Representations of the Crystal Palace in Mayhew, Dickens, and Dostoevsky." *Nineteenth Century Contexts*, vol. 20, no. 1, 1997, pp. 27–59.

Leckie, Barbara. "Henry Mayhew: Urban Ecologist." *Victorian Literature and Culture*, vol. 48, no. 1, 2020, forthcoming.

——. *Open Houses: Poverty, the Novel, and the Architectural Idea in Nineteenth-Century Britain*. U of Pennsylvania P, 2018.

Levy, Michelle, and Tom Mole. *The Broadview Introduction to Book History*. Broadview, 2017.

——, editors. *The Broadview Reader in Book History*. Broadview, 2017.

Loftus, Donna. "Work, Poverty and Modernity in Mayhew's London." *Journal of Victorian Culture*, vol. 19, no. 4, 2014, pp. 507–19.

Martin, George. "London Labour and the London Poor." *Reynolds's Newspaper*, vol. 7, September 1851, p. 7.

[Masson, David.] "Recent Aspects of Socialism." *British Quarterly Review*, vol. 11, no. 22, 1850, pp. 467–99.

Maxwell, Richard. "Henry Mayhew and the Life of the Streets." *Journal of British Studies*, vol. 17, no. 2, 1978, pp. 87–105.

Mayhew, Augustus. *Paved with Gold; or, the Romance and Reality of the London Streets: An Unfashionable Novel.* Chapman and Hall, 1858.

Mayhew, Henry. *Labour and the Poor. Report of the Speech of Henry Mayhew.* London, 1850.

——. *London Labour and the London Poor*, vols 1–4. 1851–61. Dover, 1968.

[——. "Nature"] "That Man Gets...." *Morning Chronicle*, 1 October 1849, p. 6.

——. *The Unknown Mayhew: Selections from the* Morning Chronicle *1849–50*, edited by E.P. Thompson and Eileen Yeo. Penguin, 1973.

Menely, Tobias, and Jesse Oak Taylor. "Introduction." *Anthropocene Reading: Literary History in Geologic Times*, edited by Tobias Menely and Jesse Oak Taylor, Pennsylvania State UP, 2017, pp. 1–24.

Morrison, Arthur. *A Child of the Jago*. 1896. Edited by Diana Maltz. Broadview, 2013.

Münch, Ole. "Henry Mayhew and the Street Traders of Victorian London—A Cultural Exchange with Material Consequences." *London Journal*, vol. 43, no. 1, 2018, pp. 53–71.

Nead, Lynda. *Victorian Babylon: People, Streets and Images in Nineteenth-Century London.* Yale UP, 2000.

O'Connor, Erin. *Raw Material: Producing Pathology in Victorian Culture*. Duke UP, 2000.

O'Day, Rosemary. "Introduction." *London Labour and the London Poor*, by Henry Mayhew. Edited by Rosemary O'Day and David Englander. Wordsworth Editions, 2008, pp. xiii–xlviii.

O'Day, Rosemary, and David Englander, editors. *London Labour and the London Poor*, by Henry Mayhew. Wordsworth Editions, 2008.

Pemberton, Neil. "The Rat-Catcher's Prank: Interspecies Cunningness and Scavenging in Henry Mayhew's London." *Journal of Victorian Culture*, vol. 19, no. 4, 2014, pp. 520–35.

Pike, David Lawrence. *Subterranean Cities: The World Beneath Paris and London, 1800–1945*. Cornell UP, 2005.

Poovey, Mary. *Making a Social Body: British Cultural Formation, 1830–1864.* U of Chicago P, 1995.

Prasch, Thomas. "Eating the World: London in 1851." *Victorian Literature and Culture*, vol. 36, no. 2, 2008, pp. 587–602.

——. "Ethnicity as Marker in Henry Mayhew's *London Labour and the London Poor*." *Fear, Loathing, and Victorian Xenophobia*, edited by Marlene Tromp, Maria K. Bachman, and Heidi Kaufman, The Ohio State UP, 2013, pp. 231–48.

Price, Leah. "The Book as Waste: Henry Mayhew and the Fall of Paper Recycling." *How to Do Things with Books in Victorian Britain.* Princeton UP, 2012, pp. 219–57.

Prizel, Natalie. "The Non-Taxonomical Mayhew." *Victorian Studies*, vol. 57, no. 3, 2015, pp. 433–44.

Reynolds, George W.M. *The Mysteries of London*, vol. 1. G. Vickers, 1846.

Reynolds's Newspaper, "London Labour and the London Poor." 15 June 1851, p. 14.

Roddy, Sarah, Julie-Marie Strange, and Bertrand Taithe. "Henry Mayhew at 200—The 'Other' Victorian Bicentenary." *Journal of Victorian Culture*, vol. 19, no. 4, 2014, pp. 481–96.

Rose, Jonathan. *The Intellectual Life of the British Working Classes*. Yale UP, 2001.

Rosenman, Ellen Bayuk. "Rudeness, Slang, and Obscenity: Working-Class Politics in *London Labour and the London Poor.*" *Victorian Vulgarity: Taste in Verbal and Visual Culture*, edited by Susan David Bernstein and Elsie B. Michie, Routledge, 2016, pp. 55–70.

Samalin, Zachary. "Plumbing the Depths, Scouring the Surface: Henry Mayhew's Scavenger Hermeneutics." *New Literary History*, vol. 48, 2017, pp. 387–410.

Samuels, Raphael. "Mayhew and Labour Historians." *Society for the Study of Labour History*, vol. 26, 1973, pp. 47–52.

Scanlan, John. "'In Deadly Time': The Lasting On of Waste in Mayhew's London." *Time and Society*, vol. 16, 2007, pp. 189–206.

Schroeder, Janice. "The Publishing History of Henry Mayhew's *London Labour and the London Poor*." 2019. *BRANCH: Britain, Representation, and Nineteenth Century History*, edited by Dino Franco Felluga, branchcollective.org. (Extension of *Romanticism and Victorianism on the Net.*)

Schülting, Sabine. "Dirt and Victorian Thing Culture." *Dirt in Victorian Literature and Culture: Writing Materiality*. Routledge, 2016, pp.15–48.

Seed, John. "Did the Subaltern Speak? Mayhew and the Coster-girl." *Journal of Victorian Culture*, vol. 19, no. 4, 2014, pp. 536–49.

Shannon, Mary L. *Dickens, Reynolds, and Mayhew on Wellington Street: The Print Culture of a Victorian Street*. Ashgate, 2015.

Smith, Sheila Mary. *The Other Nation: The Poor in English Novels of the 1840s and 1850s*. Clarendon, 1980.

Stallybrass, Peter, and Allon White. *The Politics and Poetics of Transgression*. Methuen, 1986.

Steedman, Carolyn. "Mayhew: On Reading, About Writing." *Journal of Victorian Culture*, vol. 19, no. 4, 2014, pp. 550–61.

——. *Strange Dislocations: Childhood and the Idea of Human Interiority, 1780–1930*. Harvard UP, 1995.

——. "The Watercress Seller." *Past Tenses: Essays on Writing, Autobiography, and History*. Rivers Oram, 1992, pp. 193–202.

Taithe, Bertrand. *The Essential Mayhew: Representing and Communicating the Poor*. Rivers Oram, 1996.

Taylor, Jesse Oak. *The Sky of Our Manufacture: The London Fog in British Fiction from Dickens to Woolf*. U of Virginia P, 2016.

Thackeray, William Makepeace. "Waiting at the Station." *Punch*, 9 March 1850, pp. 92–93.

Thompson, E.P. "Mayhew and the *Morning Chronicle*." *The Unknown Mayhew: Selections from the* Morning Chronicle *1849–50*, by Henry Mayhew, edited by E.P. Thompson and Eileen Yeo, Penguin, 1973, pp. 9–55.

——. "The Political Education of Henry Mayhew." *Victorian Studies*, vol. 11, no. 1, pp. 41–62.

Vincent, David. *Literacy and Popular Culture: England 1750–1914*. Cambridge UP, 1989.

Williams, Daniel. "The Clouds and the Poor: Ruskin, Mayhew, and Ecology." *Nineteenth-Century Contexts*, vol. 38, no. 5, 2016, pp. 319–31.

Williams, Karel. *From Pauperism to Poverty*. Routledge and Kegan Paul, 1981.

Williams, Raymond. *The Country and the City*. Oxford UP, 1973.

——. *Culture and Society: 1780–1950*. Columbia UP, 1983.

Wohl, Anthony S. *Endangered Lives: Public Health in Victorian Britain*. Cambridge UP, 1983.

——. *The Eternal Slum: Housing and Social Policy in Victorian London*. Transaction, 2002.

Yeo, Eileen. "Mayhew as a Social Investigator." *The Unknown Mayhew: Selections from the* Morning Chronicle *1849–50*, by Henry Mayhew, edited by E.P. Thompson and Eileen Yeo, Random House, 1971, pp. 51–95.

From the Publisher

A name never says it all, but the word "Broadview" expresses a good deal of the philosophy behind our company. We are open to a broad range of academic approaches and political viewpoints. We pay attention to the broad impact book publishing and book printing has in the wider world; for some years now we have used 100% recycled paper for most titles. Our publishing program is internationally oriented and broad-ranging. Our individual titles often appeal to a broad readership too; many are of interest as much to general readers as to academics and students.

Founded in 1985, Broadview remains a fully independent company owned by its shareholders—not an imprint or subsidiary of a larger multinational.

For the most accurate information on our books (including information on pricing, editions, and formats) please visit our website at www.broadviewpress.com. Our print books and ebooks are also available for sale on our site.

broadview press
www.broadviewpress.com

This book is made of paper from well-managed FSC® - certified forests, recycled materials, and other controlled sources.

FSC www.fsc.org MIX Paper from responsible sources FSC® C103567

PCF

BIO GAS® ENERGY

PERMANENT